In the National Interest

Joseph A. Kayne

Amelia Island, Florida

Dedication

To my mother, who just turned 100 years old. When asked the secret to her longevity, she replies, "Waiting for my son to finish writing this book."

Because the eye gazes but can catch no glimpse of it, it is called elusive. Because the ear listens but cannot hear it, it is called the rarefied. Because the hand feels for it but cannot find it, it is called the infinitesimal. These are called the shapeless shapes, forms without form, vague semblances. Go towards them, and you can see no front; go after them, and you see no rear.

—C. G. JUNG
SYNCHRONICITY: AN ACAUSAL CONNECTING PRINCIPLE

Preface

Imagine a more perfect world than the one you live in and then engage in making that happen.[1]

Randy Komisar/Venture Capitalist
Kleiner Perkins, Menlo Park, California

I adopted the above quote as the central theme for the "Imagination and Entrepreneurship" course I taught for nine years at Miami University in Oxford, Ohio. Class instruction began with two exercises. #1: Fill in a table of desired outcomes for each decade of your life. #2: Pick the one you think is most improbable and create a path to achieve it.

Each semester I shared one item from my personal decennial bucket list. In my sixties, I hoped to write the "great American political novel." At 73 years of age, I am half-way there, though a tad late. Whether it is "great" or not, I will leave to readers and critics. I approached "making it possible," much like a doctoral dissertation. It had to be unique and well researched.

When I began drafting the following narrative, there were more than 500 books, articles, documentaries and movies about John F. Kennedy's assassination. Most challenged the Warren Commission findings and presented alternative versions of the circumstances leading to the president's murder. The rare exceptions were books such as

---

[1] Interview with Rudy Poe for the documentary *ImagineIt*[2], n3TV, February 27, 2007.

Gerald Posner's *Case Closed* which affirmed the Commission's official explanation by debunking many of the major conspiracy theories.

For my story to be unique, I had to find open space in this over-developed landscape. What if I could combine the approaches employed in previous works? First, hand the protagonist a previously unexplored version of the events leading up to November 22, 1963. Then, charge him with the responsibility of determining the document's veracity.

I decided to construct the most far-fetched conspiracy, one rarely if ever included in compilations of the many alternative accounts that gained traction over the half-decade following JFK's death. To give credence to the implausible, my next challenge required lacing the storyline with factual information from the public record.

To be clear, the following is a work of fiction. However, it references real people and events. Any fact, event or quotation for which I provided a cited source is true and accurate. Any content for which there is no citation is solely a product of the author's imagination.

I must confess, on occasion I dream FBI agents knock on my front door. When I ask the purpose of their visit, they reply, "We need to know how you figured it out." At best, my dream is a subliminal self-assessment. I achieved what I set out to do, to make something highly preposterous seem possible. But the true test is not what I think, but whether you the reader finds the resulting story both satisfying and entertaining.

Joseph A. Kayne

CONTENTS

PROLOGUE

There was one thing I never understood. How the participants in an operation of such historical importance and impact kept it a secret for more than half a century. Yet, that may be exactly what they did. If what I now have in my possession is fact, not fiction, the answer is obvious. Anyone inclined to share such an implausible version of the events leading up to November 22, 1963, would appear either a deranged conspiracy theorist or living in an alternate universe.

Imagine yourself in that person's place. What would you do? Walk into the editorial board room of the *Washington Post* or *New York Times* and announce you know what lay behind the crime of the 20th century? And tell the editor everything ever said or written about the assassination of President John F. Kennedy, including the official record, was either intentionally fabricated or the result of shoddy, hasty efforts to explain what really happened? You claim to be the last surviving member of the team that planned and carried out the assassination of the chief executive of the United States. You are now coming forward to clear your conscience.

Imagine the barrage of questions. Are you insane? What proof do you have? Is there anyone else who can corroborate your story? Do you expect us to believe a former Secret Service agent who, every year for more than three decades, had been interviewed on the anniversary of Kennedy's trip to Dallas? And each time, expressed remorse that he was unable to protect his primary charge?

Finally, imagine the person who possesses this knowledge never chose to reveal it. Instead, upon his death, he entrusts you with what might be the only written chronicle of this incredible account. He then encourages you to do with it whatever you believe is in the best interest of the country and history.

To my consternation, I am the person who now faces that exact dilemma. My name is Jonathan Sheppard. Nineteen years ago, former Secret Service agent Mason Rhodes posthumously anointed me guardian of what might be the best kept secret in American history.

Jonathan Sheppard
January 14, 2023

CHAPTER ONE

THE JOURNAL

"Where do these things begin?" You may recognize this opening line from the long-running, off-Broadway musical *The Fantasticks*. Unlike playwright Tom Jones' script (no, not *that* Tom Jones), my story is not about two lovers who defy fathers who they believe disapprove of their deep, mutual affection. My story is about a different kind of love, or should I say obsession. First with politics, then, history.

Carl Jung would describe my story as a textbook example of his theory of synchronicity, which the Swiss psychiatrist insisted was an often overlooked but critical element in each of our life narratives. Synchronicity refers to connections between seemingly unrelated events, those happenings we often refer to as coincidences. So, let me commence by taking a cue from Glinda, the good witch in *The Wizard of Oz*. "It's always best to start at the beginning."

Tuesday, November 8, 1960.

My initial foray into electoral politics. I passed out "Kennedy for President" brochures at the Church of the Holy Comforter, the polling place where my parents voted. If the weather that day was an omen, it foreshadowed an equally abrupt change in America's political environment. When I arrived at the church just before 7:00 a.m., it was clear and quite cold, 27 degrees to be exact. However, by noon the temperature topped out at 60 degrees. It did not matter Richard Nixon carried my home state of Virginia by 5.4 percentage points. The nation was on the cusp of something new, even radical, and I cherished the small part I played in it.

I still have tangible keepsakes of the 1960 presidential campaign. Several Kennedy/Johnson buttons. A PT-109 tie clip. And my prized possession, a 45 RPM record of Frank Sinatra singing, "High Hopes with Jack Kennedy," which I framed and, to this day, hangs on the wall in my home office. Each is a reminder how I once viewed myself as a member of that "new generation" to which Kennedy claimed the torch had been passed.

Friday, November 22, 1963.

My recollections of the 36 months, 14 days between JFK's election and death are a blend of what I saw and heard in real time and a collage of published accounts and photographs to fill in the gaps. That all changed during mid-day recess on a late-November Friday when a man approached the playground at my middle school and told us the president had been shot. We immediately retreated to our respective homerooms where my teacher Mrs. Oliver was in tears, having just learned Kennedy had died. Afternoon classes were cancelled.

At the time I could not appreciate the long-term personal impact this single event would have on my life. In their book *Generations*, William Strauss and Neil Howe describe the arc of American history as a series of generational "crucibles," seminal occasions which shape the direction and psyche of those for whom these events are the defining moments of their young lives. World War II for the "greatest generation." September 11, 2001, for millennials. And of course, for baby boomers like me, the Kennedy assassination.

Thursday, March 27, 2003

Memories of that tragic day forty years ago do not fully explain my nearly two-decade obsession with the events in Dallas, Texas in November of 1963. It began in earnest eight days after the funeral of a man who, for purposes of this narrative, I refer to by the alias "Uncle Mason." He was not a blood relative, but a much older acquaintance who I called "uncle" because addressing him by his first name or Mr. Rhodes (again, not his real name) inadequately defined our relationship.

He was a mentor, role model and most importantly a friend. The full importance of our relationship surfaced when I received a phone call, summoning me to the reading of his will.

Thus began the latest and longest chapter of this Jung-like, synchronistic tale, a more than 19-year effort to separate fact from fiction about one of the defining moments in United States history. Or should I say two stories. The one Uncle Mason bequeathed to me. The other, my journey to understand the first and how the two became intertwined.

Monday, March 31, 2003

Disappointment. It is the only word to describe how I felt as I departed the conference room at the law offices of Reuben, Reuben and Whitman.

I had never attended the reading of a will. I expected something akin to the many accounts I saw in movies and on television. The room was always filled with people, seated in straight-back wooden chairs. As the deceased's estate was divided among potential heirs, each quickly learned who was favored and who was not. Money always tells a story.

In this case, I was the sole attendee. Mason Rhodes had never married. He had no surviving members of his nuclear family. Uncle Mason lived a modest lifestyle. For the most part, he avoided the notoriety or infamy which came with being one of the Secret Service agents in Dallas on November 22, 1963.

With one exception. Every year, on the anniversary of the Kennedy assassination, local media outlets invited him to share his own memories of that day. I often wondered why they kept reaching out to him. He had not been assigned to the motorcade as it snaked its way through Dealey Plaza. Instead, he was stationed at the Dallas Trade Mart awaiting the president's arrival for a luncheon with civic and business leaders.

Yet, he had a story to share. How he learned Kennedy's limousine had been diverted to the nearest hospital. Being ordered to go to Parkland Memorial and report to the leader of the vice-president's detail. The 48 hours of constant chaos, first at the hospital, over jurisdiction of the dead president's body, and later at the Dallas police station, culminating with Jack Ruby shooting Lee Harvey Oswald. Each time he would recount his experience almost *verbatim*. As the years passed, local televisions stations skipped the on-air interview, choosing instead to replay excerpts of previously recorded ones.

Unlike Clint Hill, the agent credited with restraining Jacqueline Kennedy when she climbed on the trunk of the presidential limousine, you would never know Uncle Mason was part of the Dallas Secret Service contingent. He does not appear in a single photograph or film clip. And as you will learn, he never testified during any of the official investigations into the assassination. Some people might begrudge the fact they narrowly missed their 15 minutes of fame. But somehow, I sensed Uncle Mason was satisfied with being an uncredited extra in the tragi-drama that unfolded shortly after 12:00 p.m. in Dealey Plaza.

On those occasions when asked to give a live interview, it became more and more of a rote exercise, a memorized script. His goal seemed not to convey the emotion of that fateful day but to make sure there was no deviation from his previous accounts.

I was 15 years old when I realized Uncle Mason was a minor celebrity in my hometown. He moved there in 1965 to take a job as director of security at a local Fortune 100 corporation. Of more consequence, he bought a house in the neighborhood where I grew up.

The first time I saw him on the local news I immediately made the connection. He had been THERE. My curiosity got the better of me. The next afternoon I knocked on his door and introduced myself. I told him I had been a "Kennedy for President" volunteer in 1960, hoping he would tell me what it was like to be in the presence of someone who had been a personal inspiration. I knew better than to ask about Dallas.

Decades later, as his health began to deteriorate, we developed a special bond. Whatever occasion brought me back to my hometown, I would make time to spend a few hours with him. My visits occasionally included a chess match, but mostly consisted of conversation about current events and updates on my personal life. Over time the latter evolved from news about my career to the latest adventure with my wife and daughter.

I made a special trip back to celebrate his 80th birthday. It would be the last time we would be together. Did he have a premonition this might be our final encounter? As I walked out the front door, he gave me a hug and said thank you. "Why?" I asked. He explained I was the one person who, over so many years, had been part of his life. Despite the age difference, he considered me among the few individuals with whom he felt comfortable, with whom he could be at ease.

The feeling was mutual. He would encourage and inspire me, often complimenting me to the point of embarrassment. So, as his appointed executor began to read from the will, I fully expected Uncle Mason would entrust me with one or more artifacts to add to my Kennedy era collection.

Here comes that word again. Disappointment. Uncle Mason instructed his modest savings go to help maintain the Secret Service Wall of Honor, a memorial to agents who died in the line of service.[2] Personal memorabilia collected during his time on the presidential detail, especially items from the trip to Dallas, would go to the Smithsonian or the National Archives.

Only a single item remained. A sealed cardboard box, the kind that might contain letterhead or reproduced documents from a copy shop. The Reuben who officiated at the reading (I cannot remember which) made a joke. "See, you didn't make this trip for nothing. He did not forget you. Here." He handed me the package, closed his portfolio and left the room.

Normally, I cannot wait to rip open a present or newly delivered package to see what it contains. But I was deflated. So deflated, that

---

[2] The Wall of Honor acknowledges the sacrifice of 37 agents who died in the line of duty, the first of whom, William Craig, died on September 3, 1902, in Pittsfield, Massachusetts when a streetcar collided with President Theodore Roosevelt's carriage. Leslie W. Offelt is the only agent who died during an assassination attempt, an assault on President Harry Truman by two Puerto Rican dissidents in front of Blair House on November 1, 1950.

when I got home, I put the box on the end table by my reading chair and did not think about it again until later that evening. However, curiosity is a strange animal. It can be managed, but never tamed. And eventually mine got the best of me.

As seemed appropriate for the occasion, I used the pocketknife Uncle Mason gave me as a high school graduation present to break the seal. No surprise. Just as I suspected, it was half-filled with letter sized sheets of type-written paper. The one exception, a hand-printed note.

> *Jonathan,*
>
> *If this is now in your possession, you already know I am no longer alive. And if we did not get the chance to say goodbye, I am sorry. I will miss you greatly.*
>
> *This box is my most valued possession. It contains something I have shared with no one. Maybe I should have, but I was afraid.*
>
> *Maybe I should have burned the contents. Let historians keep on believing whatever they want. Would the truth be too much for people to accept? Or would it be a crime to destroy the record of what really happened? I did not have the confidence or courage to make that decision. I leave that up to you.*
>
> *I am sure you will make the right choice.*
>
> *Forever grateful for your friendship,*
> *Uncle* ████

Underneath the note was the first typewritten page which I again redacted.

```
                Personal Journal
          Special Agent  ██████████
         United States Secret Service
        December 4, 1962 – November 22, 1973
```

Whatever I planned for that evening no longer mattered. I poured a glass of wine, adjusted the reading lamp and turned the page. As the time frame on the cover page promised, the first entry was from late fall of

1962. Just two months earlier, the U.S. and Soviet Union had averted a potentially disastrous confrontation over the deployment of offensive missiles in Cuba. Had Uncle Mason been privy to some unknown element surrounding that Cold War stand-off? Time to stop speculating and start reading.

When I realized I wanted to capture and possibly present my own take on Uncle Mason's story, I needed a way to differentiate my analysis from the journal. I first consulted a font designer who confirmed the document was produced on an Underwood manual typewriter, most likely the one I observed in Uncle Mason's study. To reproduce a digital version, he recommended I use "Underwood Champion," which most closely mimicked the original typeface.

You might ask, "Why didn't you just scan the journal?" When Mason (I will drop the "uncle," since you know he was not a blood relative) wanted to correct or edit the text, he would x-out a word, phrase or even an entire sentence, interrupting the flow of the narrative. It was my first indication of the journal's contemporaneous nature. Mason's method of self-editing gave credence to whether the document was drafted in real time. If he had used an alternative such as dry correction tape, not commercially available until the 1970s, or a self-correcting typewriter, even later, it would impeach the contemporaneous nature of his work. The only other option at the time would have been Liquid Paper, available since Bette Nesmith Graham brewed the first batch in her kitchen in 1951. Mason seemed more interested in the document's content than its appearance.

The following is a scanned copy of an excerpt from the first entry exactly as it appears.

December 4, 1962

I wish I had started this journal months ago.
Something is not ~~rihgt~~ right, but I cannot tell
what it is. ~~Should I have paid more attention?~~
Had I missed something? I am trying to remember
exactly what he said that caught my attention.

Perhaps it began ~~around~~ on August 6th. It was
clear ~~Lancer~~ Kennedy had something on his mind. I
accompanied the first family on a long weekend to
Hyannis Port. That morning we took AF One back to
Andrews and then Marine One from there to the ~~WH~~
White House. The President asked ~~maxa~~ what seemed
to be an interesting but not significant question. "If you had a choice, would you rather have
been President Woodrow Wilson or Abraham Lincoln?" I ~~remember feeling~~ was flattered. Lancer
knew I was interested in presidential history.
But this was a first. I did not know how to respond ~~And probably made some lame comment.~~

When you compare it to my digitally produced version, you see I only
removed what Mason personally expunged.

December 4, 1962 (digitally reproduced)

I wish I had started this journal months ago.
Something is not right, but I cannot tell what it
is. Had I missed something? I am trying to
remember exactly what he said that caught my
attention.

Perhaps it began on August 6th. It was clear
Kennedy had something on his mind. I accompanied
the first family on a long weekend to Hyannis
Port. That morning we took AF One back to Andrews
and then Marine One from there to the White
House. The President asked what seemed to be an
interesting but not significant question. "If you
had a choice, would you rather have been
President Woodrow Wilson or Abraham Lincoln?" I
was flattered. Lancer[3] knew I was interested in

---

[3] John F. Kennedy's Secret Service code name.

presidential history. But this was a first. I did not know how to respond.

The December 4 entry continued:

> Over the past three months, I have not been able to get this incident out of my head. Was it just a way to pass the time during the 13-minute helicopter ride? Or was the President preparing me for something yet to come?
>
> I wondered whether Kennedy already knew about the buildup of Soviet missiles in Cuba. Was he deciding on a course of action? Did he want to look at the situation through the eyes of two other war time presidents? Lincoln knew the Civil War was inevitable and prepared from his first day in office. Wilson avoided entering WWI until he had no choice. Two different approaches. Was Kennedy facing similar options?
>
> The Cuban crisis was resolved when the Soviets did not challenge the U.S. blockade and withdrew their missiles. But lately he seemed as preoccupied as he had been last October. Was there a new national security threat? That was always a possibility. There is seldom a day the president isn't dealing with a potential danger to the country.

I put down the page and took another sip of wine. He called it his most valuable possession. Why? And why such detail? Mason was meticulous to a fault, most likely a byproduct of his military, and later, Secret Service training. Of course, he would know the flight from Andrews to the White House was exactly 13 minutes. Or where the president was every minute of every day.

How many times had I begged Mason to tell me what it was like to be so close to a president, especially John F. Kennedy? Was this his way of fulfilling that request, a detailed chronicle based on his hands-on experience as a member of the president's Secret Service detail? A unique viewpoint where policies and programs are of little interest. A factual record or story where the person for whom you are responsible is not John Kennedy or even Mr. President. To you, he is only known by his code name "Lancer."

There was only one way to find out. Keep reading.

CHAPTER TWO

AN UNEXPECTED TWIST

Among my lesser bad habits is a compulsive need to go immediately to the end of a mystery novel to see "whodunnit." I blame this on Richard Levinson and William Link, who today would be called the "showrunners" for *Columbo,* the NBC mystery that debuted in February 1968. Unlike a traditional crime novel, movie or television series, the premise of Peter Falk's television show did not require viewers to figure out who committed the crime. At the beginning of each episode the audience was privy to the murderer's motive and watched the crime as it was planned and executed. Instead, the task was to identify the clues or the perpetrator's missteps Lieutenant Columbo would eventually use to solve the case.

I needed to know how Mason's story ended. I pulled the manuscript from the box, laid the pile on the kitchen table face down and flipped over the last couple sheets of paper.

```
November 22, 1973

The 10th anniversary of the assassination. It is
time to bring this to a close. A time to face
some old demons and consider what might have
been.

Kennedy was a student of history. I still find it
hard to believe he ignored the lessons in his own
books. While England Slept. Profiles in Courage.
```

Abraham Lincoln once said a lawyer who represents himself has a fool for a client. Maybe it also applies to authors who pay no attention to what they write.

Didn't it all go back to that question he asked me almost 11 years ago? Lincoln or Wilson? Had these moments in history clouded his vision? Was Lincoln's assassination necessary to unite the country? Did Wilson's deteriorating health make that much difference in the long run?

What will historians say about Kennedy's post assassination legacy? Will they focus on his proposed civil rights legislation and the Cuban missile crisis? Or will they question why he did not do more to avoid a ground war in Southeast Asia when he had the chance? Or his many affairs? Will they let us continue to believe in Camelot or that JFK was just another flawed politician who conducted business as usual?

I wonder whether anyone will ever understand what may have been the lasting impact of that day in Dallas. It had been 62 years since President McKinley was shot in Buffalo, New York. He died seven days later. There had been other attempts on presidents after that, all unsuccessful. I'd like to think those incompetent assassins may have discouraged others. But nothing encourages imitation like success. Did Dallas lead to Los Angeles and Memphis? Or even the recent attempt on Governor Wallace in Maryland?

Is that the true Kennedy legacy? And mine? Did we make political assassination acceptable again?

This journal includes everything I knew at the time or learned later about Kennedy's death with one exception. The planning and execution of the events in Dallas involved only 4 agents, none who were among the 30 assigned to the president's personal detail in November of 1963. I have not identified my three accomplices or our White House contact. That is not up to me.

They are not aware I kept this journal. Nor do I
know if any of them created their own. Maybe they
were able to put the past behind them. Or, by the
time anyone reads this, they may all have died.
When we met, following the release of the Warren
report, we agreed never to talk again about our
role in the assassination. There was one
exception, a dinner following the appointment of
a special counsel to investigate the break-in at
the Watergate Hotel. Since then, we have not.

The country's obsession with the Kennedy
assassination has been replaced by Watergate.
America has moved on. Maybe it is time I do the
same.

Someday I may share this journal. And leave it to
historians to decide our legacy.

So much for clearing up the mystery. I sensed Mason suspected I would jump to the ending. If he wanted to make sure I was hooked, he succeeded. I re-read this final entry a dozen times. And each time, my attention was drawn to four words. "And mine? Did we…" As a member of the Dallas Secret Service contingent, Mason always lamented the Secret Service did not do enough to prevent the assassination. Yet, there was not much he could have personally done that day. He was at the Dallas Trade Mart, two and a half miles away when Oswald fired his rifle. Maybe he was referring to his role in planning the visit to Dallas, especially the motorcade route through Dealey Plaza. Did he see this failure as his legacy? Did he believe if he and the other agents had done more to protect Kennedy in 1963, Bobby Kennedy and Martin Luther King would not have been targets of future assassins? That the course of the nation would have been altered?

Or was there more to it? There was one thing about Mason; he was always careful how he expressed himself. It would have been more like him to write, "If only we had been able to stop Oswald, we might have changed the course of history." But that's not what he said. "Did we make political assassinations acceptable again" suggests something different, even sinister.

But what? Were Warren Commission doubters justified in their skepticism? Was it possible Oswald did not act alone? Was there a conspiracy? Were members of the Secret Service complicit? Was everything Mason previously said about the assassination a lie? And were his annual TV interviews a cover story, fulfilling a promise he made at a dinner with former colleagues?

Hooked? Hell, I was reeled in, landed and fileted. No chance I would throw this one back in the water. I went back to the handwritten note. "My most valuable possession…I was afraid." What did he mean by "valuable?" Did he believe there was some monetary worth to this document? And what exactly was he afraid of? What the contents might disclose? Evidence of his own malfeasance? Mistakes made before, on the day of and after November 22, 1963?

Despite my training and three degrees in political science, I initially forgot everything I ever learned about how to analyze information and events. You do not jump around randomly. You start with a hypothesis. Then design a process to prove or disprove your supposition. Mason charged me with responsibility to determine the fate of what took him more than a decade to compile. "I leave that up to you." I felt obligated to faithfully abide by this last request.

Faced with my first collegiate social science research assignment, I believed starting with the right hypothesis was the key to any successful research project. But that discounts the likelihood an investigator's biases, even unintended ones, often result in selection of a predisposed outcome the researcher hopes to substantiate. It also assumes there is a right and a wrong interpretation of the facts. In truth, there are always multiple explanations, some better than others, but most containing a kernel of truth. And as my analytical skills improved, I found it best to consider the most unlikely conclusion first. Otherwise, it might be overlooked when compared to simpler or more rational explanations. When it comes to intellectual curiosity, Occam's Razor[4] is a blunt instrument.

---

[4] A scientific rule which requires the simplest of competing theories be preferred to more complex ones.

So, I began this quest as I always do, by acknowledging the most likely scenario and setting it aside. Before me lay hundreds of typewritten pages which appeared to be a journal or diary of events beginning in the fall of 1962 and ending more than ten years later. It was written by a Secret Service agent who had been on duty in Dallas on November 22, 1963. No doubt someone in that situation would want to capture the experience from the unique vantage point he had that day. And to memorialize how that experience affected him from that moment forward.

Logical, but the wrong starting point. If Mason only wanted to capture what it felt like to be part of a tragic episode in American history, it would not take 11 years or fill half a ream of paper. There had to be another motive for such a conscientious and painstaking undertaking. All of which pointed to an impetus beyond mere guilt, failing to do that for which he was hired and paid, protecting the life of the nation's chief executive.

What did I already know that might point me in the right direction? First, he was one of several Secret Service agents on duty that day. Second, he was barely a footnote in the history books, in stark contrast to Clint Hill. Any voiceover accompanying Abraham Zapruder's grainy 8mm film identifies Hill, by name, as the man who jumped on the trunk of Kennedy's limousine and forced Mrs. Kennedy back into the vehicle. Third, Hill was the Secret Service agent the major national media outlets wanted to interview while Mason was relegated to local TV appearances. Fourth, Hill received offers from numerous magazines and book publishers to tell his story. In response, he and his wife Lisa McCubbin Hill co-authored four books covering different aspects of his career spanning six presidential administrations.[5]

What if Mason was driven by envy or jealousy? What if he wanted some of the attention reserved for those in closer proximity to the president when the shots were fired? One way would be to create an alternative

---

[5] Five Days in November (2013), My Travels with Mrs. Kennedy (2022), Mrs. Kennedy and Me (2012) and Five Presidents: My Extraordinary Journey with Eisenhower, Kennedy, Johnson, Nixon and Ford (2017).

version of the events in Dallas and their aftermath. One in which he was a central character.

Mason would not be the first person to dispute the official version of the events of November 22. Mark Lane made headlines by challenging the Warren Commission's findings in his book *Rush to Judgment.* David Lifton, in *Best Evidence: Disguise and Deception in the Assassination of John F. Kennedy,* questioned why doctors' notes from Parkland Memorial Hospital in Dallas and the official autopsy conducted at Bethesda Naval Hospital were, in many ways, contradictory. Sustained interest in the assassination over the years made these books and many others best sellers.

Maybe Mason wanted to emulate author Gore Vidal. Perhaps the journal was destined to become the basis for a historical novel about the assassination, not unlike Vidal's treatment of Aaron Burr. In that case, he must have known even the most implausible retelling of history had to be grounded in fact. Therefore, his journal could add to the credibility of his novel's story line.

Eventually, I chose the following hypothesis to pursue first. The journal was not initially written in real time like a diary. It was designed to add authenticity to some future work, one that Mason never completed; possibly never started because he was "afraid." Afraid he might spend months or years on a project which would be summarily rejected by publishers or the public. Afraid there were too many flaws in his supporting documents to quiet potential critics. Afraid he might be seen as just one more conspiracy theorist, and a poor one at that, out to make a quick dollar on a tragic chapter in American history.

As I started reading Mason's journal, I made lists of easily verifiable facts using records from the National Archives, the John F. Kennedy Presidential Library, other public sources and news reports. If Mason had manufactured an alternative account of the who, what and why of the assassination, one would expect inconsistencies between his narrative and the public record.

I never anticipated that process would take 19 years nor believed it could hold my attention for so long. I soon realized, however, every page contained a fact, no matter how trivial, that piqued my curiosity.

Furthermore, I could take nothing for granted. Consider one example from the initial entry on December 4, 1962. Was the president on his way back to Washington on August 6 when Mason claims to be with him? Easy enough to confirm. The Kennedy Presidential Library in Boston retained scanned copies of the White House daily log, maintained in excruciating detail by JFK's personal secretary Evelyn Lincoln. It contained the following item for August 6.

```
President Kennedy departed from Hyannis Port,
Massachusetts at 9:10am. He arrived at Andrews
AFB, Maryland and boarded a helicopter for the
White House at 10:10am. The helicopter landed on
the South Lawn at 10:23am.6
```

I would frequently return to Lincoln's chronological account of Kennedy's daily schedule to verify the president's itinerary. Especially those occasions when Mason claimed to accompany him. However, at this early juncture of my research, I had no inkling how important she would become.

The next example illustrates the importance of having multiple secondary sources, i.e., official documents, books and articles. Everything had to be verified, even on those occasions when there was no reason to believe Mason had created some element out of whole cloth. Like the final November 22, 1973, entry when Mason explains he and his three compatriots were not part of the 30 agents who made up Kennedy's personal detail in late November.

I had no reason to believe Mason would not know the number of agents assigned to the presidential rotation. But what if that was the inaccuracy that might cast doubt on the larger narrative? I had to be sure. Confirmation of this minor data point appears in an appendix to the Warren Commission Report. A transcript of the March 9, 1964, testimony of special agent Roy Kellerman includes the following.

> Mr. KELLERMAN. At the time of the assassination, the president's Secret Service detail consisted of three eight-hour shifts of 10 agents each. Every two weeks the agents assigned to each shift were

---

6 Evelyn Lincoln, "Monday, August 6, 1962," PDF of President's Daily Activity Report, John F. Kennedy Library and Museum, Boston, Massachusetts.

rotated so no member of the detail was permanently assigned to the least desirable midnight to 8:00am berth.[7]

Another match. Two for two. Little consolation once I realized I needed to replicate this painstaking procedure hundreds of times if I ever chose to share the journal with a larger audience. Planning a research project and establishing the procedural guidelines are the easy parts. It was time to roll up my sleeves and get my hands dirty.

---

[7] Testimony of Roy H. Kellerman, Special Agent, Secret Service, Hearings before the Presidential Commission on the Assassination of John F. Kennedy, Volume II, March 9, 1964,

CHAPTER THREE

THE TEAM

All poker players, even the best, have a tell. It can be a quivering hand or a wrinkled brow. Once detected, the ability to know when a gambler is bluffing or holding a strong hand becomes relatively effortless. What if you cannot observe your opponent? What if all you see are the backs of the cards? What would you want to know about them? Are they randomly distributed? Is the order in which a player arranges the cards in one direction or the other based on value? Are they constantly being rearranged?

Among the most common tells a professional gambler looks for is "the double-check,"–how often opponents take a second or even third glance at their hands. However, frequency tells only half the story. Timing completes the picture. Did the double-check occur prior to placing a bet? After the bet? Once before, once after? Yet, even with all this information, poker experts admit there is no guarantee the tell is a sign of strength or weakness. Fortunately, I was not looking for guarantees. Of more importance was any clue which would help me better understand both Mason's motive for keeping a journal and the veracity of its contents.

Suppose Mason's journal *was* his hand. What did he see when he first looked at his cards? And did a second look, after tossing his chips into the pot, change his assessment? I again read the journal's first and last entries. And there it was.

In both passages, Mason referred to Abraham Lincoln and Woodrow Wilson. It is one thing to find a key. Quite another to discover what it opens. Kennedy mused about which of his predecessors he wished to emulate. What was it about that particular conversation that made Mason regret not starting the journal earlier? And compelled him to create and maintain a detailed record over the next 11 years? Of the 34 presidents who preceded Kennedy, why these two? What did they have in common? Or perhaps, more importantly, when and how did their respective life experiences diverge, making Kennedy's preference an either/or choice?

The most indisputable similarity was the characterization of each as a "war-time president," although 52 years apart. Both believed once the military conflicts which defined their time in office were resolved, there was an opportunity for a new national or world order in the form of Reconstruction and the League of Nations, respectively. Kennedy was also at the center of a global conflict; however, this time it was a "cold war," largely dependent on a nuclear deterrence strategy based on the principle of "mutually assured destruction." Except for a few "police actions," a euphemism for war on a regional rather than global scale, these engagements were more about diplomacy and brinksmanship than military power.

Mason was not the only person to connect Kennedy to these previous occupants of the Oval Office. On the 50th anniversary of Kennedy's death, Princeton historian Maynard Barksdale linked the slain president to his same two predecessors.

> *Both Lincoln and Wilson were lawyers before becoming the nation's chief executive. And even though one (Lincoln) had little formal education while Wilson was a product of Princeton and Johns Hopkins University, both were known for their masterful articulation of the American ideal through oratory and prose. In terms of his own education, Kennedy shared one thing with Wilson. Although biographies focus on his undergraduate degree from Harvard, the future president*

had originally enrolled at Princeton only to leave after two months due to a severe gastrointestinal illness.[8]

Additionally, one could argue neither Lincoln nor Wilson completed his second term in office. One literally by assassination. The other figuratively due to a series of strokes which resulted in his inability to perform the simplest of tasks during his last year and a half in the White House. According to Wilson biographer Edwin A. Weinstein, the 1919 seizures were just the culmination of a history of cerebrovascular disorders dating back to 1896, 16 years before he was elected president.[9] As I would learn from subsequent journal entries, the distinction between death and disability lay at the heart of Kennedy's obsessive curiosity about the 16th and 28th occupants of the Oval Office.

Following his death, Kennedy's presidency was compared most often to Lincoln's, fueled by the tributes and eerie numerological coincidences associated with two assassinations a century apart. Within 48 hours of Kennedy's death, the Chad Mitchell Trio performed a musical eulogy to the fallen president, "In the Summer of His Years," on *BBC's* "That Was the Week That Was." To forever bind Kennedy and Lincoln in folksong lore, the original was later combined with George Frederick Root's (1820-1895) Civil War anthem "Rally Round the Flag," sung in support of the Lincoln/Andrew Johnson ticket in 1864.

As Mason soon discovered, Kennedy was preoccupied with the possibility his legacy would be more akin to the second coming of Woodrow Wilson.

December 15, 1962

At the invitation of a colleague, I joined him
and two other agents on a trip to the Liberty
Bowl between the University of Oregon and
Villanova. On the drive from DC to Philadelphia,
I told the others about my conversation with the

---

[8] Maynard W. Barksdale, "Mourning a Former Son," *Princeton Alumni Weekly,* November 13, 2013
[9] Weinstein, Edwin A., *A Medical and Psychological Biography,* Princeton University Press, 1981

President and his question about Lincoln and
Wilson. I was curious if Kennedy had similar
discussions with any of them.

One of my road-trip companions jumped in. He said
he could understand the reference to Wilson and
asked if any of us was aware of the President's
most recent medical issues. He told us he had
noticed a difference in the President's physical
appearance during and after the Cuban missile
crisis. Also, Dr. Max Jacobson, on whom Kennedy
relied for less conventional pain-relieving
drugs, had been making more frequent White House
visits in the past two months.

I know Kennedy's many health issues are being
kept from the public as not to undermine his
image as a young, energetic alternative to recent
predecessors Roosevelt, Truman and Eisenhower.
But is he in poorer health than even we who spend
so much time with him are led to believe? Does
Kennedy believe, like Wilson, he might become
totally incapacitated before the end of his first
term?

For the record, Oregon State 6 Villanova 0.

My first reaction to this entry had nothing to do with the substance. It
was the style. Was Mason a poker player who had again, either
intentionally or subconsciously, shown his hand? It would have been
easy to simply record the fact he had a conversation with fellow agents
about Kennedy's health. Of what value was information about the car
ride to Philadelphia to watch a football game and his closing the entry
with the score? Was this level of detail about peripheral facts included
to support the veracity of the events or to make a fictional narrative
more credible?

Or were they put there to make sure I would not accept the journal at
face value? Was this an intentional error? For as long as I could
remember, the annual Liberty Bowl was played in Memphis. However,
a Google search of the phrase "1962 Liberty Bowl," confirmed the

game was played at Philadelphia Municipal Stadium. The annual contest moved to Memphis in 1965.[10]

If nothing else, I now understood Mason was doing his best to make the document historically accurate even if it were not grounded in truth. I made a mental note about the need to question and research even the most seemingly insignificant references as I parsed each entry.

---

[10] Fuqua, Brad, "A Look Back at Oregon State's 1962 Liberty Bowl Victory," *Corvallis Gazette-Times,* August 9, 2012

CHAPTER FOUR

ANOTHER CLUE

The entry immediately following the trip to Philadelphia demonstrates how the discussion concerning Kennedy's health affected Mason's commitment to "faithfully discharge the duties of the office on which I am about to enter," an oath to which he swore upon joining the Secret Service.

December 17, 1962

Final preparation for Lancer's two-week stay at the compound in Palm Beach. As usual, the advance team prepared a thorough "threat report," which includes the movements of any individuals in the area who might want to harm the president. For this trip, I requested one more briefing. If Lancer's health was as uncertain as I and my colleagues now suspected, I needed to be equally prepared in case of a medical emergency.

Lancer's personal physician Dr. Janet Travell kept detailed records of Kennedy's condition and treatments. I obtained a copy of the file covering the past 90 days which included entries during the Cuban missile crisis. The daily updates covering the 13 days between October 16 and October 28 went beyond anything I expected.

Travell reported she administered treatment for several ailments including anti-spasmodics for colitis, antibiotics for a urinary-tract infection as well as hydrocortisone and

> testosterone to control Addison's disease and
> increase his energy levels.
>
> In early December, there was a notation Mrs.
> Kennedy asked a gastronomic specialist to
> reevaluate the effect of antihistamines Kennedy
> was taking for food allergies. She felt they had
> a "depressing action" on her husband's behavior.
> Travell's notes reveal Dr. Richard Boles, the
> gastroenterologist on her staff, prescribed one
> milligram of Stelazine twice a day. Stelazine is
> an anti-psychotic for the treatment of anxiety.
>
> My responsibilities now included more than
> stopping threats to the president from
> overzealous critics or mentally disturbed
> individuals. They also required watching for
> changes in behavior caused by Lancer's
> potentially competing drug regimen.

Although Mason never directly addresses the question, he must have wondered how long Kennedy's inner circle could hide the president's deteriorating health. Historic precedence suggests there are two distinct ways public knowledge of a president's medical condition is disclosed. Sometimes it is a single dramatic event, impossible to spin. In September 1955, Dwight Eisenhower suffered a massive heart attack. He was in Colorado with the First Lady who wanted to spend their vacation near Denver, her childhood home. During a golf outing at Cherry Hills Country Club, Eisenhower complained of what he thought was indigestion. Following an evaluation by his personal physician, the president was rushed to Fitzsimons Army Hospital in Aurora.[11]

Prior to ratification of the 25th Amendment to the Constitution in 1967, there was no provision for the temporary transfer of power to the vice-president. An announcement of Eisenhower's cardiac event was made public within hours of his hospitalization, and procedures were established by which Eisenhower could continue to perform his

---

[11] The military hospital closed in 1999 in response to recommendations under the Base Realignment and Closure (BRAC) process. The building now is part of the Colorado Anschutz Medical Campus and Suite 8002, where Eisenhower stayed, has been preserved as a historical site including the Secret Service sitting room.

executive duties first from the hospital and later during recuperation at his farm in Gettysburg, Pennsylvania.

Kennedy's situation, like Wilson's, was akin to the "boiling frog syndrome," a principle wherein a situation increases in severity incrementally and reaches catastrophic proportions before the eventual victim or observers are cognizant of the potential danger. In each case, there was no singular trauma. Instead, deterioration in the health of these two occupants of the Oval Office was years in the making.

Yet, the comparison of the young president's short time in office to "Camelot," a mythical saga about unfulfilled promises, remained intact for decades. Any perceived discomfort was attributed to Kennedy's service aboard PT 109 in World War II. The famous JFK rocking chair, a duplicate of which traveled with him whenever he left Washington, D.C., was intended to reinforce public perception his constant back pain was a result of his highly touted military service.

Public knowledge of JFK's physical dystopia did not materialize until 2003 when Boston University professor of history Robert Dallek, assisted by Dr. Jeffrey Kelman, devoted a chapter of his book *An Unfinished Life: John F. Kennedy, 1917-1963* to the subject's physical condition. Dallek was the first researcher to obtain access to JFK's medical records stored at the Kennedy presidential library. Dallek's account confirmed Mason's assessment that the president's medical status required close monitoring.

Although more obvious examples would later emerge as I learned what Mason and his colleagues were up to, this entry was the first to alter the way I viewed my primary objective, to either validate or refute the journal. Whether the contents were true or not, I soon found myself pondering the ethical questions associated with various elements of the narrative. Had Mason done the same?

At the outset, it appears not. The December 17 entry had the look and feel of a disinterested bystander. He admitted the medical records included information "beyond anything I expected." Yet, there was no evidence he questioned whether Dr. Travell had violated her Hippocratic oath in terms of both the president's treatment and her participation in a coverup of his physical maladies.

Nor did Mason seem to consider, in light of this newly acquired knowledge, any responsibility to challenge concealment of a commander-in-chief's questionable health. Or whether JFK's medical condition and the drug regimen administered by his doctors posed a national security threat. Instead, he viewed his decision not to question the public's right to know about Kennedy's medical issues as a Secret Service agent's obligation to "take one for the boss."

This entry also established the course of my narrative. It now involved not one, but four avenues of inquiry. Of primary importance was still affirmation or repudiation of the account. Second, if true, how might history judge the participants and their actions? Third, were there clearly identifiable long-term impacts as suggested in Mason's final post?

And finally, how important was the time frame in which the events of November 1963 occurred? Would advances in medicine and treatment of Kennedy's health issues over the intervening years have made a difference in the president's physical capacity to govern? Or was a tragic end to the Kennedy presidency inevitable? Was JFK's health only one of several undisclosed factors which would stain the well-polished veneer of Camelot?

CHAPTER FIVE

THE CALL

If I had concerns about the ethical implications of the December 17 entry, they paled in comparison to those contained in the subsequent one.

January 9, 1963

My first morning back in DC after the trip with Lancer to Palm Beach. I was eating breakfast when I got the call. A senior White House advisor asked me to join him for lunch in the Treaty Room in the OEOB. [12] Such calls usually signal an upcoming trip. But this was different. My host instructed me not to mention the meeting to anyone else. My first thought. Lancer would be meeting with one of his mistresses and I would again be asked to either arrange for a room at a DC hotel or sneak her up to the private residence on the second floor of the WH. Not the favorite part of my job, but one any agent was expected to do without question.

---

[12] OEOB is an acronym for the Old Executive Office Building, located on 17th Street, immediately west of the White House. The French second empire architectural structure was commissioned by President Ulysses S. Grant and completed in 1888. It initially housed the Departments of State and War (now Defense). In 1999, President Bill Clinton, by executive order, renamed the building the Eisenhower Executive Office Building following the death of the 34th president. The Indian Treaty Room originally served as the Navy Department Library and was the venue for Eisenhower's first televised news conference.

When I arrived shortly before noon, it was clear
this was not a one on one. Sitting outside the
Treaty Room were my three traveling companions to
the Liberty Bowl. This could not have been by
accident.

At precisely 12 o'clock our host arrived. After
the meal was served our host asked all staff to
leave the room. He then spoke to the four of us.
(I will try to capture his exact words.)

"The President is not well. His health is
deteriorating rapidly, and he has been informed
that it is unlikely he will survive the end of
this term. He is concerned his political rivals
will see his failing health as a weakness and an
opportunity to seize power. I know that Kennedy
has talked with each of you about his perspective
on Lincoln and Wilson. (I was not the only one.)
He is concerned about two things. First, that his
agenda goes forward even if he is not here to
lead it. Second, his personal legacy."

"The President has made a choice. He wants to be
a Lincoln, not a Wilson. I don't know how else to
say this. He wants to be a martyr for the cause.
Last week, he personally asked me to assemble a
team to plan and carry out his assassination."

My first response, you can't be serious. But he
reminded us Kennedy was still commander-in-chief,
and this was not a request, but an order.

Our host continued, "He also specifically named
the four of you to lead the operation based on
his assessment of your competence, integrity and
loyalty. I told him I would reluctantly proceed
with the planning but would continue to try and
talk him out of it. He said that was fair even
though he doubted anything would change his mind.
No one outside this room must ever know why or
how this plan was hatched. No one is to keep a
record of these events. (Perhaps I am not as
loyal as Lancer believes.)"

<blockquote>
He told us he arranged for office space in the
Navy Annex in Arlington to serve as our
operations center. We would have no assistants.
Secured phones had already been installed. Each
of us had been assigned an alias with
identification documents. All of us would remain
on the President's detail to maintain the
appearance of business as usual. However, our
schedules would be modified so at least two of us
would be available at all times to focus on the
new assignment.

He ended the meeting by giving us the rest of the
day off. "Get some rest. You're going to need
it."

No chance. I had been ordered to murder the man
whom I had taken an oath to protect.
</blockquote>

I still find it hard to fathom the lack of emotion in Mason's account of that day. His words were so matter of fact. I was called to a meeting. I am told I have been chosen to kill the president of the United States. I am given the rest of the day off. But maybe this is the first indication the journal is a contemporaneous document. A Secret Service agent is trained not to question an assignment. In real time, that training kicks in. Personal reflection might come later.

Or maybe he chose not to record his emotional response or the many questions he now contemplated. Was the Philadelphia road trip part of a selection process? Had the agent who invited him already been chosen as the team leader? Was the outing a test of compatibility among four would-be co-conspirators?

What else about the request might be a test? Maybe there was no presidential directive. Could this be a way to ferret out possible defections within the Secret Service ranks? Were other small groups of agents going through the same process? Were each being given a slightly different version of the order so any leaks could be attributed to a specific quartet of agents?

Or maybe, Mason was simply beyond surprise. After all, Kennedy's health issues were not news. And his first thoughts about a "secret" meeting centered on the president's extramarital dalliances. Was he so accustomed to "business as unusual," nothing about this White House shocked him?

One thing in the White House contact's instructions made complete sense. Concerns about Kennedy's political foes using the president's physical condition against him were not unfounded. It happened once before. On November 3, 1960, five days before the presidential election, Richard Nixon recruited Franklin Roosevelt's youngest son John to issue a challenge to both presidential candidates "to disclose any medical difficulties that might impair their ability to serve as president." The Kennedy campaign countered by resurrecting a five-year-old story by columnist Walter Winchell that Nixon had once been under the care of a psychiatrist Dr. Arnold Hutschnecker. Caution prevailed on both sides, and neither camp released their potentially damning information during the final days of the campaign. [13]

During a campaign, competing opposition research and its timely release are common practice. Any attempt by Kennedy's political foes to undermine a sitting chief executive in the middle of his term would impact governance, not electoral outcomes. It might be designed to pump the brakes on the incumbent's policy agenda. Or even, sabotage the country's faith the president is physically or mentally up to the job. Kennedy did not intend to let that happen.

---

[13] Robb, David L., "Richard Nixon's Secret War on JFK's Health," *The Wrap*, March 15, 2012

CHAPTER SIX

THE COMMAND CENTER

[As individual journal posts grew in length and often covered multiple topics, it no longer made sense to present those entries in their entirety, followed by an analysis or commentary. In some cases, supplemental information and my analysis are interwoven with the original text. In others, excerpts from multiple entries are aggregated.]

When I read the January 16, 1962, journal entry for the first time, two things caught my immediate attention. First, the precision and detail involved in planning an event, whether a presidential trip or his assassination, is second nature to a Secret Service agent. The second was a by-product of the meticulous way in which Mason recorded this process. A real-time, comprehensive chronicle of a single event could open a broader window into other aspects of the times. In this case, the technology of the early 1960s.

January 16, 1963

First day at the mission center in the Navy
Annex. No Taj Mahal, but comfortable. Lots of
room, windows with a view of Arlington cemetery,
four large desks each with a secured phone and
IBM Selectric typewriter, and a Xerox 914 copier.
The gray walls were covered with blackboards and
bulletin boards. One wall was lined with file
cabinets. On each desk was a sealed manila folder
stamped CONFIDENTIAL in red ink.

The Navy Annex was originally built as a one million square foot warehouse. Located just west of the Pentagon, over time it was converted to office space, first for the Marine Corp in 1941 and then as headquarters for base realignment and closure in 1963. Following the 9/11 attack on the Pentagon, several dislocated operations were temporarily reestablished in the Annex. In 2013, the building was demolished to make room for the southern expansion of Arlington Cemetery. [14]

Compared to the workspace I occupied in my home office these past 19 years, the Navy Annex "war room" was straight out of the dark ages. The agents' rotary landline phones[15] have been replaced by my series of perpetually updated, multi-functional smart devices. Vocal communication is the least used application. Instead, it is the camera, capturing photos of locales referenced throughout the journal which can later be viewed to compare with Mason's description. Or the voice recorder on which I memorialized even the most insignificant thoughts for fear I could not later retrieve them from memory. But most importantly, it is a readily available connection to an abundance of multiply sourced, online information, accessible regardless of my location.

The IBM Selectric[16] typewriters have given way to my Dell desktop computer with dual monitors. The one on the left contains a digitized, searchable copy of the journal on which I could add comments or document sources. On the right is an always open, oft-referenced Chrome browser or PDF reader. Replacing their three and a half foot tall, 650-pound Xerox 914 (available since 1959) is an all-in-one HP OfficeJet printer (25.4 pounds) which doubles as a copier and scanner.

However, some technological advancements outpace others. The team's blackboards contained constantly updated information, flow charts and checklists as emerging plans were sketched out, amended

---

[14] Steve Vogel, "Navy Annex being razed after 70 years of service," *Washington Post*, December 30, 2012.

[15] The first commercial phone with touch-tone dialing was made available to customers in Carnegie and Greensburg, Pennsylvania by Bell Telephone on November 18, 1963, following several years of testing.

[16] The original IBM Selectric was less than two years old at the time of this entry having been introduced on July 23, 1961, based on a design by Eliot Noyes.

and occasionally dismissed. In what can only be characterized as the "yin and yang" of technical evolution, the only difference between the erasable board in their command center and my office is the background color. The black surface designed for white or yellow chalk is now white with content added via a rainbow of dry markers.[17]

Likewise, the following description of the team's living accommodations are not dissimilar to the lifestyle I chose while I dissected Mason's journal.

```
The adjoining room seemed like a better fit for
the clandestine nature of our assignment. Four
twin beds, a small kitchen, a large supply of
non-perishable food and drinks. A reminder this
was as much a bunker as a workspace. We need to
prepare for the long haul.
```

In one sense, the team operated out of a "home office" away from home. There would be days when I, too, felt I was in a bunker, under a siege of uncertainty and apprehension of what lay ahead.

I never got used to the tenor of the next several passages in the January 16 entry. "…we began the process required for any presidential event." Why did I increasingly find this cold, unemotional approach so disturbing? This was not the typical presidential event. Had Mason's training and previous years of service stripped him of his humanity? Was there no room for compassion or empathy? Did fulfilling the mission overshadow all other considerations?

Or did the enormity of the task ahead demand a heightened devotion to protocol and discipline? Total dependence on one's memory of each critical step might jeopardize the mission. Mason and his comrades-in-arms needed to see it laid out in black and white, as no margin of error was tolerable.

```
After everyone arrived, we began the process
associated with any presidential event.
```

---

[17] Although whiteboards were invented in the early 1960s, they did not come into common use until the invention of the dry-erase marker in 1975.

Step #1. Make sure you know exactly what you are
being asked to do.

We simultaneously broke the seal on the envelopes
in front of us. It was clear this assignment
would challenge the assumptions on which the
service approaches its primary function. After
years of trying to prevent such crimes, I thought
I understood the process someone would use to
take down the president of the United States.
Track the target. Pick the best time and place to
act. Eliminate the target. Escape.

Killing a president is hard enough. Restrictions
on how it must be done makes it more difficult.
Our assignment included five caveats.

1) The assassination could not be carried out by
a Secret Service agent or anyone currently
associated with the U.S. government or military.

2) Lancer cannot know when and where the
assassination will take place.

3) The assassin must be eliminated immediately.

This was perhaps the least onerous of the conditions. None of the 13
men and women who either assassinated or tried to assassinate a sitting
U.S. president escaped. All either died at the hand of law enforcement,
were executed following their trials or sentenced to prison.[18]

4) The assassin's background and motivation must
support the dead president's policy agenda and
add to his legacy.

5) No one else could be harmed. This final
criterion would require the assassin be a skilled
marksman or someone who could get face-to-face
with his target.

Put simply, we have been asked to recruit an
assassin who has a grievance against the

---

[18] "Hunting the President: Threats, Plots and Assassination Attempts," *History on the Net,* Salem Media.

```
president, somehow convince him to carry out a
felony crime, make sure he does not survive and
do it in such a way the operation will never be
revealed.
```

Was this one more example of the skill set required of a Secret Service agent? The ability to boil down a complex, perhaps impossible task into terse, unequivocal directives. I could imagine, if their planning started to go off-track, a member of the team would stop the conversation and say, "Remember," followed by those 43 words starting with "Put simply…"

```
After reading the file, no one in the room needed
to say a word. Our silence said it all.

Step #2. Establish communications protocols. It
was agreed we would refer to ourselves as "the
team." The mission would always be called "the
assignment." Each of us would be identified by a
familiar code name. Since there were four of us,
we decided these aliases should be associated
with a quartet of fictional characters. After
several false starts, someone suggested the
assignment was a journey, much like a trip down
the yellow brick road in The Wizard of Oz. That
was it. Our code names would be Dorothy, Tinman,
Scarecrow and Lion. Our WH contact would be
Wizard. Having been chosen team coordinator, I
was now Dorothy.
```

As the journal entries increased in length and complexity, the tedious nature of parsing each sentence began to weigh heavily on my ability to concentrate. It reminded me of an English class, when asked to analyze a Shakespearean tragedy. And how much I welcomed the bard's introduction of comic relief. However, I doubted Mason or other members of the TEAM[19] would include a Rosencrantz or Guildenstern as peripheral characters in this drama. I would have to create my own whimsical respites.

---

[19] For purposes of this narrative, I chose to capitalize the words TEAM and ASSIGNMENT to differentiate their generic use from specific references to Mason, his compatriots and their task.

Imagine if the time frame had been different. For example, 45 years later, would *The Wizard of Oz* still be the inspiration for code names? Or would the eventual choice emerge when Mason or one of his colleagues suggests, "We need to make this operation look like **nothing** to see here." Who would know more about nothing than Jerry, George, Kramer and Elaine?

These humorous breaks proved few and far between. Curiosity and my sense of duty to my benefactor remained the driving force. There would perhaps be time for witty asides later.

```
Step #3: As with any assignment, we divided the
mission into milestones and assigned each to a
member of the team. I was tasked with identifying
potential candidates to carry out the
assassination. Once identified, each member of
the team would be responsible for grooming one or
more of the candidates to eventually complete the
assignment.
```

Nothing yet to discredit the account. Still a long way to go.

CHAPTER SEVEN

MOTIVES

The January 18 journal entry mimics a memorandum written by the CEO or planning director of any major corporation. Of the five prerequisites in the January 16 posting, only one could be called strategic. "The assassin's background and motivation must support the dead president's policy agenda and add to his legacy." This is the "what," the desired outcome. The others are the "how," the tactics. Find an assassin. Pick a time and place for him to act. Arrange for his immediate elimination. Make sure no one else is harmed.

To link tactics to the overall strategy, the TEAM needed a motivated assassin, someone whose reason for killing the president would enhance his victim's image or policy agenda. That is where Mason and the TEAM began.

```
January 18, 1963

An unusually light WH schedule this weekend.
Tonight Volunteer[20] is hosting the Jefferson-
Jackson Day dinner at the Armory. Saturday and
Sunday the WH is holding events to celebrate the
second anniversary of Lancer's inauguration.
Scarecrow, Lion and Tinman are taking my shifts
so I can spend the next three days on the
assignment.
```

---

[20] Vice-president Lyndon Johnson's Secret Service code name.

> Although I have been given responsibility for
> identifying potential assassins, the team agreed
> the sign-off on any recommendations presented to
> Wizard required our unanimous approval. To build
> a case for the eventual selection of an assassin,
> we decided to start with motive. Why would the
> chosen individual want to kill Kennedy? The team
> agreed on three possibilities, which I listed at
> the top of one of the blackboards: civil rights,
> national security and organized crime.
>
> Civil Rights. Last fall, Lancer sent federal
> troops to the University of Mississippi to ensure
> James Meredith, the first Negro to enroll there,
> could register peacefully. The day before
> Meredith's scheduled enrollment riots broke out
> resulting in two deaths. Four days ago, newly
> elected Alabama governor George Wallace promised
> to continue the fight against desegregation.
> Would assassination by an opponent of the civil
> rights movement create more support for this
> cause?

Maybe you find the use of the term "Negro" a bit awkward, or even offensive. For me, these contemporaneous accounts only increased my appreciation for Mason's gift. Not only did the journal provide a fresh glimpse at a significant moment in U.S. history; it often chronicled the evolution of American culture.

Until the late 1960s, the capitalized word "Negro" was the commonly accepted means of classifying individuals of black African heritage, especially residents of the sub-Saharan region. In his August 28, 1963, "I Have a Dream" speech on the steps of the Lincoln Memorial, Dr. Martin Luther King, Jr. used the term 15 times. To this day, the single largest benefactor of financial support for students at historically Black colleges and universities remains the United Negro College Fund. Reading Mason's words evoked images of the decades-long struggle to settle on an appropriate descriptor to capture the legacy of one-time slaves and their descendants, including Negro, Colored, Black and African-American.

It is also a reminder of what has not changed, the *de jure* and *de facto* treatment of some Americans as second-class citizens. Take, for example, Mason's citing of George Wallace's inauguration speech. It was just a single line in a speech given 50 years ago. But that one phrase, "segregation now, segregation tomorrow and segregation forever," still echoes in some of the darkest corners of American society.[21]

> There was no lack of possibilities. The Klan had
> re-emerged in several southern states. More anti-
> Negro groups had formed following the 1954
> Supreme Court decision which declared school
> segregation to be unconstitutional. There had
> also been an increase in the number of violent
> crimes targeting Negroes since 1954. Most of the
> suspects, even those who were charged and tried,
> were not convicted by all-white juries. No one
> would be surprised if someone motivated to kill
> Kennedy was a member of the Klan, a
> segregationist or someone who already used
> violence to prevent integration.
>
> National Security. Cuba has haunted Lancer since
> the Bay of Pigs disaster. Withdrawal of Russian
> offensive weapons from Cuba has not eased
> concerns about a Communist regime so close to the
> U.S. Is liberating Cuba still a foreign policy
> objective? Would JFK's death at the hands of a
> pro-Cuban sympathizer justify action against
> Castro?

Consideration of a Cuba-linked motive indicates the TEAM had no knowledge of the multiple attempts by the CIA to assassinate Castro following the Bay of Pigs invasion and continuing as late as March 1963. These covert operations, which included five additional attempts on the Cuban leader's life, were first exposed by *Washington Post* columnist Jack Anderson in June 1971.[22] And documented in 1975 by the Senate Select Committee to Study Government Operations with

---

[21] "Segregation Forever: A Fiery Pledge Forgiven, But Not Forgotten," *All Things Considered,* National Public Radio, January 10, 2013.
[22] Jack Anderson, "6 Attempts to Kill Castro Laid to CIA," Washington Post, June 18, 1971.

Respect to Intelligence Activities, chaired by Idaho Senator Frank Church.[23] From the vantage point of hindsight, I wondered if prior knowledge of these covert operations would have influenced the TEAM's contemplation of an assassin with pro-Castro sympathies.

Imagine the impact on Kennedy's legacy if an investigation immediately following the assassination had exposed the CIA's efforts to kill Castro. Kennedy's death at the hands of a pro-Cuban gunman would no longer be viewed as an unprovoked attempt by the Havana government to intervene in American foreign policy. Instead, it could be regarded as an understandable, if not justified, response to Kennedy's green-lighting unlawful use of the nation's intelligence apparatus.

```
Organized Crime. Attorney General Robert Kennedy
declared a war on organized crime which would not
have been possible if he was not the President's
brother. At the top of his list was Teamsters
Union president Jimmy Hoffa. RFK seemed even more
determined to bring Hoffa down after he was re-
elected union president in July 1961. Many
believed the union election was rigged. Would a
Mafia attack on JFK provide cover and public
support for RFK to expand his prosecution of
organized crime and union corruption?
```

As was the case with the Cuban related motive, knowledge of CIA efforts to eliminate Castro might have tempered the TEAM's consideration of the organized crime option. While Mafia dons cursed the Kennedy administration for its prosecution of organized crime, the CIA recruited crime bosses Momo Salvatore (Sam) Giancana and Santos Trafficante, Jr. as conduits between the agency and business associates in Havana who could assist with Castro's demise.[24]

The lack of internal communication between U.S. intelligence agencies was not surprising considering the siloed nature of each agency's

---

[23] *Foreign and Military Intelligence: Final Report,* Senate Select Committee to Study Governmental Operations with Respect to Intelligence Activities, Government Printing Office, April 26, 1976.

[24] Steve Holland and Andy Sullivan, "CIA tried to Get Mafia to kill Castro: Documents," *Reuters,* June 26, 2007.

operations. This was more than the left hand not knowing what the right hand was doing. It was akin to an octopus with tentacles totally independent of one another. As later exposed by the Church Committee, many of the president's closest advisors knew nothing about CIA attempts to kill Castro. If Wizard had such information, he surely would have forewarned the TEAM.

```
For now, we decided to keep all three options on
the table. The next task was to identify
organizations or individuals identified with each
motive. Whether we could entice or manipulate one
of them to carry out the assignment would come
later.
```

Without the benefit of highly classified intelligence information, the decision to pursue all three options made sense.

Not so, if the TEAM had prior knowledge of the CIA/Mafia alliance to assassinate Castro. The TEAM's options would have been significantly restricted. They probably would have been forced to eliminate the Cuba option. Or the Mafia connection. Oswald's pro-Cuba activities might have disqualified him as a potential assassin. Would rejection of these alternatives make an already difficult task next to impossible? If Mason had continued the journal beyond November 1973, I imagine his response to the Church Committee report might have been, "It was a good thing we did not have access to this information. Sometimes ignorance really is bliss."

CHAPTER EIGHT

CIVIL RIGHTS

With each succeeding entry, the journal provides one more retrospective about America during the Kennedy era. The January 19 description of Mason's time in the FBI records room is a window into how much the nation's capital physically changed from 1963 to the present. Some transformations resulting from new construction to accommodate an expanding federal government. Others associated with honoring the past.

Compare the nature and location of Mason's research in January 1963 to how he might describe it today. FBI headquarters are no longer housed in the Department of Justice building (renamed for Robert F. Kennedy in 2001). Since 1974, the Bureau resides in the J. Edgar Hoover building, across Pennsylvania Avenue from its original home. Some things, however, remain the same. The FBI's Central Records System (CRS), established in 1921, survives although physical analog files gave way to digital ones.

January 19, 1963

As a matter of course, agents check with our internal Protective Research Section prior to each presidential trip for any individuals who might represent a threat based on background or previous activity. PRS records are less than complete. To fill in the gaps, I will be spending most of my time reviewing FBI/CRS files at the Department of Justice.

This entry reaffirms the lack of coordination among federal law enforcement agencies. Did the Secret Service really need to maintain its own records of potential threats to the president? Was this not duplicative of what was available in the more comprehensive FBI files? However, this proved to be to the TEAM's advantage. Keeping the assignment confidential and avoiding suspicion would prove more difficult if there were better coordination between the full range of investigative and security services.

Testimony before the Warren Commission confirmed this absence of cooperation between the Secret Service and FBI as well as the inadequacy of the service's internal files. During an April 1964 hearing, Commission assistant counsel Samuel Stern asks agent Winston Lawson, a member of the president's detail in Dallas, about the threat assessment in advance of the trip to Texas. Imagine the look on Stern's face if agent Lawson answered, "There was no need to look for potential threats. We already knew who the threat was. Us."

Of course, that assumes Lawson was a member of the TEAM, which was impossible based on the November 22 journal entry. Mason later specifies that TEAM members were intentionally assigned to locations other than the motorcade. Lawson, who was credited with planning the route was a rider in the car immediately in front of the presidential limousine.

In fact, Lawson's reliance on information available from the Protective Research Section demonstrates the informal and non-rigorous nature of the process of identifying presidential threats. This lack of concern was even more onerous considering the known hostile environment in Dallas toward Kennedy.

> Mr. LAWSON. I went--on November 8, after leaving Mr. Kellerman's office, I went to the office in the Executive Office Building where our agents of the Protective Research Section are, and notified agents at that location that I was being assigned the advance for Dallas, Tex. trip, the date of this trip, and that I requested them to check their files and determine as to whether I should have the name of any individual in the Dallas area who was of record to us as an active subject.
>
> Mr. STERN. Was this request made in writing?

Mr. LAWSON. It was oral, sir.

Mr. STERN. Is it usually made that way, orally? Do you ever make a written request?

Mr. LAWSON. I have never done so. I don't know about the other individuals.

Mr. STERN. What did they tell you?

Mr. LAWSON. I was told after waiting there a little while that there were no subjects of record in the Dallas area, of active PRS individuals that we would expect to harm the President.[25]

With three options on the table, where does one begin the search for a motivated killer? Perhaps in alphabetical order: civil rights, national security, organized crime. Or the order in which they appeared on the TEAM's blackboard (long ago erased). Instead, Mason indicates he acts on the TEAM's initial discussion with Wizard and the emphasis on JFK's legacy.

The president's national security agenda was the most complex. It consisted of a long-term undertaking focused on containing the spread of Communism, especially in the Western Hemisphere, while simultaneously negotiating with the Soviet Union to reduce the threat of nuclear conflict. Attorney general Robert Kennedy, not the president, took the lead when it came to prosecuting organized crime and associated corruption in Mafia-infiltrated unions. Civil rights was much more straightforward. Although the Kennedy administration responded to violent incidents resulting from enforcement of *Brown v. Board of Education of Topeka, Kansas*, civil rights activists argued the president had not done enough to support their broader agenda.

Washington insiders believed Kennedy wanted to wait until his second term to pass new legislation which would codify violations of constitutional protections affirmed by the Supreme Court. However, the increase in organized civil rights protests and violent responses by opponents would force Kennedy to accelerate his timeline.

---

[25] Testimony of Secret Service special agent Winston Lawson, Hearings before the Warren Commission, April 23, 1964, Volume IV, p. 342.

On June 11, 1963, JFK announced his intention to send civil rights legislation to Congress. This promise came during an address to the nation following the deployment of National Guard troops to safeguard the enrollment of two African-American students at the University of Mississippi. The TEAM assumed the president's death at the hands of an avid segregationist would increase public and Congressional support for any forthcoming legislation.

Having prioritized the order in which he would tackle each of the options, Mason's search for potential assassins began in earnest with a probe of suspects who opposed Kennedy's commitment to alleviate race-based social and economic injustice.

```
I organized my search based on our initial three
options. Among the three categories, I started
with civil rights. There was already evidence
Lancer's support of the civil rights movement
would not sit well with those who opposed
integration, especially in the deep south.

Each document in the FBI/CRS files has a three
number code. The first number is the
classification code which indicates the statutory
basis for FBI jurisdiction. Civil rights cases
fall under Classification 44.
```

When needed, the FBI creates a new classification code following a presidential executive order or passage of a specific act of Congress. I assumed FBI engagement in civil rights cases originated after World War II in response to Executive Order 9981, by which President Harry Truman, in 1948, ordered integration of the U.S. armed services. Archive records, however, attribute the classification to Reconstruction era legislation, which prohibited "actions or conspiracies of two or more people to stop citizens in their free exercise of Federal rights secured by the Constitution and laws of the United States."[26] The classification was later amended to include violations of the Voting Rights Act of 1965, Civil Rights Act of 1968 and the Voting Rights Act of 1975.

---

[26] Classification 44 was officially established and originally labeled "Civil Rights and Domestic Violence" in a memorandum from FBI director J. Edgar Hoover. (Source: "Records of the FBI—Classification 44: Civil Rights," National Archives.)

The case list under classification 44 included two categories of people whose backgrounds might be considered a threat to JFK. Leaders of segregation groups and individuals believed to have committed violent acts against Negroes.

The files confirmed that after years of decline, white supremacy organizations such as the Ku Klux Klan began to resurface in the late 1950s. FBI interest in Klan activity was triggered by the 1957 Alabama murder of Willie Edwards Jr., a Negro, who had been hired as a driver for Winn-Dixie.

Klan membership continued to increase in the 1960s in response to the civil rights movement. In 1961, Robert Shelton, the son of a former Klan member, established the United Klans of America merging several local chapters of the KKK.

A brief review of Shelton's file suggests he is an unlikely candidate for the assignment. He has spent much of his life moving from one job to another, none for any significant length of time, including car tire salesman and operating a printing business. He has no demonstrated skill using a firearm. There is no record of violent behavior as he sees himself as the legal and political leader of the movement.

A file on Edgar Ray Killen, a sawmill operator and ordained Baptist minister, documented his strong ties to the KKK in two Mississippi counties: Neshoba and Lauderdale. Like Shelton his Klan responsibilities were administrative, recruiting new members and organizing protests. There is no record of his ever being charged with a violent crime.

Another possibility is Byron De La Beckwith. Unlike Shelton or Killen, De La Beckwith is not a native southerner. He was born in 1920 in Colusa, California. He goes to live with his maternal uncle's family after his father dies of pneumonia when he is five. His mother dies of lung cancer

when he is 12. He enlists in the Marines in 1942,
serves as a machine gunner in the Pacific and
fights in the battle of Guadalcanal. He is
honorably discharged in August 1945.

After the war he marries and settles in
Greenwood, Mississippi. In 1954 he joins the
White Citizens Council, an organization formed to
resist school integration after the Supreme Court
decision in Brown v. Board of Education. Unlike
the Klan, the WCC does not engage in violence.
Instead, it organizes boycotts of Negro
businesses and urges others to fire Negro
employees.

Although De La Beckwith has experience with
military firearms he has no history of violent
behavior. There is nothing to suggest he would
agree to be the triggerman.

The references to Killen and De La Beckwith provide additional
evidence the journal is a contemporaneous account. While accurate at
the time Mason reviewed their files, the assessment of both men as non-
violent would later prove to be inaccurate. Mason admits this error in
judgment when he learns De La Beckwith is charged with the murder
of the NAACP's Mississippi field secretary Medgar Evers in June 1963
and Killen's role in the deaths of civil rights activists James Chaney,
Andrew Goodman and Michael Schwerner in 1964.

There is no shortage of files covering violent
crimes against Negroes since the Brown decision.
Those responsible fall into five categories.
Never identified. Since deceased. Charged but not
indicted. Tried and acquitted. Tried and
convicted.

Based on the number of cases in the last three
categories, there is no need to reopen
investigations to identify suspects in the
unsolved cases. Or spend time researching those
who have died.

One example in this last category is Luico Flowers who killed Dr.
Thomas Brewer, a prominent Black doctor and founder of the

Columbus, Georgia chapter of the NAACP. Less than a year after the February 28, 1956, incident, Flowers was shot and killed. Suspects in Flowers murder were never identified.[27]

Those still in prison can also be eliminated.

One such case involved the assault on a mentally disabled handyman named Judge Edward Aaron[28] who was abducted, beaten and castrated by six members of the Asa Carter chapter of the KKK. The leader Jesse Mabry was also among the Klan members who attacked singer Nat King Cole during a performance in Birmingham on April 10, 1956.[29] Mabry was convicted for his role in the Aaron assault and sentenced to 20 years in prison. After several unsuccessful appeals, Mabry began serving his sentence at the state penitentiary in 1959.

I then reviewed the files of several individuals charged with crimes against Negroes but were never convicted or had been released after serving minor sentences.

On August 13, 1955, Lamar Smith, a WWI veteran and civil rights activist, was murdered in front of the Brookhaven, Mississippi courthouse. Noah Smith, Mack Smith and Charles Falvey were arrested. A grand jury heard testimony from more than 30 witnesses who were present at the courthouse on the day of the shooting. All denied having seen anything.

The FBI contacted local police who said the victim was selling absentee ballots. They also claimed he was in possession of a .32 caliber pistol when he was shot.

On September 13 an all-white grand jury announced it would not indict the three suspects. The file contains an article from the Alabama Tribune

---

[27] "Notice to Close File," Civil Rights Division, Department of Justice, File No. 144-19M-1752.

[28] "Judge" did not refer to a magisterial appointment. It was the victim's given first name.

[29] Associate Press, "Alabamans Attack 'King' Cole on Stage," *New York Times*, April 11, 1956, p. 1.

dated September 30, 1955, which states the grand
jury was unable to get so much as one witness to
testify against the three white men charged with
the murder.

The file provides no information about their
current location.

The FBI revisited the case in 2008 under the "cold case" provision of the Emmett Till Unsolved Civil Rights Crime Act of 2007. Despite additional evidence the murder may have been a premeditated ambush, the FBI officially closed the case on April 22, 2010, as all three suspects had since died. Noah Smith on June 17, 1975, Mack Smith on September 14, 1992, and Falvey on December 26, 1987.[30]

Department of Justice lawyers conceded, even if the suspects were still alive, the statute of limitations prevented any federal attempt to retry the case. Prior to 1994 amendments to the Civil Rights Act, federal criminal civil rights violations were not capital offenses, and therefore, remained subject to a five-year statute of limitations.

Emmett Till's kidnapping and murder were among
the most reported racial crimes. The FBI file
contained an August 30, 1955 article in the
Jackson-based Clarion Ledger which first reported
Till's disappearance. It identified two suspects
J. W. Milam and Roy Bryant who police arrested
for kidnapping the 14 year old Negro. They denied
any involvement and claimed several other people
saw Till threaten Bryant's wife who worked at the
family-owned grocery store. Till's body was found
two days later in the Tallahatchie River.

The trial began on September 18. Five days later
an all-white, all male jury took just over an
hour to acquit Milam and Bryant.

After the trial, Milam rented a farm in Sunflower
County but abandoned the business when locals,
especially Negroes, would not work for him. On
February 14, 1958, the New York Post reported

---

[30] "Lamar Smith – Notice to Close File," Civil Rights Division, U.S. Department of Justice, File #144-41-3581, April 12, 2010.

Milam was seen in a bread line in Washington
County. Milam and his wife Juanita moved to
Orange, Texas later that year.

Bryant was forced to give up his store following
a boycott by the Negro community. He and his wife
moved to Indianola, Mississippi where he is
working as a mechanic.

There are three other relevant documents in the
file. There is a copy of an article in the
January 24, 1956, issue of Look magazine which
included an interview with Bryant and Milam. They
confess to the murder. There are also two
releases dated October 28, 1955 signed by
Bryant's wife and Milam in return for $3,150 from
Look for their story.

I was initially surprised at Mason's summary of Till's murder and the subsequent trial, considering the wealth of information I found in the FBI files and newspaper accounts. Milam and Bryant could not be retried for murder after publication of the *Look* magazine article. However, on November 7, 1955, they came before a LeFlore County grand jury after the county district attorney sought to indict the pair for kidnapping. The DA argued a second trial would not constitute double jeopardy since Till's kidnapping and murder occurred in two different legal venues, LeFlore and Tallahatchie Counties, respectively. On November 9, the grand jury decided not to indict Milam and Bryant on the kidnapping charge.

From Mason's perspective, details of the murder, trial or any attempt to re-litigate the case were irrelevant to his mission. He had no interest in the alleged murderers' guilt or innocence. He was looking for an assassin. Furthermore, the heinous details of Till's torture and death had been widely reported by every major national newspaper. The outcry based on news coverage became a catalyst that increased demand for racial justice. Therefore, he likely felt no need to duplicate information that was already publicly available. Instead, Mason reviewed additional files in search of motivated candidates with the skills and temperament to carry out the ASSIGNMENT.

On October 22, 1955, a young Negro boy John Earl
Reese was shot and killed in a Longview, Texas
cafe. It appeared to be a random killing when the
cafe was sprayed with bullets from a passing car.
Two other people were injured.

Texas Rangers arrested Perry Dean Ross and Joe
Simpson who were indicted for Reese's murder.
Simpson's charges were dismissed in exchange for
testimony against Ross. On April 23, 1957, Ross
was convicted of the murder without malice and
the all-white jury recommended a two to five year
suspended sentence. Ross was released in 1959. No
information about other criminal activity or
current location.

Like Lamar Smith, the FBI reopened the case in 2008 under the "cold case initiative" but terminated the investigation after obtaining copies of death certificates for both Ross (Panola County, Texas/January 8, 1976) and Simpson (Maricopa County, Arizona/June 30, 1998).

The 2008 review affirmed, without evidence of kidnapping or the use of explosives, there was no statutory justification for federal intervention. FBI director Hoover did explore the possibility Ross and Simpson violated U.S. postal law when they damaged several mailboxes during the shooting. However, legal counsel at the Postal Service determined this was insufficient to justify pursuing the lesser charge.[31]

Emmett Till was not the only victim of racial
violence in Tallahatchie County. On December 3,
1955, Elmer Otis Kimbell shot and killed a Negro
Clinton Melton. He worked at a service station
where Kimbell stopped to get gas. The shooting
followed an argument over how much gas Melton had
pumped. Witnesses claimed Kimbell asked Melton to
fill his tank. When Melton gave him the bill,
Kimbell insisted he had asked for just one

---

[31] "John Earl Reese – Notice to Close File," Civil Rights Division, Department of Justice, File #144-73-4749, updated July 26, 2021.

```
dollar's worth. Kimbell left the station, later
returned with a gun and shot Melton three times.

On March 13, 1956 an all-white, all-male jury
acquitted Kimbell. Newspaper clippings in the
file indicate Kimbell returned to his job as
manager of a cotton gin in Glendora, Mississippi.
```

Mason's description of the Melton case explains the fear in which Black Americans lived in northeast Mississippi.

Location was not the only coincidence linking the Till and Kimbell murders. Kimbell lived next door to J. W. Milam. The fan Milam and Bryant tied to Till's body before tossing him in the Tallahatchie River reportedly came from the Glendora Gin where Melton was employed. Kimbell's trial was held in the same courthouse as the Till trial. Furthermore, Kimbell was represented by J. W. Kellum, the same defense attorney hired by Milam and Bryant months earlier.

```
The last file I pulled was Robert Chambliss,
another member of the United Klans of America.
Chambliss was suspected of firebombing the homes
of several Negro families earning him the
nickname Dynamite Bob. Although he was never
convicted of any of the bombings, he reportedly
bragged about them in local bars. The last thing
we need is someone who cannot be trusted to keep
silent about the assignment.
```

Like De La Beckwith and Killen, Chambliss' most infamous crime came years later when he was identified as one of the four Klan members responsible for the September 15, 1963, bombing death of four African-American girls while attending Sunday school at the 16th Street Baptist Church in Birmingham, Alabama. On September 29, 1963, Chambliss was charged with illegally purchasing and transporting dynamite. He was fined $100 and given a suspended 180-day jail sentence.

Newly elected Alabama attorney general William Baxley reopened the investigation in January 1971. Based largely on testimony by several eyewitnesses, a grand jury indicted Chambliss on four counts of murder on September 24, 1977. Chambliss was convicted on November 18 and sentenced to life in prison where he died in 1985.

> Today has not been as productive as I had hoped. Although I found several possibilities based on motive, most have something in their backgrounds that suggests further consideration would be a waste of time. Chambliss is a braggart who is likely to share what he is doing with others. Bryant and Milam have already sold their story once and would surely do it again. Even De La Beckwith, the only one who appears to have the necessary temperament and experience with firearms, has nothing in his background that suggests he would commit a violent crime.

I always thought of Mason as someone who could connect the dots or see the big picture. This time, however, his focus on individuals prevented him from recognizing the fertile environment which could seed and nourish wave after wave of rabid segregationists. True, each person Mason researched had a potential dealbreaker in their background. But the fact so many of the cases occurred within such a narrow slice of American geography suggested these were only the most recent by-products of a local culture steeped in racial animus and violence. What was it about northeast Mississippi that made it the epicenter of mid-20th century racial conflict?

Then aspiring journalist David J. Halberstam provided one possible answer. Seventeen years before he won the Pulitzer Prize for *The Best and the Brightest*, Halberstam penned an article for *The Reporter* titled, "Tallahatchie County Acquits a Peckerwood." Following the acquittal of Elmer Kimbell for the alleged murder of Clinton Melton, Halberstam wrote:

> *A friend of mine divides the white population of Mississippi into two categories. The first and largest contains the good people of Mississippi, as they are affectionately called by editorial writers, politicians, and themselves. The other group is a smaller but in many ways more conspicuous faction called the peckerwoods.*

> *The good people will generally agree that the peckerwoods*
> *are troublemakers, and indeed several good people have told*
> *me they joined the Citizens Councils because otherwise the*
> *peckerwoods would take over the situation entirely. But while*
> *the good people would not act with the rashness of and are*
> *not governed by the hatred of the peckerwood, they are*
> *reluctant to apply society's normal remedies to the*
> *peckerwood. Thus it is the peckerwoods who kill Negroes and*
> *the good people who acquit the peckerwoods.*[32]

Maybe Bryant, Milam, Mabry, Kimbell, Smith, Falvey and Chambliss did not fit the bill. But there were likely others where they came from. Even if Mason had not immediately found a suitable candidate to be the gunman, his research suggested there were untapped possibilities in the vicinity of Greenwood who might be willing to commit murder in the name of the South's "lost cause."[33]

Mason missed one other prospect due to an aberration in the FBI/CRS classification system. Files covering white supremacists were split between Classification 44/Civil Rights and Classification 157/Extremist Matters and Civil Unrest. Focusing only on CRS 44, Mason never reviewed an Atlanta field office file (#157-608) in which an undercover police informant William Somersett kept tabs on Joseph A. Milteer, a leader associated with the ultra-right National States Rights Party and other white supremacist organizations.

Somersett recorded a conversation during a November 9, 1963, meeting with Milteer in Miami, during which Somersett tells Milteer, "I think Kennedy is coming here on the 18th," leading to the following exchange.

> MILTEER: Whenever he goes anyplace, he knows he is a marked man.
>
> SOMERSETT: You think he knows he is a marked man?

---

[32] David Halberstam, "Tallahatchie County Acquits a Peckerwood, *The Reporter*, April 19, 1956.

[33] A myth perpetrated by Southerners "to cast the Confederate defeat in the best possible light which celebrates an antebellum South of supposed benevolent slave owners and contented enslaved people." (Source: Britannica.com/topics/lost cause, written by David W. Bright)

> MILTEER: Sure he does.
>
> SOMERSETT: They are really going to try to kill him?
>
> MILTEER: Oh yeah, it is in the works. Brown himself, [Jack] Brown is just as likely to get him as anybody in the world. He hasn't said so, but he tried to get Martin Luther King.[34]

Milteer also told Somersett he believed Jack Brown, a Dixie Klan Imperial Wizard, had participated in the bombing of the 16th Street Baptist Church. In reference to Brown's unsuccessful attempt to kill Martin Luther King, Jr., Milteer added, "He followed him for miles and miles, and couldn't get close enough to hit him."[35]

Milteer eerily predicted any assassination attempt would involve a high-powered rifle from a perch in a multi-story building. In *Zero Fail: The Rise and Fall of the Secret Service,* author Carol Leonnig writes:

> *(Milteer) was right. Given the Secret Service's small size, it was impossible to check the hundreds of buildings along any motorcade route. If there was a reason to suspect a specific problem, or a structure was very close, buildings could be checked or shuttered, as (Secret Service agent Winston) Lawson had done in Binghamton. But otherwise, the agents would do nothing about the buildings they passed.[36]*

Not only could Milteer have identified Jack Brown as a willing assassin. He identified a security gap which Lee Harvey Oswald would later exploit to target the president.

Even if Mason had pulled the file on Milteer in January 1963, it would not, at that time, contain the transcript of the November 9 conversation with Somersett. The only information he would have found was background on Milteer's hate-group activities. These included distribution of leaflets in Atlanta on May 18, 1962, a "White Christians, Believing in White Supremacy" meeting on May 20, a meeting of the local White Citizens Council in his hometown of Quitman, Georgia,

---

[34] Dan Christensen, "Assassinations: Miami Link, Part 1," *Miami Magazine*, Volume 27, Number 11, September 1976.

[35] Ibid.

[36] Carol Leonnig, "Chapter 2: Tempting the Devil," *Zero Fail: The Rise and Fall of the Secret Service*, Random House, New York, 2021, pp. 42-43.

and a September 24 advisory from the Quitman Police Chief William R. Elliot that describes Milteer as an "agitator."[37]

If Milteer's name had surfaced in advance of Kennedy's November 16-18 trips to Palm Beach, Cape Canaveral and MacDill Air Force Base, would the TEAM have considered South Florida a more serendipitous location to pull off the ASSIGNMENT? Especially since Somersett had placed Milteer in the region as late as November 9. Upon learning of the taped conversation between Somersett and Milteer, Miami special agent Robert Jamison immediately notified the head of protective services Robert Bouck, putting Milteer on a watch list.

Milteer's treatment significantly differed from that of Lee Harvey Oswald. Despite all the information Mason found in Oswald's FBI files, none of it was forwarded to the Protective Research Section. Therefore, when Agent Lawson queried the PRS, as he testified before the Warren Commission, Oswald did not appear on their radar screen.

The difference between the handling of information about Milteer and Oswald raises the question whether someone was intentionally violating standard operating procedures when it came to the FBI updating the Protective Research Section about Oswald. If so, why? I made a note to look for similar anomalies in other advance preparations for Kennedy's trip to Dallas.

---

[37] Report of FBI Special Agent Royal A. McGraw, "Joseph Adams Milteer," Atlanta Field Office, January 22, 1964, pp. 6-7.

CHAPTER NINE

NATIONAL SECURITY

The following day, Mason confirmed a lack of confidence in finding a suitable candidate under the civil rights umbrella. He discontinued his search of files under Classification 44, skeptical it would lead him to additional possibilities motivated by racial animus. Instead, he moved on to the next option, someone with a national security motive, especially one with Cuban, Russian or other Communist associations.

January 20, 1963

Today, I focused on individuals whose motive might be linked to American foreign policy or national security. I started with files of Americans who left the U.S. to live in Communist countries.

FBI/CRS Classification 105 Foreign Counterintelligence has files on almost 400 Americans who match this profile going back to the mid-1950s. I immediately eliminated those who still live in their adopted countries. Of those who returned to the U.S. or were in the process of repatriation, over half are not natural born Americans. I quickly narrowed the list down to 12 persons of interest. Mollie and Morris Block. Harold Citrynell. Bruce Frederick Davis. Shirley Dubinsky. Joseph Dutkanicz. Martin Greendlinger. Nicholas Petrulli. Lee Harvey Oswald. Libero

Ricciardelli. Vladimir Sloboda. Robert E.
Webster.

These individuals have several things in common.
They all denounced their American citizenship
while visiting or living in the Soviet Union.
Many had military training prior to defecting.
Spent more than a year in the USSR. Made anti-
American statements in the Soviet press. Many had
personal relationships with Soviet citizens. Were
known to have been in contact with KGB personnel.
Most eventually sought repatriation.

I further reduced the number of potential
candidates based on their current status
according to the most recent FBI updates. Only 3
of the 12 are currently living in the U.S.:
Citrynell. Oswald. Petrulli.

Harold Citrynell with his wife and child traveled
to the USSR as tourists in February 1958. While
in Moscow he applied for permanent residence and
Soviet citizenship at the Office of Visas and
Registration. On his application he claimed he
had been unable to find employment in the U.S. He
was offered a job at a mining instrument factory
in Kharkiv in the Ukraine.

In the fall of 1958, Citrynell wrote U.S.
officials he was being involuntarily detained and
wanted to return to the U.S. With assistance from
the Red Cross, he left the Soviet Union on June
29, 1959 after agreeing he would never speak
badly about his time there.

Lee Harvey Oswald was a Marine who traveled to
the USSR in September 1959 following a hardship
discharge a month earlier. He immediately applied
for Soviet citizenship. His application was
rejected and he was scheduled for deportation.
His departure was delayed due to a self-inflicted
foot wound. On October 31 he went to the American
embassy in Moscow and denounced his U.S.
citizenship. Oswald was assigned a job as a lathe
operator in a Minsk electronics plant. Early in

1961, Oswald openly expressed dissatisfaction with Soviet life and considered returning to the U.S.   However, in March 1961 he chose not to leave Minsk after he met and soon married Marina Prusakov. Marina gave birth to a daughter in February 1962.

Three months later Oswald applied for repatriation and a visa for Marina. After returning to the U.S. they settled in Dallas where Oswald's mother Marguerite lived.

The next tab contained information about his Marine service. Oswald joined the Marines in October 1956. His specialty was radar operations. It required a security clearance which he received in May 1957. During his time at El Toro AFB in the fall of 1956, an officer's performance review described Oswald as "a very competent crew chief and brighter than most people." His service record included the fact he taught himself Russian.

The next document caught my attention. In December 1956 he was tested for marksmanship. Oswald received a score of 212 which qualified him as a sharpshooter.

The last tab in his folder covered Oswald's early childhood. He was born in New Orleans on October 18, 1939. His father Robert Oswald died on August 19, 1939, two months before Lee was born. Although he never met his father, Lee's interest in the Marines was the result of stories about Robert's service as a Marine in WWI.

In January 1944 Marguerite moves the family to Dallas where she marries Edwin Ekdahl. In October 1946 Lee begins school at Benbrook Elementary. Marguerite and Edwin separate in early 1948 after she learns he was having an affair. She divorces him in June 1948.

After the divorce, Lee begins to exhibit aggressive behavior including an incident when he threatens his half-brother John Pic with a knife. After John joins the Coast Guard and his older brother Robert Oswald joins the Marines in 1952, Marguerite takes Lee to New York. They move in with John and his new family. They are asked to leave when Lee threatens John's wife with a pocketknife.

Marguerite and Lee settle in the Bronx where Lee enrolls at PS 117. In January 1953 Lee is the subject of a truancy hearing. After additional absences, Lee is classified as a habitual truant and receives a psychological evaluation by Dr. Renatus Hartogs. He shows signs of schizophrenia and passive-aggressive tendencies.

While Oswald's Russia connection and rifle skills make him a good prospect, his mental stability is a concern but does not totally disqualify him as a potential assassin. Incidents of threatening behavior and Dr. Hartogs' assessment are several years old and his file includes no recent instances of similar conduct.

Nicholas Petrulli traveled to the USSR in 1959 under a 7-day visitor visa while on an organized tour of western and eastern Europe. The tour ended on August 18 in Moscow when the group was to leave by train. Petrulli did not show up at the Moscow station. Instead he made arrangements through an Intourist[38] guide to stay at the Hotel Ukraina in Moscow.

On August 28 he informed the U.S. embassy in Moscow of his intention to defect. The next day he sent a letter to the Supreme Soviet requesting citizenship. Petrulli returned to the U.S. embassy on September 2 and took an irrevocable oath of renunciation.

---

[38] At the time, Intourist was a state-owned entity created to facilitate business and tourist travel in the USSR. It was privatized in 1992 and is currently operated by Anex Tours.

> After failed attempts to find work, Petrulli was
> told he should have applied for Soviet
> citizenship at the Soviet embassy in Washington
> before coming to the USSR and was told to leave
> the country. Petrulli returned to the U.S.
> embassy where he was given a one-way passport and
> arrived in New York on September 22.
>
> I spent the remainder of the day scanning more
> FBI files. There were other possible candidates,
> but none had Oswald's potential. I made a note we
> should start tracking him.

Although he may not have realized it at the time, January 20, 1963, is the first consequential milestone in Mason's story and mine. I anticipated Lee Harvey Oswald's introduction but was not prepared how my curiosity about the journal would shift. Whether true or not, I was now captivated by the narrative. Oswald could no longer be viewed as the self-motivated, disenchanted loner portrayed in the Warren Report. He had been chosen by the TEAM who, in less than a year, would somehow transform a repatriated Russian defector into a presidential assassin.

Before digging deeper into that metamorphosis, I needed to review Mason's exploration of the third option under motives.

CHAPTER TEN

ORGANIZED CRIME

The January 26 entry provides a clear sense of what to expect in the rest of Mason's journal. As with every previous page, the narrative is presented in meticulous detail as he pursued the immediate task, creating a list of individuals with the motive and skill to assassinate a president. Yet, it lacked any indication of the plotters' mindset or how the TEAM would reconcile the conflict between loyalty to their oath and what the person they pledged to protect had asked them to do.

What mechanisms might Mason and other members of the TEAM use to compartmentalize this moral struggle? I thought about comedian Dana Gould who once used the Kennedy assassination as an example of how stand-up comics inject humor into the darkest situations.

> *I was born on August 24, 1964, which is exactly nine months and two days after the Kennedy assassination which tells you all you need to know about how my father processes grief. And now when I watch the Zapruder footage, I have very mixed emotions because I realize if he misses, I wouldn't be here.* [39]

Did any member of the TEAM bring anything like Gould's graveyard sense of humor to the ASSIGNMENT? There must have been opportunities. Imagine the moment when Mason adds the words

---

[39] Dana Gould, "Anything Can Be Funny," *I Know It's Wrong,* Comedy Dynamics, 2013.

"organized crime" to the list of potential motives. Did one of his colleagues interject, "Come on Mason. Organized crime? What makes you think the Mafia would be interested in or capable of pulling off a hit job?" Or, without the benefit of Mario Puzo's yet unpublished saga of the Corleone family, would one of them come up with an idea to incent the assassin similar to consigliere Tom Hagen's explanation how he convinced movie producer Jack Woltz to cast singer/actor Johnny Fontane in his next movie. "I made them an offer they couldn't refuse."

Would everyone laugh? Or would a member of the TEAM remind the others, "This is serious business. We don't have time for jokes."

```
January 26, 1963

The Kennedys are spending the next two days at
Glen Ora with the children. I had the weekend off
from the presidential detail which meant I could
spend Saturday and Sunday in the FBI records
room.
```

In February 1961, JFK leased Glen Ora, a 400-acre estate near Middleburg, Virginia from Grady Byfield Tartiere as a weekend family retreat.[40] Was this one more peripheral fact about the Kennedy years that Mason included in his journal to add to its veracity?

```
My new focus was organized crime. The FBI had a
ready-made list of potential targets. It was
created when approximately 100 Mafia leaders met
in Apalachin, New York in November 1957. The
meeting was called following the contract killing
of Albert Anastasia, one of the leaders of what
was known as Murder, Inc. Anastasia's murder was
ordered by Vito Genovese, the don of one of New
York's five families. Genovese set up the
Apalachin meeting to arrange a truce among
warring crime organizations and divide up
Anastasia's operations.
```

---

[40] "Houses: Glen Ora, Middleburg, Virginia, 1960-63," Clark Clifford Personal Papers, Archives, John F. Kennedy Presidential Library, Digital Identifier: CCPP-MF02-005-p0024.

Local and state police became suspicious when
several expensive cars with out of state license
plates arrived in the southcentral New York town.
More than 60 attendees were detained and 20 were
indicted and convicted of conspiring to obstruct
justice. Sentences ranged from 3 to 5 years and
each was fined $10,000. In November 1959 a U.S.
appeals court reversed the conspiracy convictions
as there was no evidence any state or federal law
was violated during the meeting.

Despite the vacated convictions, the Apalachin gathering became a turning point in the federal government's effort to stem organized crime. Prior to the confab, J. Edgar Hoover plausibly denied the existence of a vast, nation-wide Italian-American criminal enterprise. That all changed after Apalachin. Jerry Capeci, a journalist who covered Mafia activities in New York City, made the following observation.

It was a watershed moment. Hoover and the FBI had to acknowledge the existence of the Mafia--this Italian-American organized crime syndicate. And the American people also became aware of it. It was no longer like the boogeyman in the closet. It was real.[41]

As Mason then explains, this "watershed moment" presented its own challenges for the TEAM. His immediate concern with the organized crime option was not a lack of potential confederates. As Mason points out, there were too many.

The attendance list from Apalachin was a who's
who of organized crime. It included the heads of
the major syndicates in New York City, Buffalo,
Tampa, Chicago, Cleveland, Dallas, Kansas City,
Pennsylvania, Colorado and Los Angeles. Many were
accompanied by their underbosses and
consiglieres. If not already an FBI target, a CRS
file was created for each major player at
Apalachin.

---

[41] Michael Hill, "Busted Hoodlum Conclave Made N.Y. Hamlet a 'Crime Shrine,'" *Associated Press*, November 19, 2000.

Finding a Mafia accomplice required a different strategy from the civil rights and national security options. Instead of looking for the eventual hitman, we needed to find a willing ally who would do that for us. That made the Apalachin list with names of second tier leaders for each family more valuable. Direct contact with one of the mob bosses was too risky. We needed to find an intermediary.

I called Lion and Scarecrow to ask their advice where to start. We decided that location was not an issue with one possible exception. New York City. The disrupted meeting in Apalachin did not resolve the rivalry among the five NYC based families whose in-fighting could compromise the assignment. However, we agreed it was too early to completely eliminate them.

The FBI files suggested an incentive the team could use to enlist their services. Several prominent members of the five families were currently in prison. The files documented successful DOJ prosecutions of Carmine Galante, John Ormento, and Frank Palermo. What if we could reverse their convictions or commute their sentences in return for ending Kennedy's presidency? There was one additional incentive. Aware of the open animosity between RFK and the vice-president, it was unlikely the president's brother would stay on as attorney general.

In addition to Galante, Ormento and Palermo, we agreed to include the leaders of families in the other major cities represented at Apalachin, cities that were likely campaign stops in the coming year. The list included:

-Frank DeSimone, Los Angeles
-Sam Giancana, Chicago
-John T. Scalish, Cleveland
-Joseph Civello, Dallas
-Santo Trafficante Jr., Tampa
-Joseph Ida, Philadelphia

-James Colleti, Denver
-Nicolas Civella, Kansas City

I asked Lion to share the list with Wizard. Were there any we should give priority or could eliminate?

Lion returned the call with Wizard's input. The WH priority is political. He suggests we focus on states Democrats need to win in 1964. Kennedy lost California and Florida to Nixon. He barely won in Illinois and Texas despite Johnson being on the ticket. Although Kennedy won New York easily, Wizard said it might be harder next time if Rockefeller is the Republican nominee.

Eager to narrow my search I used this information to eliminate Scalish, Ida, Colleti and Civella. That left DeSimone, Giancana, Civello and Trafficante plus one or more of the New York bosses.

Frank A. DeSimone. The file on DeSimone was more useful than I expected. Not because what it said about DeSimone. It clarified what I needed to look for in each subsequent folder, information about which family we could trust to carry out the assignment and keep it confidential.

DeSimone's status in the LA family rose when he was a lawyer, representing John Roselli. Roselli oversaw entertainment operations for the Chicago Mafia. DeSimone became don of the LA crime family in 1957 following the death of Jack Dragna. He inherited the loyalty of Frank Bompensiero who was the most feared Mafia hit man in southern California. Dragna repaid Bompensiero when he chose him to manage the family's San Diego operations. Despite his successful hits, Bompensiero had been involved in failed assassinations of Dragna's rivals including an attempt on Bugsy Siegel capo Mickey Cohen in 1948. Dragna's reputation suffered and DeSimone proved to be equally incompetent. This made DeSimone's LA operations including those in the

> entertainment industry an opportunity for rival
> families.
>
> Bompensiero's current status. He was convicted on
> three counts of bribery in 1955 and was released
> on five years probation in 1960. There is no
> record of post-release offenses. If he has gone
> straight, he may not be the potential hitman his
> past indicates.
>
> I realized the size of the folder was important.
> Those targets with less complete files would
> require more team follow-up to assess their
> potential. But like DeSimone there was often
> enough to eliminate them.

I constantly reminded myself Mason only had access to information about each potential alliance with organized crime as of January 1963. His assessment might have differed based on post-1963 FBI addenda to the files. Subsequent FBI documents suggest DeSimone was not as inept and disrespected as previously believed. A January 1965 memo from the LA field office to director Hoover described DeSimone as the go-between linking the bosses in several western U.S. states to their Midwest and East Coast counterparts. FBI surveillance of Nick Licata, a DeSimone lieutenant, produced this updated assessment.

> *(Licata) pointed out that since the publicity of the Apalachin Meeting, that such large meetings no longer occur. In this connection he mentioned that FRANK DESIMONE "Boss" of the Los Angeles "Brugad" represented the smaller Western "Brugads" on those occasions when a Western U.S. representative was necessary.*[42]

Until his death by natural causes in 1967, the FBI viewed DeSimone more as an intermediary between the entertainment industry and the more powerful Midwest and New York City families.

Updates on post-DeSimone organized crime in California tapered off following his death. Beginning in the mid-1960s, the FBI field office

---

[42] "La Cosa Nostra Anti-Racketeering Conspiracy," Memo from SAC, Los Angeles to Director, FBI, via AIRTEL, January 15, 1965.

in Los Angeles no longer considered Mafia activities their primary interest. Protests against the Vietnam war led to a new focus, surveillance of radical, anti-war organizations such as Students for a Democratic Society.

The full text of the interview confirms the relationship. It further corroborates most of these trips were related to their grocery and beverage businesses. With one exception. Civello claimed he had not been invited to the Apalachin meeting. His attendance resulted from DeSimone inviting him to come along, although at the time DeSimone claimed he "did not know the purpose of the meeting."[43]

Despite on-going FBI surveillance of Civello following his release from prison, the records support Mason's assessment. Civello maintained a

---

[43] Interview of Joseph Civello, File No. 92-4225-14, January 2, 1958.

low-profile when it came to running the Dallas syndicate. It must have made for quite dull reading. After Civello filed an "Application for Pardon after Completion of Sentence," he and partner Russ Musso purchased the Love Field Grocery, then opened another business, Civello's Imports. Civello often traveled to Midland, Texas on weekends. He hung out at the law offices of James Robert Todd whose practice included representing area prostitutes.[44] Of little interest to federal law enforcement before November 1963, attention to Civello and Dallas organized crime would re-emerge following the assassination and Jack Ruby's assault on Oswald.

> Santo Trafficante, Jr. Trafficante inherited the crime organization and connections put together by his father who died in 1954. In the early 1950s, he was arrested several times and charged with bribery and running illegal lotteries in the Cuban and Puerto Rican districts of Tampa where his operation was based. His only conviction in 1954 was overturned by the Florida Supreme Court.
>
> The family's primary source of income was legal gambling operations in Cuba before Castro. In 1955 Trafficante moved to Cuba to oversee and invest in several Mafia-owned hotels and casinos. Among his co-investors were Sam Giancana/Chicago and Joseph Bonanno/New York. Trafficante retained a presence in Tampa as the owner of several restaurants and bars.
>
> Before Castro took power, Mafia investments in Cuba were well documented and indirectly supported through cooperation between the Cuban Bureau of Investigation, the Cuban Treasury Department and the IRS. In 1958 the CBI listed eight hotels and casinos either owned or operated by U.S. Mafia families. When Castro took over, he ordered the casinos closed.
>
> A July 21, 1961, memo drafted by U.S. narcotics agent Eugene Marshall suggested Castro began disrupting Trafficante's lottery operations in

---

[44] FBI, Central Records System, Folder 92-2824.

```
Tampa. Marshall believed Castro's actions pushed
Trafficante back into narcotics trafficking. In
an August 1961 follow-up memo, agent Oscar Davis
shared unconfirmed reports that Trafficante
became a Castro agent and agreed to be "Castro's
outlet for illegal contraband" into the U.S.

Trafficante may have another reason to want
Kennedy dead. His consigliere Frank Ragano also
represents Teamster president Jimmy Hoffa. Hoffa
was a constant target of RFK's investigation of
organized crime going back to RFK's time as
counsel to the McClellan Committee. Would
Trafficante risk killing JFK as a favor to Hoffa?

The FBI files contained no evidence of a personal
vendetta against the Kennedys. The Tampa
syndicate seems preoccupied with regaining its
Havana casinos. It is unlikely they would use any
of their resources to carry out the assignment.
```

After reviewing the January 26 entry, I realized I mistakenly focused only on the content of the journal to assess its veracity. What did the presentation of the content say about the timing and spontaneity of the document? What assumptions would help me understand the process by which Mason created the narrative?

The journal entries related to Mason's FBI research differed from those prior to January 19, 1963. They captured secondary information whereas earlier ones were based on events in which Mason claimed to be a participant. The conversation with JFK in Marine One. The road trip to the Liberty Bowl with the other future members of the TEAM. Their first meeting with Wizard. Setting up shop in the Naval Annex.

The earlier entries were prologue, not unlike Act I of a Shakespearean tragedy, what the Sydney Theatre Company (STC) refers to as the exposition phase. "The exposition introduces important information to the audience that is vital to the unfolding action of the play." Mason's research of the three options is the beginning of Act II or what STC calls the rising action. "Throughout the rising action a series of events occur that lead to the climax." [45]

There was a second major difference. The earlier entries were much shorter. I could imagine Mason sitting down at his typewriter each evening to capture his fresh recollection of each day's development. The same could not be said of his research of FBI records. Were the entries covering his two weekends at FBI headquarters derivative of the report he prepared to share with the TEAM?

I doubted this would be the last time I would encounter an issue which needed to be tabled for further consideration. Before moving on to the next entry, I added an "Outstanding Issues" column to the white board in my office.

```
January 27, 1963

Returned to the FBI records room to review files
on Giancana and NYC bosses.

Momo Salvatore aka Samuel Mooney (Sam) Giancana.
Giancana has been on the FBI's radar screen for
quite some time. The records consist mainly of
telegrams and faxes between the FBI Chicago field
office and DC headquarters.

Of particular interest was a classified folder
which included surveillance summaries which
documented Giancana's attitude toward JFK. The
first dated 12-20-62 was a field report on a
reopened restaurant The Villa Venice Club
allegedly owned by Giancana. The cover sheet
includes an underlined sentence in all capital
letters. "GIANCANA SHOULD BE CONSIDERED ARMED AND
DANGEROUS." Much of the report focused on Mafia
attempts to influence local Chicago politics. An
important ally was Congressman Roland Libonati
who led the opposition to anti-corruption
legislation proposed by RFK.
```

---

[45] "Dramatic Structure of a Tragedy," Sydney Theatre Company Education worksheet, sydneytheatre.com.au/education/resources.

> An earlier coded teletype memo addressed to
> Hoover, dated 10-31-62, claims Giancana expressed
> displeasure with JFK during a card game with
> other Chicago crime figures. "GIANCANA TOOK OFF
> AGAINST DEMOCRATIC ADMINISTRATION, CRITICIZED
> PRESIDENT'S HANDLING OF CUBA, STATES IF
> ADMINISTRATION SPENT LESS TIME ATTEMPTING TO PUT
> PEOPLE IN JAIL AND MORE ON INTERNATIONAL
> SITUATION THIS COUNTRY WOULD NOT BE IN ITS
> PRESENT SHAPE."
>
> Giancana may have more than one reason to want
> JFK gone. While Castro remains in power the Mafia
> is unlikely to reestablish its gaming interests
> in Havana.

I immediately noticed something different about the January 27 entry. Mason had largely summarized the information in the FBI files when it came to the Russian connection, civil rights option and the previous day's analysis of other Mafia prospects. In this posting, there were *verbatim* quotes. He also included metadata about communications between the Chicago field office and FBI headquarters, including the author, the recipient, method of transmittal and the date.

The metadata was a godsend as it saved my having to flip through the entire file to locate a document which could verify or rebut the journal. The referenced December 20, 1962, field report[46] and the October 31, 1962, memo to Director Hoover[47] were exactly as Mason described them.

Which raised still another question. Mason knew he needed to share everything he learned with the other TEAM members as they had previously agreed to collectively sign off on each step. But, when it came to the Chicago crime boss, did Mason's more precise sourcing signal his personal preference for Giancana if the TEAM settled on the Mafia option?

---

[46] Memo to the Chicago FBI Office files from the service agent in charge, field office file # 92-349, December 20, 1962.
[47] Coded memo from Chicago field office service agent in charge to the FBI director, date/time stamp October 31, 1962, 5:52 AM.

Mason now had evidence of the Chicago crime boss' motivation. But what incentives could the TEAM provide to solidify his participation? Giancana would never believe Hoover and especially RFK would magically drop their pursuit of organized crime. An economic incentive seemed more plausible. Fidel Castro's rise to power in Cuba had decimated organized crime's lucrative gambling enterprise in Havana. One need not be a McArthur Foundation Genius Award winner to understand the mob's financial interest in overthrowing the Castro government. Or their dashed hopes for a quick resolution of the situation following the failed Bay of Pigs invasion in April 1961. Or Kennedy's "hands off" pledge in return for withdrawal of Soviet missiles in October 1962.

What the TEAM did not know at the time was the extent to which Giancana, Santo Trafficante and John Roselli became active participants in efforts to remove Castro from power. The CIA's alliance with organized crime to assassinate the Soviet-aligned dictator remained a closely guarded secret until reported by the Senate Select Committee on Government Operations with Respect to Intelligence Activities, often referred to as simply the Church Committee for chair Idaho Senator Frank Church. Details of CIA/Mafia collaboration first appeared in an interim report "Alleged Assassination Plots Involving Foreign Leaders," released by the Committee on November 20, 1975.[48]

Understanding the totality of the relationship between Giancana and the Kennedys was complicated by conflicting, and often undocumented, accounts of *quid pro quos* and broken promises. Giancana's daughter Antoinette provides the most complete list in *JFK and Sam: The Connection between the Giancana and Kennedy Assassinations*, which she co-authored. Ms. Giancana alleges the following instances in which the two families were either collaborators or adversaries.

- During prohibition, JFK's father Joseph P. Kennedy was a target of the Detroit Mafia, which controlled rum-running in the region. When the elder Kennedy began importing wine and hard liquor

---

[48] "Alleged Assassination Plots Involving Foreign Leaders," An Interim Report of the Senate Select Committee on Government Operations with Respect to Intelligence Activities, U.S. Government Printing Office, Washington, D.C., November 20, 1975.

to the East Coast via the Canadian-Detroit border, he relied on Chicago mob contacts to negotiate a settlement.

- Following the 1929 stock market crash, Joseph Kennedy began investing in the movie industry. He engaged Giancana and the Chicago mob to handle labor disputes since they had ties to the leadership of several Hollywood unions.

- The first *quid pro quo* occurred in 1960 when Ms. Giancana claims Joseph Kennedy sought her father's help in securing union support during the West Virginia primary. In return, the elder Kennedy promised Senate investigations into her father's activities, in which both JFK and Robert Kennedy had a role, would cease.

- Giancana also ensured union support for Kennedy in Illinois during the general election.

- Ms. Giancana claimed her father was responsible for destroying annulment documents related to JFK's rumored 1947 marriage to Palm Beach socialite Durie Malcolm.

- In 1961, the CIA recruited Giancana, Trafficante and Rosselli to participate in authorized attempts to assassinate Cuban president Fidel Castro. After the Communist leader's demise, Giancana fully expected to recoup his lost investment in Havana casinos and a Cuba-based shrimping company.

- Judith Campbell, whom Frank Sinatra introduced to both men, had simultaneous affairs with Giancana and JFK. Ms. Giancana made an unsubstantiated claim Campbell discovered she was pregnant with JFK's child shortly after the president ended the relationship. Her father offered to marry Campbell, and when she refused, arranged for an abortion.[49]

Ms. Giancana's account must be taken with a grain of salt as it relies solely on personal recollection and hearsay with little, if any, sourced documentation. For example, her father's destruction of documents which purported to annul JFK's rumored marriage to Durie Malcolm is questionable on multiple counts. In a 1997 exposé of the Kennedy family, *The Dark Side of Camelot*, Seymour Hirsch claims long-time

---

[49] Antoinette Giancana, John R. Hughes & Thomas B. Jobe, *JFK and Sam: The Connection between the Giancana and Kennedy Assassinations,* Cumberland House Publishing, Nashville, Tennessee, 2005, pages 81-88.

JFK friend Charles Spalding confirmed the union although Malcolm repeatedly denied the allegation. Although she refused to be interviewed for Hirsch's book, she had a close friend deliver the following message.

> *Tell [Hirsch] one thing. I've never been married to John Kennedy and there's nothing to discuss. Just call him up and say we were never married.*[50]

Even if the marriage took place, Sam Giancana could not have been responsible for disposal of an annulment. Father James J. O'Rourke, pastor of a parish church in Brighton, Massachusetts, told Hirsch, there was no need for an annulment since Malcolm was not Catholic and a justice of the peace reportedly officiated at the ceremony.

> *An annulment only comes into play when a Catholic is involved and the marriage has taken place in the Catholic Church.*[51]

However, if a fraction of what his daughter claims is true, Sam Giancana had more than enough motivation to kill Kennedy. At the time Giancana's name rose to the top of the TEAM's list of potential Mafia accomplices, little if any of this information was available. Considering the justification for the ASSIGNMENT included solidifying the president's legacy, any disclosure of Mafia associations, marital infidelity or illegal CIA black ops resulting from an investigation into Kennedy's murder would have had the opposite effect.

Antoinette Giancana's wilder allegations aside, we know two things were true. The Church Committee provided proof of Mafia participation in CIA efforts to assassinate Castro. And Judith Campbell Exner's simultaneous liaisons with JFK and Sam Giancana were substantiated during hearings by the House Select Committee on Assassinations.

---

[50] Seymour Hirsch, *The Dark Side of Camelot*, Little Brown and Company (Boston), 1997, p. 329.
[51] Ibid., p. 330.

Disposition of those who attended the Apalachin conference, and its aftermath, provides additional justification for this choice of "finalists." All became targets of FBI surveillance after being detained by state and local police on November 14, 1957. Of those on Mason's list, only DeSimone, Civello and Scalish were indicted and tried for conspiracy. Why them and not Giancana and Trafficante? Were prosecutors aware the Chicago and Tampa dons were aligned with members of Congress who could short circuit any FBI inquiry? Or did they believe DeSimone, Civello and Scalish were low-hanging fruit? Did the FBI and DOJ assume it would be easier to make examples of these three lesser-known members of the Mafia network because they lacked the stature and resources to contest the charges?

Apalachin was DeSimone's coming out party upon his promotion to Los Angeles crime boss following Dragna's death. Likewise, Civello was an equally unknown figure pre-Apalachin. The exception was Scalish whose tenure predated the New York mob gathering. He ruled the Cleveland Mafia from 1944 until his death in 1976. However, his sphere of influence was limited to northern Ohio, consisting largely of gambling, loansharking and union corruption.

In contrast Giancana had strong ties to several prominent politicians in Chicago's First Ward. Additionally, Trafficante shared Giancana's responsibility for gambling operations in Havana on behalf of several New York-based mob bosses. In 1957, that connection meant major Mafia figures were aligned with U.S. policy toward Cuba including support of the U.S.-backed government headed by military dictator Fulgencio Batista. The Eisenhower administration viewed Batista as a buffer against Communist revolutionaries led by Fidel Castro. Giancana and Trafficante feared a Communist takeover would result in nationalization or closure of their casinos and hotels. Thus, the U.S. intelligence community and the Mafia became unlikely bedfellows.

Regardless of the reason for their presence on the TEAM's list of potential allies, Mason selected three data points which would further narrow the list: documented animosity toward Kennedy, experience eliminating adversaries and willingness to take one for the team if captured. Those criteria led to reconsideration of one or more of the New York-based families.

The CRS files were limited to surveillance of the men at the top of the organization charts in cities like Cleveland and Dallas. New York was a different story. In some cases, underbosses and capos were as infamous as the dons and were constantly under FBI scrutiny. To Mason's advantage, the FBI had already done the research to help identify not only the organizations most likely to join the conspiracy, but potential hitmen.

CRS files on the NY crime families include extensive histories of capos and soldiers, including confidential memos from FBI field offices to the director. Among the most extensive was a March 7, 1958, NY field office summary of Carmen Galante's illegal activities dating back to an attempted holdup in 1930.

Galante had ties to the NYC-based Genovese and Bonanno families. In the 1940s Galante allegedly participated in dozens of murders as one of Vito Genovese's most reliable hit men. In the 1950s he managed the Montreal drug business for Joseph Bonanno and Vicenzo Cotroni. In 1959, Galante was arrested by New Jersey state police and indicted in May 1960 on drug conspiracy charges. On July 10, 1962, Galante was convicted of all charges and sentenced to 20 years in a federal prison.

The files also describe how Galante became a trusted associate of several Mafia bosses. A March 1958 memo from the New York office referenced an unnamed informant who had known Galante for more than 25 years. "No matter what illegal activities Galante might be caught in or charged with, he has the reputation of not talking." Doesn't that make him an ideal candidate to be our hitman? Someone who is willing to accept any assignment and if caught will remain silent.

Was Mason's reading of the FBI assessment wishful thinking? Could someone like Galante be that skilled at taking down adversaries without being caught? In *Five Families: The Rise, Decline and Resurgence of America's Most Powerful Mafia Empires*, Selwyn Raab references over 80 murders in which Galante was involved. He also confirms Galante's connection to more than one of the five New York crime organizations.[52]

The above journal passage stands out as one of the few times Mason included direct quotes for an obvious reason. He wanted to differentiate between his personal opinion and that of a documented source. It was the FBI, not Mason, who believed Galante was a willing gun for hire and someone who kept his business to himself.[53]

```
Giovanni Ormento aka Big John Ormento is part of
what became known as the "dope trio," which
includes Galante and Joseph Di Palermo. The FBI
believes this trio is responsible for most of the
Mafia's heroin distribution. They were arrested
after being betrayed by one of their lieutenants
who was recruited to expand the narcotics market
in his native Puerto Rico.

Ormento was charged and convicted of violating
the Harrison Narcotics Act in 1937, 1941 and
1951. He was released in 1953 after serving two
years.
```

The Harrison Narcotics Tax Act, regulated "the registration of, with collectors of internal revenue, and to impose a special tax on all persons who produce, import, manufacture, compound, deal in, dispense, sell, distribute, or give away opium or coca leaves, their salts, derivatives, or preparations, and for other purposes." Enacted in 1914, its intended purpose was to facilitate physicians' use of prescription narcotics "in the course of normal treatment."[54]

---

[52] Selwyn Raab, Five Families: The Rise, Decline and Resurgence of America's Most Powerful Mafia Empires, St. Martin's Press, 2005.
[53] "Carmine Galante, Anti-Racketeering," Special Agent in Charge, New York Field Office, March 7, 1958, page 91.
[54] Harrison Narcotics Tax Act of 1914, Chapter 1, signed into law by President Woodrow Wilson on December 17, 1914.

My own background research on Ormento provided one more "Forrest Gump moment" involving a chance encounter between Ormento and comedian Billy Crystal. In his book *700 Sundays*, Crystal recounts a confrontation between his father and the mob underboss. The encounter took place following an incident when a drunk Ormento swerved his car into the Crystals' brand new 1957 Plymouth Belvedere they had parked outside a Chinese restaurant. Crystal writes Ormento surveyed the damage, ran to his car and left the scene. He continues:

> *The five of us sat in the living room bemoaning the loss of the Belvedere. The doorbell rang and I got it. When I opened the door, there was an overcoat, a neck and an eyebrow. Big John Ormento was in the doorway.*

Ormento offered to replace the Plymouth with "a new car, any car you want, the car of your choice." But Crystal's father did not want to be indebted to someone the comedian referred to as "our Luca Brasi." He told his son, "Let's just get this car fixed."[55]

This sidebar represents one more opportunity to compare Mason's account of the assassination to a Shakespearean play. Like the Bard of Avon's darkest tragedies, here lay an additional opportunity to inject comic relief. According to Tom Stoppard's 1990 film, Rosencrantz and Guildenstern may be dead, but Ormento and Crystal live on.

```
The final decision is not up to me, but I am more
convinced Mafia anger directed at the attorney
general is not motive enough to kill the
President. RFK is the more likely target for
revenge. Although killing RFK might not make a
difference. Investigation and prosecution of the
Mafia has taken on a life of its own. The DOJ
section responsible for pursuing organized crime
```

---

[55] Billy Crystal, *700 Sundays,* Grand Central Publishing, October 31, 2005, pages 9-11.

has grown from a handful of lawyers to more than
60.

Without knowledge of Mafia participation in CIA efforts to assassinate Castro or the JFK, Giancana, Campbell Exner triangle, I understood and agreed with Mason's evaluation Robert Kennedy was the more logical target. RFK had a long history of prosecuting the mob. Before his brother became president, RFK served as special counsel to the Senate Select Committee on Improper Activities in Labor and Management.[56] As attorney general, he ordered investigations of major crime syndicates.

Just prior to Mason's two weekends among the FBI/CRS records, RFK updated his brother and the nation on DOJ's progress in a publicly released memo. The Department's record of success during RFK's tenure as attorney general was acknowledged during congressional debate of the Racketeer Influenced and Corruption Act of 1970 (RICO) which gave the department new authority to go after the heads of crime families even if they were not personally engaged in any illegal activities.

In Frank Palermo's case, animosity toward the attorney general included personal considerations. Palermo, a Philadelphia crime family associate, was best known for fixing the Jake LaMotta-Billy Fox middleweight championship fight in 1947 and as majority owner in the syndicate that controlled heavyweight champion Sonny Liston. In 1961, Palermo was charged with extorting welterweight champion Don Jordan. Following a three-month trial, at which Attorney General Robert Kennedy served as lead prosecutor, Palermo was sentenced to 25 years in prison.

Although the organized crime option would not produce the eventual assassin, it remained a viable option for several reasons. The motive was obvious. Crime bosses would surely welcome a reduction in on-going DOJ investigations and prosecutions. Additionally, several major organized crime figures were currently behind bars. When

---

[56]The U.S. Senate established the Select Committee on Improper Activities in Labor and Management on January 30, 1957. Chaired by Arkansas Senator John McClellan, the Committee's primary focus was efforts by Jimmy Hoffa to oust Teamsters president Dave Beck and his union's connections to organized crime.

Galante was convicted of narcotics trafficking in July 1962, he was sentenced to 20 years in prison. Any reduction or commutation of his incarceration represented an attractive *quid pro quo* for arranging Kennedy's murder.

However, the existing FBI surveillance and background on Sam Giancana proved too seductive. There was documented evidence of Giancana's displeasure with JFK plus three additional factors. His interest in reestablishing Mafia gaming interests in Havana. A sense of personal betrayal by the president's father Joseph Kennedy, a perceived compatriot in black market exploitation. And the importance of Illinois in the 1964 election per Wizard's assessment of the electoral landscape.

The concealed relationship between Giancana and the president was much more complex. FBI files contained no information which might alert Mason of the triangle involving Giancana, JFK and Judith Campbell. If FBI director J. Edgar Hoover was aware of these facts, he buried them in his private files along with equally damaging information about Richard Nixon, Martin Luther King, Jr. and others to be used, if needed, to protect his own interests.

In addition to the typewritten journal, I wondered if Mason kept a separate checklist of the conditions attached to the team's assignment. If so, the Mafia option, and particularly Giancana, checked all the boxes.

- Motive? Multiple players had personal vendettas against Kennedy and his brother.
- The assassin must not be anyone tied to the U.S. government or military. Although arranged by a prominent Mafia boss, the assassin would be an unknown hitman.
- The assassin must be eliminated. On numerous occasions crime families had knowingly offered up one of their own to achieve a desired outcome. Sacrificing a family soldier to protect a member of the senior leadership was not beyond the pale.
- Would this add to the president's legacy? Once authorities or the press announced the assassin had connections to organized crime, DOJ could justify further investment of time and money

to prosecute Mafia-supported corruption, whether Robert Kennedy was heading the agency or not.

- No one else could be harmed. Seldom was collateral damage a consequence of a Mafia-directed hit. The typical modus operandi of a contract killing by a crime family lieutenant involved either a highly proficient sharpshooter or a point-blank assault.

Mason had been flying solo for more than a week. It was time to share his research with the other TEAM members.

At first, I was surprised at the brevity of the February 6 journal entry. In hindsight and context, it made perfect sense. Mason had already captured major findings from the FBI files in the four previous entries. Nor did I expect him to share the TEAM's reaction to his research. This was not a diary in which emotions or feelings played any role. Mason's only interest lay in preserving the facts. Then, determining how those facts would influence the next steps.

```
February 6, 1963

I arrived early this morning to add the most
relevant information under each option for my
presentation to the team.

Under civil rights, I added Byron De La Beckwith.
I do not see him as the eventual trigger man.
However, through his membership in the White
Citizens Council, he could lead us to someone
willing to be a martyr for the cause.

Lee Oswald remains the best possibility under
national security. He has both the motive and
skill to carry out the assignment.

The organized crime option is more complex. I
confirmed the on-going rivalry among the New York
families and recommended Giancana and the Chicago
syndicate as my first choice.
```

The team asked few questions. They were ready to
move on, looking deeper into the background of
the primary candidate in each category. Of the
four of us, Tinman was the only one with previous
experience in corruption cases. He volunteered to
take the lead with Giancana. Despite the "armed
and dangerous" warning, Tinman doubted Giancana
would risk being the trigger man. We would need
to convince Giancana that eliminating JFK is in
his business interests and have him arrange the
assassination. This would also add another layer
of separation between us and the killer.

Scarecrow volunteered to be Oswald's primary
contact. He knows Dallas and his southern accent
is an asset. He also knows he cannot approach
Oswald directly. He will need to identify an
intermediary who can make the introduction.

By elimination, Lion agreed to connect with De La
Beckwith. Before leaving for Mississippi, he
needed a cover story which included a false
record of his segregation credentials in case
someone questions his interest in killing JFK.

I will remain at the command center to coordinate
field operations and be available as a
"reference" if needed.

CHAPTER ELEVEN

A FULL TIME JOB

The second week in February marked a turning point in the ASSIGNMENT. To date, the TEAM's activities, consisting largely of setting up shop and researching secondary sources, did not require travel outside the immediate Washington, D.C. area. That was about to change.

February 12, 1963

After working on the assignment for just over a month it was clear we could not continue providing regular protective services for the president and plan the operation. The team requested a meeting with Wizard. Yesterday he confirmed his availability this morning. Lancer was meeting with the national security council at 10:00am. Afterwards he planned a swim and late lunch. Wizard did not need to be in the WH until late afternoon for a meeting with the Commission on Civil Rights followed by a reception commemorating the 100th anniversary of the Emancipation Proclamation.

Again, Mason begins an entry with what some people might consider extraneous details. Did he really need to do that and how might it be relevant? There were two possible explanations. It could just be his nature and training kicking in. It might also be his way of convincing readers the journal was drafted in real time. A skeptical audience, however, might describe it as overkill, an attempt to deceive rather than illuminate.

> I do not believe in omens, but there was something eerie about discussing a presidential assassination on Lincoln's birthday. When Wizard arrived, we immediately addressed the issue at hand. We told him we needed to be relieved of our regular detail rotations. In addition to the time element, the next phase of the assignment involved undercover work. We could not risk being seen with the president where someone might make a connection between our regular jobs and the assignment.
>
> Wizard was two steps ahead of us. He had already talked with the director. We would be reassigned to work with the re-election campaign staff to plan what would be an extensive travel schedule for the next 18 months. The director signed off with one exception. The team must brief the director monthly on the campaign schedule, even if it was tentative. Agreed.

The TEAM's reassignment to the campaign made sense logistically. Campaign trips 18 months prior to the election were not a security priority. Agents only accompanied the president during reelection-related travel. Their primary responsibility was advance work. Therefore, this switch in assignments ensured the TEAM's absence would not be seen as out of the ordinary or suspicious.

Although Wizard did not explicitly say as much, his recommendation that the TEAM operate as an arm of the campaign staff seemed to include a subliminal message. Was Wizard suggesting the assassination take place while Kennedy engaged in a political activity rather than official business? If so, why?

First, the presence of large crowds and relatively unfettered access to the candidate were desirable during any election cycle and would not be viewed as contrary to normal protocol. Second, the TEAM would be involved in scheduling details which included the selection of venues, decisions that would facilitate their ability to synchronize the assassin's movements with those of his target. Third, with almost total control over campaign travel security, the TEAM could minimize random factors that might complicate or even derail the effort.

Relieved of their regular shifts on the presidential detail, the TEAM could now launch the next phase of the ASSIGNMENT, field operations to verify secondary information about each potential assassin needed to make the final selection.

```
February 13, 1963

Scarecrow arranged to fly to Dallas the next day.
Tinman took off for Chicago. Lion is heading for
Greenwood, Mississippi.

I stayed behind to provide support when needed. I
will also maintain the files and update the
options blackboard.
```

To this point, I have shared each journal entry, except for the last page, in chronological order. However, the TEAM's deeper dives into each of the three options became stories within themselves. For that reason, I chose a different tack, aggregating relevant entries or excerpts as they applied to the three options.

CHAPTER TWELVE

BYRON DE LA BECKWITH

What turns an otherwise non-violent white supremacist into a killer?

At the outset of the three on-site investigations to gather more detailed information on Oswald, Giancana and De La Beckwith, the TEAM never viewed the Mississippi segregationist as the eventual assassin. According to every available FBI document in early 1963, his role in the White Citizens Council was limited to legal and promotional activities. There was no evidence of his ever having engaged in physical assaults or bloodshed involving African-Americans. The following excerpts from Mason's journal reveal why the FBI felt no need to track Medgar Evers' murderer and what changed leading up to June of 1963.

February 18, 1963

Lion found the Greenwood Library's microfiche collection of archived newspapers to be a valuable resource. It contains articles about De La Beckwith, the White Citizens Council and several of DLB's letters to the editor.

Lion identified three things he believes are important. DLB sees himself as the leader of the fight against integration in Greenwood and gets angry when others do not. DLB was overlooked as a gubernatorial appointee to the Mississippi Sovereignty Commission, established to defy the Brown decision based on the Commission's belief it was a violation of states rights. Following

```
this snub, he devoted more effort to making the
WCC the leading segregation power in the state.
```

The Mississippi Sovereignty Commission was established by the state legislature in 1956 for the specific purpose of preserving segregation in the wake of *Brown v. Board of Education of Topeka, Kansas.* The Commission, led by then Governor James P. Coleman, recruited state and local law enforcement officials to monitor civil rights activities and intimidate the organizers. Among the Commission's prime targets were Fannie Lou Hamer, co-founder of the Freedom Democratic Party and an organizer of Mississippi's Freedom Summer; Dr. Gilbert R. Mason, co-founder of the Biloxi chapter of the NAACP and Medgar Evers, the first NAACP Mississippi field secretary.[57]

```
DLB tried to increase his influence in Greenwood
and the state through membership in several civic
organizations. Lion's conversations with people
who knew DLB suggest there was a second reason he
joined the WCC. He felt like an outsider after
moving to Greenwood from California. In addition
to membership in the WCC, DLB joined the Moose
Lodge, Knights of Pythias, Masons, Greenwood
Historical Society, Sons of Confederate Veterans,
Sons of the American Revolution and the local
Church of the Nativity.

Articles in the local newspapers identified other
segregationist leaders. Lion used them to create
a list of future contacts who could provide
additional information about DLB or might be
considered as the assassin.

February 20, 1963

After Lion arrived in Greenwood, four Negro owned
businesses were destroyed by fire. One of the
buildings was next to the headquarters of the
Student Nonviolent Coordinating Committee which
was leading a voter registration drive in Leflore
County. Instead of investigating whether the fire
was arson, local police arrested the SNCC field
```

---

[57] Leo Carney, "The Vestiges of Jim Crow and the Mississippi Sovereignty Commission," *Mississippi Free Press*, May 20, 2021.

    secretary after he suggested the fires were
    deliberately set. He was charged with making
    statements which could incite violence.

Sam Block's arrest on February 20 was his seventh since arriving in Greenwood to organize the voter registration campaign. He was tried, convicted and sentenced to six months in jail for "making statements calculated to incite the breach of the peace."[58] The presiding judge offered to suspend the sentence if Block agreed to terminate SNCC's voter registration efforts and leave town. Block's response? "Judge, I ain't gonna do none of that."[59]

    February 22, 1963

    Lion contacted a member of the WCC who also
    belongs to DLB's church. He described DLB as a
    troublemaker, more interested in prohibiting
    Negro membership than spiritual pursuit. He told
    Lion DLB claimed to be a leader of the WCC though
    he held no formal position. He also suggested DLB
    used membership in the WCC to associate with
    local business leaders.

In his 1994 biography of De La Beckwith, author Reed Massengill, a nephew of his subject's first wife Mary Williams, confirms how De La Beckwith used membership in community organizations as introduction to local power brokers. This was particularly true of the Greenwood chapter of the White Citizens Council, whose membership included the owners of many local businesses and elected officials. "With a renewed sense of purpose, and–through the Council–access to some of Mississippi's leading businessmen, [Beckwith] began to gain a feeling of self-importance."[60]

[58] "Violence Stalks Voter-Registration Workers in Mississippi," SNCC Press Release, New York, NY, March 12, 1963.
[59] Douglas Martin, "Samuel Block, 60, Civil Rights Battler, Dies," *New York Times*, April 22, 2000, p. C7.
[60] Reed Massengill, *Portrait of a Racist: The Real Life of Byron de la Beckwith*, St. Martin's Griffin, New York, page 101.

February 24, 1963

Lion is not sure the FBI assessment of DLB
aversion to violence is accurate. Several of his
contacts mentioned that DLB and his wife Mary
have twice divorced and remarried. Both are heavy
drinkers and often engage in physical abuse.

The most recent episode occurred in August 1962.
Mary filed for a second divorce and restraining
order after she claimed DLB tried to drown her in
the community swimming pool. However, they
married for a third time on October 9. One of
DLB's neighbors told Lion that it happened so
fast most people did not know they divorced
again.

Marital problems did not deter DLB's anti-
integration efforts, particularly when it came to
education. He was outraged by the forced
integration of the University of Mississippi.
Rallies in support of the Negro students were
held in several cities including Greenwood. DLB
showed up at the rallies and would try to
intimidate attendees by taking photos of them.

Except for the intervention of Oxford, Mississippi police, DLB might
have been a more prominent actor on the day Black students eventually
enrolled in classes at Ole Miss. According to Mary De La Beckwith,
her husband planned to join the thousands of protesters from across the
state who converged on the campus. That morning he loaded several
guns in his car before making the 80-mile trip from Greenwood to
Oxford. An anonymous tipster warned local police. They intercepted
De La Beckwith outside of Oxford and ordered him to return home.[61]

February 29, 1963

Lion reports more violence in Greenwood. Another
SNCC organizer and two volunteers were wounded
when an unknown assailant shot at their car.
Jimmy Travis, one of the volunteers, was taken to

---

[61] Massengill, page 116.

a local hospital where he is in critical but
stable condition.

Lion also mentioned DLB recently changed jobs. He
was hired as a sales representative for the Delta
Liquid Plant Food Company.

March 7, 1963

A car occupied by four SNCC workers including
field secretary Sam Block was damaged by gun fire
while parked in front of SNCC headquarters. No
one was seriously injured.

March 20, 1963

Lion reports SNCC said it will not be intimidated
by the increase in attacks on volunteers. Today
more than 100 Negroes attempted to register to
vote at the courthouse but were turned away.

March 27, 1963

Lion reports continuing efforts to stop the SNCC
voter registration project. Yesterday a fire
destroyed the interior of the SNCC headquarters
on McLourin Street. Today police used dogs to
disperse Negroes gathering at the county
courthouse to register to vote.

The *Atlantic Constitution* documented the March incidents in Greenwood. Of note were eyewitness accounts of the March 25 fire at SNCC headquarters.

*About midnight, March 24, Curtis Hayes SNCC field
secretary and Joe Lee Lofton, a Greenwood high school
student, drove by the SNCC office at 115 E. McLourin Street
and noticed a light on. Both tried to enter the office but were
stopped by someone holding the door on the other side. As
Hayes and Loften left they noticed smoke and went to call the
fire department. Negroes in the neighboring building said*

*they heard glass break and saw two whites slip out of the
building and run down an alley.* [62]

Less than 24 hours after the fire was reported, Greenwood Fire Chief J.
C. Evans determined there was no evidence of arson and dismissed the
possibility anybody had exited the building through a broken window.
"Anyone coming in that way would have been severely cut by jagged
glass around the window and there are no traces of blood anywhere."[63]

March 31, 1963

Today DOJ petitioned a federal court to order
city officials and police to release SNCC workers
arrested on March 27, to stop interfering with
the voter registration project and to allow the
peaceful assembly of Negro protestors.

April 9, 1963

Lion reports DLB is producing and distributing
pamphlets which warn about the dangers of sex
between Negroes and whites. He appears to be
promoting violence, calling for action by local
residents. He says Negroes who tell other Negroes
they are equal to whites must be punished.

Reed Massengill confirms this account, especially De La Beckwith's
use of miscegenation to create fear among the white population. De La
Beckwith reportedly distributed flyers at the Church of the Nativity on
Palm Sunday 1963 which included the following:

*It is noted throughout history that the master of the house, his
sons (and yes, even his daughters) consorted with slaves.
Even present-day white women have been found guilty of
enjoying a wide variety of carnal entertainment provided by
black menservants.*

---

[62] Hearings on Miscellaneous Proposals Regarding the Civil Rights of Persons within
the Jurisdiction of the United States, House Judiciary Committee, Eighty-Eighth
Congress, Government Printing Office, 1968, page 1295.
[63] "Fire Chief Nips Negro Arson Talk," *The Greenwood Commonwealth,* March 25,
1963, page 1.

The race mixing in our church has got to stop now. The black race in America must not be permitted to enter the white bedchamber through the open doors of the integrated church.

De La Beckwith's brochures singled out "renegade Christians," those who increasingly joined with civil rights activists, and advocated "physical force, if necessary, to halt further spread."[64]

April 19, 1963

Lion called. DLB has cut back on his anti-Negro activities. He is devoting more time to his job selling fertilizer and chemicals for Delta Liquid Plant Foods.

April 24, 1963

Lion reports DLB and his wife are having marital problems again. Last night the police were called to their home after neighbors heard a gunshot. His wife said they both had been drinking when Byron fired his gun at her. She also claimed he broke a window, threw her clothes on the front lawn and told her to get out.

May 9, 1963

More news about DLB's personal situation. DLB's wife and son spent the night at the Greenwood Leflore Hotel.

May 10, 1963

Lion says the DLBs separation may be permanent. His wife rented an apartment on West President Street.

May 26, 1963

Although I did not expect to hear from Lion over the Memorial Day weekend, he called to say DLB is again distributing flyers at the church. He says

---

[64] Massengill, p. 123.

    the flyers again call for violence to stop
    integration.

The leaflet to which Mason refers is among the last De La Beckwith distributes before targeting Medgar Evers. It includes an ominous message. "The two ideologies [segregation and integration] are now engaged in mortal conflict and only one can survive."[65]

June 8, 1963

    Lion reports he overheard several people talking
    about a concert and voting rally in Jackson. When
    he asked someone how they knew about the event,
    he learned DLB had been there.

This event was part of a voter registration campaign sponsored jointly by the NAACP, Congress of Racial Equality (CORE) and Tougaloo College faculty. Jackson Mayor Allen Thompson hoped to derail the effort when he issued an injunction on June 6, banning parades and mass demonstrations without a permit. To bolster attendance singer Lena Horne and comedian Dick Gregory hosted a benefit concert at the Masonic Temple the night of June 7. One of the speakers at the event was NAACP field secretary Medgar Evers.[66]

NAACP Southeastern regional director Ruby Hurley reported seeing De La Beckwith at the concert, standing in the back of the room with a white Jackson police officer. Hurley added she occasionally observed De La Beckwith hanging around NAACP offices in Jackson. Lillian Louie, Evers' personal secretary, also identified De La Beckwith as someone she had seen there on at least two occasions.[67]

June 13, 1963

    This morning radio and tv are covering the murder
    of civil rights activist Medgar Evers who was
    shot in front of his home in Jackson. A rifle

---

[65] Massengill, p. 123.
[66] "Case Study: Black students, community, allies begin desegregating Jackson, Mississippi, 1962-63," Global Nonviolent Action Database, Swarthmore College.
[67] Massengill, pp. 150-51.

Kennedy delivered the speech to which Mason refers following the peaceful enrollment of two Black students at the University of Alabama. Despite the need for Alabama National Guardsmen, the president applauded the conduct of students who witnessed the event. "That they were admitted peacefully on the campus is due in good measure to the conduct of the students of the University of Alabama, who met their responsibilities in a constructive way."[68]

There is no evidence the timing of De La Beckwith's murder of Medgar Evers was in direct response to Kennedy's speech. However, the president's inference Alabama students accepted the campus' integration must have angered him. If De La Beckwith's efforts to energize white residents to oppose integration were flailing, did he now believe he needed to set an example?

Mason's two questions about the effect Evers' death might have on the three motive-based options characterize the fluid nature of the TEAM's identification of the eventual assassin. By June 13, Oswald emerged as the most likely choice. Still, the TEAM continued to go down all three tracks in case a new variable changed the odds.

---

[68] "Televised Address to the Nation on Civil Rights," June 11, 1963, Historic Speeches, John F. Kennedy Library, Boston, Massachusetts.

```
us in New Orleans to help him keep an eye on
Oswald.

This evening Lion called to say he has been in
touch with Scarecrow and will drive to New
Orleans in the morning.

June 21, 1963

Lion learned De La Beckwith's wife has been
hospitalized.
```

A brief notice in *The Greenwood Commonwealth* confirms Mary De La Beckwith's hospitalization. Under the headline "Undergoes Treatment at Local Hospital," the paper reports, "Mrs. Byron DeLa (sic) Beckwith is a patient in room 313 at the Greenwood Leflore Hospital. She is undergoing treatment and will remain there through the weekend."[69] The article contained no reason for her hospitalization nor mention of her estranged husband's reaction.

```
June 22, 1963

I called a contact at the FBI and asked for an
update on the Evers case. I tell him the Secret
Service is concerned about the timing of JFK's
civil rights speech and Evers' murder. Especially
since JFK is planning campaign trips for late
fall.

They have a suspect. The FBI was able to trace
the serial number on the telescopic sight to a
U.S. distributor in Chicago. Then to a gun and
tackle shop in Grenada, Mississippi. The shop
owner says he swapped the scope for two pistols
in May to one of his regular customers Byron De
La Beckwith. He also told me that early this
morning an FBI fingerprint examiner has made a
match with DLB's Marine service records.
```

---

[69] "Undergoes Treatment at Local Hospital," *The Greenwood Commonwealth*, June 21, 1963, p. 3.

    I do not tell him I had previous knowledge about
    DLB. I immediately shared the information with
    the rest of the team.

The FBI traced the rifle to De La Beckwith in response to a June 13, 1963, request from the office of Jackson, Mississippi mayor Allen Thompson signed by W. D. Rayfield, chief of police, and M. B. Pierce, chief of detectives. They told director Hoover local law enforcement pulled several latent fingerprints from a rifle and scope they found "in a clump of honeysuckle vines at the Southeast corner of Joe's Truck Stop parking lot in the vicinity of the residence of Evers." They requested the FBI laboratory assist in the investigation by searching its fingerprint files for a match to fingerprints on the rifle and bullets found near the Evers residence.[70]

The next day Hoover replies to Rayfield via a collect telegram.

    MEDGAR EVERS MURDER CASE.

    LATENT FINGERPRINT FROM TELESCOPIC SIGHT OF RIFLE
    NOT IDENTIFIED IN OUR SINGLE FINGERPRINTNG FILE.

    HOOVER[71]

On the morning of June 22, an FBI fingerprint examiner discovered a January 5, 1942, print in a St. Louis military database matching that of De La Beckwith. Latent fingerprint expert George Goodreau verified a match between the military records and the prints on the rifle and scope used to shoot Evers.[72]

    June 23, 1963

    De La Beckwith is arraigned for the murder of
    Medgar Evers.

    I called Lion in New Orleans. While DLB is
    eliminated as the possible assassin are there any

---

[70] Letter to FBI director J. Edgar Hoover from Jackson, Mississippi chief of police W. D. Rayfield and chief of detectives M. B. Pierce, June 13, 1963. (Source: Massengill, p. 321-22.)
[71] Telegram to W. D. Rayfield from J. Edgar Hoover, June 14, 1963. (Source, Massengill, p. 322.)
[72] Massengill, p. 153.

    of his associates who should be considered? He
    had no immediate answer but promised to get back
    to me ASAP.

Was the term "ASAP" an anachronism? A quick Google search traced its origins to the Korean War. The first literary reference appears in Captain Annis G. Thompson's book *The Greatest Airlift,* published in 1954.[73] Since Mason served in the military prior to joining the Secret Service he likely heard or even used this acronym on numerous occasions.

    June 25, 1963

    Lion continues to monitor coverage of Evers
    murder and DLB's arrest. An article in the
    Jackson Clarion Ledger congratulates local police
    and the FBI for their efforts, especially how
    quickly they identified DLB as a suspect based on
    fingerprints on the rifle and scope.

During a June 26, 1963, FBI interview with John W. Goza, owner of Turk's Tackle shop in Grenada, Mississippi, he confirmed what Mason had learned from his FBI contact three days earlier. Goza admitted he gave De La Beckwith the rifle scope in exchange for a .45 caliber automatic pistol. This contradicted statements he made during an earlier FBI interview. A summary of the June 26 interrogation includes the following. "He said he remembered this deal when interviewed by FBI Agents on June 20, 1963, but did not want to mention BECKWITH's name as he is a friend and did not want to get BECKWITH in trouble."[74]

    July 9, 1963

    Lion reports the Greenwood WCC has created a
    legal fund to help pay for Beckwith's defense.
    WCC says the fund is similar to the one
    established by the NAACP to cover costs of
    plaintiffs in civil rights cases. Several

---

[73] "What's the origin of the phrase 'ASAP – As soon as possible?'" The Phrase Finder, phrases.org.uk/meanings/as-soon-as-possible.html.
[74] FBI notes from June 26, 1963, interview of John W. Goza.

```
prominent Greenwood residents are listed as
directors of the fund.

Lion believes Evers murder and DLB's arrest and
future trial have compromised his work in
Greenwood. He offers to help Scarecrow and Tinman
with the other options. I agree. Lion will stay
in New Orleans and continue to observe Oswald.

Today, I also learned the campaign is planning a
second trip to Texas.
```

The decision to abandon the field operation in Greenwood proved to be a wise one. Despite the forensic evidence pointing to De La Beckwith, pre-trial motions assured the case would take months if not years. An August 9, 1963, teletype message from the FBI field office to director Hoover reported the reversal of a lower court order for De La Beckwith to receive a thorough mental evaluation. Circuit court Judge O. H. Barnett ruled the district attorney's request "was too broad in that it permits an examination of Beckwith's mental capacity at time of alleged crime, whereas under Mississippi law mental examination can only go into Beckwith's mental competency to conduct a defense."[75]

De La Beckwith's trial commenced on January 27, 1964. In response to the prosecution's evidence, De La Beckwith took the stand and reported the rifle missing sometime after June 10, the last time he used it for target practice. The jury deliberated the afternoon of the sixth and the morning of the seventh before informing the judge they were hopelessly deadlocked. On February 7, 1964, UPI issued the following bulletin.

```
UPI-84

(BECKWITH)

JACKSON, MISS.  AN ALL-WHITE JURY WAS UNABLE TO
AGREE ON A VERDICT IN THE BYRON DE LA BECKWITH
MURDER TRIAL TODAY AND A MISTRIAL WAS DECLARED.

2/7  MJ1239PES
```

---

[75] Urgent memo from SAC, New Orleans to Director, FBI, August 9, 1963, via teletype at 4:30 PM CST.

The copy of the UPI bulletin in the FBI files includes a handwritten note, "Do we know how votes stood? K." Could "K" have been the attorney general trying to assess whether there was any chance of a conviction in a retrial?

A second 1964 trial also ended in a hung jury. In 1994, despite arguments a third prosecution would violate De La Beckwith's Fourth Amendment guarantee to a speedy trial, the Mississippi Supreme Court ruled against him. The basis for dismissing the defense motion was evidence the Mississippi State Sovereignty Commission, a state agency violated ethics rules. The Commission improperly aided De La Beckwith when it provided personal information on members of the jury pool to help the defense lawyers identify sympathetic panelists.

De La Beckwith was convicted of first-degree murder on February 5, 1994, and sentenced to life imprisonment. After unsuccessful appeals to the Mississippi Supreme Court and the U.S. Supreme Court, he remained in prison until his death on January 21, 2001.

CHAPTER THIRTEEN

SAM GIANCANA

Adding Chicago Mafia don Sam Giancana to the mix of potential conspirators introduced a new challenge for the TEAM. Unlike Oswald and De La Beckwith, he had a public persona and the backing of a sophisticated crime syndicate. Furthermore, Giancana knew he was already a target of federal law enforcement and would be suspicious of being approached by anyone outside his inner circle. Infiltration of his network would require more subtle and intricate methods than those employed with the other two prospects.

Fortunately, a list of portals into Giancana's world already existed. A field office summary of FBI surveillance of the Chicago crime boss dated December 20, 1962, covering the period between October 8 and December 14, included the names of 15 informants who had contributed to the report.

Tinman warned about the downside of relying on an informant identified in the December 20 memorandum. They all had relationships with federal law enforcement agents. If they became suspicious of the TEAM's operations, they might share their concern with their FBI handlers. Tinman needed what would today be referred to as a "back channel" to Giancana, a way to exchange information with Giancana outside the normal protocols. While one of the informants might help set up the communications network, the person on the other end of the call had to be an extremely loyal and trusted Giancana ally.

February 11, 1963

Tinman has the toughest assignment. And the most dangerous. He cannot simply show up on Giancana's doorstep. He can never have an in-person meeting with Giancana. Engaging Giancana must be done through intermediaries he trusts. Tinman's knowledge of FBI tactics to penetrate organized crime families should be valuable.

I gave Tinman the folder of copied FBI records I put together in January. Several refer to FBI informants. A December 1962 summary of Giancana's connection to the Villa Venice, a Chicago supper club frequented by area Mafia, included references to several FBI sources. There is also detailed information about where Giancana conducts private meetings with his top lieutenants.

Tinman assumes this kind of information could only come from someone inside the organization. Contacting one or more of these individuals is a priority when he gets to Chicago.

February 13, 1963

Update from Tinman. To explain his presence in Chicago, Tinman met with agents in the FBI field office to discuss what he said was an upcoming campaign trip to Illinois. The Secret Service is concerned about potential Mafia threats. He references the December 20 summary prepared by Chicago special agents. Based on Giancana's statements about RFK targeting organized crime and JFK foreign policy, Tinman said the advance team needed to monitor Giancana.

When Tinman asks which of the 15 informants has been the source of the most reliable information, it was Charles English, one of Giancana's deputies. The FBI agents told Tinman that English spends much of his time at one of two places. The armory lounge and a Quonset hut that had been converted into a casino.

The existence of the makeshift casino is documented in the December 1, 1962, edition of the *Chicago Daily Tribune*.

> *The casino was housed in a Quonset hut near Milwaukee Avenue and River Road, less than two blocks from the Villa Venice, at 2855 Milwaukee Avenue, near Northbrook. The gambling joint was set up, investigators said, by the syndicate chief Momo Salvatore (Sam) Giancana, to tap the bankrolls of patrons drawn to the Villa Venice by night club acts like Frank Sinatra, Sammy Davis Jr., and Dean Martin.[76]*

February 15, 1963

Last night, Tinman tested English's value in establishing a link to Giancana's operation. Tinman placed an anonymous call to English. When English asked about his interest in Giancana, Tinman claimed to be an anti-Castro activist who was angry the U.S. government did not use the missile crisis to eliminate the Communist leader. He understands Giancana, who had casino investments in Havana, shares this view.

Tinman then told English there are rumors the FBI is planning to raid the casino, which is not true. He suggested English warn Giancana and gave him a phone number where he could be reached if they wanted more information.

February 20, 1963

Tinman finally heard back from English. The false tip about RFK's plans to target the Chicago casino produced some unexpected intelligence. English told Tinman Giancana was quite angry when he heard about the raid. According to English, Giancana said something to the effect, "How many times are Kennedy and his brother going to betray me?"

---

[76] "Mob Gamblers Make $200,000 in Big Hut," *Chicago Daily Tribune*, December 1, 1962, p. 44.

Tinman asked English if he had any idea what
Giancana was referring to. English said Giancana
had often talked about how, at the request of
Frank Sinatra, he used his ties to organized
labor to get union workers to support JFK over
Hubert Humphrey in the West Virginia primary. In
return, Sinatra arranged for friends such as Dean
Martin and Sammy Davis, Jr. to appear at
Giancana's Villa Venice Club in Chicago.

In a *CBS News* interview, Sinatra's daughter Tina confirmed her father
was a go-between for the Kennedys and Giancana during the 1960
campaign. She said JFK's father Joseph Kennedy met with Sinatra
before the West Virginia primary and told him, "We know the same
people," referring to Giancana. The senior Kennedy wanted Giancana's
help with the coal unions and recruited Sinatra to be the go-between.[77]

Since Giancana had been the subject of FBI
surveillance and Kennedy's brother made organized
crime a priority at Justice, Giancana felt he had
been double-crossed. Was it enough to order a hit
on the president? Even with a clear motive, this
option may be less viable. RFK's organized crime
task force already proved it could turn Mafia
subordinates into government informants. We could
not take a chance one of them would learn of and
disclose the assignment.

Despite these concerns, Tinman's exchange with
English was a successful first effort to
indirectly communicate with Giancana. The team
agreed to take the next step.

February 24, 1963

Tinman placed another anonymous call to English.
This time to inform him of a pending campaign
trip to Chicago. If Giancana wants detailed
updates about the trip, he needs to designate a
contact.

---

[77] "Tina Sinatra," 60 Minutes, *CBS News*, October 8, 2000.

As expected, Tinman gets a call from the Chicago
FBI field office. English warned his FBI handlers
he had received a tip that JFK was coming to
Chicago and the caller wanted an inside
connection to Giancana. Tinman said this was
consistent with what originally concerned the
advance team. The situation needed to be closely
monitored. He then suggested the best way to
expose the source of this leak was for the FBI to
instruct English to play along and keep them
informed.

February 26, 1963

English called Tinman. He is willing to help
identify a contact to Giancana. There is one
condition. Tinman must also update English about
the president's visit.

February 27, 1963

Tinman called late this evening to report on the
day's activities.

English again called Tinman. Giancana had
designated one of his capos as the contact.
English gave Tinman a phone number to use to set
up a meeting with the contact. Tinman promised to
call English as soon as the meeting was
scheduled.

Tinman next called the contact. Neither
identified himself. The two exchanged a second
set of phone numbers for future calls. The
contact then suggested they meet for lunch the
next day at the armory lounge. Tinman reluctantly
agreed, not sure if he was being set up.

He was relieved when the contact immediately
called him at the second phone number. The
contact told him the lunch invitation was a decoy
in case either of their phones was tapped. He
said it was not wise for them to be seen in
public and they should only communicate by phone.

Tinman then called English to thank him for
making the connection and told him about the
"lunch" at the armory on Thursday.

I congratulated Tinman on his brilliant scheme.
Tomorrow he would accompany a team of FBI agents
who would case the armory wondering at which
table a Giancana lieutenant and a disgruntled
anti-Communist activist might be plotting to harm
the president. Tinman would be among the hunters
who had no idea he was their prey.

February 28, 1963

Tinman called English to report on his fabricated
lunch with the Giancana contact. He tells English
the Chicago mob has no interest in Kennedy's trip
to Chicago. Even if they wanted to take him down,
they would not do it so close to home. Giancana
would be an immediate suspect.

English shared this information with the FBI
field office. An agent immediately called Tinman
to pass on their informant's news. Tinman thanked
the agent and suggested his work in Chicago was
done.

Tinman now has a contact inside Giancana's
organization while English and the Chicago FBI
office are out of the picture.

At this point the TEAM must feel good about the progress being made
with the organized crime option. That would soon change.

March 1, 1963

Tinman called to say he had confidence in his
relationship with his Giancana contact. They were
now on a first name basis (both aliases). The
contact referred to himself as Mario, while
Tinman used Stefano as his AKA.

Although Tinman had no specific date for JFK's
next visit to Chicago, he assured Mario there
would be one. The last time Kennedy came to
Chicago was October 1962. He appeared at a last-

minute rally for congressional candidates in the November general election. A return visit was on the campaign's tentative schedule for late 1963 or early 1964.

Mario told Tinman the location was not important. In fact, the farther away from Chicago the better. That would make it harder to trace anything back to Giancana.

Mario then gave Tinman the bad news. All he needed to know was Kennedy's schedule. He would take it from there. When Tinman asked what he meant by that, Mario explained that Giancana does not take orders from anyone. Tell us what you want done and we will make it happen.

Tinman admitted there was not much he could say in response. If he told Mario he needed to get back to him, that would suggest Tinman was not the lone wolf he claimed to be. Challenging Mario might also raise suspicions. With no other choice, he told Mario he understood.

After I hung up with Tinman, I scheduled a conference call the next morning with the team and Wizard.

March 2, 1963

We started our meeting with progress reports from Lion and Scarecrow. Lion recounted the increasing number of violent attacks in Greenwood. However, De La Beckwith had not participated in any of them. Scarecrow repeated what he already told me about meeting Oswald at the dinner party at Everett Glover's home.

Tinman provided a detailed account of his discussion with Mario. There was a difference of opinion about continuing to pursue this option. The cons were obvious. Turning the assignment over to Giancana would mean a loss of control. The team would not be involved in critical decisions of timing and location. Nor would we be able to limit who might be involved or have knowledge of the operation. Our role would be limited to feeding Giancana's people the information they needed to carry out the assassination.

On the other hand, there were advantages to farming out the assignment. Lion pointed out how turning the operation over to a third party eliminated the need to frequently communicate with Giancana's people by phone or in person. That would make it more difficult to connect any member of the team to the assassins.

Wizard identified four more pros of turning over the assignment to Giancana's people. They, not the team, would be responsible for monitoring the assassin. We would not have to make sure the gunman remained motivated and committed to the plan. Nor would we have to arrange for his movements to be coordinated with Kennedy's. Additionally, if we had the lead, there would be expenses which might leave a money trail.

As the discussion ended, Tinman laughed. What did he find so funny? He compared the assignment to heart surgery. You would not ask anyone with a medical degree to perform that operation. You'd look for a specialist. Secret service agents specialize in preventive medicine. We needed someone who is good at killing the patient. Giancana and his people are the specialists in that field.

None of us could argue with that kind of logic. The team unanimously agreed using the Chicago mob was still an option but might be our second choice depending on Scarecrow's progress with Oswald. Wizard instructed Tinman to tell Mario we had a deal on two conditions. The assault on the president had to be done without injury to anyone else. And they could plan the assassination but not act without a signal from Tinman. In return, Wizard authorized Tinman to tell Mario the promised compensation would be honored even if he never got the go ahead.

March 4, 1963

Tinman called Mario with the offer. Mario said he
would get back to him within the week.

March 7, 1963

Mario called back. Giancana signed off on
everything. Mario said he does not need to hear
from Tinman again until he has specific
information about Kennedy's trip to Chicago.

There is no reason for Tinman to remain in
Chicago. He booked a flight back to DC.

When I first read the March 2, 1963, journal entry, something about the TEAM's outsourcing the ASSIGNMENT seemed strangely familiar. Entrepreneurship curricula include the concept of "strategic resource management," how successful enterprises obtain critical factors of production at minimal cost. The goal is to create a competitive advantage in the marketplace.

Although the TEAM was the only player in the presidential assassination business, they looked for advantages, not against competitors, but among their options. This required identifying opportunities to maximize their limited resources.

At the early stages of many startups, the founders lack the collateral to obtain loans or the credit history to negotiate leases. Instead, they secure services or inputs through *quid pro quos* such as stock options, profit sharing or royalty agreements, eliminating the need for up-front cash payments. The arrangement between the TEAM and Giancana involved acquiring a service for which compensation would come later.

I now viewed Mason's account of the ASSIGNMENT in a different context. It was more than a benevolent conspiracy to protect and enhance the legacy of a physically declining president. It was also a high-risk entrepreneurial venture. And the founding team was conducting business using the same principles employed by the architects of any for-profit start-up.

CHAPTER FOURTEEN

LEE HARVEY OSWALD

The TEAM used four tactical criteria to rank contenders to carry out the assassination, regardless of the option. Motive. Capability. Incentive. Inability to be traced back to the TEAM. However, when the TEAM compared the three "finalists" side-by-side, they recognized none was an ideal candidate.

Although the TEAM must have continuously analyzed each new piece of information and its impact on the ASSIGNMENT, Mason did not record the content of those discussions. The journal was more akin to a fact-based, page one news story, leaving the punditry to the editorial board or op-ed columnists. The February 6, 1963, entry is a perfect example. Mason's recollection of the TEAM's review of his two weekends digging through FBI memoranda and exhibits consisted of just six sentences, followed by:

```
The team seemed satisfied with my work. They are
ready to move to the next step, deeper analysis
of the most likely candidate who has emerged in
each category.
```

It is hard to believe the TEAM's only response was "Great work! What now?" There must have been a more thorough assessment of Mason's findings. What information could they accept as irrefutable? What gaps needed to be filled? What questions did the FBI records raise? Perhaps the TEAM's internal assessment included the following.

De La Beckwith had publicly expressed a desire to eliminate or at least intimidate anyone who did not share his fear of minority encroachment into white society. He was an experienced rifleman. His personal connections were limited to local and state networks. As of January 1963, he had no criminal record or indication of violent behavior. What incentive could the TEAM offer De La Beckwith to raze the barrier between blunt, outspoken support of white supremacy and lethal force? Surely, he was not naïve enough to believe replacing Kennedy with Johnson would stem the growing public support for racial equality. He too must have realized it was more likely a martyred president would energize the civil rights movement.

In contrast, Giancana's dissatisfaction with the administration's enmity toward organized crime and its hands-off policy after the Cuban missile crisis was a matter of record. Getting the president's brother off his back was more than enough incentive. Moreover, eliminating rivals is what Giancana and his underlings did. The uncertainty in this case centered on the probability of exposure. Giancana was under constant FBI surveillance. What's more, this would be an organizational effort. Would the involvement of multiple players increase the odds of someone sharing information with the wrong people? Finally, why was Giancana one of the few attendees at the Apalachin meeting neither detained nor indicted? Did he have allies among federal law enforcement officials who were looking out for him? If so, why?

Where did Oswald fit into this equation? At the outset, he satisfied only two of the four criteria. He was a skilled marksman. And he was an introvert, a loner with few friends.

Could the TEAM make a reliable evaluation of Oswald's potential based solely on two factors? Although disappointed with American policy towards Russia and Cuba, Oswald never openly attributed his displeasure directly to Kennedy. The Cold War was a non-partisan fact of life, and any change in U.S. response was unlikely, regardless of who occupied the White House. Finally, his restlessness and tendency to constantly uproot his own life suggested it might be difficult to determine what it would take to keep Oswald in tow at any point in time.

With each entry leading up to Oswald's selection and grooming as the eventual assassin, I realized these ambiguities were what made him more attractive. His lack of conviction made him more malleable and open to suggestion. I wondered if the TEAM grasped this potential at this early stage or whether it emerged later, after Scarecrow arrived in Dallas. I could only speculate as Mason rarely diverged from his *Dragnet*-like, "just the facts," style.

Scarecrow's first task was to identify someone who could discreetly introduce him to Oswald.

```
February 14, 1963

Scarecrow arrives in Dallas. Using a list
provided by the Immigration and Naturalization
Service, he begins contacting Soviet immigrants
who had settled in the Dallas area. He tells them
he recently took a new job in Dallas. He adds he
had spent time at the U.S. embassy in Moscow
after President Eisenhower sent a letter to
Khrushchev in 1958 to suggest the two countries
expand trade. He says he greatly enjoyed his time
there and was looking for opportunities in the
Dallas area to connect with Soviet immigrants.

Two of these contacts refer him to George de
Mohrenschildt, a petroleum geologist from the
Russian region of Mozyr. De Mohrenschildt has
been helping former Soviet citizens settle in the
Dallas/Fort Worth area and is a regular attendee
at community gatherings. He often sponsors
Russian cultural events.
```

De Mohrenschildt confirmed his attachment to the Soviet community in Dallas when interviewed by Albert Jenner, Jr, assistant counsel to the Warren Commission.

> Mr. JENNER. Now, before we get to that, what I would like to have you do for me is tell me about what I will describe in my words, and you use your own, the Russian emigre group or community or society in Dallas at or along about that time.
>
> Mr. DE MOHRENSCHILDT. Yes. There I knew them all, because both my wife and I like to speak Russian, and we like Russian

cooking, mainly. This is our main interest in Russian society. They are all of the same type— in other words, they are all people who carry memories of Russia with them, and who became, I think, perfect American citizens.[78]

February 18, 1963

Scarecrow contacted de Mohrenschildt. He repeats the story about his time in Moscow and tells de Mohrenschildt he is surprised at the number of Soviet emigrants who have settled in the Dallas area. De Mohrenschildt invites Scarecrow to join him for lunch at the Dallas Petroleum Club on Wednesday.

February 20, 1963

Scarecrow called this morning to discuss his noon lunch with de Mohrenschildt. He needed a cover story that might get his host to talk about Oswald. He will ask whether Russians who have relocated to the Dallas area have issues with the conservative Southern culture.

Scarecrow called again in the afternoon to brief me on his lunch with de Mohrenschildt. The cover story provided the needed opening. De Mohrenschildt tells Scarecrow he shares many of the same concerns about newly arrived Russians fitting in. Many of them talked about increased animosity toward Soviet nationals during and after the Cuban missile crisis.

De Mohrenschildt also expressed concern many of the latest arrivals could not find jobs. He mentions this is particularly true for Americans who defected, married Soviet citizens, then returned to the U.S. with their wives and children. He does not mention the Oswalds by name.

---

[78] Interview with George de Mohrenschildt, Warren Commission Hearings, Volume IX, April 22, 1964.

```
Scarecrow offered he may be able to help with job
searches. De Mohrenschildt thanks Scarecrow and
says he will let him know when the next community
event will be.
```

The February 24, 1963, journal entry might be described as "the beginning of the end." It documents the first time a member of the TEAM directly interacts with Lee Harvey Oswald. It exceeded expectations. Not only did Scarecrow get a chance to personally observe Oswald. He also identified a potential path by which the TEAM could incent Oswald to be the assassin.

```
February 24, 1963

This morning Scarecrow checks in and reports he
received a call from de Mohrenschildt yesterday.
He invited Scarecrow to accompany him to a dinner
party at the home of Everett Glover that night.
Lee and Marina Oswald were there. He had a chance
to briefly talk with Lee. During their
conversation, Lee mentioned how disappointed he
was that U.S.-Cuban relations had not improved
after the missile crisis last October. He also
expressed an interest in going to Cuba and
meeting Castro. Scarecrow said he understands how
Lee could feel that way and tells him he might be
able to help. They exchange phone numbers.

Scarecrow notices Marina spent much of the
evening talking with another guest Ruth Paine. He
asks Lee about Paine. He says they have never met
before.
```

As I delved deeper into Mason's journal, I looked for two things. First, could I corroborate each specific claim using public records. Second, and equally important, was whether the complete narrative was internally consistent. Or were there later entries that contradicted previous assertions. Scarecrow's initial contact with Oswald provided a baseline of information against which future interactions with the eventual assassin could be juxtaposed.

Although Oswald voices concern about U.S. policy vis-à-vis Cuba and his experience post-repatriation, Kennedy's name does not come up in the conversation. Certainly, Scarecrow would have communicated if Oswald indicated any ill-will toward the president. Convincing Oswald to carry out the ASSIGNMENT, absent such inclination, the TEAM would have to find a way to turn his attitudes about repatriation or policy toward Cuba into a personal vendetta against JFK. Was that truly the case or was Oswald just being cautious? After all, this was the first encounter between Oswald and a member of the TEAM. No one would expect Oswald to confide in a new acquaintance, "I hate the president and I'd welcome the chance to take him down."

I needed to understand Oswald's sentiment toward Kennedy in February 1963. That information lay in testimony by Oswald's family and acquaintances before the Warren Commission. In every instance, they confirmed Oswald's feelings about U.S. policy toward Cuba did not translate into a vendetta directed at JFK. While he was not elated about life in the United States following his return from the Soviet Union, he never attributed his dissatisfaction to Kennedy.

During a March 24, 1964, deposition conducted by Warren Commission assistant counsel Wesley J. Liebeler, Dallas businessman Samuel Ballen suggests just the opposite. In the latter part of 1962 or early 1963, Ballen scheduled a meeting with Oswald at the request of his friend de Mohrenschildt who hoped Ballen might help Oswald find employment. Ballen differentiated between Oswald's disappointment about how hard it had been to re-assimilate into American society and bitterness toward the U.S. government or Kennedy.

> Mr. LIEBELER. Did he (Oswald) ever demonstrate or indicate to you any particular hostility toward any official of the U.S. Government?
>
> Mr. BALLEN. None whatsoever; none whatsoever. My own subjective reaction is, that the sum total of these 2 hours that I spent with him, I just can't see his having any venom towards President Kennedy.
>
> Mr. LIEBELER. Did President Kennedy come up in any way during the course of your discussion?
>
> Mr. BALLEN. No; it did not. The sum total of his reaction, limited as it was that I got from this individual, is that this man would have—this is subjective, I can put no concrete support in there, but

I would have thought that this is an individual who felt warmly towards President Kennedy.[79]

If Ballen's assessment was correct, someone or something else turned Oswald's sentiments toward Kennedy between late-1962 and November 1963. At this point, all the TEAM had to work with was Oswald's interest in visiting Cuba and meeting Castro. How that could work to their advantage would come later.

```
March 8, 1963

It has now been two weeks since Scarecrow had
contact with Oswald. The team fears we may have
reached a dead-end. We agree Scarecrow should
again reach out to de Mohrenschildt.

March 11, 1963

De Mohrenschildt returned Scarecrow's call. He
has only talked by phone with Oswald since the
dinner at the Glovers. Oswald seemed a bit testy.
One issue seems to be Marina. Since the dinner
party she spent a lot of time with a new friend
she met there. Scarecrow asks if that might be
Ruth Paine. Very likely. Scarecrow then asked if
it would be okay if he used de Mohrenschildt's
name when he calls Paine to see if everything is
okay. De Mohrenschildt said that would be fine.

Scarecrow called Paine. She tells him Lee is not
very happy with his job and is thinking about
quitting. Otherwise, they seem to be fine.
Scarecrow tells Paine he knows how tough it must
be for Marina and offers to help any way he can.

March 24, 1963

Scarecrow has good news. Ruth Paine just called
him. She invited him to a dinner on April 2 and
said the Oswalds will also be there.
```

---

[79] Deposition of Samuel Ballen, Warren Commission, March 24, 1964.

April 1, 1963

Scarecrow called to tell us he just got off the
phone with Ruth Paine. She confirmed the Oswalds
would be at dinner the next day. Paine asked
Scarecrow if he knew Lee had just been fired. He
did not.

Oswald often tended to move to another city when
he was unhappy. This dinner has new importance.
But it is also an opportunity. No longer
employed, he might be more likely to listen to an
offer to get to Cuba.

The journal provides no evidence Scarecrow, Tinman or Lion saw
themselves as advocates for the respective options to which they had
been assigned. However, I believe Scarecrow now felt as if the table
was set to make Oswald the guest of honor.

CHAPTER FIFTEEN

PRIMING THE PUMP

Any enthusiasm Scarecrow may have shown about Oswald was tempered by the effort needed to take advantage of the situation. Furthermore, Wizard had provided no timetable for future events. Was timing of the essence, dependent on the president's rate of physical decline? On the other hand, Scarecrow must have known Oswald could not be rushed. Oswald needed to reach any decision to become part of the ASSIGNMENT on his own.

April 2, 1963

Lee and Marina Oswald do attend Ruth Paine's dinner. After dinner Scarecrow pulled Oswald aside. He asked Lee if he was aware of the Fair Play for Cuba Committee based in NYC. Its purpose was to protect Cuba and Castro from further U.S. interference. Oswald was not. Scarecrow tells Oswald the founder Vincent Lee is trying to establish local chapters in other cities and gives him the information for the NY office.

April 17, 1963

Scarecrow reports Oswald contacted Lee and offered to work for FPCC. Scarecrow expected Oswald would be asked to open an FPCC office in Dallas. However, Oswald surprised him when he said he had been asked to start an FPCC program in New Orleans. Someone needs to be there before

> Oswald arrives. It cannot be Scarecrow. If Oswald
> sees Scarecrow in New Orleans, he will realize he
> is being monitored.
>
> I called Lion. He believes something is about to
> happen and wants to stay in Greenwood. Tinman
> says he needs to stay in Chicago. Whether I want
> to or not, it's my turn to do some field work. I
> book a morning flight to New Orleans.

Relocating to New Orleans may have been Oswald's idea since there was another reason Oswald felt compelled to leave Dallas in April. Unknown to either Mason or Scarecrow, a week after the dinner at Ruth Paine's house, Oswald attempted to assassinate retired U.S. Major General Edwin Walker, an avid segregationist and anti-Communist. Although the assault was widely reported in Dallas, the perpetrator had not been identified. Therefore, Scarecrow had no reason to assume it impacted his work as he never raised the incident in any communications with Mason. Oswald's identity as Walker's assailant would not have come to light without Ruth Paine's and Marina Oswald's cooperation with the Warren Commission in 1964.

> April 24, 1963
>
> My first week in New Orleans is uneventful. I use
> the time to update the status of each option.
> This afternoon I got a call from Scarecrow who
> reports Ruth Paine has taken Oswald (without
> Marina) to the bus station where he boards a bus
> to New Orleans.
>
> April 25, 1963
>
> Scarecrow calls Ruth Paine. He tells her he heard
> Oswald is heading to New Orleans and wants to see
> how he is doing. He asks if she knows how he can
> be contacted. Paine tells Scarecrow Oswald is
> staying with his aunt Lillian Murret and gives
> him the phone number.
>
> April 28, 1963
>
> Scarecrow calls Oswald and learns he has been
> unable to find work. Oswald says he plans to

visit the local unemployment office that
afternoon.

May 9, 1963

Oswald has been hired by the Reilly Coffee
Company. Also, he moved out of his aunt's house
after finding an apartment at 4905 Magazine
Street.

Scarecrow received a call from Ruth Paine. She
wanted to let him know that Marina will be
joining Lee in New Orleans. She asked Ruth if she
would drive her and their daughter there.

May 11, 1963

I may be here longer than I planned. Ruth Paine
arrived in New Orleans with Marina and their
daughter June. Marina appears to be pregnant. All
three stay at Lee's apartment. Is this a
permanent move?

I have another new concern. Oswald has done
nothing related to Cuba. Now that he has a job
and his family has joined him, has he changed his
mind about visiting Cuba?

May 14, 1963

My concern grows. Paine left New Orleans without
Marina. Have we wasted our time on Oswald?

May 29, 1963

After two weeks, the situation in New Orleans
turns in our favor. I observed Oswald entering a
print shop. After Oswald left, I went in the
store and asked the owner if I can see some
samples of color paper stock. While the owner was
in the supply room, I looked at Oswald's order.
1000 handbills for the Fair Play for Cuba
Committee except the order was signed by A. J.
Hidell.

This is the first time Mason refers to the alias Oswald used multiple times after returning to the U.S. We do know Oswald's alter ego was not a spur of the moment creation. The wallet on Oswald's body when he was arrested at the Texas Theatre contained two forged government documents issued to "Alex James Hidell." The first was his notice of classification under the Selective Service System which includes a photograph of a younger Oswald.

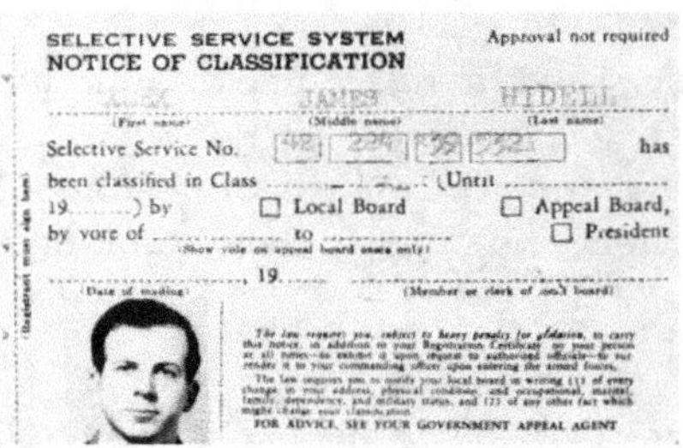

The second was proof of service in the armed services.

Exactly why Oswald chose this pseudonym remains a mystery. One possibility emerged during Marina Oswald's testimony before the Warren Commission during questioning by general counsel J. Lee Rankin.

> Mr. RANKIN. Have you ever heard that he used the fictitious name Hidell?
>
> Mrs. OSWALD. Yes.
>
> Mr. RANKIN. When did you first learn that he used such a name?
>
> Mrs. OSWALD. In New Orleans.
>
> Mr. RANKIN. How did you learn that?
>
> Mrs. OSWALD. When he was interviewed by some anti-Cubans, he used this name and spoke of an organization. I knew there was no such organization. And I know that Hidell is merely an altered

Fidel, and I laughed at such foolishness. My imagination didn't work that way.[80]

Later in her testimony Marina recalls a radio interview during which her husband suggests he and Hidell are two different people.

Mr. RANKIN. But it was in regard to some interview for radio transmission, and he had identified himself as Hidell, rather than Oswald, is that right?

Mrs. OSWALD. No--he represented himself as Oswald, but he said that the organization which he supposedly represents is headed by Hidell.

Mr. RANKIN. He was using the name Hidell, then, to have a fictitious president or head of the organization which really was he himself, is that right?

Mrs. OSWALD. Yes.[81]

Marina's distinction between Oswald and Hidell led to speculation "Alex J. Hidell" was a reference to his being akin to "Jekyll and Hyde." A November 1, 1964, article in the *New York Times* included an analysis by Dr. Joseph A. Kochen, a professor at the Albert Einstein College of Medicine. He suggests, "Oswald might have conceived the pseudonym as an anagram with 'sufficient insight to recognize the schizoid features of his own personality.'" However, the same article contains a more likely explanation. "Alek" was the nickname Oswald used while living in the Soviet Union. It appeared in several letters to Marina and friends. [82]

June 3, 1963

```
More encouraging news. This morning Oswald rented
a post office box. I contacted post office
headquarters in DC and asked if it was possible
to get information about someone who might
represent a threat to the president. This is
standard procedure and should not raise any
```

---

[80] Testimony of Marina Oswald before the Warren Commission, February 3, 1964, Hearings, Volume I, p. 64.
[81] Ibid., p. 65.
[82] "AN OSWALD ALIAS SEEN AS ANAGRAM; The Name of 'Alek J. Hidell' Linked to Jekyll and Hyde," *New York Times*, November 1, 1964, page 50.

> flags. The New Orleans branch confirmed Oswald
> filled out the application. There was only one
> new rental that morning to A. J. Hidell. It
> appears Oswald is using the same alias for any
> transaction related to the FPCC.

Still looking for anachronisms or inconsistencies which might challenge the authenticity of Mason's journal, the phrase "raise any flags" caught my attention. What if the origin of this idiom post-dated the timing of this journal entry? Would that be proof positive the document was not created contemporaneously?

While the exact origin of the term is unclear, "raise a flag" appears in the *Journal of the American Bar Association* in September 1955. In an article titled "Treaty-Made Law: A Case in Point on Procedural Deficiencies," Donald Beelar writes, "Publishers of legal services should announce or cite applicable treaties which affect statutory law or ***raise a flag*** in the preface that no consideration is given to treaty-made law."[83]

> My time in New Orleans is about to end. The re-
> election campaign staff is now focused on Texas.
> I am scheduled to accompany Lancer on a trip to
> El Paso, one stop on a four day campaign tour to
> Colorado, Texas, California and Hawaii.
>
> I called Scarecrow to inform him of my departure
> and suggested he again take the lead in tracking
> Oswald's activities. I ask if De Mohrenschildt is
> still a viable intermediary. Scarecrow informs me
> de Mohrenschildt is no longer in Dallas. He was
> hired to work on an oil exploration project in
> Haiti.

Although this is the last time Mason mentions de Mohrenschildt, he became a central figure in alternative versions of the assassination based on suspicious, but potentially legitimate, associations and actions. Warren Commission critic and future Minnesota governor Jesse Ventura, without evidence, believed de Mohrenschildt was

---

[83]Donald Beelar, "Treat-Made Law: A Case in Point on Procedural Deficiencies, *Journal of the American Bar Association*, Volume 41, September 1955, p. 819.

Oswald's CIA "handler." In his 1988 book *On the Trail of the Assassins*, New Orleans district attorney Jim Garrison describes de Mohrenschildt as "one of Oswald's unwitting baby-sitters…assigned to protect or otherwise see to the general welfare of Oswald."[84]

It was his many other U.S. and foreign relationships which made him of interest first to the Warren Commission and later the House Select Committee on Assassinations. A November 1964 article in the *New York Times* summarized de Mohrenschildt's testimony before the Warren Commission including a surreal revelation.

De Mohrenschildt claimed he met Kennedy's future wife in 1938, then Jacqueline Bouvier, when she was a young girl growing up on Long Island. De Mohrenschildt testified his initial contact with Mrs. Kennedy's family occurred while on summer vacation in Belport, Long Island after finding employment in New York City.

> Mr. DE MOHRENSCHILDT. I think as soon as I arrived we went to spend the summer on Long Island, Belport, Long Island.
>
> Mr. ALBERT E. JENNER. And at Belport, you made what acquaintances?
>
> Mr. DE MOHRENSCHILDT. Lots of people, but especially Mrs. [Janet] Bouvier.
>
> Mr. JENNER. Who is Mrs. Bouvier?
>
> Mr. DE MOHRENSCHILDT. Mrs. Bouvier is Jacqueline Kennedy's mother, also her father and her whole family. She was in the process of getting a divorce from her husband. I met him, also. We were very close friends. We saw each other every day. I met Jackie then, when she was a little girl. And her sister, who was still in the cradle practically. We were also very close friends of Jack Bouvier's [Jacqueline's father John Vernou Bouvier III] sister, and his father.[85]

Adding to this unimaginable journey in which de Mohrenschildt crossed paths with both an assassin and his target's wife, supplemental information provided to the Warren Commission details his continuing

---

[84] Jim Garrison, *On the Trail of the Assassins*, Sheridan Square Press, NY, 1988, pp. 55-56.

[85] Testimony of George de Mohrenschildt before the Warren Commission, April 23, 1964, Hearings Volume IX, p. 179.

connection to Jackie Kennedy. Both of de Mohrenschildt's sons by first wife Wynne Sharples died of cystic fibrosis. In 1960, he and his ex-wife established a chapter of the National Foundation for Cystic Fibrosis in Dallas "for which Jacqueline Kennedy served as the honorary chairman."[86]

Additional documentation of de Mohrenschildt's connection to JFK and his assassin surfaced during the Warren Commission investigation. Following the assassination, de Mohrenschildt sent now-divorced and remarried Janet Bouvier Auchincloss a letter of condolence dated December 12, 1963, and postmarked Port-au-Prince, Haiti.

> *Since we lived in Dallas permanently last year and before, we had the misfortune to have met Oswald and especially his wife Marina sometime last fall. Both my wife and I tried to help poor Marina who could not speak any English, was mistreated by her husband; she and the baby were malnourished (sic) and sickly. We took them to the hospital.*[87]

Following a thorough investigation of de Mohrenschildt's background, career, and links to both Oswald and Jackie Kennedy, the Warren Commission dismissed the possibility de Mohrenschildt had any knowledge of or role in the assassination.

> *The Commission's investigation has developed no signs of subversive or disloyal conduct on the part of either of the De Mohrenschildts. Neither the FBI, CIA, nor any witness contacted by the Commission has provided any information linking the De Mohrenschildts to subversive or extremist organizations. Nor has there been any evidence linking them in any way with the assassination of President Kennedy.*[88]

There seemed, however, to be an important inconsistency between de Mohrenschildt's post-assassination letter to Janet Auchincloss and Ruth Paine's willingness to help reunite Lee and Marina Oswald in New

---

[86] Ibid, p. 199.

[87] Warren Commission Report: Volume XIX: De Mohrenschildt Exhibit 14.

[88] Report of the President's Commission on the Assassination of President John F. Kennedy, U.S. Government Printing Office, Washington, D.C., September 24, 1964, pp. 283-284.

Orleans. Paine affirmed multiple instances of marital conflict and described Lee as overbearing, demanding and jealous. However, she never mentions his mistreating their daughter June and shows no concern when Marina informs her of the pending birth of a second child. In a June 5, 1963, letter to Paine, written while she was living with Lee in New Orleans, Marina tells her Lee has suggested she return to the Soviet Union even though the due date for her second child is early to mid-October.

> *With us everything is as it used to be. A gloomy spirit rules the house. The only joy for me and for Lee (I think) is June.*[89]

In contrast, de Mohrenschildt's letter to Janet Auchincloss makes it sound as though his sole justification for associating with the Oswalds was to protect Marina and the baby. Yet there is no corroboration of his claim that the child was "malnourished and sickly." Lee's possible mistreatment of Marina seems more valid. On the third day of testimony before the Warren Commission, Marina admitted Lee had physically abused her. In response to reports neighbors had raised concerns Lee had beat her, Marina testified, "The neighbors simply saw that because I have a very sensitive skin, and even a very light blow would show marks."[90]

Was De Mohrenschildt trying to distance himself from the president's assassin? If so, was he hiding something? Or did he now suspect his helping Lee and Marina had somehow contributed to the assassination? Had someone within his circle of friends and acquaintances been part of the chain of events leading to November 22? What if the Warren Commission asked de Mohrenschildt if he had introduced others to Oswald? Then Scarecrow might also become a person of interest, making him subject to additional scrutiny and possibly incriminating the TEAM.

---

[89] Letter from Marina Oswald to Ruth Paine, June 5, 1963, Warren Commission Exhibit 409-B.

[90] Testimony of Marina Oswald, Warren Commission, Washington, D.C., February 4, 1964.

June 4, 1963

I arrived at National Airport around 10:00 am and took a cab to the Navy Annex where I met Wizard.

I updated him on all three field operations and told him I now believe Oswald is the most promising prospect. He has been open to Scarecrow's direction so far and has followed through on every suggestion. We have a plan that will put Oswald back in Dallas by the fall. A campaign trip to the Dallas area would be the most likely chance for Oswald and Lancer to cross paths. We need Wizard to suggest a second Texas campaign trip for late November or early December.

June 5, 1963

This morning I joined Lancer at Andrews AFB for the flight to Colorado Springs. This is the first time I have been with him since reassignment to the campaign committee in February. We exchanged greetings as he walked past on his way to his private quarters in the rear of the plane. If he knew I was part of the assignment he did not show it.

After an address to the Academy graduates, we departed Colorado Springs and arrived in El Paso around 6:00 pm.

June 6, 1963

Wizard has done his part. Last night he had dinner with Lancer, Volunteer and Governor Connally at the Cortez Hotel. Wizard reminded them Lancer had spent little time in Texas since the 1960 campaign. The reception in El Paso had been excellent. The campaign needed to do this more often. Connally agreed. He told Kennedy the trip would also help with a political problem he was having. He needed the President's help to patch up an intraparty dispute with Senator Yarborough.

The Warren Commission confirmed the location, participants and purpose of the meeting at the Cortez Hotel.

> *The basic decision on the November trip to Texas was made at a meeting of President Kennedy, Vice President Johnson, and Governor Connally on June 5, 1963, at the Cortez Hotel in El Paso, Tex. The President had spoken earlier that day at the Air Force Academy in Colorado Springs, Colo., and had stopped in El Paso to discuss the proposed visit and other matters with the Vice President and the Governor. The three agreed that the President would come to Texas in late November 1963.* [91]

The next paragraph in the June 6 journal entry is a reminder the Giancana option had not been eliminated. Later, I would learn how it may have set in motion a series of critical events immediately following Oswald's arrest.

```
The location of the assault on Lancer is no
longer in question. It will take place in Texas.
I called Tinman and asked him to share this
information with Mario.

June 10, 1963

Mario told Tinman that Giancana was relieved by
the news about Texas. He had been concerned from
the start Chicago was too close to home. If the
assassin had any connection to the Mafia, as head
of the Chicago crime family, Giancana would
immediately be considered a suspect.

This news had another unexpected effect on Mario.
Though he did not divulge specifics, Mario talked
about how the mob is able to recruit a hitman for
a job like this. Tinman opened this conversation
by asking Mario a question. I know why you are
willing to help but what incentive does the
gunman have? Mario laughed. Mario then told him
we do favors for a lot of people. They do not pay
```

---

[91] Report of the President's Commission on the Assassination of President Kennedy, "Chapter 2: The Assassination," September 24, 1964, pages 28-9.

> us for helping them. But they know sometime in
> the future we may ask them to do us a favor.

As I read Tinman's description of his conversation with Mario, I realized it was one more occasion in which life imitated art. The exchange mimicked the opening scene in *The Godfather*. On the day of his daughter's wedding, Don Corleone promises Amerigo Bonasera he will bring justice "to those scum who ruined your daughter." When Bonasera offers to pay Corleone, the don replies, "Someday, and that day may never come, I will call upon you to do me a service in return."[92]

> Creating distance between the site of the
> assassination and Giancana also resolved another
> problem. If Giancana was implicated, any post-
> assassination investigation would likely uncover
> past associations between Giancana, Lancer and
> his father. Something that would damage Kennedy's
> legacy and embarrass the family. Even if the
> Mafia was implicated, investigators would likely
> assume the assassin was linked to a Texas crime
> organization, not Giancana.

Always looking for that significant clue as to the true nature of the journal, the phrase "damage Kennedy's legacy and embarrass the family" seemed worthy of precise and painstaking scrutiny. Much that linked Giancana to the Kennedy family did not become public knowledge until years after the assassination. Mafia participation in CIA covert operations to assassinate Fidel Castro did not surface until 1974. And Judith Campbell Exner did not confirm her relationships with Kennedy and Giancana until three years after disclosure of the CIA connection.

Was this passage a flaw or gaffe that would challenge whether Mason created the content in real time? Had he referenced something of substance he could not possibly know in June 1963? I scoured the journal in hopes of finding further evidence to what Mason might have referred. There was none.

---

[92] Mario Puzo and Francis Ford Coppola, *The Godfather*, Paramount Pictures, March 1, 1971, p. 5.

A contemporaneous account would not have referenced CIA activities in Cuba. To maintain secrecy, the operation was conducted out of the former CIA offices in Coral Gables, Florida which now operated under the name Zenith Technical Enterprises, Inc. Military historians still debate whether JFK, who authorized the project in November 1961, was privy to the unit's specific activities. Regardless of the commander-in-chief's level of participation, only those with the highest security clearance and "need to know" authorization would have knowledge of this undertaking.

Judith Campbell, her name at the time, was a totally different situation. Not only were Secret Service agents aware of Campbell and Kennedy's other paramours, they were expected to facilitate the president's trysts both inside and outside the White House. In *Zero Fail*, Carol Leonnig explains the code of silence which existed among those responsible for the commander-in-chief's safety.

> *All agents knew that discretion was part of their duty. They weren't supposed to share the inner workings of the White House or the private moments they witnessed between the president and his family. Kennedy's agents had to keep some darker secrets as well.*[93]

A member of Kennedy's detail Tim McIntyre told Leonnig about the night his supervisor Emory Roberts gave him the following advice. "You're going to see a lot of shit around here. Stuff with the president. Just forget about it. Keep it to yourself. Don't even talk to your wife."[94]

JFK was not the first or last president engaged in extramarital affairs. But his actions differed from his peers in two important aspects. First, his appetite for casual sex was legendary, ranging from movie stars to White House staff. In the June 2013 issue of *Harper's Bazaar*, Caitlin Flanagan described the extent of JFK's sexual escapades:

> *Throughout the marriage, [Kennedy] always had girls: there were girlfriends and comfort girls; call girls and showgirls;*

---

93 Leonnig, p. 37.
94 Ibid, p. 37.

> *girls on the campaign trail and girls who seemed to materialize out of thin air wherever he was.*[95]

During his time in the Oval Office, there were only three long-term relationships, the most serious being Mary Pinchot Meyer, sister-in-law of *Washington Post* editor Ben Bradlee. An October 1963 handwritten note from Kennedy to Meyer, which surfaced in 2016, confirmed the intensity of their relationship.

> *Why don't you leave suburbia for once—come and see me—either here—or at the Cape next week or in Boston the 19th. I know it is unwise, irrational, and that you may hate it—on the other hand you may not—and I will love it. You say that it is good for me not to get what I want. After all of these years—you should give me a more loving answer than that. Why don't you just say yes.*[96]

JFK's secretary Evelyn Lincoln was supposed to deliver the note to Meyer but never got a chance following the assassination. It remained in Lincoln's possession for more than a half century until it was sold at auction on June 23, 2016, to an undisclosed buyer for $88,870.[97]

Meyer became fodder for assassination conspiracy theorists when, on October 12, 1964, she was shot and killed walking the towpath along the Chesapeake and Ohio Canal near her Georgetown home. Raymond Crump, Jr., whom a police officer spotted near Meyer's body, was arrested and tried for the murder. However, he was acquitted in July 1965 due to a lack of evidence. Meyer's homicide remains unsolved.

The most pervasive theory about Mary Meyer's possible role in the assassination centers on her ex-husband Cord Meyer, Jr. In 1949, he began working for the CIA, eventually rising to the position of Assistant Deputy Director for Planning. Adding fuel to the fire was the fact Mary

---

[95] Caitlin Flanagan, "Jackie and the Girls," *The Atlantic*, July/August 2012 Issue.

[96] Megan Friedman, "A Scandalous Love Letter from JFK to His Mistress Has Been Unearthed," *Harper's Bazaar*. June 3, 2016.

[97] Mark Shanahan, "JFK love letter to his alleged mistress sells for big money," *Boston Globe*, June 24, 2016.

remained close to a college friend Cicely, wife of James Angleton, head of the CIA counterintelligence division.

Ben Bradlee also contributed to the mystery surrounding his sister-in-law's murder in his memoir *A Good Life*. He recounts a phone call from Mary's best friend, an artist living in Tokyo, imploring him to retrieve Meyer's private diary. As he soon discovered, he was not the only one in pursuit of his sister-in-law's personal records.

> *We didn't start looking until the next morning, when [my wife] Tony and I walked around the corner a few blocks to Mary's house. It was locked, as we had expected, but when we got inside, we found Jim Angleton, and to our complete surprise he told us he, too, was looking for Mary's diary.* [98]

In February 1976, the *Washington Post* reported Angleton destroyed the diary.[99] That did not stop conspiracy theorists from speculating what it contained. Some believe it merely confirmed her relationship with Kennedy. Others, aware of Meyer's friendship with psychedelic drug advocate Dr. Timothy Leary, believe she introduced the president to LSD. Most, however, think the diary included information about the CIA covert activities in Cuba, which would explain James Angleton's presence at Mary's townhouse the morning after her death and his interest in her diary.

Two more documented affairs raised concerns whether JFK's infidelity represented a threat to national security. The U.S. intelligence community believed Communist operatives constantly sought avenues by which they could blackmail or harm the president. Larry Newman, a member of Kennedy's Secret Service detail told Carol Leonnig, "We were in the middle of the Cold War, for Christ's sake. We anguished over the possibility of that happening."[100]

One suspect was Bertha Hildegard Elly a native of Kleinitz, East Germany. In 1955, her family moved to Schwelm, West Germany

---

[98] Benjamin Bradlee, *A Good Life*, Simon and Schuster: New York, 1975, p. 267.
[99] Don Oberdorfer, "JFK, Artist 'Affair' Reported," *Washington Post*, February 23, 1976, p. 2.
[100] Leonnig, p. 41.

where she pursued a modeling career and married Rolf Rometsch, a German air force sergeant. She came to America when her husband was assigned to the German Logistics Office in Washington, D.C. Using the moniker Ellen Rometsch, she met Kennedy while working as a hostess at the Quorum Club, a watering hole near the U.S. Capitol, frequented by members of Congress.

After learning about the affair from an FBI informant, the agency began an investigation into Rometsch's East German background including her having belonged to a Communist youth group. On July 3, 1963, Director Hoover shared his confidential file on Rometsch with attorney general Robert Kennedy.

In a 2000 biography of the former attorney general *Robert Kennedy: His Life*, Evan Thomas writes, "[Robert] Kennedy instantly saw the danger."[101] In July 1963, the FBI concluded, "Security allegations concerning subject not substantiated. No further investigation warranted."[102] Despite this determination, Ellen Rometsch was deported to West Germany on September 26, 1963.

Perhaps Kennedy's most reckless sexual liaison was his 18-month affair with Judith Campbell. As had been the case with Ellen Rometsch, Hoover warned the president's brother of potential national security issues stemming from JFK's extramarital activities. On February 27, 1962, Hoover sent a memorandum to RFK detailing what the FBI knew about the JFK/Campbell/Giancana triangle after which RFK arranged a March 22, 1962, lunch between Hoover and the president.[103]

The meeting with Hoover had the intended effect. In her autobiography, *Judith Exner: My Story*, she records how, in that exact time frame, her interest in the president waned.

> *The weight of the office was getting heavier on his shoulders*
> *and he was changing. He wasn't as happy-go-lucky, not as*

---

[101] Evan Thomas, *Robert Kennedy: His Life*, Simon & Schuster: New York, 2000, p. 155.
[102] FBI memorandum from W. R. Wannall, "Ellen Rometsch, Internal Security-East Germany," July 12, 1963.
[103] Taylor Branch, "Affairs of State," *The Washington Post*, October 30, 1988.

> *relaxed, and cheerful...By early 1962, I dreaded going to the White House.*[104]

Public knowledge of the affair did not surface for 13 years, until the *New York Times* noted a discreet reference to Campbell, now Exner, in the final report issued by the Senate Select Committee on Covert Intelligence Activities. *Times* reporter John M. Crewdson received a tip that the FBI had evidence Exner's ties to Kennedy and two Mafia kingpins were not unrelated. Crewdson sought comment from committee chair Frank Church, asking why the final report did not reference the FBI disclosure. Church told Crewdson the committee voted unanimously to exclude that assessment from their final report after "the evidence showed that [Campbell] had no knowledge of assassination activities [directed at Fidel Castro] on the part of the Mafia leaders." He added the panel therefore decided, "...it would not be appropriate to wade into the personal life of the President."[105]

FBI memoranda contradict the Church Committee's assessment. Following publication of the *Times* story, Crewdson sent a request to the FBI seeking verification of additional information previously obtained by the *Times*. In response, the FBI undertook an investigation "...to determine the veracity of the aforementioned stories," which included a 1961 or 1962 conversation between Campbell and JFK intercepted via an FBI wiretap on Giancana's home phone.

Knowledge of the Giancana/Kennedy/Campbell triangle may have influenced the TEAM's preference for Oswald over Giancana as the most viable option. They continued to allocate their time and resources in that direction.

```
June 16, 1963

Lion reports Oswald distributed the FPCC
handbills at a location near the naval shipyard.
Lion walked by Oswald who offered him a handbill.
```

---

[104] Judith Campbell Exner, *My Story*, Grove Press, 1977, p. 245.
[105] John M Crewdson, "Church Denies Cover-Up of a Kennedy Friendship," *New York Times*, December 16, 1975, p. 1.

After reading it, Lion talked with Oswald about his support for Cuba and Castro.

June 24, 1963

Lion observed Oswald entering the U.S. consulate in New Orleans. A call to the State Department revealed Oswald had applied for a new passport.

Scarecrow then called Ruth Paine. He asked if she had heard from Marina? Did she know how they were doing in New Orleans? Paine volunteered the Oswalds are having marital issues and she is hoping Marina will come stay with her until they are resolved.

The FBI's psychological profile of Oswald suggests stress is a positive factor in our ability to manipulate him. Oswald is more susceptible to suggestion when he is unhappy or under pressure. His relationship with Marina is already under stress. Is there something more we can do?

July 10, 1963

At my request, Scarecrow places an anonymous call to the Reilly Coffee Company asking if they are aware of Oswald's pro-Castro activities. They are not.

July 19, 1963

Lion reports Reilly Coffee fired Oswald.

July 22, 1963

Lion observed Oswald entering the local unemployment office.

Just as the TEAM appears to be making progress with Oswald, Mason learns their activities do not exist in a vacuum. Kennedy's presidential duties could influence their choice of options and the timetable for completing the ASSIGNMENT.

July 24, 1963

```
I received a call from Wizard. He needs an update
on Oswald. He says Lancer has just left a meeting
with the Joint Chiefs concerning the final
language in a nuclear test ban treaty which is
likely to be approved by the Soviets. Lancer has
a meeting scheduled with Secretary of State Rusk
this afternoon to discuss a possible announcement
by the weekend. Wizard is afraid if the president
is killed by someone with Soviet connections
before the treaty is ratified by the Senate, it
might prevent approval. The target date for a
Senate vote is early October.
```

Evelyn Lincoln's recap of the day's activities confirm the meetings with the Joint Chiefs and Dean Rusk.[106] And as Wizard predicted, the three signatories to the treaty–the United States, Great Britain and the Soviet Union–sign off on the proposed language the following day. On Friday, July 26, Kennedy addresses the nation, claiming "a limited test ban treaty is safer by far for the United States than an unlimited nuclear arms race."[107]

There is one more appointment on the July 24 daily recap, which at the time seemed of little historical significance. Prior to Kennedy's meeting with the military leadership, Lincoln records:

```
9:45-10:00 am/The President greeted the
delegates to the 18th Annual American Legion BOYS
NATION in the Rose Garden of the White House.
```

It is at this event, White House photographer Arnold Sachs takes a picture of Kennedy shaking hands with the future 42nd president of the United States, 17-year-old William Jefferson Clinton.

---

[106] Among attendees at the meeting with Secretary Rusk was journalist Edward R. Morrow whom Kennedy appointed as director of the United States Information Service in March 1961.

[107] John F. Kennedy, "Statement announcing postponement of underground nuclear testing," JFK Presidential Library, JFKPOF-046-009, July 26, 1963.

August 1, 1963

Tinman received a call from Mario. Everything is
set to go in Dallas. There are two options. They
can take out the president from a distance or up
close. All they need to know are the best
opportunities for each option. Tinman assured
Mario he would update him as Lancer's schedule is
finalized. We agreed there was no reason to tell
Mario we are pursuing a second option or that his
is the backup. That can wait.

One more epiphany. Occasionally, Mason's journal satisfied my
original objective when I stopped by his home for the first time. I
wanted to know what it was like to have observed and interacted with
my childhood political idol. I knew I had a better-than-average
understanding of the presidency due to my undergraduate and graduate
education. But the parsing of each journal entry alongside the historical
record, especially Evelyn Lincoln's minute-by-minute recap of
Kennedy's three years as chief executive, provided a degree of
awareness one could never obtain from a lecture or text.

The events of August 7-9, 1963, were a somber reminder the official
responsibilities of any commander-in-chief occasionally take a back
seat to those of spouse and parent.

August 7, 1963

Mrs. Kennedy went into premature labor. She was
taken by helicopter from the compound on Cape Cod
to the hospital at Otis AFB.

Lancer was notified around noon and immediately
departed the WH. Due to the last minute nature of
this trip, off-duty agents were recruited. Tinman
and I will accompany him.

August 8, 1963

Mrs. Kennedy remained at Otis AFB while the baby
was transferred to Boston Childrens Hospital for
treatment of a breathing disorder. It is unclear
how long Lancer will stay in Massachusetts. His

schedule has been cleared for the next several
days.

August 9, 1963

Not a good day. The WH announced Patrick Kennedy
died at 4:04am this morning. No word on funeral
arrangements and no update on Lancer's schedule.

Patrick Bouvier Kennedy was delivered by cesarean section at 12:52 p.m. on August 7. He was just short of 34 weeks old, measured 17 inches, and weighed four pounds 10 and a half ounces. The timing of his birth suggests that he was likely conceived during the Kennedys' 1962 holiday vacation in Palm Beach. Is it possible this was the first stop on the president's legacy tour? Was Patrick supposed to be a farewell gift to Jackie? And did Mason make the connection but decided not to put it in the journal out of deference to the family? Or did he omit it because it was irrelevant to the task at hand?

Meanwhile, Lion and Scarecrow were preoccupied with keeping the ASSIGNMENT on track.

In New Orleans, the team has a potential problem.
Lion reports Oswald got into a fight with an
anti-Castro Cuban refugee while distributing FPCC
literature on Canal Street. Oswald was arrested.

August 10, 1963

After spending the night in jail, Oswald requests
an FBI interview. His request is granted and he
is questioned by agent John Quigley from the New
Orleans office. His aunt arranges bail that
afternoon.

Tinman and I are having a hard time focusing on
the assignment. We are informed Lancer will
remain in Boston with Mrs. Kennedy through
Tuesday. The team has scheduled a call for
Wednesday morning to discuss whether the events
of the past week will affect the assignment.
Tinman, always looking for the silver lining,
thinks Mrs. Kennedy's safety is one less thing we
need to worry about. It is unlikely she will

accompany Lancer on campaign trips after losing
the baby.

One more data point in support of the contemporaneous nature of the journal. Mason would not have included Mrs. Kennedy's anticipated absence from the campaign trail if the August 10 entry was written after Dallas.

August 12, 1963

Oswald pleads guilty to one charge of disturbing
the peace, a misdemeanor, and is fined 10
dollars.

August 14, 1963

Back to the assignment after accompanying Lancer
to DC last night.

If Oswald is going to be the assassin, we need to
move quickly before he does something that takes
him off the street. Scarecrow suggests we use
Oswald's interest in meeting Castro in Cuba to
gain his trust and increase his animosity toward
Kennedy.

Step 1. Scarecrow will tell Oswald he can help
him get to Cuba by way of Mexico. Step 2. He goes
to Mexico but is denied a visa. Step 3. Scarecrow
tells Oswald the visa denial was the result of
intervention by the U.S. State Department. It is
the Kennedy administration which is keeping him
from Cuba and Castro. Step 4. Scarecrow also
informs Oswald that Khrushchev believes Kennedy
still wants to overthrow the Cuban government.
Step 5. Oswald is told U.S.-based Castro
supporters are looking for someone to kill
Kennedy. The assassin will be well compensated
and relocated in either Havana or Moscow.

The team signs off on Scarecrow's plan.

August 17, 1963

    Another potential complication. Oswald's arrest
    and court appearance are noticed by a local radio
    talk show host Bill Stuckey. He invites Oswald to
    appear on his WDSU program Latin Listening Post.
    Lion thinks this can help us. His interview will
    probably be recorded and could become evidence of
    Oswald's motive for killing Kennedy.

August 21, 1963

    Oswald appears again on WDSU. This time he is
    asked to debate U.S./Cuba relations with Ed
    Butler, a member of a right-wing group which
    opposes Castro.

The following journal entry raises the possibility Oswald's involvement with the Fair Play for Cuba Committee may have backfired. Oswald seems increasingly comfortable being in New Orleans, which creates two problems. First, it takes him away from Dallas which is now confirmed for a November campaign trip. Second, he seems less interested in going to Havana and meeting Castro.

August 24, 1963

    Scarecrow calls Oswald from Dallas. He reminds
    Oswald about their discussion at Ruth Paine's
    dinner party and asks if he is still interested
    in going to Cuba. Oswald says yes. Scarecrow
    tells him he knows other people who have made it
    to Cuba via the Cuban embassy in Mexico City.
    Oswald says he will consider it.

Meanwhile, integration efforts in deep-south states produce violent responses in several cities, the most prominent being the September 15 bombing of the 16th Street Baptist Church in Birmingham, Alabama. As they did on numerous occasions, the TEAM reassessed its options based on current events.

September 16, 1963

    The bombing of a Negro church in Birmingham
    killed four young girls. Lancer instructs the FBI

to help identify those responsible. He also says
it increases his commitment to civil rights. By
targeting innocent victims, opponents of racial
integration have already advanced Lancer's
agenda. Would their assassination of the
president still make sense?

Kennedy acknowledges as much in his September 16 statement.

*If these cruel and tragic events can only awaken that city and
State--if they can only awaken this entire Nation--to a
realization of the folly of racial injustice and hatred and
violence, then it is not too late for all concerned to unite in
steps toward peaceful progress before more lives are lost.*[108]

The church bombing reinforces JFK's commitment to introduce civil
rights legislation during the 1963-64 session of Congress.

September 17, 1963

Oswald goes to the Mexican consulate in New
Orleans and obtains the necessary documents to
travel to Mexico on a tourist visa.

Oswald calls Scarecrow to thank him for his help
and tells Scarecrow he has invited Ruth Paine to
come to New Orleans and stay with Marina who is
expecting their second child. Scarecrow shares
this with Lion and suggests he travel to Mexico
City before Oswald arrives.

September 20, 1963

Lion reports Ruth Paine is now in New Orleans.

September 23, 1963

Lion observes Ruth and Marina leaving the house
with suitcases. It appears Marina will stay with
Ruth in Dallas while Lee is in Mexico.

---

[108] John F. Kennedy, Statement by the President on the Sunday Bombing in
Birmingham, September 16, 1963.

```
September 25, 1963

Lion reports Oswald briefly stopped at the
unemployment office. Then goes to the bus station
and buys a ticket to Houston.

September 26, 1963

Oswald calls Scarecrow from the Houston bus
station where he spent the night. He then
purchased a ticket to Laredo, Texas. After
crossing the border into Nuevo Laredo, he will
catch a bus to Mexico City. He will be staying at
the Hotel del Comercio.

September 27, 1963

Lion arrived in Mexico City last night. Oswald
arrived this morning and checked into the hotel.
In the afternoon, he went to the Cuban Embassy
but left shortly afterwards. He left the embassy
rather hurriedly and appeared to be upset. He
then walked to the Soviet Embassy.
```

On September 27, Oswald learns getting to Cuba will not be as easy as Scarecrow suggested. According to the Warren Commission report, Oswald made a series of visits to both the Cuban and Soviet embassies in Mexico City. His first stop was the Cuban embassy where he requested an "in-transit" visa which would allow him to travel to the Soviet Union via Cuba. This is contrary to what Marina Oswald told the Warren Commission. She assumed he always intended to stay in Cuba. Silvia Duran, a Mexican native who worked at the Cuban Consulate, told Oswald that Cuba could not issue a visa until he had permission to enter the USSR. This infuriated Oswald.

According to Duran, "...he became very excited or angry, and requested to speak directly to the Cuban Counsel Eusebio Azcue Lopez." In testimony before the House Select Committee on Assassinations, Azcue Lopez described Oswald's demeanor. "He always had a face which reflected unhappiness. He was never friendly. He was persistent. And he was not pleasant."[109]

```
October 2, 1963

Oswald failed to obtain the necessary travel
documents from either the Soviet or the Cuban
embassy in Mexico City. He makes plans to return
to the U.S. Lion heads back to New Orleans.
```

Between September 27 and his departure from Mexico City on October 2, Oswald visited the Soviet embassy repeatedly. The last time, a Soviet official informed him that it could take up to four months to process his visa application. He reenters the U.S. and heads to Dallas to be with Marina rather than return to New Orleans. In testimony before the Warren Commission, Marina described Lee as "disappointed and discouraged" at his inability to secure entry into Cuba.[110]

```
October 4, 1963

My first day back in the WH since February. Just
past noon, Lancer met with Texas Governor John
Connally about the President's campaign trip in
November. I was on call in case there were any
questions about security arrangements. After
Connally left the Oval Office, Wizard briefed me
on what Lancer and the governor agreed to. In
turn, I updated him on the team's progress. It
was almost 7:00 pm when I left Wizard's office.
As I passed through the reception area outside
the Oval Office, Lancer was escorting the Vice
President to the door. They exchanged an extended
handshake, the kind that says, "I've got your
back" or "Don't worry, I get it." Was this to
assure Volunteer the Texas trip would resolve the
in-fighting between Connally and Yarborough? Or
does Volunteer know something else?
```

---

[109] Testimony of former Cuban Counsel in Mexico City Eusebio Azcue Lopez, September 18, 1978.
[110] Warren Commission Report, p. 301.

Evelyn Lincoln's recap of Kennedy's activities on October 4, 1963, confirms the meeting with Johnson beginning at 6:50 p.m. and ending 20 minutes later.

```
October 7, 1963

Despite Lee and Marina expecting their second
child, Marina is still living with Ruth Paine.
Lee decides not to go back to New Orleans. He is
living in a rooming house in the Oak Cliff
section of Dallas.

Oswald called Scarecrow to share his experience
in Mexico City. He tells him he still hopes to
get to Cuba but does not know what to do next.
Scarecrow offers to make a couple of calls.

Oswald told Scarecrow he interviewed for a
typesetting job with Padgett Printing. He thought
it went well. This could create a problem because
Padgett is almost two miles from what is the most
likely motorcade route. We must find a way to
prevent Oswald from getting the job.
```

This would not be the first time Oswald sought employment in the printing industry. In October 1962, he applied for a similar position in the photographic department at Jaggars-Chiles-Stovall, a typesetting company. He was hired on October 12. His employment was terminated on April 6, 1963. According to his immediate supervisor John Graef, Oswald's dismissal was due to the number of times his work did not meet company standards and his hostile relationships with other employees.[111]

Some problems solve themselves. Despite being dismissed at Jaggars-Chiles-Stovall, Oswald listed Robert Stovall as a reference on his Padgett Printing job application. In testimony before the Warren Commission, Stovall described his conversation with Ted Gangel, Padgett's superintendent.

---

[111] Testimony of John G. Graef before the Warren Commission, March 30, 1964, Hearings, Volume X, pages 174-194.

> Mr. STOVALL. He called me and asked me and I told him I did not know [Oswald], so I asked John Graef and they said this fellow was kind of an oddball, and he was kinda peculiar sometimes and that he had some knowledge of the Russian language, which—this is all I knew, so I told Ted, I said, "Ted, I don't know, this guy may be a damn Communist. I can't tell you. If I was you, I wouldn't hire him." So he didn't.[112]

Having removed one potential roadblock, the TEAM still needed to check two more boxes. First, convert Oswald's disapproval of U.S. policy toward Cuba into enough motivation to take it out on the sitting president. Second, ensure Oswald will be at the appointed location where he can carry out the ASSIGNMENT. The key to achieving the first goal was to convince Oswald the Kennedy administration had intervened in his efforts to get to Cuba.

```
Later Scarecrow gets back to Oswald. Scarecrow
tells Oswald he learned the Soviet ambassador in
Mexico contacted his U.S. counterpart who advised
them to reject Oswald's visa application. Oswald
is furious.

Scarecrow also tells Oswald he is not alone.
Other Cuban sympathizers think Kennedy is trying
to have it both ways. While he promised
Khrushchev the U.S. would not intervene in Cuba
after the Soviets removed their missiles, he is
still squeezing Castro with the trade embargo and
travel ban.

Scarecrow tells Oswald there may be someone who
can help him get to Cuba. He will contact Joseph
Hansen, a member of the American Socialist
Workers Party national committee who has close
ties to members of the Soviet politburo. Hansen
is a pro-Cuba activist who believes Castro
aligned with the Soviets only because of the
hardline response by both Eisenhower and Kennedy
to Batista's overthrow. The peaceful resolution
of the missile crisis was an opening to convince
```

---

[112] Testimony of Robert Stovall before the Warren Commission, March 30, 1964, Hearings, Volume X, pp. 170-1.

    Castro his interests were better served aligning
    with the U.S. rather than the Soviets. Oswald
    agreed.

Introducing Hansen as someone who could intervene on Oswald's behalf was a logical choice. Hansen's ascension to a leadership position within the Socialist Workers Party (SWP) begins when his parents emigrate to the United States from Norway after converting to Mormonism. While under the tutelage of his English literature professor Earle Birney at the University of Utah, Hansen embraced socialism and associated with an American Trotskyist group. In 1937, he and his wife Reba travelled to Mexico where he served as Leon Trotsky's personal secretary and bodyguard following the Communist leader's exile from Russia. Hansen was with Trotsky when he was assassinated by Ramon Mercader and assisted in Mercader's capture and interrogation.[113]

In 1961, Hansen traveled to Cuba with the SWP presidential nominee Farrell Dobbs after which he helped launch Fair Play for Cuba Committees in the United States and Canada. The following year, he moved to Paris where he served for three years as the SWP representative in Europe. While there, he and Reba launched a journal called *World Outlook*. Hansen remained active in the SWP until his death in January 1979 at age 68.[114]

    Scarecrow informs Oswald members of the SWP have
    become increasingly critical of Kennedy. Some
    have called for his removal from office. Oswald
    says he can understand how they feel. Scarecrow
    promises to get back to Oswald as soon as
    possible.

    October 10, 1963

    Oswald did not wait for Scarecrow to call him. He
    called Scarecrow to see if he had any success
    reaching Hansen.

---

[113] Joseph Hanson, The Socialist Worker Workers Party: What It Is, What It Stands For, Pioneer Publishers, October 1948, p. 2.
[114] Wolfgang and Petra Lubitz, "Bibliographical Sketch of Joseph Hansen," TrotskyanaNet, revised August 2012.

> Scarecrow sensed Oswald was upset about
> something. Oswald confirmed he did not get the
> job at the printing company. He thinks someone
> told the owner about his pro-Cuba activities.
> Scarecrow suggests it is possibly someone at the
> FBI or state department. Oswald agrees this could
> be one more instance of Kennedy administration
> intervention.
>
> Scarecrow was surprised how quickly Oswald took
> the bait. Maybe too quickly. Scarecrow wondered
> if Oswald realized he was being used and was now
> playing along, becoming the manipulator rather
> than the manipulated.

In hindsight, Oswald's immediate and rash response seems consistent with past behavior. As Ruth Paine and Marina Oswald would later testify, it had not taken much more to spark Oswald's April 1963 failed assassination attempt of retired general Edwin Walker. However, on October 10, the assault on Walker was still an open case with no identified suspect. Nor was it likely Oswald talked about Walker to bolster his credentials as a motivated assassin. If known, Scarecrow surely would have shared that critical information with the TEAM and Mason would have noted it in his journal.

> Scarecrow stuck to the plan. If the SWP was as
> anxious to get rid of Kennedy as they claimed,
> would Oswald help them? Especially if it resulted
> in his getting to Cuba. Oswald was skeptical and
> asked if someone could really make that happen.
>
> Scarecrow decided it was time to take a risk. He
> told Oswald he had not been able to reach Hansen.
> But had talked to other members of the SWP who
> wanted Kennedy gone. They mentioned a tentative
> campaign trip to Dallas as an opportunity. All
> the opposition to Kennedy's visit was coming from
> anti-Castro activists who believed Kennedy was
> soft on Communism. No one would suspect an
> assassin would be a Castro supporter.
>
> Oswald did not balk. Scarecrow told Oswald he had
> done as much as he could for now, but to expect a
> call from someone from the SWP.

```
I set up a call with Wizard and the rest of the
team. Scarecrow repeated the details of his
conversation with Oswald. He was confident Oswald
was now all in. Wizard gave the okay to proceed.
Meanwhile, Tinman would let Mario know their
services were needed only if the preferred option
fell through.

October 11, 1963

Tinman informed Mario the Mafia alternative is
now the backup plan. Mario's response surprised
Tinman. It appears the assignment's success is as
important to Giancana as it was to Lancer. Mario
said rather than call off his people, he would
ask them to stand by. Everything will be in place
up until the last minute. All he needs is a phone
call.
```

Of all the surrealistic twists in Mason's journal, I still found passages related to the TEAM's unconditional trust in the Mafia to be among the most questionable. Would they have turned over total control of the operation to a third party, especially a criminal organization? And not push back when Mario tells Tinman his forces will still mobilize just in case, not knowing who, when or where this back-up unit would strike?

The journal includes no evidence Tinman told Mario the assassination was scheduled for noon in Dealey Plaza. As the presidential motorcade gets within minutes of the Trade Mart, might the individual overseeing the Mafia operation unilaterally decide Plan A had failed and green light his own shooter to act? Could the crossfire on Elm Street, reported by several witnesses, have been the result of both Oswald and a Mafia gunman independently targeting Kennedy?

Trying to make sense of each entry as Mason's account approaches a climax on November 22, Occam's razor again has little value. Apart from the "magic bullet" striking both Kennedy and Connally, the Warren Commission's conclusion Oswald acted alone is the simplest explanation. Conversely, Mason's version defies credulity. Yet the level of detail and complexity laid out in his journal make it equally hard to believe someone could create such a tale out of whole cloth. The best example of this paradox of specificity versus credibility appears in the October 14 entry.

```
October 14, 1963

Yesterday, Scarecrow paid a boy in Ruth Paine's
neighborhood to distribute flyers listing several
downtown companies with job openings. Among them
was the Texas School Book Depository. This
evening he called Paine to ask if Oswald had
found a job. She told him he applied to a local
bakery and a gypsum plant, but both required
driving and Oswald did not have a license. Paine
then mentioned she and Marina were having coffee
with a neighbor who knew Lee was looking for
work. She asked if they had seen the flyer. The
neighbor said her brother recently got a job he
liked at the school book depository.
```

Was it a coincidence Ruth Paine's neighbor Linnie Mae Randall's brother worked at the depository? Or had Scarecrow already identified that connection when he added the depository to the list of companies hiring new employees? Either way, Paine called Roy Truly, a supervisor at the depository and scheduled an appointment for Oswald. Neither his Soviet defection nor his pro-Cuban activities came up during the interview, after which Truly immediately offered Oswald a job filling book orders.

On the 51st anniversary of the assassination Paul Brandus, founder of the White House-based newsletter *West Wing Reports*, suggested Oswald's employment at the schoolbook depository could not have been a random event.

If it was a conspiracy, then everyone, at each point along the way, would have had to be in on it. One boss checked references, another didn't. Neighbors gossiping over coffee and cigarettes. The wrong skills for one job, the right skills for another. A warehouse here, or a warehouse there. Had

*any one of these minor footnotes to history been slightly
different, what would our world be like today?*[115]

If Scarecrow's use of Randall, her brother, Paine and Truly is accurate, Brandus was half right. Each milestone from identifying the opening at the schoolbook depository to Oswald's hiring was more than a coincidence. However, none of the players were necessarily knowing participants. What they all had in common was susceptibility to manipulation.

```
October 16, 1963

Oswald reports to work at the depository. He is
now where we need him to be. Can we keep him
there until Lancer's arrival?
```

The October 16 entry is the first in a series of posts where Mason has doubts about the TEAM's ability to keep Oswald committed to the task. Perfectly understandable considering his restless nature and history of quitting jobs on a moment's notice.

```
October 18, 1963

Our next task, to make sure everything is in
place for Oswald to act. Another member of the
team, someone with whom Oswald has had no
previous contact, needed to take the lead from
here. I was the obvious choice having never
spoken directly to Oswald.

I called Oswald and introduced myself as one of
Joseph Hansen's associates. I told Oswald I would
be his contact as Hansen was in Europe
representing the SWP. I also told him I was aware
of his interest to go to Cuba in return for
helping to eliminate Kennedy. Oswald was not
totally convinced and asked how he could be sure
I was someone he could trust.

I took another big risk. I asked Oswald if he
thought it was a coincidence he got a job at the
```

---

[115] Paul Brandus, "The Kennedy Assassination: How Did Oswald Get His Job at the Book Depository, Anyway?" *West Wing Reports*, November 22, 2014.

depository. I then told him how we made that happen when we found out the president's motorcade would come through Dealey Plaza. And why it was important he be hired so far in advance of any public announcement of the motorcade route. The police would want to identify anyone who was hired after publication of the exact route. Oswald would not be on that list.

That seemed to assure Oswald. When I asked him what else he needed, he talked freely. He told me he already had a rifle and scope that would do the job. And that he would check out different floors and windows to determine the best vantage point to target Kennedy.

I then gave Oswald a general description of the escape plan. There would be a car waiting for him near the depository. The driver would have fake credentials for him to use for the trip to Mexico City. The Soviet embassy had already processed his Russian visa and informed the Cuban embassy to expedite his tourist visa for entry into Havana. A ticket for ship passage from Cozumel to Havana would be purchased and given to him at the Cuban embassy.

I promised to get back to him with updates. Holding back on details was something the team agreed was important since there were still 36 days before Lancer's trip to Dallas. More than enough time for Oswald to back out. Occasional phone calls with additional information were a way to monitor whether Oswald was having second thoughts.

With just over a month before Kennedy's trip to Texas, all the pieces were in place. But would they stay there?

CHAPTER SIXTEEN

THE COUNTDOWN

As the presidential trip to Texas approached, the TEAM believed the one variable beyond their total control was Oswald's commitment to the ASSIGNMENT. There was always the chance he might reconsider at the last minute. However, there was another potential disruption on the horizon.

```
October 24, 1963

There is a report out of Dallas that United
Nations ambassador Adlai Stevenson was jeered and
physically attacked following a speech at the
Dallas Memorial Auditorium. This is the latest
example of anti-Kennedy sentiment in Texas.
```

Following his introduction by Stanley Marcus, co-founder of the luxury retail store which bears his name and that of his partner Al Neiman, one attendee Frank McGehee, leader of the ultra-right National Indignation Convention, challenged Stevenson. "Mr. Ambassador, why do you insist on negotiating with Communist dictators?" Although local police escorted McGehee out of the building, protesters continued to interrupt Stevenson with noisemakers and fake coughing. The demonstration reached a crescendo when another attendee shouted, "Kennedy will get his reward in hell." [116] Police had to shield Stevenson and Marcus as

---

[116] Bill Minutaglio and Steven L. Davis, "A Month Before JFK's Assassination, Dallas Right Wingers Attack Adlai Stevenson," *The New Republic*, November 18, 2013.

they left the building to shouts of "Communist" and "traitor."

By "latest sign of anti-Kennedy sentiment in Dallas," Mason implicitly acknowledged a series of incidents going back to the 1960 presidential campaign. Then vice-presidential candidate Lyndon Johnson and his wife faced protesters leaving their hotel during a campaign visit. A year later E. M. Dealey, publisher of the *Dallas Morning News*, during a White House event, challenged Kennedy's leadership, describing the president as someone "riding Caroline's tricycle, not a man on horseback." [117]

Dealey was not the only prominent Dallas resident to accuse Kennedy of being soft on Communism. Among them was General Walker who resigned from the army after being reprimanded for distributing John Birch Society brochures to his troops. In protest, Walker flew an American flag upside down at his home to warn the country it was in extreme danger while Kennedy was commander-in-chief.

This right-wing, anti-Kennedy sentiment made Mason rethink the TEAM's focus on pro-Cuban or Communist sympathizers as the more credible threat.

```
Had we overlooked the possibility the most likely
suspects to assassinate Kennedy in Texas were not
leftist with pro-Cuba sympathies, but right-wing
extremists who thought the president was soft on
Communism? It is too late to start over now. The
more important question is whether the WH will
postpone or cancel the Dallas trip as a
precaution after the Stevenson incident.
```

Mason's angst was not unfounded. Bill Kemp, archivist for the McLean County (Illinois) Museum of History, penned a May 2016 article in which he quoted a conversation between Stevenson and then White House special assistant and speechwriter Arthur Schlesinger, Jr. Stevenson tells Schlesinger:

---

[117] E. M. Dealey was the son of George Bannerman Dealey for whom Dealey Plaza is named. The elder Dealey was publisher of the *Morning News* from 1926 until his death in 1948. He was instrumental in the redevelopment of downtown Dallas including the plaza that was dedicated in his honor in 1949.

...there was something ugly and frightening about the atmosphere. Later I talked to some of the leading people there. They wondered whether the president should go to Dallas, and so did I.[118]

Several Dallas officials shared Stevenson's apprehension. Mayor Earl Cabell urged residents to be on their best behavior during the president's visit. As a precaution, Dallas chief of police Jesse Edward Curry requested 100 off-duty police to stand by as extra security.

The Warren Commission did not eliminate the possibility of an assassin with right-wing leanings as quickly as Mason had. Due to Walker's disdain for Kennedy and his association with the John Birch Society, he was among those initially considered as someone who may have been involved in a conspiracy to kill the president. When the Warren Commission directed its focus on Oswald as the sole gunman, Walker was exonerated of any role in the president's murder. However, the more ominous connection between Walker and Oswald emerged during the investigation.

At approximately 9:00 p.m. on the evening of April 10, 1963, Walker barely avoided an assassin's bullet while seated at the desk in his home study. A retrieved slug provided little evidence about the gunman's identity. The case remained unresolved until December 1963, when Ruth Paine, at whose house Oswald spent the night of November 21, turned over several items belonging to the Oswalds to the Warren Commission staff. Among them was a note, in Russian, from Lee Harvey Oswald to his wife Marina, with 11 instructions in the event "something" happened to him. Item #11 read in part, "If I am alive and taken prisoner, the city jail is located at the end of the bridge through which we always passed on going to the city."[119]

Anyone could logically assume the note was written in anticipation of his fate following Kennedy's assassination. However, other items on the list indicated Oswald drafted the instructions months earlier. Of particular note, Item #1 references a key to a post office box which

---

[118] Bill Kemp, "Stevenson Faced Anti-UN Mob in 1963," *The Pantagraph,* Bloomington, Illinois, May 15, 2016.
[119] *Warren Commission Report,* Chapter 4, pages 183-84.

Oswald rented from October 9, 1962, to May 14, 1963, clear evidence Lee's instructions for Marina pre-dated the November assassination.

Four photographs belonging to Oswald provided more evidence the "something" for which he anticipated his death or arrest was the attempt on General Walker's life. Three of the pictures were of Walker's home including one of the windows through which Oswald targeted Walker. The fourth was a section of railroad tracks less than a half-mile from Walker's residence.[120]

In her February 1964 testimony before the Commission, Marina Oswald confirmed her husband attempted to kill General Walker.

> Mrs. OSWALD. No, I didn't understand anything. On the note it said, "If I am arrested" and there are certain other questions, such as, for example, the key to the mailbox is in such and such a place, and that he left me some money to last me for some time, and I couldn't understand at all what can he be arrested for. When he came back I asked him what had happened. He was very pale. I don't remember the exact time, but it was very late. And he told me not to ask him any questions. He only told me that he had shot at General Walker.[121]

Furthermore, she told the Commission the picture of railroad tracks marked the spot where Oswald had buried the rifle after he fired it at Walker. At some point Oswald retrieved the rifle though the time frame is unclear. Marina's last reference to the rifle came when questioned whether she believed her husband when he promised he would not engage in any similar activity.

> Mr. RANKIN. When he promised you that he would not do anything like that again, did you believe him?
>
> Mrs. OSWALD. I did not believe him inasmuch as the rifle remained in the house.
>
> Mr. RANKIN. Did you ask him to get rid of the rifle at that time?

---

[120]Warren Commission Report, Chapter 4, page 186.
[121] "Hearings Before the President's Commission on the Assassination of President Kennedy," Volume 1, Marina Oswald, p 16.

Mrs. OSWALD. Yes.[122]

Although Mason acknowledges this revelation later in the journal, he does not reflect on how earlier awareness of Oswald's attempt on Walker's life might impact the ASSIGNMENT. As Mason states in the October 4 entry, it was too late to reopen the search with a new focus on anti-Communist activists.

Nevertheless, how ironic two individuals with opposing views of U.S.-Cuban relations could share such diverse, yet kindred animosity when it came to U.S. foreign policy pertaining to Cuba. Furthermore, it was the anti-Cuba element who appeared more motivated by Kennedy's resolution of the October 1962 standoff with Nikita Khrushchev. They were the ones who felt Kennedy had betrayed the country after the limited blockade and a subsequent agreement which ensured Fidel Castro's status as leader of a Communist regime within 100 miles of the U.S. mainland.

There was also the possibility Oswald was not the marksman he was reported to be. If the TEAM had known Oswald had missed his intended victim in General Walker's case, would they have questioned whether he was still the sharpshooter described in his military service records? If he could not hit a sitting duck, could they trust him to succeed when it came to a moving target? Again, one might consider the TEAM's lack of awareness about Oswald's attempt on Walker as more proof of the adage, "Ignorance is bliss."

Wizard anticipated the TEAM's concern about the Stevenson incident and placed a call to the Naval Annex the next day.

```
October 25, 1963

Wizard just called. Lancer is taking the report
about Stevenson in stride. He even had an aide
call Stevenson who joked about not knowing his
job description included being Kennedy's stand-in
at a riot.
```

---

[122] "Ibid, p 18.

The call with Wizard did not end after Wizard provided reassurance Stevenson's experience would not derail the operation. Before hanging up, Mason raised another issue which must have plagued the TEAM from the day Wizard called them to have lunch in the Treaty Room.

```
While I had Wizard on the phone, I took the
opportunity to raise an issue the team discussed
on several occasions. Our training taught us to
view everything as a potential threat. As
unlikely as it may seem, what if Wizard made up
the story about JFK ordering his own
assassination as a cover for something more
heinous? What if we were being played?

I told Wizard we needed direct confirmation from
the President. Wizard said he was surprised we
had not asked for Lancer's confirmation sooner
and offered to see what he could do.
```

While waiting for Wizard to schedule the face-to-face meeting with Kennedy, the TEAM got its first indication Oswald might not be totally committed to the plan.

```
October 26, 1963

Oswald called. He is not sure he can make it at
the depository for four more weeks. He is bored
with the work and unhappy with his pay.
```

Buell Wesley Frazier, the co-worker who occasionally drove Oswald to the schoolbook depository including the morning of November 22, did not observe any signs of workplace anxiety. In an interview on the 50th anniversary of the assassination, he described Oswald as showing no signs of distress even on the day of Kennedy's murder.

I needed to reconcile Frazier's observation with Mason's concern Oswald was on the verge of jumping ship. Testimony by Marina Oswald and Ruth Paine suggested his personal life was in shambles. His marriage was falling apart, his wife and two daughters were living with Paine, and he was holding down a job he did not want for a salary of just $1.25/hour.[123] Was it possible he could hide these inner feelings from those unaware of his situation?

Psychologist Margaret Rutherford's research into "perfectly hidden depression" suggests behavior, like Oswald's, is often the norm. She describes this syndrome, as follows:

> *Perhaps you have a perfect-looking life outwardly, yet inwardly you struggle with a sense of something being wrong, or even more dangerously, you have fleeting thoughts of suicide or escaping your very busy life.[124]*

Based on Dr. Rutherford's research and patient experience, the discrepancy between the two accounts of Oswald's demeanor is understandable, if not predictable. Dr. Rutherford's explanation would not deter conspiracy theorists using Frazier's description of Oswald's demeanor on the day of the assassination as one more data point to challenge the Warren Commission's conclusions.

During a 2013 interview with *Richmond Times-Dispatch* reporter Markus Schmidt, Frazier sprinkled yet more crumbs for Warren Commission skeptics to follow. Frazier described how Dallas police believed he was Oswald's accomplice. He was fingerprinted, photographed and subjected to a lie detector test but never charged with a crime. Cleared of his own participation in a plot to kill Kennedy, he told Schmidt he believed Oswald was also innocent. His evidence? He maintained the package Oswald carried to work on the morning of November 22 could not have been the murder weapon. "It wasn't long enough to put that type of rifle in that bag."[125]

```
I assured Oswald it will all be worth it. I gave
him a more detailed update on the escape plan. A
member of the SWP will meet him at the corner of
Market and Pacific. His contact will be driving a
black Buick Riviera with a Kennedy/Johnson
```

---

123 "Co-worker who drove Oswald to schoolbook depository recounts Dallas' darkest day," *The Dallas Morning News*, April 1, 2013.
124 Margaret Rutherford, Ph.D., *Perfectly Hidden Depression*, New Harbinger Publications, 2019.
125 Markus Schmidt, "Buell Wesley Frazier: A commute with Oswald, then a harsh interrogation," *Richmond Times-Dispatch*, November 17, 2013.

    sticker on the rear bumper. He has agreed to
    drive Oswald all the way to Mexico City. And if
    necessary, to stay in Mexico and drive him to
    Cozumel to catch the ship to Havana. Also, Hansen
    confirmed he is arranging a meeting between
    Oswald and Castro soon after his arrival.

    Oswald says he appreciates everything we are
    doing and will try to hold on.

Mason will soon learn "everything" refers only to those elements he and the TEAM can control. That did not include the FBI who had been trailing Oswald since the street altercation and his arrest in New Orleans.

    November 1, 1963

    Oswald called. He is quite angry. An FBI agent
    showed up at Ruth Paine's house to interview
    Marina. At first, I was afraid they had made the
    connection between Oswald's recent hiring at the
    school book depository and the motorcade route.
    But Marina told Lee all the agent's questions
    were about his FPCC activity in New Orleans.
    Though she was not sure since the agent did not
    bring a translator.

The FBI did not know of Marina's minimal command of English. And Ruth Paine's narrow grasp of Russian was of little help. During her Warren Commission testimony, Marina commented on Paine's limited translation skills. "She does not interpret quite exactly. She is hard to understand."[126]

Meanwhile, the White House and Secret Service began finalizing the itinerary for Kennedy's Texas trip.

    November 4, 1963

    Special agents Winston Lawson, WH detail, and
    Forrest Sorrels, agent in charge at the Dallas
    office, were notified Lancer will be in Texas

---

[126] Testimony of Marina Oswald, Warren Commission, Washington, D.C., February 24, 1964.

```
beginning November 21. The trip will include a
stop in Dallas including a speech to local
business leaders. At Wizard's request, Sorrels is
asked to check out three potential sites, Market
Hall, the Women's Building at the state
fairgrounds and the new Dallas Trade Mart.
```

Wizard's participation in planning the venue for Kennedy's noon speech was consistent with standard procedures. The specifics, including time and location, associated with a campaign event always included political considerations which required the input of the president's senior advisors. Only after choosing the final site would the Secret Service advance team take the lead, arranging to secure the designated location. What's more, this division of labor and degree of separation between the TEAM and their White House contact made their collaboration less obvious. In case one or more of the conspirators were compromised, it would be difficult to prove any collusion between the advance team and the White House or the role each played to ensure a gunman and his target would eventually rendezvous in Dealey Plaza.

Meanwhile, the FBI's continued interest in Oswald's time in New Orleans prompted additional handholding on Mason's part.

```
November 5, 1963

Oswald called late this evening. The same FBI
agent returned to interview Ruth Paine. Oswald
tells me he will be visiting Marina and the
children over the weekend. He will talk to Marina
and Ruth about this.
```

The November 8 entry demonstrates how the involvement of additional Secret Service agents in Washington and in the Dallas field office might derail the arrangement by which Kennedy's and Oswald's paths would intersect.

```
November 8, 1963

Lawson and Sorrels receive the tentative schedule
which includes alternate motorcade routes from
Love Field through downtown Dallas to each of the
three potential locations for the luncheon
speech. If either makes a strong case for
```

avoiding Dealey Plaza, we may need a contingency
plan.

On Saturday, November 9, the TEAM tied up the last loose end. As promised, Wizard arranged a face-to-face meeting between Kennedy and the TEAM in New York. The choice of location and timing was likely designed to minimize public notice of the encounter.

November 9, 1963

Lancer agreed to meet with the team. Everything
under our control was locked in place. To set the
plan in motion, all we needed was a green light.

The team prepared for the meeting at breakfast.
We agreed we were there to listen, not talk. Even
if asked, we would not share anything about the
assignment.

Around noon we arrived at the presidential suite
at the Waldorf-Astoria Hotel. Lancer was seated
in a replica of his Oval Office rocking chair. [127]
He did not stand up when we entered the room.

There was no small talk. Scarecrow spoke for the
four of us. He first reminded Lancer we were
honored to be part of his WH and would do
anything he asked of us. If that included his
assassination, we would carry out the order. But
the team's instructions always came from Wizard.
We needed to hear it from you directly.

Lancer said he understood. He even agreed he
would have wanted to hear it directly from the
horse's mouth. He offered to share his reasons
for his decision, but assumed we knew most of
them already. Instead, he spent the remainder of
the time assuring us this was the best thing for
the country. Since we were not allowed to record
or take notes, this is my best recollection of
what he told us.

---

[127] The rocking chair remains a permanent fixture in the hotel's presidential suite.

"When I was campaigning for president, I made a lot of promises. Maybe more than I should have. My goal was to lay out a vision of a better America and a safer world. Where we no longer lived under the shadow of nuclear war. A strong economy in which everyone could earn a decent living and fewer people lived in poverty. An America where every individual was equal in the eyes of the law and in society."

"Unfortunately, progress has been slower than I hoped. For whatever reason, too many people did not buy into my agenda. I don't want to sound crass, but what better way to increase support for those policies than by honoring a president who was not given the chance to fulfill his promises. You may think you are doing this for me. That is not the case. You are doing this in the national interest, not mine."

"Pay attention to everything I do from now until my last day in office. Every meeting, every statement will confirm what I just told you. This is what I want. That's an order."

That afternoon, I accompanied Kennedy back to D.C. Instead of taking Marine One to the White House after landing at Andrews, we went directly to the country home he and Mrs. Kennedy had built just west of the capital. We did not speak during the flight from NY to DC or on the helicopter ride to Atoka.

Considering the likelihood JFK knew his time was running out, why would he go to the trouble and expense of building an elaborate family refuge outside the nation's capital? When her husband became president, Jacqueline Kennedy wanted a place where she and Caroline could ride their horses and the Kennedys could entertain guests somewhere other than the White House. The 166-acre retreat in the township of Atoka was completed in May 1963 and occupied for the first time in October. Jacqueline Kennedy dubbed the estate "Wexford" after the Kennedy's ancestral home in Ireland. The weekend of

November 9, guests included future *Washington Post* editor Ben Bradlee and his wife Antoinette. [128]

Was Wexford a legacy gift to his wife? If so, Mrs. Kennedy did not view it as such. Following the assassination, she moved into a Georgetown home which was made available to her by former New York governor Averell Harriman. She seldom spent time at Wexford and sold it in 1964.

With Kennedy's personal confirmation in hand, there was a distinct change in tone in subsequent journal entries. First, the narrative seesaws between last minute details as the Texas trip approaches and Mason's desire to spend time with the president. Knowing the plan for Dallas required his being nowhere near Kennedy, Mason asked Wizard if he could be assigned to Lancer's detail one last time, during a trip to Florida. This was the first time Mason asked Wizard if he could be part of the normal rotation since the trip to Boston for Kennedy to be with Jackie following Patrick's difficult birth.

The journal provides no indication Mason's desire for proximity to his charge involved anything more than a normal service rotation. However, I cannot help but wonder if Mason thought he might use the Florida trip as one last opportunity to convince Kennedy to rescind the order. Did he still believe he could make Kennedy reconsider? Or was it simply a case of creating memories as evidenced in the November 11 post.

```
November 11, 1963

I asked if I could accompany Lancer to Arlington
cemetery for the laying of the wreath at the Tomb
of the Unknown Soldier. I had done this for the
past two years and wanted to participate in this
event one more time. As I stood behind him, I
could not help but consider the possibility, if
all went according to plan, sometime in the next
```

---

[128] The property served as residence and transition headquarters for Ronald and Nancy Reagan following the 1980 presidential election.

```
two weeks I might be attending a funeral for the
35th president of the United States.
```

The following day, Mason must again focus on his other responsibility, keeping Oswald in the fold.

```
November 12, 1963

I called Oswald to ask about his weekend with
Marina and the children. As promised, Oswald
queried Marina about the FBI visit which led to
an argument when she told him agent James Hosty,
Jr. asked whether Lee was still using the alias
Alek Hidell. Marina told Hosty the only time Lee
used the alias was in New Orleans.

Since Hosty had asked about the alias, Oswald was
convinced the FBI's interest was his FPCC
activities and had nothing to do with JFK's
visit. He did say he sent a note to the Dallas
FBI asking them to leave Marina alone. If they
wanted to know anything they should talk directly
to him.
```

Marina Oswald confirmed Lee spent Veterans Day weekend (November 9-11) at Ruth Paine's home in Irving, Texas. Lee would normally begin weekend visits after work on Friday and return to his apartment in Dallas on Sunday afternoon. This time, due to the long three-day holiday weekend, he arrived around noon on Saturday and stayed through Monday.

Oswald spent most of the weekend at the house, playing with their oldest daughter June and watching television. One exception was a trip to Hutchinson's grocery store with Marina and Ruth Paine on Monday. A second exception involved his typing an envelope. It was shown to Marina during her Warren Commission hearing, to which she testified:

> Mrs. OSWALD. This was typed on the typewriter belonging to Ruth.
>
> Mr. RANKIN. You can tell that by the looks of the typing, can you, Mrs. Oswald?
>
> Mrs. OSWALD. No, I don't know, but I know that he was typing there. I don't know what he was typing.

> Mr. RANKIN. And it is Ruth Paine's typewriter that you are referring to, when you say Ruth?
>
> Mrs. OSWALD. Ruth Paine. Because Lee did not have a typewriter, and it is hardly likely that he would have had it typed somewhere else.

The envelope was addressed to the Soviet embassy in Washington, D.C. In the enclosed letter, Oswald first apologized for having to leave Mexico City before he could complete the paperwork for his Russian visa. He also informed the embassy he was under FBI surveillance. He closed with a request that Marina and his two children be allowed to remain in the United States.[129]

I found it strange Oswald told Mason about the note to the FBI but not the letter to the Soviet embassy. Did this signal some lack of trust? Or did Oswald, once he was out of the U.S., want to totally separate his new life from the events which made it possible?

Satisfied the FBI interference was merely a distraction that would not derail the ASSIGNMENT, Mason returns to his documentation of Kennedy's last days in office. This time he adds even more detail, perhaps to justify to himself Kennedy's rationale for what was to come.

```
November 13, 1963

Even when I am not on duty, I find myself paying
close attention to Lancer's schedule. Is it more
than pure curiosity? Did Lancer mean what he said
about using his remaining time to push an agenda
he hoped would continue after his death?

This morning he hosted a delegation from Kentucky
to highlight poverty in the eastern region of the
state. Afternoon meetings included a debriefing
by the chairman of the Civil Rights Commission.
```

---

[129] Letter from Lee Harvey Oswald to Consular Division, USSR Embassy., Washington, D.C., dated November 9, 1963.

With just over a week before Kennedy's departure for Texas, Mason continues the back-and-forth listing of the president's activities and final preparations for Dallas.

November 14, 1963

Lancer maintained a normal schedule with a press conference at the State Department and a WH meeting with the National Committee on Health Care for the Aged.

I remained in contact with the Dallas field office as the Texas trip approached. Today Sorrels called and again questioned the location of the Dallas speech. Wizard and I assured Sorrels any concerns about holding the lunch at the Trade Mart can be addressed by adding security in locations where he thinks there is a potential threat. Sorrels forwards this information to the WH detail. Later in the day, they sign off on the Trade Mart for the noon luncheon.

November 15, 1963

We leave for Florida with a brief stop in New York. The schedule is packed with a combination of campaigning, official business and a personal stop in Palm Beach. Kennedy makes two appearances in NYC at the national conventions of the AFL-CIO and the Catholic Youth Organization.

From NY, we flew to the residence in Palm Beach where his parents were staying. No one questioned the timing of this trip even though he originally planned to spend Thanksgiving there. Does he know or suspect the assassination will take place before Thanksgiving?

November 16, 1963

Lancer did not mention the space program during our meeting on November 9 but added a visit to Cape Canaveral to the schedule. I was not surprised. Was this his way of reminding

Americans he promised to put a man on the moon by
the end of the decade? Perhaps he knew NASA
needed a morale boost since the Soviet space
program had several major achievements following
the last Mercury mission.

On May 15, 1963, astronaut Gordon Cooper spent a U.S. record 34 hours aboard Faith 7, the sixth and final Mercury space flight. Within a month the Soviet Union set a new endurance record on June 14 when cosmonaut Valery Bykovsky began a five-day mission aboard Vostok 6. Three days later Valentina Tereshkova became the first woman in space.

November 18, 1963

Possibly Lancer's last official act as commander-
in-chief. A briefing by General Paul Adams on the
operations of the U.S. STRIKE Command at MacDill
AFB.

Established in September 1961, STRIKE's primary mission was "to be prepared to respond swiftly, and with whatever degree of force may be necessary, to threats against the peace in any part of the free world."[130] As a unified operation, STRIKE could draw from combat-ready elements of the Tactical Air Command and the Continental Army Command. Defense Secretary Robert McNamara recommended STRIKE after Kennedy expressed concern American armed services were ill-prepared to respond to the increasing numbers of limited, regional conflicts versus major global confrontations. STRIKE provided a more flexible, on-demand alternative to large mobilizations.

Before leaving the Tampa area, Lancer spoke at a
Chamber of Commerce event. I was disappointed
this stop and the next one did not receive more
coverage. After leaving Tampa, AF One landed at
MIA where Lancer held a rally on the tarmac.
Police estimate over 3,000 people attended the
event. The Texas trip three days later was
described by the press office as a series of
events to shore up the president's southern

---

[130] Allan R. Schollin, "STRIKE: Newest Unified Command," *Air Force Magazine*, May 11, 1962.

support going into the 1964 campaign. Similar
events in Florida put the Texas trip in the
context of a broader re-election strategy.

Sorrels called to ask if I knew Lancer's Dallas
itinerary had made the local papers. The Dallas
Times-Herald was first to report the potential
route to the Trade Mart. [131]

The WH and Dallas field office had no choice but
to confirm the motorcade route and notified the
host committee they could publicize it. This
plays well into our cover story. If Oswald is
identified as the assassin, it is important his
hiring at the school book depository precedes any
official word of the motorcade route. Oswald will
look like an angry opportunist rather than
someone engaged in a coordinated conspiracy.

On Tuesday, November 19, the *Times-Herald* published the precise
route.

*From the airport, the President's party will proceed to
Mockingbird Lane to Lemmon and then to Turtle Creek,
turning south to Cedar Springs. The motorcade will then pass
through downtown on Harwood and then west on Main,
turning back to Elm at Houston and then out Stemmons
Freeway to the Trade Mart.* [132]

I checked in with Oswald for the last time. He
did not go to Irving to be with Marina last
weekend but said he would be spending the night
there on Thursday.

He told me the rifle was still in Ruth Paine's
garage. He had arranged a ride to work Friday
with Ruth's neighbor who also worked at the

---

[131] Reporting by the *Dallas Times-Herald* is confirmed in the Warren Commission
Report, Chapter Two, p. 39.

[132] "Yarborough Gets JFK Table Spot," Dallas Times-Herald, November 19, 1963,
page 13. (Source: Warren Commission Exhibit #1362)

Marina described their last night together in detail during her final day of testimony before the Warren Commission. When asked about his mood that evening, she said he was focused on her having her own place to live with the children. He even offered to buy her a washing machine if the apartment did not come with one. At the time, she believed it was his way of broaching the possibility of their moving back in together.

> Mrs. OSWALD. He then stopped talking and sat down and watched television and then went to bed. I went to bed later. It was about 9 o'clock when he went to sleep. I went to sleep about 11:30. But it seemed to me that he was not really asleep. But I didn't talk to him. In the morning he got up, said goodbye, and left, and that I shouldn't get up--as always, I did not get up to prepare breakfast. This was quite usual.
>
> [General Counsel] RANKIN. Then did he say anything to you that morning at all, or did he get up and go without speaking to you?
>
> Mrs. OSWALD. He told me to take as much money as I needed [from his wallet] and to buy everything, and said goodbye, and that is all. After the police had already come, I noticed that Lee had left his wedding ring. [133]

Oswald knew he would not return home after work on November 22. Either he would be on his way to Cuba via Mexico, in police custody or dead. If he and Marina had any chance of reuniting, it would be much later, most likely in the Soviet Union.

Mason's last two days in the Kennedy White House were uneventful. At this point, matters were out of the TEAM's hands. Sorrells and Larkin were already in Dallas with the rest of the advance team. Mason would leave early Thursday morning for San Antonio where he would await Kennedy's arrival later that day.

---

[133] Ibid, February 5, 1964.

```
National Board. Credential presentations to newly
appointed ambassadors. Meetings with cabinet
members and WH advisors. An unscheduled visit
from Lena Horne, Carol Lawrence and Richard Adler
accompanied by DNC chairman John Bailey. Most
likely to raise campaign funds.

Nothing more the team can do.
```

The brevity of this journal entry, the only one covering multiple days, suggests Mason's White House presence before departing for Texas must have been excruciating. He was relegated to the reception area outside the Oval Office where he observed a parade of staff and visitors. With little to do, he was left to his thoughts about the coming events.

The only major news story coming out of the White House involved the turkey. While Harry Truman is credited with holding the first South Lawn photo op with a Thanksgiving fowl, neither he nor Dwight Eisenhower showed their guests any mercy. To the contrary, in 1953, Eisenhower implored National Turkey Federation president Roscoe Hill to slaughter the 39-pound bird "in plenty of time because I hope to spend Thanksgiving with my youngsters and I want to take him along." The now traditional pardon, as reported by Christopher Klein of *The History Channel*, is credited to Kennedy just days before the assassination.

> *A president finally took pity on a gifted bird in 1963 when John F. Kennedy spared the life of a mammoth 55-pound white turkey wearing a sign around its neck—clearly not of its own volition—that read "Good Eating, Mr. President!" "We'll just let this one grow," Kennedy said with a grin. "It's our Thanksgiving present to him."* [134]

Did Mason hope Kennedy might still commute his own death sentence?

---

[134] Christopher Klein, "A Brief History of the Presidential Turkey Pardon," History.COM, November 25, 2014.

CHAPTER SEVENTEEN

DALLAS

Since January 9, 1963, the day Wizard summoned members of the TEAM to the Treaty room in the Old Executive Office Building, Mason had documented each step in the planning and execution of the ASSIGNMENT sans reflection or emotion. It read more like a step-by-step instruction manual than a personal memoir. The 11/22/63 journal entry and those for the days that followed start to differ significantly.

I compare it to the transformation at the end of any major sporting event. During the post-game press conferences, the players shift gears from being gladiators in the arena to eyewitnesses and analysts. It reminded me of those occasions when a competitor who has spent days preparing and then executing a plan for the big game, suddenly is at a loss for words. The pent-up emotions that come after winning or losing rush to the forefront.

November 21, 1963

This morning, as I left to join the advance
detail at Brooks AFB, my apprehension grew.
Lancer followed on AF One arriving around 11am.

It was a busy day. A dedication of the new
Medical Health Center at Brooks. A quick stop in
Houston for a meeting with the League of United
Latin American Citizens and a dinner in honor of
Congressman Albert Thomas. Then on to Ft. Worth.

> By the time we had the president secured at the
> Texas Hotel, it was well past 11pm.
>
> Once we passed responsibility to the night shift,
> the team talked about joining other agents for a
> few drinks. Lion joked no sober man could do what
> we were about to do. I decided not to join them.

The Warren Commission considered possible malfeasance by Secret Service agents the night before the assassination. The final report confirmed the agents' questionable judgment exhibited by a "night on the town" the evening of November 21.

> *It is conceivable that those men who had little sleep, and who had consumed alcoholic beverages, even in limited quantities, might have been more alert in the Dallas motorcade if they had retired promptly in Fort Worth. However, there is no evidence that these men failed to take any action in Dallas within their power that would have averted the tragedy.*[135]

The Commission's finding was further corroborated by then *Fort Worth Star-Telegram* reporter, Bob Schieffer, who reached national prominence as anchor of the "CBS Evening News." During a 2015 interview in *Vanity Fair*, Schieffer described how several Secret Service agents, including Clint Hill, joined him and other local reporters the night of November 21 at the Cellar Café.

> *The Cellar was an all-night, San Francisco-style coffeehouse down the street, and some of the visiting reporters had heard about it and wanted to see it. So we all went over there, and some of the agents came along. The place didn't have a liquor license, but they did serve liquor to friends — usually grain alcohol and Kool-Aid.*[136]

---

[135] Warren Commission Report, page 451.
[136] "Secret Service's 1963 night in Fort Worth's Cellar recalled," *The Dallas Morning News,* February 10, 2015.

If not for 50 years of reporting and analysis as spoilers, a first read of the November 22, 1963, journal entry would shock any reader. Yet, as I initially picked it up and scanned the first sentence, I wondered if this was the "gift" Mason had left for me and me alone. Was he finally sharing what he never felt comfortable communicating in person?

```
November 22, 1963

The reality of the assignment is finally starting
to sink in. After breakfast, we left for our
designated locations. Had Wizard thought that far
ahead when he suggested we be transferred to the
campaign? Did he wisely anticipate we should not
be at the scene of the crime? If we were still in
the presidential rotation, we would most likely
have been assigned to the motorcade from Love
Field to the Dallas Trade Mart.

Each of us manned one of the several stops on
JFK's itinerary to ensure each venue was secured.
Today, those included the eighth floor of the
Hotel Texas in Fort Worth where he and the First
Lady spent the night (Scarecrow). The hotel's
grand ballroom for a breakfast speech to the FW
Chamber (Lion). Love Field (Tinman) for the
arrival in Dallas. And the Trade Mart (me) for
the midday lunch.

You know how the day ends. We did what we had
been asked to do. With unfortunate exceptions,
the operation came off as planned. Governor
Connally was an unintended casualty. Reports from
Parkland Hospital say he is in critical but
stable condition and is expected to recover.

We also should have anticipated Mrs. Kennedy's
reaction. Without Clint Hill's quick response,
she too might have been injured.

But those are not our immediate problem. Oswald
is still alive. He has no idea the extent to
which he was manipulated. If authorities learn
the series of events which led to his being in
the depository it is only a matter of time before
someone makes the connection. Ruth Paine or de
```

Mohrenschildt might recognize Scarecrow if his picture appears in a Dallas newspaper or on TV. What if Lawson and Sorrels start to question how much Wizard and I influenced details about the trip to Dallas, especially the motorcade route.

The team wrongly assumed Oswald would not be captured alive. We expected police would immediately trace the shots to the depository. They would then rush the building and find Oswald with the rifle. Knowing Oswald's temperament, we expected he would try to defend himself at which point the police would return fire. No one would fault the police. There would be no doubt they got the right man and had saved the nation and the Kennedy family from having to relive the day's events during an investigation and the assassin's trial.

What we did not anticipate was confusion about the direction of the rifle shots when the discharge sound echoed through Dealey Plaza. Instead of looking immediately behind them, Secret Service agents and police focused on an area that is being called the grassy knoll. It was to the right and in front of the limousine when Kennedy was struck. The delay in searching the school book depository gave Oswald time to follow the instructions we gave him.

Even if Oswald made it out of the depository, we thought the situation was covered. How could we have been so confident Tinman would be at the rendezvous location in time despite traffic created by the crowd that came downtown to see Kennedy and the chaos immediately after Oswald fired his rifle? When Oswald showed up at the corner of Pacific and Market Street, he must have panicked and thought he had been double crossed. There was no car to take him from downtown Dallas. Or anyone who had arranged for travel to Cuba. He was on his own. Which led to another unintended victim, a Dallas police officer. And Oswald's eventual capture at the Texas Theatre.

The team met for dinner at Angelo's BBQ in Fort
Worth and then went back to our hotel. We
gathered in Scarecrow's room to discuss next
steps. When we got to the hotel, there was a
message from Win Lawson. Agents except those in
Volunteer's detail needed to stay in Dallas to
help the Dallas field office and local
authorities with the investigation. Scarecrow
returned the call. Before hanging up, he asked
Win what the Dallas police would do with Oswald.
All he knew was Oswald had been arraigned for
killing Officer Tippit and had twice been taken
to a police captain's office for questioning.

We needed to act quickly. Oswald's custody at the
Dallas police station was temporary. Eventually
he would be moved to a more secure location. It
had taken months to identify, recruit and prepare
a presidential assassin. Now we had just days or
even hours to silence him.

There was only one option. Was Mario telling
Tinman the truth when he said Giancana wanted a
backup in case our plan failed? If so, they never
would have ceased preparations or told their
designated hitman to stand down. Even after they
were told they were not needed. Was there a
hitman in waiting to eliminate Oswald? Tinman
made the call.

Chapter 5 of the Warren Commission report provides a minute-by-minute account of Oswald's detention at the Dallas police department. After his arrest he was taken to the third floor until Captain John William Fritz, head of the Homicide and Robbery Bureau, returned after participating in the initial inspection of the Texas School Book Depository.

On the day of the assassination, Oswald was searched and fingerprinted, participated in two line-ups, questioned by Captain Fritz multiple times and arraigned for the murder of officer Tippit. Shortly after midnight he was moved to a maximum-security cell on the fifth floor. An hour later he appeared before Justice of the Peace David L. Johnston and was arraigned for killing the president. [137]

```
November 23, 1963

Mario called Tinman before we left the hotel.
Everything is set to go. Mario told Tinman he
wished he had contacted him earlier. Last night,
the police briefly brought Oswald before the
press. That would have been the perfect
opportunity. They have several individuals in
Dallas who are friendly with both the police and
press. It would have been easy for one of their
guys to get lost in the crowd. All we needed to
do was let Mario know when there might be similar
opportunities.
```

This brief passage includes harbingers of what is to come in the next 48 hours. Oswald's killer would need to be in close proximity to his mark. The only thing Mario wanted from the TEAM was inside information about additional opportunities for the killer to confront his target. Except for those updates, this is the last time Tinman communicates with Mario until Mario assures him, on the afternoon of November 24, Ruby will not be a problem.

In hindsight, the access given reporters and photographers to a presidential assassin at the Friday night press conference defies reason. The Warren Commission Report documents the lack of security and chaos that night.

Oswald's most prolonged exposure occurred at the midnight press conference on Friday night. In response to demands of newsmen, District Attorney Wade, after consulting with Chief Curry and Captain Fritz, had announced shortly before midnight that Oswald would appear at a press conference in the basement assembly room.

In the words of an FBI agent who was present, the conditions at the police station were "not too much unlike Grand Central

---

[137] "Chapter 5: Detention and Death of Oswald," Warren Commission Report, September 24, 1964, pp. 198-199.

Station at rush hour, maybe like the Yankee Stadium during the World Series games...." [138]

Based on Friday night's experience, why didn't the Dallas police or federal monitors limit or completely ban further public access to Oswald? Fortunately for the TEAM, negligence by local police ensured Jack Ruby would have the opportunity he needed to confront Oswald.

```
When we arrived at the Dallas field office
briefing, Sorrels told everyone that Service
agents in Dallas were not going to handle the
investigation. That would be done by the FBI and
Service headquarters in DC. Our role was to
assist local law enforcement and monitor how they
handled Oswald. Sorrels had received a call from
deputy attorney general Nicholas Katzenbach at
Justice. He told Sorrels Oswald's incarceration
and trial needed to be done strictly by the book.
It made sense. I could only imagine the public
outrage if a presidential assassin was freed on a
technicality.
```

There are two passages in this paragraph that underscore the legal environment at the time. First, it seems inconceivable, as late as 1963, the arrest and prosecution of a suspect in the felony murder of an American president fell under the jurisdiction of local law enforcement officers in the municipality where the crime took place. It made a bit more sense if the nation never previously dealt with this exact situation. But that was not the case. This was the fourth presidential assassination.

After Abraham Lincoln's murder, one could assume future assailants would be quickly tracked down and brought to justice as had John Wilkes Booth. Even if that had not been the case, the crime occurred in the District of Columbia, a federal enclave in which federal authorities had jurisdiction by default.

This was also the case with the assassination of James Garfield by Charles Guiteau. The June 30, 1881, assault on President Garfield occurred at the Baltimore and Potomac Railroad Station in Washington,

---

[138] Ibid, p. 209.

D.C.[139] Garfield was struck in the back by two bullets, after which Guiteau immediately surrendered to authorities. After Garfield's death on September 19, Guiteau was charged with murder and tried in what was then known as the Supreme Court of the District of Columbia. In 1948, Congress renamed the judicial body the District Court for the United States for the District of Columbia and changed the presiding officials' title from justice to judge.

The more relevant precedent was the assassination of William McKinley, the first to occur outside the nation's capital. The venue was Buffalo, New York. On September 6, 1901, McKinley was scheduled to speak at the Pan-American Exposition, when anarchist Leon Czolgosz shot the president twice at close range. Czolgosz was arrested and held at Buffalo police headquarters before being transferred to the Erie County Women's Penitentiary.

Upon McKinley's death on September 13, Czolgosz was indicted on one count of murder by an Erie County grand jury. The prosecution was led by county district attorney Thomas Penney. The trial began on September 23 and lasted nine days, during which Czolgosz pleaded insanity, claiming the choice of a public location and assault at close range were not the actions of a sane man.

Further evidence of local jurisdiction over the trial came when Judge Truman C. White referenced New York state law when he instructed the jury on the legal definition of insanity. The jury pronounced Gzolgosz guilty of murder after less than 30 minutes of deliberations. He was executed on October 29 by a state electrician and buried on the prison grounds.

At the time of the Kennedy assassination, killing a president was handled differently from crimes against other federal officials. Federal criminal law covered the murder of federal judges, U.S. attorneys and marshals who died in the line of duty. More ironically, it was a federal

---

[139] The station was decommissioned in 1907 and later demolished. In 1937, the site was designated for construction of what is now the West Building of National Gallery of Art.

offense to *threaten* a president or anyone in line to the presidency through the mail although *actual harm or murder* was not.

In the summer of 1965, Congress addressed this disparity, responding to a recommendation from the Warren Commission. The House and Senate passed, and President Johnson signed HR 6097 which amended Title 18 of the U.S. Code making assassination of a president a federal crime. The act also established penalties and provided for preemption of local and state authority in such instances.[140]

Second, the reference to how Dallas police handled Oswald re-centered my attention on the credibility of the narrative. Was this the "smoking gun" that would challenge the contemporaneous nature of Mason's journal? Nicholas Katzenbach's warning made perfect sense in a post-*Miranda v. Arizona* environment. However, the Supreme Court did not hand down the *Miranda* decision until June 12, 1966, an apparent discrepancy that needed to be reconciled.

Katzenbach's interest in the consequences of Oswald's treatment in custody could be explained since Ernesto Miranda's arrest occurred on March 13, 1963, a full eight months prior to the assassination. At issue in *Miranda v. Arizona* was a failure by Phoenix police to inform Miranda of his right to legal counsel prior to his interrogation, a line-up and obtaining a signed confession. Following Miranda's conviction on June 12, 1963, his public defender Alvin Moore appealed the decision claiming a violation of Miranda's Sixth Amendment right "to have the assistance of counsel for his defense."

This was just one in a series of cases in which the Supreme Court confirmed Sixth Amendment protections for criminal suspects. On March 18, 1963, in *Gideon v. Wainwright*, the Court unanimously expanded the right of indigents to legal counsel in other than capital cases. Speaking for the Court, Justice Hugo Black wrote:

> *[L]awyers in criminal courts are necessities, not luxuries. The right of one charged with crime to counsel may not be deemed*

---

[140] Public Law 89-141, enacted August 28, 1965.

> *fundamental and essential to fair trials in some countries, but it is in ours.*[141]

The ACLU took up Miranda's cause after the Arizona Supreme Court denied his appeal. In a 6-3 decision, the U.S. Supreme Court found the lack of a defendant's request for counsel was insufficient to satisfy Sixth Amendment guarantees. Arresting officers needed to proactively inform suspects of their right to an attorney. And, consistent with *Gideon*, arresting officers should also inform suspects that, if they could not afford an attorney, the court would appoint a public defender prior to questioning.

In March 1966, Miranda was retried and again found guilty. This second conviction was based on testimony by his former common-law wife Twila Hoffman. Miranda was sentenced to 20-30 years in a state prison and released on parole in December 1975. A month later Miranda was fatally stabbed following an argument at the La Amapoia Bar in downtown Phoenix. An unfortunate end for someone whose name is forever etched in the annals of constitutional law. Ironically, in accordance with the landmark decision, Phoenix police dutifully read Miranda's assailant Ferando Zamora Rodriguez his mandated legal rights which bore the victim's name.

Katzenbach was not the only person concerned about Oswald's treatment during his two days in Dallas police custody. While Warren Commission general counsel J. Lee Rankin was questioning Dallas police chief Jesse Edward Curry, commission chair Chief Justice Earl Warren jumped in.

> CHAIRMAN WARREN. May I interrupt just to ask the chief a question? Chief, on your arraignments does the magistrate advise the petitioner of his right to counsel?

Rankin later picked up on the same line of inquiry. Curry told the Commission that Louis Nichols, president of the Dallas Bar Association, showed up at the police station. Rankin asked, "What did he do?"

---

[141] *Gideon v. Wainwright,* 372 U.S. 335, March 18, 1963.

> Mr. CURRY. He said he had heard that [Oswald] was not being allowed the right to counsel, and they wanted to see and so I took him myself up to Lee Harvey Oswald's cell and let him go in the cell and talk to Lee Harvey Oswald.

What I thought might be a chronological anomaly in Mason's account again proved consistent with the public record.

```
Next, Sorrels told us about meeting a man who
filmed the assassination on his movie camera.
Abraham Zapruder first contacted a local reporter
who then introduced him to Sorrels. They had the
film developed and made three copies. Sorrels
gave the original and one copy to Zapruder. He
then sent the other two copies to Secret Service
headquarters in DC.
```

This excerpt from the November 23 entry is another example where Mason's priorities departed from my own. First and foremost, the TEAM had to silence Oswald. Second, per instructions from Washington headquarters, they needed to help manage potential jurisdictional conflict between the FBI, Secret Service and local authorities. I, however, was drawn to the paragraph detailing the process by which federal authorities discovered and obtained the Zapruder film. Had the film been reported and secured as rapidly as Mason suggested?

Mason claimed the Secret Service knew about and had copies of the Abraham Zapruder film within 24 hours of the assassination. The circumstances under which the exchange took place are documented in Forrest Sorrels' testimony before the Warren Commission. After leading the motorcade to Parkland Hospital, Sorrels returned to Dealey Plaza and spoke with several eyewitnesses including some who were in the Texas School Book Depository. *Dallas Morning News* reporter Harry McCormack approached him and said, "Forrest, I have something over here you ought to know about…I have a man over here that got pictures of the whole thing." To which Sorrels responded, "Let's go see him."[142]

They met Zapruder at his office where he showed McCormack and Sorrells the Bell & Howell Zoomatic camera and the spool of Kodak 8mm color film. Sorrells suggested they have the film developed immediately. They first took the camera to the *Dallas Morning News* and then to the nearest local television studio WFAA. Neither had the necessary equipment to process the footage. They then proceeded to the local Eastman Kodak facility which developed the original print but could not make copies. That required assistance by a third party, the Jamieson Film Company.[143]

```
Sorrels ended the briefing with an update on
Oswald's schedule while in custody of Dallas
police. Captain Fritz had arranged more
interrogation. The rest of Saturday was reserved
for Oswald to meet with family members and his
lawyers. On Sunday morning Oswald would be
transferred to the county jail where he would be
held pending trial. Sorrels handed out an
assignment sheet to ensure at least two service
agents monitored local authorities at all times.

The team grabbed dinner on its way back to the
Hotel Texas where we played cards until midnight,
still wondering if Mario would deliver as
promised. This will be another sleepless night.
```

Records of Oswald's detention on November 23 include the following. Two interrogations in Captain Fritz' office, the first at 10:25 a.m. for 80 minutes and another at 12:35 p.m. for an additional 30 minutes. He twice entertained brief visits with family, first at 1:10 p.m. with his wife and mother and later at 3:30 p.m. with his brother Robert. The rest of the afternoon consisted largely of phone calls. One, an attempt to reach New York attorney John Jacob Abt, and two to Ruth Paine's home to speak to Marina. In between phone calls he again met with the president

---

[142] Testimony of Secret Service Agent Forrest Sorrels, May 7, 1964, Hearings of the Warren Commission, Volume VII, pages 332-592.
[143] Vincent Bugliosi, *Reclaiming History: The Assassination of President John F. Kennedy*, W. W. Norton & Company, May 2007, pages 452-453.

of the Dallas Bar Association. His day ended with another round of questions from Captain Fritz and one more phone call to the Paine residence.[144]

The story behind Oswald's pursuit of legal counsel is another example how my sense of curiosity would sometimes take me away from the primary task at hand. Since Mason never mentioned Abt; it made no difference in determining whether the journal was fact or fiction. Still, I wanted to know who he was and why Oswald wanted a New York lawyer as his advocate.

John Abt had a history representing left-wing causes. In 1948, he joined the staff of Progressive Party presidential candidate Henry Wallace. In 1960, he represented the Communist Party of the United States of America (CPUSA) before the Supreme Court to overturn sections of the McCarren Act which required domestic Communist organizations to register with the federal government. Although the Court decided against the CPUSA by a 5-4 margin, the issue was eventually resolved in their favor in 1965 when the Court ruled the registration requirement violated the constitutional right against self-incrimination.

After being advised by Louis Nichols and the Dallas ACLU he needed legal counsel, Oswald told the Dallas police:

> *I want that attorney in New York, Mr. Abt. I don't know him personally but I know about a case that he handled some years ago, where he represented the people who had violated the Smith Act, [which made it illegal to teach or advocate the violent overthrow of the U.S. government] ... I don't know him personally, but that is the attorney I want.[145]*

Abt and his wife were spending the weekend at their cabin in Connecticut when Oswald tried to reach him on November 23. Abt reported he began receiving phone calls from the press asking him if Oswald had requested his services.

---

[144] "Chapter 5: Detention and death of Oswald," Warren Commission Report, pp. 198-99.
[145] Interrogation by Dallas police captain John William Fritz on the evening of November 22, 1963.

> Mr. ABT. I informed them—and these calls kept on all day and night Saturday and again Sunday morning—I informed all of the reporters with whom I spoke that I had received no request either from Oswald or from anyone on his behalf to represent him, and hence I was in no position to give any definitive answer to any such proposal if, as and when it came."[146]

Oswald was not the last of the famous defendants with whom Abt was associated. In 1970, he participated in the defense of Angela Davis and members of the Black Panthers who disrupted the Soledad Brothers[147] trial and freed the defendants at the Marin County, California courthouse. Thus, Abt joined the parade of cameo appearances of individuals on the periphery of the events in the fall of 1963.

---

[146] Testimony of John J. Abt, April 17, 1964, Warrant Commission Hearings. Volume 10, p. 116.

[147] George Jackson, Fleet Drumgo and John Clutchett were charged with murdering Soledad prison guard John Vincent Milles.

CHAPTER EIGHTEEN

AN ASSASSIN'S ASSASSIN

Why and how Jack Ruby wound up in the basement of the Dallas police station on the morning of November 24, 1963, was one more opportunity to compare Mason's narrative to the public record. This task, however, proved much more complicated compared to scrutinizing Mason's detailed description of Oswald. First, since the TEAM allegedly delegated Oswald's elimination to Giancana via Mario, the journal contained minimal baseline information. Second, the public record is littered with inconsistencies about Ruby's contacts and movements during the two days immediately following the assassination.

These discrepancies lay at the heart of the many theories about Ruby's participation in some grand conspiracy and who orchestrated it. Piecing the story together would require evaluating assumptions, reconciling conflicting accounts and creating a scenario in which Giancana establishes a *quid pro quo* with Ruby. At a minimum, a circumstantial case would require two things to be true. Ruby had previous Mafia connections. And Ruby needed something Giancana could provide.

As had been true so many times, my research agenda was sidetracked by an unanticipated historic artifact. This time it came while reviewing testimony by Dallas police chief Jesse Edward Curry before the Warren Commission. I was still focused on Oswald's detention when I came upon the following passage in reference to the night of the assassination and the lax security at the Dallas police station.

> Mr. CURRY. An estimated 70 to 100 people, including Jack Ruby,
> and other unauthorized persons, crowded into the small downstairs
> room. No identification was required. [148]

Was this just one more coincidence? Or did Ruby's presence so early after Tinman's call to Mario substantiate his claim that he already had everything under control.

```
November 24, 1963

I had breakfast with the team then returned to my
hotel room to watch TV. Lion and Tinman left
after breakfast as they were scheduled to be at
the Dallas police station until Oswald was
transferred to the county jail. Scarecrow and I
would take the afternoon shift to monitor
Oswald's handling once he arrived at the county
jail.

Regular programming was replaced with tributes
and updates on tomorrow's state funeral. Around
11:30 the coverage switched to Oswald's departure
from the police station just before he was shot.
```

Mason must have been watching KRLD-TV, the local NBC affiliate, the only network that broadcast the Oswald transfer live. Frank McGee anchored the coverage and turned it over to Tom Pettit in Dallas after Oswald was shot. Pettitt interviewed witnesses who described the shooter "as wearing a dark hat" and "appears to have emerged from a green car." Approximately 14 minutes after the single shot is fired, a Dallas police officer tells reporters the suspect is in custody. When asked if he knows the suspect, the officer says yes but he is not at liberty to release the name. [149]

```
Oswald was taken to Parkland Hospital and
pronounced dead just after 1:00. We did not know
whether the gunman was associated with Mario and
Giancana or someone else who wanted to kill
```

---

[148] Testimony of Jesse E. Curry, Warren Commission Hearings, Volume IV, April 22, 1964.
[149] "Lee Harvey Oswald is Shot," NBC-TV LIVE COVERAGE, November 24, 1963. Source: David Von Pein's JFK Channel/YouTube.

Oswald. Either way, Oswald's death crossed off
one more item on our to do list.

This evening, Win Lawson contacted all the DC
agents and said we were no longer needed in
Dallas. Everything would now be handled by the
local field office. Federal jurisdiction did not
apply to Ruby. His arrest and trial would be
conducted by local authorities under Texas law.
And Secret Service interests would be represented
by agents in the Dallas field office. There was
no need for additional support.

After dinner, we spent the evening preparing to
return to D.C.

Mason's limited account of Jack Ruby's assault on Oswald represented one of my last chances to crosscheck Mason's supposed contemporaneous narrative with other sources. And as previously noted, for the most part, I was flying blind, something I could not lay at Mason's feet. Having allegedly left the entire operation to a third party when it came to Ruby, Mason lacked detailed knowledge of how the desired outcome was achieved.

Despite delegating Oswald's silencing to others, excerpts from the journal entries covering November 22-24 help recreate the arrangement. Mason begins with the decision to re-engage Giancana and the subsequent call from Tinman to Mario on Friday evening. Mario returns the call on Saturday morning and assures Tinman, "Everything is set to go." Finally, Mason shares his seeing the Oswald shooting on TV on Sunday morning. Aware of these parameters, my challenge consisted of filling in the timeline between Tinman's initial call to Mario and Oswald's murder. I began with a list of questions.

- Did Ruby have Mafia connections and specifically ones to Sam Giancana?
- Why would the mob choose Ruby?
- Were there any discernible changes in Ruby's behavior before and after he became the designated hitman?
- How did Ruby so easily gain access to the Dallas police station following the assassination?

- Did Ruby make extraordinary efforts to advance his claim the shooting was a crime of passion, triggered by his concern Jackie Kennedy would be required to come back to Dallas for Oswald's trial?

Answers to these questions would not provide definitive proof of Mason's account. They would, however, support the possibility Jack Ruby was a Mafia hitman in waiting, authorized to act following Tinman's call to Mario. This quest depended on whether this scenario was consistent with the public record, a conclusion obscured by the conflicting witness accounts and varying theories posited during official inquiries and independent investigations.

One example of these inconsistencies is Ruby's movements on the morning of November 24. John Smith, a remote video operator for WBAP-TV claimed to have seen Ruby on the Commerce Street side of the Dallas police station shortly after 8:00 a.m.[150] Ira Walker, another WBAP employee in the mobile van, told the FBI Ruby "…came to the window of the truck and asked, 'Has he come down yet?'"[151] However, before the Warren Commission, Walker offered a different time frame, estimating the encounter with Ruby occurred closer to 10:30 a.m.[152]

Further muddying the record is the following sample of at least eight more accounts related to Ruby's location and actions that morning. Elnora Pitts, Ruby's cleaning lady, called between 8:30 and 9:00 a.m. to tell Ruby she was coming sometime that Sunday. According to her testimony before the Warren Commission, Ruby told her to call back as he "was going out."[153] Ruby's roommate George Senator told Secret Service agents Ruby woke up around 9:30 a.m., dressed and said he was going to the Carousel Club, which he owned.[154] Two neighbors in

---

[150] FBI Interview with John A. Smith, conducted by agents Earle Haley and Robley Madland, December 4, 1963, Warren Commission Exhibit 5317.

[151] FBI Interview with Ira Walker, conducted by agents Earle Haley and Robley Madland, December 4, 1963, Warren Commission Exhibit 5315.

[152] Testimony of Ira Walker, April 15, 1964, Warren Commission Report, Volume 13, pp. 294-96.

[153] Testimony of Elnora Pitts, April 15, 1964, Warren Commission Report, Volume 13, pp. 232.

[154] Interview with George Senator by Secret Service special agent Elmer Moore, December 3, 1963, Warren Commission Exhibit 5402.

Ruby's apartment building Sidney Evans and Malcolm Slaughter remembered seeing Ruby in the hall carrying laundry.[155]

Despite these conflicts in the details, was there enough reliable evidence to support the possibility Tinman's call to Mario set in motion a series of events which culminated in Ruby's killing Oswald? I started with the following assumption. For Giancana or one of his surrogates to engage Ruby on such short notice, there had to be a connection prior to the assassination. Without one, it made little sense Ruby would have been in the picture other than as a self-motivated actor.

Although the Warren Commission concluded there was no "significant link between Ruby and organized crime," the final report laid out his 25-year association with mob elements beginning in 1947. The relationship first emerged when Ruby met a former member of the Chicago syndicate shortly after relocating from the Windy City to Dallas.[156]

In 1979, the House Select Committee on Assassinations (HSCA) described the Warren Commission's investigation of possible Mafia complicity in the assassination and Oswald's murder as "limited." Its more extensive scrutiny concluded:

> *The evidence available to the committee indicated that Ruby
> was not a "member" of organized crime in Dallas or
> elsewhere, although it showed that he had a significant
> number of associations and direct and indirect contacts with
> underworld figures, a number of whom were connected to the
> most powerful La Cosa Nostra leaders. Additionally, Ruby
> had numerous associations with the Dallas criminal
> element.[157]*

From my perspective, "…associations and direct and indirect contacts" were insufficient to place Ruby within Sam Giancana's sphere of

---

[155] Testimony of Sidney Evans, Jr. and Malcolm R. Slaughter, March 31, 1964, Warren Commission Report, Volume 13, pp. 198-99, 263-64.

[156] FBI interview with Paul Rowland Jones with agents James Underhill and James Morgan, Charlotte, North Carolina, June 26, 1964.

[157] "Ruby and Organized Crime," Final Report, House Select Committee on Assassinations, March 29, 1979, p. 150.

influence. It was time to play "six degrees of separation" between Ruby and the Chicago crime boss. Fortunately, the HSCA had already done most of the preliminary research.

> *The committee also established associations between Jack Ruby and several individuals affiliated with the underworld activities of Carlos Marcello. Ruby was a personal acquaintance of Joseph Civello, the Marcello associate, who allegedly headed organized crime activities in Dallas; he also knew other individuals who have been linked with organized crime, including a New Orleans nightclub figure, Harold Tannenbaum, with whom Ruby was considering going into partnership in the fall of 1963.*[158]

The HSCA also established a link between Ruby and Tampa crime boss Santo Trafficante, Jr. In 1959, Ruby traveled to Cuba to visit a close friend Lewis McWillie. At the time McWillie managed the Tropicana hotel and casino in Havana. Trafficante was among the resort's investors.

Trafficante represents the missing link between Ruby and Giancana. He was a member of the trio of Mafia kingpins recruited by the CIA to help assassinate Fidel Castro, later exposed during the 1975 Senate investigation into covert intelligence activities. This was likely one more reason why Mario tells Tinman that Giancana was more comfortable with Dallas as the assassination locale. Not only would Chicago have raised immediate suspicion about Mafia complicity; Giancana knew he had Dallas associates capable of managing the operation. Once you stipulate Ruby's ties to organized crime and Giancana, the other pieces of the puzzle start to fall into place.

Still, it did not answer the question, "Why Jack Ruby?" He could not have been the only person in Texas indebted to Joseph Civello or Carlos Marcello. What made Ruby the mob's preferred choice for this specific task? Perhaps it was a combination of four factors.

One, Ruby never expressed any animosity toward the president. Just the opposite. Joe Cavagnaro, a sales manager at the Dallas Statler Hilton

---

[158] Ibid, p. 171.

and one of Ruby's best friends, told *Texas Monthly* writer Gary Cartwright about a conversation he had with Ruby just hours after the assassination. In that exchange Ruby shared his opinion of Kennedy and the impact of his death on Dallas.

> *Jack [Ruby] was a true patriot. He was also a Democrat. He thought Kennedy had done a lot for the minorities. Just from a business standpoint, he said, something like that (the assassination) could kill a city.[159]*

Two, unlike Kennedy's exposure in the open presidential limousine, it was unlikely a sharpshooter would ever get a similar line-of-sight opportunity to fire at Oswald from a distance. Any assailant would need to get within point-blank range, something Ruby could achieve without suspicion. Being owner of the Carousel Club, a somewhat seedy strip joint, Ruby's interaction with Dallas police and journalists was a common occurrence. According to Cartwright:

> *Cops and newspapermen, that's who Ruby wanted in his place. Dallas cops drank there regularly, and none of them ever paid for a drink.[160]*

Three, in the fall of 1963, Ruby desperately needed help. The American Guild of Variety Artists, the union which represented exotic dancers filed complaints against Ruby for exceeding regulations which limited the number of hours a performer could work per day. On top of his general labor problems, a newly hired stripper from New Orleans, hoping to increase her tips, caught the attention of local law enforcement when she began removing more clothing than the law allowed.

However, Ruby's most pressing concern was the $39,000 (equivalent to $350,000 in 2022) he owed the IRS in back excise and income taxes. Ruby knew the Mafia could make all his problems disappear in return for "a favor." This *quid pro quo* represented two more checked boxes, a solid motive for Ruby and enough Mafia leverage to procure his allegiance. They could make his federal tax situation go away. Solve

---

[159] Gary Cartwright, "Who Was Jack Ruby," *Texas Monthly,* November 1975.
[160] Ibid.

his problems with the artists union. And assure him the best legal counsel at no cost. Again, I found myself in Mario Puzo territory. Reminiscent of the Corleone family's consigliere Tom Hagen, I was convinced Giancana could "make Ruby an offer he couldn't refuse."

Four, Ruby always thought of himself as a "made man" in organized crime circles, a title of honor and pride, even though he lacked one essential requirement, being of Italian descent. The next best thing was acceptance as a respected associate which carried many of the same benefits including Mafia backing and protection. Such status followed sponsorship by a previously made man who could speak to the candidate's qualifications and participation in a contract killing. Murdering Oswald would fulfill that second prerequisite.[161]

I did find one caveat to Ruby's being the ideal candidate to eliminate Oswald. He was a gossip. He tried to impress people, presenting himself as someone privy to inside information. This behavior was so well known among his friends and acquaintances, they offered it as proof Ruby could not have been part of a conspiracy. For his 1993 book, *Case Closed,* investigative journalist Gerald Posner interviewed *Dallas Morning News* columnist Toni Zoppi whom Ruby first met in 1959. Zoppi dismissed Ruby's participation in any premeditated plot to kill Kennedy or silence Oswald.

> *[Ruby] couldn't keep a secret for five minutes ... Jack was one of the most talkative guys you would ever meet. He'd be the worst fellow in the world to be part of a conspiracy because he just plain talked too much.[162]*

Of course, Zoppi made this assessment without knowledge of any *quid pro quo* which would be null and void if Ruby ever disclosed any association with Giancana or one of his intermediaries.

This could explain why Mario assured Tinman on the morning of November 23, "Everything is set to go." In baseball parlance, it was game seven of the World Series. Jack Ruby was a modern-day Archie

---

[161] "How Do You Become a Made Man?", NationalCrimeSyndicate.com.
[162] Gerald Posner, *Cased Closed: Lee Harvey Oswald and the Assassination of JFK,* Random House, August 31, 2003, page 361.

"Doc" Graham in *Field of Dreams,* an untested benchwarmer. That was about to change. It was as if Ruby had been preparing for this turn at bat since moving from Chicago to Dallas in 1947.

There is little doubt a pre-assassination connection at some level existed between organized crime and Jack Ruby. However, without a firsthand account from one of the collaborators, e.g., Tinman or Mario, I needed a different approach to test the plausibility of Giancana's involvement. I chose one right out of the next major shock to the American political system, Watergate. In the 1976 movie *All the President's Men,* Deep Throat warns Bob Woodward he is missing the big picture focusing on activities–the break-in and the dirty tricks campaign–instead of the outcome.

> *Nationwide--my God, they were frightened of Muskie and look who got destroyed--they wanted to run against McGovern and look who they're running against.*[163]

Viewed through that lens, Jack Ruby's movements from the time he would have received the call from the Giancana camp until his arrest in the basement of the Dallas police station were either a highly improbable series of coincidences or a meticulously designed and executed game plan. More importantly, it was a total success. Oswald was dead. Oswald was the sole casualty. The media initially described Ruby as motivated by grief and concern for the Kennedy family. And neither the TEAM nor anyone in Giancana's orbit was implicated.

This appears to be a case governed by Nance's Law of Intelligence Kismet, coined by retired navy cryptologist Malcolm W. Nance. "Coincidences take a lot of planning."[164] First, the conspirators wanted the shooter to be perceived as a lone wolf, motivated by his grief over Kennedy's assassination. The best way to do that was to make sure Ruby shared his anguish over Kennedy's death with as many people as

---

[163] *All the President's Men,* screenplay by William Goldman, Wildwood Enterprises, April 1976.
[164] Malcolm W. Nance, *The Plot to Hack America: How Putin's Cyberspies and WikiLeaks Tried to Steal the 2016 Election,* Skyhorse, September 2016, p. xii.

possible. This result was perhaps the easiest to achieve as it mirrored Ruby's authentic response. He was on record voicing considerable despair from the moment Oswald fired his rifle.

Several eyewitnesses at the *Dallas Morning News* reported Ruby was both angry and emotional as he watched first reports of the shooting on a television in the advertising department lounge. Before leaving the newspaper offices, Ruby called his sister Eva Grant who he described as "crying hysterically." He next stops at the Carousel Club where he tells an employee Andrew Armstrong, "Call everyone and tell them we are not opening." From there he picked up food from the Ritz Delicatessen and headed to Eva's apartment.

This all happened before Ruby could possibly have been told he is needed to kill Oswald. Mason's journal says Tinman called Mario after the TEAM ate dinner on the evening of November 22. Mario would not have contacted Ruby until sometime later. Even if Ruby thought he had already left a sufficient trail of evidence concerning his state of mind he continued to do so throughout the next 24 hours. He attends Friday night services at Temple Beth Shearit and speaks to Rabbi Hillel Silverman who recalls:

> *We had a service, a regular Friday-night service. It became a memorial service, with a thousand people there, and I recall so vividly that he was there. And he came up to me after the service.*[165]

Around 1:30 a.m. Saturday morning, Ruby has a "chance meeting" in a parking lot with Kathy Coleman, a stripper at The Carousel Club, and Dallas police officer Harry Olsen, whom she was dating. Olsen told the Warren Commission Ruby kept referring to Jacqueline Kennedy and how tragic it was for the president's wife and children.[166] The encounter with Olsen and Coleman was just one in a series of occasions during which Ruby echoed his sympathy for Mrs. Kennedy and his outrage such a tragedy could happen in Dallas. It was as if he lined up

---

[165] Matt Potter, "Hillel Silverman—the Kennedy Assassination's Last Insider," *San Diego Reader*, November 20, 2013.
[166] Testimony of Harry Olsen, Warren Commission Report, Volume 14, pp. 631-2.

a parade of future witnesses to corroborate his assertion shooting Oswald was a crime of passion.

Outcome number two involved Ruby's presence in the Dallas police station at the time of Oswald's transfer to the county jail. He appears to have employed two tactics to produce this result. First, Ruby had a history of offering favors to local police. The Warren Commission produced evidence that when officers were at The Carousel Club, he "gave policemen reduced rates, declined to exact any cover charge from them and gave them free coffee and soft drinks."[167] Therefore, on the Friday night of the assassination when Ruby showed up at the Dallas police station with sandwiches for on-duty officers and staff, it did not create suspicion. It was merely an extension of an existing pattern of hospitality toward local law enforcement.

Second, while at the station, Ruby offered his services to both local and out-of-town members of the press as someone who could facilitate interviews with law enforcement officials. For example, Ruby arranged an interview between district attorney Henry Wade and WLIF newsman Russell Knight just minutes after Wade announced he would be charging Oswald with the president's murder. Ruby took great pride in this episode, telling the Warren Commission, "I felt that I was deputized as a reporter momentarily, you might say."[168]

As with so many of the individuals who made cameo appearances in the Kennedy assassination saga, Henry Wade would not disappear forever from the public's attention after he was denied his 15 minutes of fame as chief prosecutor in the never-to-be-held trial of Lee Harvey Oswald. Four months later he leads the successful prosecution of Jack Ruby.

Wade shows up again in 1970, in a case for which his name is forever recorded in the annals of constitutional law. That year, Norma McCorvey, a Dallas County resident, challenged Texas' ban on abortions. First among the defendants named in the case was none other than Dallas DA Henry Wade. Although he did not try the case, the 1973

---

[167] "Appendix 16: A Biography of Jack Ruby," Warren Commission Report, September 24, 1964, p. 801.
[168] Testimony of Jack Ruby, Warren Commission, Hearings Volume V, p. 189.

Roe v. Wade Supreme Court decision bears his name along with that of Jane Roe (aka Norma McCorvey).

Ruby's third challenge was ensuring his actions on the morning of November 24 could not be interpreted as premeditated. His actions that day support that outcome. Even though he had made two previous trips to the police station since Oswald's arrest, he needed an excuse to be there at the exact time of the transfer to the county jail. He had to convince law enforcement and prosecutors the Dallas police station was not his original destination.

The cover story begins when Ruby's roommate George Senator overhears a telephone call with Karin "Little Lynn" Carlin, a stripper at the Carousel Club. Senator testified before the Warren Commission that Carlin called Ruby because she needed money to pay her rent.

> Mr. SENATOR. I forgot to tell you he did get that call from this Little Lynn from Western Union.
>
> (Assistant Council) HUBERT. You remember the call?
>
> Mr. SENATOR. Yes.
>
> Mr. HUBERT. How did you know it was Little Lynn?
>
> Mr. SENATOR. I could hear him say. I heard him say Lynn, Western Union. I heard him mention Western Union. I heard about the money and that he was sending it to Fort Worth. She needed $25 for rent.[169]

In the same interview, Senator states Ruby planned to make one more stop.

> Mr. HUBERT. Did he say anything upon leaving?
>
> Mr. SENATOR. Yes.
>
> Mr. HUBERT. What did he say?
>
> Mr. SENATOR. He said, "George, I am taking the dog down to the club."

---

[169] Testimony of George Senator, Warren Commission, Hearings Volume XIV, pp. 236-7.

> Mr. HUBERT. Anything else?
>
> Mr. SENATOR. That was it, and out he went.[170]

Instead of dropping the dog at the club, Ruby first drove to Dealey Plaza and walked among the wreaths scattered at the intersection of Houston and Elm Streets. He then drove to the only Western Union office open on Sunday which serendipitously happened to be across the street from the Dallas police station. Western Union executes the wire transfer at 11:17 a.m.[171] Four minutes later Ruby shoots Oswald.

Ruby's description of the timeline between the moment he leaves his apartment and shoots Oswald addresses both his state of mind and absence of premeditation.

> Mr. RUBY. I drove down Main Street— there was a little incident I left out, that I started to go down a driveway, but I wanted to go by the wreaths, and I saw them and started to cry again.
>
> Then I drove, parked the car across from the Western Union, went into the Western Union, sent the money order, whatever it was, walked the distance from the Western Union to the ramp— I didn't sneak in. I didn't linger in there. I didn't crouch or hide behind anyone, unless the television camera can make it seem that way.
>
> There was an officer talking— I don't know what rank he had— talking to a Sam Pease in a car parked up on the curb. I walked down those few steps, and there was the person that— I wouldn't say I saw red— it was a feeling I had for our beloved President and Mrs. Kennedy, that he was insignificant to what my purpose was.[172]

However, Ruby contradicts his own account when he claims there were *two* reasons he went downtown on Sunday morning.

> Mr. RUBY. I drove past Main Street, past the County Building, and there was a crowd already gathered there. And I guess I thought I knew he was going to be moved at 10 o'clock, I don't know. I listened to the radio; and I passed a crowd and it looked— I am

---

[170] Ibid., p. 239.

[171] Western Union Receipt, November 24, 1963, Warren Commission Exhibit No. 2421.

[172] Testimony of Jack Ruby, Warren Commission, Hearings Volume V, p. 199.

> repeating myself— and I took it for granted he had already been moved.
>
> And I parked my car in the lot across from the Western Union. Prior to that, I got a call from a little girl— she wanted some money— that worked for me, and I said, "Can't you wait till payday?" And she said, "Jack, you are going to be closed."
>
> So my purpose was to go to the Western Union— my double purpose— but the thought of doing, committing the act wasn't until I left my apartment.[173]

Some conspiracy theorists assert Ruby must have been updated on the time of Oswald's transfer by one or more members of the police force. There are two other possibilities. Ruby admits he was listening to the minute-by-minute coverage of Oswald on his car radio. Did he make the side trip to Dealey Plaza because he knew the transfer was delayed beyond 10:00 a.m., the originally announced time? Did he want to assure he would not be seen in the vicinity of the police station until the last possible minute?

The second possibility might be a byproduct of the relationships Ruby developed with the press during his earlier trips to the police station Friday night and Saturday. After all, according to George Senator, Ruby left their apartment sometime between 10:15 and 10:30 a.m. That was already past the time (10:00 a.m.) the Dallas police previously informed the media as the time Oswald would appear for transfer. It is conceivable Ruby learned the revised schedule from one of his press contacts.

To further support the claim his actions lacked premeditation, Ruby's car contained two more pieces of evidence. The first were the Sunday editions of both Dallas daily newspapers, left on the front passenger-side seat. Their significance becomes apparent during the following exchange between Ruby and Elmer Moore, a Secret Service special agent assigned to the Warren Commission staff.

> Mr. RUBY. And I went home and that weekend, the Sunday morning, and saw a letter to Caroline, two columns about a 16-inch

---

[173] Ibid, p. 199.

area. Someone had written a letter to Caroline. The most heartbreaking letter. I don't remember the contents. Do you remember that?

Mr. MOORE. I think I saw it.

Mr. RUBY. Yes; and alongside that letter on the same sheet of paper was a small comment in the newspaper that, I don't know how it was stated, that Mrs. Kennedy may have to come back for the trial of Lee Harvey Oswald.

That caused me to go like I did; that caused me to go like I did.[174]

And then there was Sheba, Ruby's favorite dog, the only one of his many dachshunds he would bring home at night from the Carousel Club. There are two reasons Ruby might have taken Sheba with him to the Western Union office and left her in the car while he checked out the crowd at the police station. Ruby defenders swear he loved Sheba too much to have abandoned her, knowing he likely would not emerge from the police station basement.

On the other hand, what better way for Ruby, knowing he would be arrested or killed after shooting Oswald, to construct an air-tight case it was not premeditated. But when Vernon Smart, the Dallas police officer ordered to locate and search Ruby's car, reached the vehicle it was unlocked. He then found the trunk key in the glove compartment. When he opened the trunk, he discovered an ignition key. This sequence suggests Ruby wanted to ensure someone other than himself would be able to rescue Sheba.

```
November 25, 1963

Tinman reached out to Mario after Ruby's arrest.
Mario returned his call this morning. Tinman
asked if we needed to worry about Ruby talking.
Mario assured him Ruby had too much at stake to
talk. Ruby knew he was better off spending a
couple of years in jail than ratting out the mob.
```

It all made sense, assuming at worst, Ruby would be convicted of second-degree murder or manslaughter. But we know what happens.

---

[174] Ibid., p. 198.

"When we assume, …" Ruby's forthcoming trial would require a new assessment.

CHAPTER NINETEEN

THE WAITING GAME

Prior to reading Mason's post-assassination journal entries, I thought a typical crime consisted of three phases. Planning. Execution. Covering your tracks. Even though this ASSIGNMENT was anything but typical, I took for granted it would follow the same sequence. But Mason knew better. He more than adequately documented each step covering the twelve months between December 1962 and November 1963. Why then did he feel the need to maintain the journal for another nine years?

As I read each of the post-1963 entries, I realized there was one additional, never-ending task associated with an unlawful act–looking over one's shoulder. Despite efforts to erase each and every piece of evidence, there was always a possibility of some overlooked, unfinished business. Some relic or curio which might still point investigators in the TEAM's direction.

I can only speculate whether Mason's fears of eventual exposure were groundless. I never had the chance to ask him, "Did there ever come a time when you were convinced your secret was forever safe?" He did, however, leave clues. As time passed, subsequent posts became less and less frequent. But on those occasions when he chose to amend the journal, he returned to the detail and precision he had employed from the very start.

Each addition to the narrative was tied to one of three events. News about an individual who had participated consciously or unwittingly in the assassination. Official inquiries into the president's murder, most notably the Warren Commission. Or publication of a book or journalistic investigation by those who doubted the Warren Commission's conclusions.

That process began with the TEAM's self-assessment of their performance.

```
November 26, 1963

The team met this morning for our own internal
debrief knowing there would be many more official
ones to come. Secret Service SOP requires,
following any operation, we assess our mission
even if it was flawless. Kennedy had been
assassinated. The assassin was also dead.
Volunteer's succession process had gone smoothly.
We believed no one other than Wizard and the team
knew the whole story.

But the assignment was not without some failures.
Connally had been wounded though he was
recovering. A Dallas police officer had died when
Oswald panicked. Mrs. Kennedy could have been
seriously injured.

There was still one loose end, Jack Ruby. We knew
Tinman had been in touch with Mario who assured
him Ruby was not a problem. Ruby understood if he
ever talked about how and by whom he was
recruited he would no longer be protected. I wish
I shared Mario's confidence.
```

Some of the journal entries immediately following the assassination centered on whether Kennedy's death had the intended effect on national policy. For example, on November 27, Mason referenced Lyndon Johnson's speech to Congress and the nation the week after Dallas. Mason's purpose for doing so is obvious. He highlights Johnson's commitment to continue, and in some cases, expand the fallen president's agenda. Was this one way Mason could justify his participation in the ASSIGNMENT?

> November 27, 1963
>
> This evening I watched President Johnson's speech
> to Congress. Volunteer told viewers the best way
> to honor JFK was to pass the civil rights bill
> and other parts of his agenda. He quoted Kennedy
> a lot. Isn't this exactly what Lancer said he
> wanted when we met with him in New York?

Johnson honored the promise Mason believed he made to his predecessor. Now he needed to do the same when it came to his commitment to the nation, absent an Oswald trial, to conduct an official inquiry into the presidential assault. Among Johnson's first official acts was Executive Order No. 11130, creation of the President's Commission on the Assassination of President Kennedy.

> November 28, 1963
>
> This morning I was called to HQ. We were informed
> President Johnson would be announcing the
> formation of a commission headed by Chief Justice
> Earl Warren to investigate the assassination. We
> were instructed to fully cooperate with the
> commission and its staff.
>
> After the meeting, the team went back to the
> Naval Annex for the last time. We spent much of
> the afternoon drafting written statements and
> prepared "scripts" to be followed if called to
> testify. Each script would be consistent when it
> came to the basic story but would include minor
> differences in the details to avoid any
> appearance of coordination.
>
> We spent the rest of the day and evening
> dismantling the command center and destroying any
> evidence of the assignment.

The TEAM's liquidation of materials related to the ASSIGNMENT represented one more criminal act. The Federal Records Act of 1950 required all federal agencies to establish procedures for records management in accordance with standards set by the National Archives. The Records Act applies to the Secret Service. I was not surprised Mason did not acknowledge the illegal nature of his actions. When compared to active participation in a conspiracy to assassinate the president of the United States, destroying evidence was equivalent to jaywalking.

Mason's reference to the FBI's initial report about Dallas is more proof the journal was constructed in real time.

```
December 10, 1963

Yesterday, the FBI issued a preliminary report on
the assassination. They concluded there had been
three shots, two struck the President and one hit
Governor Connally. Their analysis of the duration
between the first and third shots raises the
possibility of a second gunman.

That should work in our favor. The more confusion
about what actually happened, the harder it will
be to uncover the truth.
```

This FBI assessment was based on a two-page memorandum dictated on November 23 by Dallas FBI Special Agent Gaston Thompson. One of the primary sources was Robert Jackson, a photographer for the *Dallas Times Herald,* who was riding with other reporters in a press car, five or six vehicles behind the presidential limousine. Jackson told Thompson, after hearing the first shot, he immediately turned toward the School Book Depository and saw a rifle in a window of one of the top floors but could not see "the person holding the rifle." Two days later Jackson took the famous Pulitzer Prize winning photograph at the exact moment Jack Ruby shot Lee Harvey Oswald.

The other source was Roy Kellerman, the Secret Service agent who was riding in the front passenger seat of the president's vehicle. According to Thompson's summary:

> *(Kellerman) stated he distinctly heard three shots. He advised he did not see the Governor get hit, nor did he observe the second bullet hit the President.* [175]

---

[175] FBI Memorandum dated November 23, 1963, prepared by Dallas special agent Gaston C. Thompson, File #83-43.

Since Thompson's summary was prepared prior to release of the autopsy report, it contained no reference to the single-bullet theory first introduced by Commission counsel and future Pennsylvania senator Arlen Specter.

```
There is nothing more to do but wait for the
Commission findings.
```

January 8, 1964 could be considered the last stop on the Kennedy legacy tour. In lieu of what would have been JFK's third state of the union address, Johnson again called on Congress to honor the slain president.

```
January 8, 1964

Tonight, as I watched Volunteer's speech, it
brought back memories of the past year.
Especially, the meeting with Lancer in New York
when he talked about his campaign promises. End
racial discrimination. Reduce the threat of
nuclear weapons. Grow the economy for everyone.

Volunteer covered each one. And told Congress
that passing JFK's legislative agenda would be
the best way to honor him. Lancer would have been
proud of his VP.
```

By continuing to call Lyndon Johnson by his code name "Volunteer," had Mason inadvertently included a reference that challenged the journal's authenticity? In 1960, the Secret Service gave then Vice President-Elect Johnson this designation because he willingly accepted Kennedy's invitation to be his running mate. It no longer seemed applicable to the new commander-in-chief, a role LBJ involuntarily inherited.

A review of the history of presidential code names proved otherwise. Beginning with Dwight Eisenhower, the "nickname" for each member of the first family would begin with the same letter. In LBJ's case, Lady Bird was "Victoria" and daughters Lynda Bird and Luci Baines were

"Velvet" and "Venus," respectively. Based on this convention, it made sense no post-assassination change was ever proposed.[176]

Mason was right about one thing. Kennedy would have been proud. Right out of the chute, LBJ challenged members of Congress to act on the late president's commitments to civil rights and economic prosperity for all Americans.

> *Let this session of Congress be known as the session which did more for civil rights than the last hundred sessions combined…as the session which declared all-out war on human poverty and unemployment in these United States.*

He promised to extend JFK's foreign policy, balancing strength where needed with continued negotiations to reduce the threat of nuclear weapons.

> *We must continue to use that strength as John Kennedy used it in the Cuban crisis and for the test ban treaty--to demonstrate both the futility of nuclear war and the possibilities of lasting peace.*

And finally, he solidified the late president's legacy. Is that not what Mason believed he saw when the two men shook hands as LBJ left the Oval Office on October 4, 1963?

> *Let us carry forward the plans and programs of John Fitzgerald Kennedy--not because of our sorrow or sympathy, but because they are right.*[177]

Mason's attention now turned to two immediate threats by which the TEAM and their participation in the ASSIGNMENT might be vulnerable to public disclosure: the Warren Commission investigation and Jack Ruby's trial. Tracking revelations resulting from Commission interviews and exhibits was problematic based on procedures and

---

[176] Ronald Kessler, *In the President's Secret Service: Behind the Scenes with Agents in the Line of Fire and the Presidents They Protect*, Crown Publishers, 2009, p.15.
[177] President Lyndon B. Johnson, "Address to Congress," January 8, 1964.

protocols established at the outset. From the foreword of the Commission's report:

> *Commission hearings were closed to the public unless the witness appearing before the Commission requested an open hearing. Under these procedures, testimony of one witness was taken in a public hearing on two occasions. No other witness requested a public hearing. The Commission concluded that the premature publication by it of testimony regarding the assassination or the subsequent killing of Oswald might interfere with Ruby's rights to a fair and impartial trial on the charges filed against him by the State of Texas.*[178]

The only public hearing was held on March 4, 1963, at the request of Mark Lane, a former New York Assemblyman, who claimed to represent Lee Harvey Oswald interests at his mother Marguerite Oswald's request. Lane's testimony included hearsay knowledge of a November 14 meeting between Dallas police officer J. D. Tippit and Bernard Weissman, a New York resident who placed an anti-Kennedy advertisement in a Dallas newspaper on the day of the assassination. He further alleged the meeting took place at Jack Ruby's Carousel Club.[179]

News coming out of the Warren Commission was sketchy at best. Although hearings were closed to the public, witnesses were not barred from discussing their testimony. And on occasion, a Commission member might give a general assessment of a witness' testimony. For example, on February 4, 1964, following the third day of Marina Oswald's questioning, Chairman Warren reported her answers were "consistent with her earlier stories, but in greater detail."[180] Relegation of the article to page 17 of the *New York Times* provided a clear indication how the paper's editors assessed the newsworthiness of these accounts.

---

[178] Foreword, Warren Commission Report, September 24, 1964, p. xiv.
[179] "Lane Gives Views to Warren Panel," *New York Times*, March 5, 1964, p. 13.
[180] William Blair, "Oswald's Widow, in Testimony for Panel, Confirms Her Earlier Statements," *New York Times*, February 6, 1964, p. 17.

In contrast, Ruby's trial became an on-going topic of evening news broadcasts and the front-pages of every major national newspaper. Mason picked up coverage with the February 14, 1964, announcement by Dallas District Judge Joe B. Brown jury selection would begin the following Monday.

```
February 14, 1964

CBS is reporting a Dallas judge heard a request
from Ruby's lawyer to move the trial out of
Dallas. Jury selection is scheduled to begin
Monday.
```

Rather than immediately addressing the defense petition to change venue, Judge Brown suggested it was too early to make that decision.

The true test of whether the defendant can obtain a fair trial rests upon the actual examination of jurors. I am withholding my ruling until the jurors have been examined.[181]

Ten days later Judge Brown officially denied the defense motion to move the trial outside Dallas County.

```
February 17, 1964

Ruby's original lawyer resigned after Melvin
Belli joined the defense team. Belli announced he
would not be charging Ruby for his services.
Belli seldom works pro bono. It is consistent
with Mario's assurances Ruby would not be a
problem. He now has one of the best defense
lawyers in the country.

February 19, 1964

After three days, the first juror was selected.
Belli challenged the selection process. He argued
Ruby could not receive a fair trial in Dallas
because potential jurors saw the shooting live on
local television.
```

---

[181] Jack Langguth, "Ruby Trial Opens in Dallas Monday," *New York Times*, February 15, 1964, p. 10.

Belli surprised no one when he employed courtroom theatrics to bolster his effort to move the trial outside of Dallas. The often-bellicose advocate had one of his assistants hand a subpoena to each prospective juror claiming he or she was a witness to the alleged crime. According to the report in the *New York Times*:

> *If the defense succeeded in subpoenaing potential jurors, to be witnesses at the trial, those subpoenaed would have to be removed from the list of veniremen (a person summoned for jury service) because a prospective witness cannot serve as a juror.*[182]

Judge Brown was not impressed. He immediately put an end to Belli's attempt to serve potential jurors, especially in the courtroom. He then warned Belli any similar efforts to disrupt jury selection would not be taken lightly.

```
February 24, 1964

Only three jurors have been chosen after eight
days. Belli said this was clear evidence Ruby
could not get a fair trial in Dallas.

Belli's appeal to the Texas Supreme Court to stop
the selection process was dismissed.

March 3, 1964

Jury selection completed. Prosecution schedules
first witnesses tomorrow.
```

The final day of jury selection was just one more example no aspect of Ruby's trial would proceed without controversy. Judge Brown, having contracted a severe cold and ordered to stay home by his doctor, was absent when the final two jurors were seated. He was replaced by Judge J. Frank Wilson, who immediately butted heads with defense lawyers. According to Homer Bigart of the *New York Times*, "Judge Wilson set

---

[182] Homer Bigart, "Ruby's Attorneys Fail in Maneuver," *New York Times*, February 20, 1964, p. 13.

out at once to show Mr. Belli who was conducting the trial. He delivered a stern reprimand to the defense counsel."[183]

In contrast to today's standards in high-profile trials, each juror was identified by name, age, residence and occupation. A March 4, 1964, article in the *Los Angeles Times* titled, "Meet the 12 Who'll Decide Ruby's Fate" included profiles of each member of the jury.

> *Here they are, in the order they were chosen and locked up to await testimony which may start today.*
>
> *1—Max E. Causey, 35, of suburban Garland, an electronics analyst with a master's degree in education, a Baptist, married and father of two sons. He saw the TV rerun.*[184]

The article contained similarly detailed sketches of the 11 other members of the panel.

Six days later, Mason received welcomed news about the Warren Commission investigation.

> March 9, 1964
>
> This morning we were told only four other members of the Dallas Secret Service detail would be called to testify before the Warren Commission: Bill Greer, Clint Hill, Roy Kellerman and Rufus Youngblood. All had been in Dealey Plaza at the time of the assassination.
>
> I was relieved. While Wizard and the team had regular contact with the advance team headed by Sorrells and Lawson, we had not talked with any of the agents who were with Lancer in Dealey Plaza. Thank goodness, I was not on the list. I do not know what I would have done if required to testify under oath.

---

[183] Homer Bigart, "Jury Completed for Ruby's Trial," *New York Times*, March 4, 1964, p. 28.
[184] "Meet the 12 Who'll Decide Ruby's Fate," *Los Angeles Times*, March 4, 1964, p. 13.

The last sentence provides one more instance in which the conflict between Mason's sense of duty and his moral compass would be tested. He participated in a conspiracy to commit murder. He had destroyed evidence. And yet, he wondered what he would do if faced with a decision whether or not to commit perjury.

Ruby's trial lasted 10 days. Late in the evening of March 13, Melvin Belli and district attorney Henry Wade made their closing statements. Judge Brown then read the jury instructions. Mason provided only a brief summary of the arguments.

```
March 14, 1964

Yesterday, Ruby's defense team rested without
calling him to testify.

From news reports both the prosecutors and
defense lawyers made closing arguments consistent
with the witnesses and evidence they presented
during the trial. No surprises. Prosecutors
focused on statements Ruby made which they
believe proved premeditation and eyewitness
reports Ruby was seen multiple times near the
police station between the time Oswald was
arrested Friday and the shooting on Sunday
morning. The defense focused on possible
neurological disorders which resulted in Ruby's
mental state following the assassination and the
morning of the shooting.
```

In his closing argument, Belli compared the credibility of his medical experts to those of the prosecution, particularly when it came to evidence of physiological disorders. Ruby would later tell the Warren Commission he opposed counsel using the mental illness defense. Yet, an autopsy following Ruby's death uncovered a "silent tumor" in his frontal lobe. Dr. Robert Kaplan, an Australian forensic psychiatrist, believes the tumor contributed to Ruby's state of mind and his desire for fame.

Without Ruby or anyone around him realising, the silent tumour altered the balance between the reality of his perceptions of the world around him and a profound feeling

that no matter what he tried, he would always be a failure, a
nobody.[185]

District Attorney Henry Wade viewed his mission differently. He paid minimal attention to Ruby or Oswald knowing the jury would not tolerate Oswald's being described as "the victim." Instead, he made the trial about the rule of law versus vigilante justice. He seldom mentioned Oswald by name with one major exception.

Jack Ruby was the Judge, the Jury and the Executioner. Now,
he and his lawyers ask you for mercy and sympathy and
compassion.

I ask you, Ladies and Gentlemen of the Jury, to show Jack
Ruby the same mercy and the same compassion, and the same
sympathy that he showed to Lee Harvey Oswald in your
Police Department and mine.[186]

March 15, 1964

The jury found Ruby guilty of murder with malice.
They recommended the death penalty. When Mario
assured Tinman that Ruby would not be a problem,
he assumed at worst he might be convicted of
second-degree murder or manslaughter.

We have a new problem. Facing death in the
electric chair, what might Ruby say or do in
exchange for a lesser sentence?

Mason would not be the only one surprised by the verdict. Jerry Flemmons, who covered the trial for the *Fort Worth Star-Telegram,* described Ruby's reaction to the jury's finding.

Ruby did not look right or left. He did not blink. He did not
lower his head. He did not take his eyes off Judge Brown. In
fact, he was so unemotional as to wonder at his show of strain

---

[185] Dr. Robert M. Kaplan, "Jack Ruby's complex: the factors driving the assassin of Lee Harvey Oswald," *Forensic Research and Criminology International Journal,* December 10, 2015.
[186] Jack Ruby Trial Transcript, March 13, 1964, p. 165.

earlier in this murder trial which had captured the world's attention.

Flemmons noted the contrast to Ruby's demeanor when he first entered the courtroom to hear the verdict.

The balding defendant, who defense attorneys claimed was temporarily insane when he fired a single shot into Lee Harvey Oswald, strolled briskly and seemingly confidently into the courtroom.[187]

Ruby's shift in demeanor was understandable. Mason alleges his Mafia handlers promised his outstanding tax bills and other debts would disappear. They would invest in his struggling strip club. They would secure the best legal defense team available. Furthermore, by promoting the fiction he acted solely in the interests of the widowed First Lady, they convinced Ruby a conviction, much less a death sentence, was unlikely.

Worst-case scenario, the jury would find him guilty of murder without malice which, under Texas law, carried a maximum five-year prison sentence. In that event, Ruby had likely been assured Giancana or Civello could find someone to run the Carousel Club until his release. A small price to pay for a fresh start for the debt-ridden, wannabe made man at age 52.

Almost everyone was shocked by the murder with malice verdict and the jury's recommendation he be executed. Jack Langguth, who covered the trial for the *New York Times*, sought reaction to the verdict from several Dallas residents. While some expressed concern Ruby did not deserve hero status, most were appalled by the death sentence. One local resident summed it up this way.

In the last few months, Ruby has become a household name in Dallas. He's like a television performer whom you feel you

---

[187] Jerry Flemmons, "Ruby Hides Emotions as Sentence Is Read," *Fort Worth Star-Telegram*, March 14, 1964, p. 1.

*know, just from hearing so much about him. You can't kill
someone like that with a clear conscience.*[188]

Immediately following the verdict, Belli ticked off a litany of alleged
procedural errors and expressed confidence Ruby would be vindicated
on appeal.

Mason's attention now shifted back to the Warren Commission,
especially pending testimony by members of the Secret Service.

```
April 23, 1964

Win Lawson is scheduled to testify before the
Warren Commission today.

April 24, 1964

I have not heard anything about Lawson's
testimony. Did he mention any member of our team
or Wizard? I contacted Wizard to see if he had
any idea what Lawson was asked. He had nothing to
share about Lawson's testimony. If my name came
up, I suspect I will soon hear from the
commission.
```

Lawson's testimony first centered on the procedures associated with
any presidential travel and the division of responsibilities between the
local Secret Service office, the advance team and the detail traveling
with the president. Next came a discussion of a Secret Service agent's
police powers if there was an individual identified as a potential threat.

There were two exchanges with Commission counsel Samuel Stern that
could potentially pull back the curtain on the ASSIGNMENT. The first
was a reference to an unnamed agent who assisted the advance team.

> Mr. STERN: Were you told anything about the assistance you
> would have in doing advance work for the Dallas trip?

---

[188] Jack Langguth, "Dallas Is Shaken by Death Penalty," *New York Times*, March 15,
1964, p. 82.

Mr. LAWSON: Oh yes, I had been told earlier, sometime between November 4 and 8, that another agent would be accompanying me, but, because the President's trips were occurring right at that time, that they would not be able to send out one at the same time, and he would have to join me later in Dallas after some of the other trips had been taken care of.[189]

The second came when Lawson was questioned about who made the decisions about the choice of the Trade Mart for the luncheon speech and the motorcade route. When asked by Stern, "Was (this) established for you by the White House?" pertaining to the Trade Mart versus the Women's Building at the Dallas Fair Grounds, Lawson replied, "Yes, sir." In reference to the motorcade route, Lawson testified, "It allowed us to go downtown, which was wanted back in Washington, D.C."[190]

May 20, 1964

This evening, I learned Forrest Sorrels had been called to give a sworn deposition two weeks ago. Most of the questions focused on the handling of Oswald following his arrest. He was the first agent to see Oswald after he arrived at the Dallas police station and briefly spoke with him there. He was often present whenever Oswald was questioned by Dallas police.

Although it has been two weeks since Sorrels' deposition, I have not heard from the Warren Commission. It again appears my name did not come up.

At the same time Mason and the TEAM focused on what the Warren Commission might uncover, President Johnson carried out a promise he made to his predecessor.

July 2, 1964

LBJ signed the Civil Rights Act today. I doubt this would have happened so quickly except for Volunteer making references to JFK's legacy.

---

[189] Winston Lawson testimony, Warren Commission Report, Volume IV, page 320.
[190] Ibid., p. 324-325.

As the 1964 presidential election approached, Johnson's popularity remained at an all-time high. The last Gallup poll taken before the Democratic National Convention at which Johnson would be the delegates' unanimous choice gave the president a 74 percent approval rating.[191] The only unresolved issue at the August Atlantic City conclave was Johnson's choice of a running mate.

```
July 30, 1964

Volunteer ended any speculation he might pick RFK
to be his vice-president. Those of us who had
observed the two of them knew this was
inevitable. It will be at least four and possibly
eight years before Kennedy might run for
president.
```

Johnson's announcement was not as straightforward as Mason suggests. Instead of referencing the attorney general by name, he eliminated Kennedy by inference. The decision was cloaked in a broader announcement of non-candidates. As reported by the *New York Times*:

Mr. Johnson went before the newsreel cameras and a hastily assembled group of reporters shortly before 6 o'clock. He announced he had decided it was "inadvisable" to choose any member of the Cabinet or anyone who met regularly with the Cabinet.[192]

After having been privately informed by Johnson prior to the public announcement, Kennedy issued a brief statement. "As I have always said, it is the President's responsibility to make known his choice for Vice President."[193] He also offered his support to help the campaign in any way he could. Following release of the statement, he sent a note to the other Cabinet members who had been mentioned as potential

---

191 "Lyndon B. Johnson Public Approval," Gallup Poll, June 26-30, 1964, Data Archive, The American Presidency Project, University of California-Santa Barbara.
192 Tom Wicker, "President Bars Kennedy, Five Others from Ticket," *New York Times, July 31, p. 1.*
193 Ibid., p. 8.

Johnson ticket mates. "I'm sorry I took so many nice fellows over the side with me."[194]

Mason's reference to "at least four and possibly eight years" was a reminder Johnson was eligible to run again in 1972 under provisions of the 22nd Amendment which limited an incumbent to two full terms. An exception was made for any person "who has held the office of President, or acted as President, for more than two years of a term to which some other person was elected President."[195] Since Johnson served less than two years of John Kennedy's uncompleted term, the only one full-term exception did not apply.

> August 7, 1964
>
> Today, Congress gave Volunteer authority to use force to protect American interests in Southeast Asia. President Johnson asked for this authority in response to attacks on two U.S. destroyers off the coast of Vietnam.
>
> Vietnam, like Korea, is divided into north and south. The boundary was established following the departure of a French colonial government in 1954. Presidents Eisenhower, Kennedy and now Johnson have supported the government of South Vietnam as a buffer against the spread of Communism in the region.

The Gulf of Tonkin Resolution (H.J. RES 1145), named after the body of water in which the naval attacks allegedly occurred, passed the House of Representatives unanimously and the Senate by a vote of 98-2. It gave the commander-in-chief broad powers which would only expire "when the President shall determine that the peace and security of the area is reasonably assured."[196] While some who supported the resolution believed it was limited to protection of U.S. assets in the region, the approved language suggests otherwise.

---

[194] Ken Rudin, "L.B.J. Rules Out R.F.K. for V.P.," NPR.ORG, July 30, 2010.
[195] Twenty-Second Amendment to the U.S. Constitution, approved by Congress on March 21, 1947, adopted on February 27, 1951, by the required 36 states.
[196] House Joint Resolution 1145, Section 2, approved by Congress on August 7, 1964.

> *Resolved by the Senate and House of Representatives of the*
> *United States of America in Congress assembled, That the*
> *Congress approves and supports the determination of the*
> *President, as Commander in Chief, to take all necessary*
> *measures to repel any armed attack against the forces of the*
> *United States and to prevent further aggression.*[197]

Labor Day signaled the end of summer and the beginning, in earnest, of the presidential and congressional campaigns. In New York state there was a new, but well-known Democratic candidate to challenge the incumbent Republican Kenneth Keating.

```
September 2, 1964

Robert Kennedy may not be leaving D.C. At
yesterday's New York Democratic Party convention,
Kennedy defeated Representative Samuel Stratton
for the U.S. Senate nomination. If he wins in
November, there will be two Senator Kennedys.
Though it is not the presidential dynasty Kennedy
supporters hoped for.
```

RFK's margin of victory was an overwhelming 968 to 153. In his acceptance speech, he addressed the elephant in the room, charges of being a Massachusetts "carpetbagger." He began by reminding those who considered him an outsider, "The first Senator from the State of New York, Rufus King, was from Massachusetts. And he served this state well."[198] With the nomination in hand, Kennedy resigned as attorney general the following day.

Meanwhile the Warren Commission continued its investigation under a veil of secrecy with few public statements and no media leaks. I can only imagine Mason's apprehension while the Commission and staff drafted its report in isolation. The lack of journal entries between May

---

[197] Ibid., Section 1.
[198] R. W. Apple, Jr., "Kennedy Swamps Stratton to Win State Nomination," *New York Times*, September 2, 1964, p. 1.

and September suggests he had no inside knowledge of the Commission's forthcoming findings or recommendations.

September **27, 1964**

President Johnson authorized public release of
the Warren Commission final report. The
Commission found Oswald was not part of a
conspiracy or acted as an agent of a federal
government. Oswald did not have any association
with the FBI, CIA or other government agency. Nor
was Jack Ruby part of a conspiracy to silence
Oswald.

The only mention of the Secret Service involved
insufficient investigation of potential threats
in advance of the trip and lack of coordination
between the Service and local law enforcement
during the visit.

The finding of most interest to the team was the
Commission's inability to determine Oswald's
motive. Will there be further official
investigations or will this unresolved question
be left to journalists and historians?

The Commission tiptoed around the question of motive. The panel referenced Oswald's propensity for violence and his ever-present discontent about his career, family situation and life in America. However, they provided no evidence of a specific incident that set the events of November 22, 1963, in motion.

> *Many factors were undoubtedly involved in Oswald's
> motivation for the assassination, and the Commission, does
> not believe that it can ascribe to him any one motive or group
> of motives. It is apparent, however, that Oswald was moved
> by an overriding hostility to his environment. He does not
> appear to have been able to establish meaningful
> relationships with other people. He was perpetually
> discontented with the world around him. Long before the
> assassination he expressed his hatred for American society
> and acted in protest against it. Oswald's search for what he
> conceived to be the perfect society was doomed from the start.*

> *He sought for himself a place in history—a role as the 'great man' who would be recognized as having been in advance of his times. His commitment to Marxism and communism appears to have been another important factor in his motivation. He also had demonstrated [through the attempt to kill General Walker] a capacity to act decisively and without regard to the consequences when such action would further his aims of the moment. Out of these and the many other factors which may have molded the character of Lee Harvey Oswald there emerged a man capable of assassinating President Kennedy."[199]*

I have no doubt Mason would have agreed wholeheartedly with the Commission assessment of Oswald's general demeanor and discontent with his life. After all, those very factors made him open to the TEAM's recruitment and manipulation.

Though the Commission Report was consistent with the FBI's preliminary findings and media coverage of the assassination, Mason realized the nation's curiosity would not end here. Even before the flood of conspiracy theories, skeptics immediately raised questions about the events in Dealey Plaza.

```
September 28, 1964

Reaction to the Warren Commission report is
mixed. Critics have focused on two topics. That a
single bullet wounded both JFK and Connally. And
eyewitness claims there was a second gunman.
```

A Harris Survey conducted shortly after release of the Commission report found 87 percent of Americans believed Lee Harvey Oswald killed the president. However, 31 percent thought he had accomplices and 45 percent felt there were still unanswered questions.[200]

Among the first critics of the report was none other than retired General Edwin Walker. Immediately after its release, he described it as a

---

[199] Warren Commission Report, pp. 423-4.
[200] Louis Harris, "31% of Public Still Feels Oswald Had Some Help." *The Washington Post*, October 19, 1964.

"farcical whitewash." Although he accepted the commission's finding that it was Oswald who had shot at him in April 1963, Walker claimed that the commission was attempting to hide "some sort of conspiracy" that included an association between Jack Ruby and Oswald.[201]

In the absence of other public investigations or trials related to the assassination, Mason's interest turned to current events directly or indirectly associated with Kennedy's death.

```
November 3, 1964

As expected, Johnson was overwhelmingly elected
to a full term. And RFK is now a New York
senator. The Kennedy family is well represented
in Congress.
```

With a newly minted electoral mandate, Johnson moved forward on two fronts, a domestic agenda he labeled "The Great Society" and expansion of America's role in the Vietnam civil war.

```
February 21, 1965

Malcolm X gunned down during a speech in
Manhattan. It is hard to feel anything for
someone who celebrated JFK's murder.
```

One week after Kennedy's assassination, Malcolm X told followers at a Black Muslim rally in New York the president's death was related to the United States having stood back while South Vietnamese president Ngo Dinh Diem and his brother were assassinated. He described Kennedy as "twiddling his thumbs," someone who did not anticipate the consequences of his actions. "He never foresaw that the chickens would come home to roost so soon."[202]

---

[201] "Probe is Whitewash: Walker," *The Courier-Journal,* Louisville, Kentucky, March 31, 1964, p. 3.
[202] "Malcolm X Scores U.S. and Kennedy," *New York Times,* December 2, 1963, p. 21.

March 3, 1965

> In response to an attack on a U.S. air base,
> Johnson ordered air strikes on a number of
> targets in both North and South Vietnam. He
> described the bombing as a defensive measure to
> disrupt supply lines to rebels trying to
> overthrow the government in the South.
>
> The Soviet Union and its support of Fidel Castro
> dominated JFK's national security concerns. There
> was no indication he thought China and its
> alliance with North Vietnam was a bigger threat.

Operation Rolling Thunder was initiated on March 2, 1965, following an assault by Viet Cong forces on the base in Pleiku, South Vietnam. Initially described as necessary to protect U.S. assets, the administration had a second policy objective. "Administration officials believed that heavy and sustained bombing might encourage North Vietnamese leaders to accept the non-Communist government in the South."[203] The bombing runs continued until October 31, 1968, when Johnson suspended the operation in hopes of negotiating a peace settlement before he left office the following January.

Was Lyndon Johnson the sole policymaker responsible for "Americanization" of the Vietnam war or had his predecessor laid the foundation for the bombings and eventual introduction of ground troops? Historians remain divided on this issue. Perhaps McGeorge Bundy, who served as national security advisor in both administrations, had the most first-hand knowledge. Gordon Goldstein, author of *Lessons in Disaster: McGeorge Bundy and the Path to War in Vietnam*, recalls an interview with the book's title subject consistent with Mason's observation Southeast Asia was not a JFK priority.

> *[Bundy] arrived at a firm conclusion that he shared with me*
> *and discussed with various colleagues . . . that Kennedy*
> *would not have deployed ground combat forces to Vietnam*
> *and thus would not have Americanized the war. What [JFK]*
> *wanted to do about Vietnam—shorthand, in political terms—*

---

[203] "Operation Rolling Thunder," HISTORY.COM, February 24, 2010.

was flush it. He didn't want it to be a big item. And he didn't think it was a big test of the balance of power. It was a test of American political opinion, but he could stand that in a second term. Kennedy didn't want to be dumb. Johnson didn't want to be a coward.[204]

Why "coward?" What did Bundy believe Johnson was afraid of? Following Mao Zedong's 1949 establishment of the Communist government in what became the Peoples Republic of China (i.e., Red China), the Truman administration published the "China White Paper," an explanation of the events which led to the Communist takeover. The document was widely criticized as an attempt to divert charges the Democratic administration had "lost" China. Johnson feared a similar blemish on his legacy if South Vietnam fell into Communist hands.

```
March 7, 1965

Another sad day for America. One Negro was
killed, and many others beaten by state police
during a march from Selma, Alabama to Montgomery
to promote Negro voter registration. ABC
interrupted its programming tonight to show
disturbing film of the police attacking the
marchers.
```

The video footage from Selma proved to be instrumental in raising public support for the pending voting rights bill. Ironically, ABC was airing the network premiere of the movie "Judgment at Nuremberg." ABC estimated as many as 50 million Americans tuned in to watch the film about Nazi war crimes when news anchor Frank Reynolds interrupted the broadcast with freshly acquired video from Selma. In their Pulitzer Prize winning book, *The Race Beat*, journalists Gene Roberts and Hank Klibanoff described the impact. "The juxtaposition [of Selma with Nuremberg] struck like psychological lightning in American homes."[205]

---

[204] Gordon M. Goldstein, *Lessons in Disaster: McGeorge Bundy and the Path to War in Vietnam*, Henry Holt and Co., New York, 2009, p. 3.
[205] Gene Roberts and Hank Klibanoff, *The Race Beat: The Press, the Civil Rights Struggle, and the Awakening of a Nation*, Knopf Doubleday, June 17, 2008, p. 389.

August 16, 1966

This morning, the New York Times published a
review of Mark Lane's book "Rush to Judgment"
which challenges the findings of the Warren
Commission. It has now been almost two years
since the Commission presented its final report
to President Johnson. Critics have spent more
time investigating the report than the Commission
spent investigating the assassination.

Lane is one of the most vocal critics of the
Warren Report. He has questioned both its methods
and conclusions from his unique perspective as
Oswald's advocate before the Warren Commission.

The Times book review suggests neither the
official accounts nor Lane's book should be taken
at face value. It encourages readers to go back
to the evidence and make their own judgment.

In his review, Christopher Lehmann-Haupt backs up his skepticism of
Lane's conclusions by demonstrating how Lane "cherry-picked"
information from the Commission Report, even when it was presented
as "speculation." A prime example is Lane's reference to the
ammunition found on the sixth floor of the Texas School Book
Depository. Lane cites the Warren Commission report which
acknowledges the bullets had not been manufactured "since the end of
World War II" and "therefore, have been at least 20 years old, making
them extremely unreliable." He omits a later passage under
"Commission Findings" which states, "In tests with the same kind of
ammunition, experts fired Oswald's Mannlicher-Carcano rifle more
than 100 times without misfire."[206]

There is no mention of possible Secret Service
involvement. I doubt this is the last rebuttal of
the Warren Commission report. That may be good
news. With each additional book or conspiracy

---

[206] Christopher Lehmann-Haupt, "Rush to the Warren Commission Report," *New
York Times*, August 16, 1966, p. 37.

```
theory, the truth becomes just one of many
versions of what happened.
```

The proliferation of competing versions of the assassination did muddy the landscape. That must have been welcomed by members of the TEAM. The confusion created by such diverse speculation about what really happened only bolstered the conspiracy theory industry.

```
January 3, 1967

Just learned Jack Ruby died this morning. The
cause is reported to be cancer. One more door is
closed. How many are still open?
```

Jack Ruby's death proved insufficient to stem theories about his involvement in a conspiracy. The first indication he might be seriously ill came when he was transferred to Parkland Memorial Hospital on December 9, 1966. Shortly thereafter, his doctors discovered cancer cells on his liver and brain. Conspiracy theorists immediately suggested his cancer was induced to permanently silence Ruby. Pulitzer Prize and National Book Award winner Norman Mailer asserted as much in a *Village Voice* op-ed.

> *He died of cancer this morning, told us the way. We do not know the cure, but son, now we know the way. We know how to give cancer now.* [207]

The TEAM had always feared exposure during a legal proceeding with its attendant discovery, exhibits and testimony. They now dodged a second bullet. Even if Oswald or Ruby could not connect all the dots, both had information that was not in the public domain. Therefore, it was always possible they might divulge clues by which a skilled investigator could build, from the ground up, a picture of what happened. Now the two lead players in this historical drama were non-factors.

---

[207] Norman Mailer, "A Requiem for the Rube," *The Village Voice*, January 5, 1967.

However, less than two months after Ruby's death, there was another trial in the offing.

```
March 2, 1967

Last night, the New Orleans district attorney
arrested Clay Shaw who he claims was part of a
conspiracy to kill Kennedy. Shaw is the former
manager of the New Orleans International Trade
Center.

I called Lion and asked if he ever met Shaw while
he was in New Orleans. He had not. I then checked
the Warren report index. The only Shaw was Dr.
Robert Shaw, the thoracic surgeon who treated
Governor Connally.

Who is Clay Shaw and what does the DA think was
his role in the assassination? Is he somehow
connected to the New Orleans mafia?
```

An *Associated Press* account of Clay's arrest included a statement by district attorney Jim Garrison suggesting a larger conspiracy. According to Garrison:

Mr. Shaw will be charged with participation in a conspiracy to murder John F. Kennedy. It should be pointed out, however, that the nature of this case is not conducive to an immediate succession of arrests at this time. However, other arrests will be made at a later date.[208]

```
March 6, 1967

Garrison served subpoenas on three more locals.
Dean Andrews, the assistant DA in Jefferson
Parish. Dante Marachini, who had been employed at
the Reilly coffee plant at the same time as
Oswald. James Lewallen, an employee at the
Chrysler-Michoud missile plant.
```

---

[208] John Lane, "Ex-Director of Orleans Trade Mart Arrested in Conspiracy Probe," *Shreveport Times*, March 2, 1967, p. 1.

    AP is reporting the presiding judge Bernard J.
    Bagert has warned Garrison about excessive
    publicity which could make it difficult to
    conduct a fair trial.

In the *Associated Press* story, Judge Bagert acknowledged he would review other high-profile cases to develop guidelines for press coverage. His sense of caution mirrored similar concerns by the judges who presided over previous assassination-related proceedings. "I don't want to go through a long trial and then have the case thrown out on technical grounds."[209]

    March 15, 1967

    There is a supposed firsthand witness at the
    center of Garrison's conspiracy case against Clay
    Shaw. His name is Perry Raymond Russo. During a
    preliminary hearing, Russo told the court he was
    present when Shaw, David Ferrie and Oswald
    planned the assassination. He claimed the meeting
    took place in Ferrie's New Orleans apartment in
    September 1963.

    News reports also suggest there is enough
    evidence to take the case before a grand jury. It
    seems Louisiana law favors prosecutors when it
    comes to meeting the probable cause standard.

This brief entry contained items that signaled Garrison's prosecution of Shaw and others would generate a host of new conspiracy theories. In February 1967, Ferrie, a retired airline pilot, told reporters he was a target of Garrison's investigation. "Supposedly, I had been pegged as get-away pilot for the assassins."[210] Ferrie denied this claim but admitted he and two friends had driven from New Orleans to Dallas, spending the night of November 22 in a Houston motel before proceeding to Dallas the next day. The trip to Dallas involved visits to several ice-skating rinks as Ferrie expressed interest in opening one of

---

[209] Jack Owens, "Shaw's Former Assistant Subpoenaed by Garrison," *Shreveport Times*, March 7, 1967, p. 4.

[210] James Phelan, "Rush to Judgment in New Orleans," *Saturday Evening Post*, May 6, 1967.

his own in New Orleans. The next morning, they headed home with stops in Galveston, Texas and Alexandria, Louisiana.[211]

Four days after that interview, police discovered Ferrie's body in his apartment from what the New Orleans coroner officially described as a Berry Aneurysm, a massive brain hemorrhage attributed to a blocked artery. Garrison used Ferrie's death to bolster his conspiracy claim suggesting Ferrie either committed suicide or was silenced.

Mason's speculation David Ferrie could be linked to Carlos Marcello was not unfounded. During an FBI interview on November 26, 1963, Ferrie admitted as much.

> *FERRIE informed that since March 1962 he has been employed by Attorney G WRAY GILL in New Orleans as an investigator and law clerk. He said that since the end of August 1963 and up until November 22 1963 he has been working on a case involving CARLOS MARCELLO who was charged in Federal Court in connection with a fraudulent birth certificate. FERRIE stated that the trial of MARCELLO began in Federal Court in New Orleans Louisiana on November 4 1963 and ended on November 22 1963.[212]*

In his book *Scandals, Scamps and Scoundrels: The Casebook of an Investigative Reporter,* James Phelan describes the relationship between Ferrie and Marcello as less adversarial.

> *[Ferrie] was an exotic fellow indeed, even for colorful old New Orleans. He was a former airline pilot, a self-proclaimed psychologist, an ex-seminary student, an amateur hypnotist, an inventor, a private investigator, and an adventurer with a penchant for cloak-and-dagger projects, some of which trailed rumors of CIA involvement. Physically, Garrison could not have picked a more ominous-looking suspect if he had ordered him up from Central Casting...Ferrie was a*

---

[211] FBI Interview with David Ferrie, November 26, 1963, by Special Agents Ernest C. Wall, Jr. and L. M. Shearer, Jr., New Orleans Field Office.
[212] Ibid.

*violent anti-Communist, and a friend of Carlos Marcello, the
reputed Mafia capo in the New Orleans area.*[213]

Instead of immediately presenting his evidence to a grand jury, Garrison
requested a preliminary hearing before Judge Bagert to determine
whether Shaw should be bound over for trial. Bagert, acknowledging
the significance of the case, recruited two colleagues--Judges Malcolm
V. O'Hara and Matthew S. Braniff—to hear Garrison's charges against
Shaw.

Perry Russo was the star witness. He testified he attended a party at
Ferrie's apartment in September of 1963. He and three other people
stayed after the other guests departed. He identified them as Ferrie,
Leon Oswald and Clem Bertrand. When asked, "Do you see the man
you knew as Bertrand in the Courtroom," Russo pointed at Clay Shaw.
When shown a picture of Lee Harvey Oswald, Russo acknowledged,
"It is the same person that I saw at David Ferrie's apartment."[214]

Russo then described the conversation he witnessed involving Ferrie,
Oswald and Shaw.

> *During the discussion, it centered around the fact that in the
> assassination attempt, they would have to use diversionary
> tactics and this was Dave Ferrie's favorite expression. He
> raised his hand showing the triangulate of cross fire involved
> that would have to be required and he pointed to this finger
> and this finger to say that there would be three people, or at
> the very minimum, two involved, but necessarily three he felt,
> and that one would shoot a diversionary shot or another,
> maybe two, one of two would shoot diversionary shots and
> third was the intended direct hit, or the good shot.*[215]

With each new theory or revelation, I am drawn back to the options the
TEAM used as it considered the three motives. Was it remotely possible
both the Secret Service TEAM and Sam Giancana, working through

---

[213] James Phelan, *Scandals, Scamps And Scoundrels: The Casebook Of An
Investigative Reporter*, (New York: Random House, 1982), pp. 141-42.
[214] Transcript, Clay Shaw Preliminary Hearing, March 14, 1967, pp. 53-54.
[215] Ibid, pp. 54-55.

Marcello, had independently singled out the same person to pull the trigger?

As preposterous as that may seem, there is a legitimate argument to be made. The TEAM was drawn to Oswald for two reasons. His dissatisfaction with U.S. policy toward Cuba and his qualifications as a sharpshooter. Did these same criteria make him attractive to organized crime? But they had one more incentive. Oswald was not Italian, nor did he have a history of Mafia-related activities. Thus, he provided one more degree of separation from organized crime during any subsequent investigation into the president's murder.

It also raises the outside possibility Mario and Marcello recruited Ferrie to fly their appointed gunman to safety, whether Oswald or someone else. I admit this is pure speculation on my part and was not surprised Mason omitted any reference to the Mario/Ferrie connection in the journal. Documentation, not speculation, remained his primary purpose for keeping the journal.

Despite his outward confidence, Garrison must have known he faced an uphill fight. Ferrie first came to the DA's attention on the day of the assassination. New Orleans resident Jack Martin raised the Ferrie/Oswald connection, claiming the two met while serving together in the New Orleans Civil Air Patrol (CAP). This assertion is bolstered by a 1955 photograph at a CAP event in which both Ferrie and Oswald were present. Michael Sullivan, executive producer for PBS' "Frontline," which obtained a copy of the photograph in 1993, explained the image's limited importance.

> *As dramatic as the discovery of this photograph is after thirty years, one should be cautious in ascribing its meaning. The photograph does give much support to the eyewitnesses who say they saw Ferrie and Oswald together in the C.A.P., and it makes Ferrie's denials that he ever knew Oswald less credible. But it does not prove that the two men were with each other in 1963, nor that they were involved in a conspiracy to kill the president.*[216]

---

[216] "Who was Lee Harvey Oswald," PBS *Frontline*, broadcast November 1993.

Immediately following the assassination, Garrison detained Ferrie and turned him over to the FBI where he was interviewed on November 26, 1963. Based on the detailed account of his travels between New Orleans and Dallas as well as interviews with 20 individuals who confirmed his itinerary, the FBI determined Ferrie was no longer a suspect.

But Garrison would get his day in court. Not only did the three-judge panel determine there was enough "probable cause" to warrant a grand jury, Judge Braniff shared his personal doubts about the Warren Commission. "It is fraught with hearsay and contradictions."[217]

March 22, 1967

Shaw was indicted by a New Orleans grand jury. The indictment refers only to a conspiracy to kill Kennedy. It does not say the assassination was planned during the alleged meeting in David Ferrie's apartment.

June 25, 1967

Garrison is accused of using questionable legal practices. Earlier this month two convicts being held in a Louisiana prison said they had been offered leniency if they helped prove Shaw's involvement in a conspiracy. John Cancler claimed Garrison offered to drop his burglary conviction if he planted evidence in Shaw's home. Garrison dismissed the accusation saying Cancler's history of criminal behavior made anything he said suspect.

Last week, the press questioned some of the methods Garrison used to build his case against Shaw.

Yesterday, one of Garrison's former investigators reportedly told RFK the Garrison case lacked substance. Garrison dismissed the report but may face a state review at the request of a local government reform group. Garrison issued a public

---

[217] Gene Roberts, "The 'Oswald Plot,' or Something," *New York Times*, March 19, 1967, p. 203.

    statement suggesting these reports were more
    evidence of a federal government coverup.

A month later, the American Civil Liberties Union charged Garrison with "gross misuse of his public office in his probe into the death of President Kennedy." In a letter to U.S. Attorney General Ramsey Clark, the ACLU highlighted instances where Garrison brought perjury charges against grand jury witnesses who did not agree with his version of the assassination.[218]

    July 16, 1967

    Last night NBC gave Garrison a chance to respond
    to attacks on his case against Shaw. The network
    provided this opportunity because its own news
    reports raised several questions about his
    methods.

Garrison's defense of his prosecution came during a half-hour special on NBC television. According to an NBC spokesman, "The program was presented on the network's own initiative and in a spirit of journalistic enterprise." As to Garrison's claims NBC had misrepresented certain facts, the network maintained its position that "…[Garrison] said nothing in the program that alters the information developed by NBC News about the methods he used in pressing his theory of the Kennedy assassination."[219]

    September 18, 1967

    Shaw defense team's attempt to dismiss the
    indictment is rejected. Judge Haggerty hoped to
    start the trial in October but gave defense
    lawyers a week to file additional pre-trial
    motions.

Efforts to quash the indictment addressed issues related to selection of the grand jury. Defense attorneys argued the court deviated from the prescribed process for choosing grand jurors by excluding women and failing to maintain the 750 required names in the container from which potential jurors were randomly pulled. During the hearing, Shaw's

---

[218] "ACLU Charges Garrison with Misuse of His Office," UPI August 4, 1967.
[219] "NBC Say Garrison Talk Still Doesn't Alter Case," UPI, July 16, 1967.

lawyers also questioned whether any member of the grand jury panel had contributed to Truth or Consequences, Inc., a fund created to help finance Garrison's probe. All responded they had not. However, one juror, the vice president of an insurance company, admitted one of his employees contributed to the fund.[220]

```
October 15, 1967

Judge Haggerty rejected the request by Shaw's
lawyers for a change of venue. He did grant
another trial delay until February 1968.
```

Appeals by defense counsel of Haggerty's decision put the Clay trial on hold for almost 12 months. During the hiatus, Mason's interest returned to politics, especially the Democratic nomination for president.

```
March 12, 1968

Tonight, President Johnson narrowly won the New
Hampshire primary with less than half the votes.
Minnesota Senator Eugene McCarthy got 42 percent
with support from voters who opposed the Vietnam
war. Johnson's nomination is less certain than it
once seemed.

March 16, 1968

Robert Kennedy announced his candidacy for
president. McCarthy called him an opportunist who
is taking advantage of his strong showing in New
Hampshire.
```

Senator Kennedy had no plans to run for higher office in 1968 despite major differences with LBJ, particularly the war in Vietnam. Deciding factors included concerns about his personal safety and his ascension to the role of family patriarch after his father's paralyzing stroke in December 1961. RFK largely attributed his change of heart to a letter from close friend and journalist Pete Hamill, urging Kennedy to come forward during what he called a "historical moment" in America. Hamill expected that Kennedy's challenging the incumbent president

---

[220] W. Galvin Scott, "Clay Shaw Indictment Attacked," Associated Press, September 12, 1967.

might tear apart the Democratic Party. To counter his own concern about party unity, Hamill recalled how so many people still associated faith in and hope for the future with President Kennedy and the family name.

> *I wanted to remind you that in Watts I didn't see pictures of Malcolm X or Ron Karenga on the walls. I saw pictures of JFK. This is your capital in the most cynical sense; it is your obligation in another, the obligation of staying true to whatever it was that put those pictures on those walls.* [221]

Hamill joined his campaign as a speech writer immediately following the March 16 announcement and was present at the Ambassador Hotel when Kennedy was shot following his victory in the California primary.

Meanwhile, Clay Shaw's attorneys continued their efforts to move the trial out of New Orleans.

```
April 3, 1968

Shaw's trial was again delayed when Judge
Haggerty held more hearings to determine whether
a change of venue was needed. Today he rejected
the defense lawyers arguments but did not set a
new trial date.
```

Shaw's lawyers cited public statements Garrison made criticizing the Warren Commission report. They feared Garrison's remarks would bias the jury based on growing public skepticism about the Commission's findings. However, Judge Haggerty rejected the petition, arguing Shaw's trial and Garrison's broader probe of the assassination were two different things. The defense unsuccessfully countered, claiming Garrison had made the connection when he showed a copy of the Zapruder film to the grand jury. [222]

---

[221] Transcript of handwritten letter from Peter Hamill to Robert F. Kennedy, *Letters of Note* on Twitter, posted August 7, 2020.

[222] Bill Crider, "Judge Refuses Shaw's Bid to Move Trial," *Associated Press*, April 4, 1968.

In the midst of the 1968 presidential election, the nation and specifically Black Americans were again reminded the darkest days of the civil rights struggle were not over.

```
April 4, 1968

CBS News just reported Martin Luther King died of
a gunshot wound. Police retrieved a rifle from a
boarding house across the street from the Memphis
motel where King was staying. Police are looking
for a white man seen running from the scene of
the shooting.
```

King's death would not be the only shock to the country's civic landscape. Sixty-two days later, Robert Kennedy became the second casualty of political violence in just over two months.

```
June 5, 1968

This morning I woke up to the news Robert Kennedy
was shot after winning the California Democratic
primary. The gunman was disarmed by campaign
advisors who were with Kennedy at the time of the
shooting. The shooter was taken away by local
police. Kennedy was taken to the hospital where
he remains in critical condition.
```

```
June 6, 1968

This morning campaign spokesman Frank Mankiewicz
announced Kennedy died around 2:00 am last night.
```

Kennedy's assassin, Sirhan Bishara Sirhan, was a Palestinian born in an Arab neighborhood in Jerusalem. At age 12, he immigrated to the United States with his parents in 1956. His motive for killing Kennedy was clear. In a 1989 interview with David Frost, Sirhan shared the reason for his animosity toward RFK. "My only connection with Robert Kennedy was his sole support of Israel and his deliberate attempt to send those 50 bombers to Israel to obviously do harm to the Palestinians."[223]

---

[223] Associated Press, "Sirhan Felt Betrayed by Kennedy," *New York Times*, February 20, 1989, p. 13.

The brevity of Mason's documentation of this event is understandable. It would have brought back memories of Dallas and reawakened the doubt and guilt he still bore from the role he claimed to play. Revisiting the events of 1963 and continuing fear of being exposed are evident in the next journal entry.

```
June 8, 1968

I had the day off and stayed home to watch
Kennedy's funeral. Another reminder of the one I
attended as an on-duty agent five years ago. Just
like 1963, this funeral did not run on schedule.
Large crowds, multiple locations and
transportation delays meant RFK's burial at
Arlington Cemetery would be held in darkness as
had the president's.

Otherwise, the funeral went off as planned except
when news anchors broke into the broadcast to
report Martin Luther King's suspected killer had
been arrested at London's Heathrow airport. Did
James Earl Ray assume he was in the clear after
just two months? Is that ever the case?
```

Five years after Dallas, Mason once again expressed concern the TEAM might still be at risk. I always assumed the best clues about the journal's authenticity would be among his description of the assassination itself. However, I found this continuing anxiety about disclosure and liability equally intriguing. Mason seemed truly distressed by Ray's capture. Would anyone be so haunted by a fictional creation? Or did Mason think ahead of his future readers, offering a detail that added nothing to a mythical tale other than to confuse skeptics? Furthermore, would he have the presence to construct such a ruse on the day Robert Kennedy was laid to rest?

While America grieved the loss of RFK and Dr. King, Clay Shaw's trial was again stalled due to his lawyers' attempts to secure a change of venue.

```
July 23, 1968

A federal district court panel refused to delay
the Shaw trial to consider the defense's request
for a change of venue.
```

Another example of the law of unintended consequences. Shaw's federal court appeal of Judge Haggerty's refusal to move the trial gave Garrison a national forum to promote his assassination theory. UPI reporter Gene Mearns speculated:

> *If Shaw's federal suit is decided by Autumn in New Orleans, say the experts, there is no reason why either Shaw or Garrison, depending on the loser, could not have the case on appeal before the Supreme Court for its winter session, beginning in October.*[224]

As expected, Shaw's attorneys served notice on August 4 they planned to appeal the district court's decision. Two days later, an unrelated event potentially altered the trial's timetable.

```
August 6, 1968

Garrison underwent surgery to correct an
abdominal hernia. It is not expected to delay the
Shaw trial now scheduled for September 10.
```

However, the appeals process had more impact on the court calendar than Garrison's hospitalization. On August 13, the federal district court acknowledged it could not act before the September 10 trial date and ordered another delay.

The nation's attention now focused on selecting the next president. The Republicans convened on August 5 in Miami to nominate Richard Nixon who ran as the "law and order" candidate. He also described himself as a representative of "the silent majority," disgruntled Americans who he believed would express their dissatisfaction with their votes, not through angry protests and street violence.

---

[224] W. Gene Mearns, "Shaw Suite Against Garrison May Provide Means for High Court to Consider Probe," UPI, July 3, 1968.

August 7, 1968

The Republicans just nominated Richard Nixon for
president. This proves anything is possible.
After losing an election for California governor
six years ago, Nixon swore he was done with
politics.

Mason was referring to Nixon's now famous closing statement at a
November 7, 1962, press conference when he blamed the media for his
disappointing loss to incumbent governor Edmond G. "Pat" Brown.
"You don't have Nixon to kick around anymore, because, gentlemen,
this is my last press conference."[225] Equally amazing was how Nixon
positioned himself as the centrist candidate between the more liberal
New York governor Nelson Rockefeller and his conservative
counterpart California governor Ronald Reagan. Both, however, would
outlast Nixon's political career. Rockefeller as Gerald Ford's vice
president following Nixon's resignation and Reagan as president from
1981 to 1989.

On the Democratic side, Senators Eugene McCarthy and George
McGovern faced off during the remaining primaries for the votes that
likely would have gone to Kennedy. Vice President Hubert Humphrey
chose a different path, skipping the primaries to court delegates chosen
by the party leaders in each state, those we now refer to as
"superdelegates."

August 30, 1968

As predicted, Democrats nominated Hubert Humphrey
as their presidential nominee.

I believe this could be the end of the
Kennedy/Johnson era. Street violence in Chicago,
protests inside the convention hall and the
party's failure to unite behind Humphrey make a
Nixon win in November likely.

---

[225] Gladwin Hill, "Nixon Denounces Press as Biased," *New York Times*, November 8,
1962, p. 20.

November 5, 1968

Nixon will be the next president after beating
Humphrey and Alabama Governor George Wallace. The
election turned out to be much closer than
expected. Wallace did surprisingly well for a
third party candidate, winning 46 electoral votes
in five southern states.

Humphrey's quest for the presidency seemed hopeless in October. An October 9 Gallop poll had the Democrat trailing Nixon by 16 percentage points (45-29) and only nine points ahead of Wallace (29-20). In what appeared to be a desperation move, Humphrey went on the attack. First, he called out Wallace as a bigot. He added "reckless" to the list of disqualifying factors when Wallace chose retired general Curtis LeMay as his running mate. LeMay made headlines at his introductory press conference when *Los Angeles Times* reporter Jack Nelson asked if he would consider using nuclear weapons to end the Vietnam war. LeMay ended his response, "I would use anything we could dream up, anything we could dream up—including nuclear weapons if necessary."[226] The impact on Wallace's campaign was immediate. Subsequent polls signaled a significant migration of Wallace supporters to Humphrey.

Next, Humphrey took on his own boss. He called for a halt to the carpet bombing in Southeast Asia and suggested the U.S. consider peace talks. Johnson followed Humphrey's lead, ordering cessation of the bombing and suggested peace talks were imminent. This policy shift had a secondary benefit when McCarthy endorsed Humphrey after claiming he never would.

The gap closed but not enough. Humphrey trailed Nixon in the popular vote by just over a half million ballots which translated into a 301-191 electoral college victory for the Republican candidate. This slim margin might have vanished but for Nixon's inappropriate tampering in the Vietnam peace negotiations. The "new" Nixon had not shed his "tricky Dick" reputation. He promised Vietnam president Nguyen Van Thieu a better deal if he refused to attend peace talks before the election, a

---

[226] Rick Perlstein, *Nixonland: The Rise of a President and the Fracturing of America,* Scribner, New York, 2008, p. 349.

precursor of questionable behavior that would eventually force Nixon to resign in August 1974.[227]

Following the presidential election, Mason's attention returned to the Shaw trial in New Orleans.

```
December 10, 1968

The Supreme Court refused to hear Shaw's appeal
of the district court decision to deny a change
of venue and said Judge Haggerty could set a new
trial date.
```

The following day, Garrison announced jury selection would begin on January 21 as he did not want the trial to overlap with events surrounding Richard Nixon's inauguration.

```
January 21, 1969

Two years after Clay Shaw was arrested, jury
selection for his trial finally began.
```

On the eve of the trial there was one more surprise to come. On January 16, in a reversal of roles, the prosecution asked Judge Haggerty for an indefinite delay. Assistant DA James Alcock, whom Garrison designated as lead counsel for the trial, claimed outgoing attorney general Ramsey Clark undercut their case against Shaw.

On January 15, Clark released a statement that a panel of experts examined the Kennedy autopsy report and confirmed the Warren Commission's opinion that all the bullets fired at the president came from above and behind the motorcade. Following a hearing before Judge Haggerty, Alcock dropped the motion stating he would "trust the good judgment, common sense and spirit which the state feels prevails among the people of New Orleans."[228]

---

[227] Ibid., p. 708.
[228] Bill Crider, "Shaw Trial Begins," Associated Press, January 21, 1969.

```
February 1, 1969

Shaw trial jury selection completed.
```

As had been the case in Jack Ruby's trial, profiles of the 12 jurors were released to the public. A UPI summary described the panel as all-male with three Negroes and only two college graduates.[229]

```
March 1, 1969

Jury finds Shaw not guilty. As with Ruby, this
trial got no closer to the truth. I should be
relieved. But Garrison seems determined to
continue his fight to disprove the Warren
Commission conclusions. I am sure there will be
others.
```

This saga did not, however, end with Shaw's acquittal. In February 1970, Shaw filed a civil suit against Garrison and others who he alleged prosecuted him in bad faith. On May 27, 1971, after three days of testimony and presentation of exhibits, a Louisiana district court issued a permanent injunction "restraining Jim Garrison, District Attorney for the Parish of Orleans, his assistants, employees, agents and all persons in active concert and participation with him from further prosecution of the pending criminal action."[230]

Garrison challenged the decision before the state appeals court and eventually in the United States District Court in Louisiana. At the time of Clay Shaw's death on August 15, 1974, the federal trial had been scheduled for the following November. On March 4, 1975, Chief Judge Frederick Heebe declared Garrison had failed to provide evidence to overturn the state court's ruling and ordered damages be paid to Shaw's estate.

The journal contains just three more brief entries before Mason turned to Richard Nixon and Watergate. All involved the fate of the men charged with Robert Kennedy's and Martin Luther King's murders.

---

[229] "Shaw Jury Names," UPI, February 2, 1969.
[230] *Shaw v. Garrison, et al*, Opinion by Chief Judge Frederick Heebe, United States District Court of Louisiana, March 4, 1975.

March 10, 1969

James Earl Ray pled guilty to murdering Martin
Luther King. In return for his guilty plea, the
prosecution offered Ray a sentence of 99 years
without parole in a state prison. If the case had
gone to trial, Ray would have faced a potential
death sentence.

Despite accepting the plea deal, Ray suggested "…others may have taken part in the April 4, 1968, sniper slaying of the Nobel peace prizewinner."[231] Three days later Ray attempted to retract his guilty plea. Until his death in 1998, Ray pursued a retrial. Among his most ardent advocates were Dr. King's family.

That same year Dr. King's widow Coretta Scott King urged President Bill Clinton to reopen the investigation into her husband's murder. Clinton referred the request to attorney general Janet Reno, who asked civil rights special counsel Barry Kowalski to review whether there was any evidence of a conspiracy. Kowalski's *bona fides* included successful prosecution of two Los Angeles police officers for the 1993 beating of Rodney King. After an 18-month inquiry, Kowalski concluded:

> *Our thorough investigation, just like four official
> investigations before it, found no credible or reliable evidence
> that Dr. King was killed by conspirators who framed James
> Earl Ray. Twenty years later, I remain absolutely convinced
> this well-supported finding is correct.*

The following month a Los Angeles jury decided Sirhan Sirhan's fate.

April 17, 1969

Sirhan was convicted of first-degree murder in
the death of Robert Kennedy. The jury will later
decide Sirhan's sentence of life in prison or
death.

---

[231] UPI, "James Ray Enters Plea of Guilty in Dr. King Slaying," March 10, 1969.

```
April 23, 1969

    Sirhan was sentenced to death in the gas chamber.
    However, there is an unofficial ban on executions
    in California. Even if the ban is lifted, appeals
    could delay carrying out the sentence for years.
```

According to Sirhan's chief defense counsel Grant B. Cooper, his client was not surprised at the trial's outcome. As they walked from the courtroom to a temporary holding cell, Cooper claimed Sirhan thanked his lawyers for doing the best they could, then added, "Even Jesus Christ couldn't have saved me."[232] On June 16, 1972, the California Supreme Court reduced Sirhan's death sentence to life imprisonment in compliance with an earlier ruling in which the Court abolished capital punishment.

Mason then set aside his typewriter for more than three years. Did he originally intend to conclude his narrative after the assassinations of King and Robert Kennedy? To test this theory, I went back to the November 22, 1973, entry. Could it have been drafted at an earlier date, then revised when Mason picked up the narrative on June 18, 1972?

There are only two references to events which took place after April 1969. One, a single sentence that adds George Wallace to the list of "copycat" assaults, possibly inspired by Oswald's and Ruby's success.

```
    Or even the recent attempt on Governor Wallace in
    Maryland?
```

The possibility Mason's mention of the Alabama governor was an afterthought is buttressed by his omission of any other reference to Wallace's May 15, 1972, shooting by Arthur Bremer during a presidential campaign stop in Laurel, Maryland.

---

[232] Douglas Robinson, "Sirhan Sentenced to Gas Chamber on 5th Jury Vote," *New York Times*, April 24, 1969, p. 1.

The second, a standalone paragraph in which Mason shares his hope Watergate is the national distraction which might forever keep the TEAM's secret from being discovered.

```
The country's obsession with the Kennedy
assassination has shifted to Watergate. America
has moved on. Maybe it is time I do the same.
```

As a separate paragraph or the last sentence of another, both could have easily been appended to an earlier version. However, without Mason's input, this becomes just one more aspect of his journal that remains a mystery.

There is one more clue the November 22, 1973, entry may have been drafted shortly following Sirhan's conviction and sentencing. This time, however, it is not what he wrote, but what he omitted. During Mason's three-year hiatus there were two major events directly tied to the Kennedy legacy. First came the successful moon landing on July 20, 1969. However, consistent with the "good news, bad news" nature of any Kennedy achievement, three days following the launch of Apollo 11, the president's youngest brother Edward was involved in the car accident which resulted in the death of the senator's aide Mary Jo Kopechne.

Although a grand jury failed to indict Kennedy, a judicial inquest characterized his actions as negligent, if not reckless, and the presiding judge James A. Boyle questioned the truthfulness of his sworn testimony.[233] Robert Kennedy was dead. Ted Kennedy's political future was on hold due to this latest scandal. Much like the emotional gut punch many felt following John Lennon's death, the dream of a Kennedy dynasty and return to Camelot appeared shattered forever.

If Mason initially planned to maintain the journal after April 23, 1969, he surely would have acknowledged both the moon landing and Chappaquiddick.

---

[233] Joseph Lelyveld, "Kennedy Veracity Questioned by Judge in Kopechne Inquest," *New York Times,* April 30, 1970, p. 1.

CHAPTER TWENTY

THE SHINY NEW OBJECT

In the short term, Mason's fear there would be other investigations and trials proved incorrect. Garrison's failure to prove his case and Shaw's successful civil litigation discouraged others from pursuing their own conspiracy theories in court. It did not, however, stop journalists and conspiracy aficionados from presenting other alternative scenarios. Though none received the attention of Mark Lane's *Rush to Judgment*.

Just as interest in the Kennedy assassination began to wane, the nation's curiosity was piqued by a new political scandal.

June 18, 1972

This morning I got a call from Scarecrow. He asked if I had seen this morning's Washington Post. I immediately thought someone had uncovered new evidence which might eventually expose us. Except Scarecrow's tone of voice suggested something less serious, more like 'you're not going to believe this.'

It seems five men were arrested Saturday night in the offices of the Democratic National Committee. They were trying to bug the office of DNC chairman Lawrence O'Brien. But that was not what caught Scarecrow's attention. The Post says one of the arrested men is a former CIA employee, three were Cuban and the fifth had a connection to the Bay of Pigs invasion.

> As he read the front-page article to me,
> Scarecrow could not help but laugh. Cuba again?
> Not very original. And they were carrying over
> two thousand dollars in sequenced $100 bills.
> It's a good thing we were not that careless.
>
> The five suspects were arraigned this afternoon
> and released on bond. No motive was given but one
> of them described their group as anti-Communists.
> A DNC official thought it had something to do
> with the upcoming national convention in Miami
> since several were from south Florida.

Why did Mason choose this day to restart the journal? After all, the last entry was dated more than three years earlier. My first memory of the Watergate scandal had not been so vivid. I was a graduate student in Baltimore, Maryland at the time. Our morning paper, the *Baltimore Sun*, had only a brief mention of the break-in on an inside page.

I pulled the article Scarecrow referenced from the *Post's* archive. The first thing I noticed was the by-line. The reporter was Alfred E. Lewis. Then unknown city desk reporters Carl Bernstein and Bob Woodward were listed as contributors at the end of the article. Lewis' 15 minutes of Watergate fame resulted from his lifetime as a police reporter. He was described in his 1994 obituary as "half cop, half reporter."[234] It was, therefore, no surprise he penned the initial Watergate article with its emphasis on the arraignment of the five men arrested early the previous morning in the offices of the Democratic National Committee.[235]

If nothing else, this offered one more opportunity to affirm or reject the journal's veracity. Either the initial accounts of the break-in were more detailed than I recalled, or Mason had recreated the Watergate timeline with information which was unavailable on June 18.

---

[234] Martin Weil, "Legendary Police Reporter Alfred E. Lewis Dies," *Washington Post*, May 4, 1994.
[235] Alfred E. Lewis, "5 Held in Plot to Bug Democrats' Office Here," *Washington Post*, June 18, 1972, p. A1.

June 19, 1972

Today, the Post reported the former CIA employee
arrested in the DNC break-in worked for Nixon's
reelection committee. He had been hired to
install the security system for the GOP offices.
That cannot be a coincidence though John
Mitchell, Nixon's campaign manager, denied any
knowledge of the operation.

The article also suggests the operation involved
more than the five men under arrest. Still no
motive.

The June 19 *Post* article, the first attributed to Woodward and Bernstein, corroborates Mason's account and provides brief profiles of the five detainees. James McCord, the former CIA employee to whom Mason refers, established his own "security consulting firm" after 19 years with the CIA. He was also a colonel in the Air Force Reserve.[236]

August 1, 1972

Watergate may prove to be a textbook example how
not to conduct a covert operation. Today, the
Post reported a $25,000 cashier's check made out
to the finance chairman of Nixon's reelection
committee was deposited in the bank account of
one of the Watergate burglars. Imagine if a large
amount of money had turned up in Oswald's or
Ruby's bank account. All it takes is one mistake
to blow a cover story. These folks seem to have
made more than their share.

Again, the *Post* report matches Mason's journal. Yet it still lacks definitive proof of the document's contemporaneous nature. Recreating an accurate account of the Watergate chronology could just as easily been accomplished by trolling the *Post* archives. After all, that is how I verified each of Mason's Watergate-related journal entries.

There is one critical difference. In 1973, *Post* coverage of Watergate existed only in the newspaper's morgue or on microfiche, neither of

---

[236] Bob Woodward and Carl Bernstein, "GOP Security Aide Among Five Arrested in Bugging Affair," *Washington Post*, June 19, 1972, p. 1.

which was searchable. I had the advantage of a digital resource in which the *Post* provided a chronological listing of Watergate-related articles beginning with Lewis' June 19, 1973, story about the arraignment of McCord and the other burglars. It ended with the death of the last surviving principal, Nixon's director of communications Herbert Klein, on July 4, 2009. Each listing included a hyperlink to the referenced article.

While it was possible Mason might have recreated the sequence based on the *Post's* reporting, it would have required a Herculean effort without the now available digital resource.

```
August 9, 1972

John Mitchell is looking for a scapegoat for the
Watergate break-in. Today the Post reported
several campaign officials are pointing the
finger at someone named Gordon Liddy who served
as finance counsel for the reelection committee.

Why am I so obsessed with this story? Is it a
distraction from the guilt I still feel about
Dallas?

September 22, 1972

This is the fourth time in five days there has
been a front-page Watergate story by Bernstein
and Woodward. This is good for our team.
Conspiracy theorists now have a new obsession.
```

Put together, the last two entries raise and answer the question about Mason's interest in Watergate. As the scandal unravels, Mason sees how it increasingly redirects the nation's attention away from Dallas. And for a brief period, from September until November, he lets go of his own lingering preoccupation with the assassination.

```
November 7, 1972

Nixon was reelected despite Watergate. Maybe it
was much ado about nothing.
```

The *Washington Post* also moved Watergate to the back burner. No more front-page articles. Carl Bernstein returned to his former status as a city desk reporter covering the December 6, 1972, homicide of a District of Columbia school teacher Dorothy Duncan.[237]

```
December 10, 1972

The Post is reporting one of the seven area
residents who died in Saturday's plane crash in
Chicago was the wife of Watergate burglar Howard
Hunt. The article said she had been subpoenaed by
the federal grand jury investigating the
Watergate break-in and was fired from her job as
a translator and speech writer because of the
publicity.
```

If Dorothy Hunt's name was on the plane's manifest, why did it take three days to confirm she was the wife of one of the Watergate burglars? One explanation was the fact that initial news reports focused on another more notable passenger, Illinois Congressman George W. Collins. He was the first victim mentioned in the *Chicago Tribune's* front page story followed by a lengthy obituary on page four.[238]

```
December 14, 1972

Dorothy Hunt's obituary in today's Times refers
to $10,000 she was carrying with her on the
plane. Nothing about that was reported in the
Post. How could they have missed it?

It is hard to believe someone would take down a
plane, killing innocent people, to silence Hunt.
Then again, I doubt anyone would believe John
Kennedy ordered his own assassination.
```

Howard Hunt told the *Times* the money was "intended for a business investment in the Chicago area…that Mrs. Hunt was taking the money

---

[237] Carl Bernstein, *Washington Post*, December 7, 1972.
[238] George Tagge, "Rep. Collins, Crash Victim, Mourned," *Chicago Tribune*, December 9, 1972, p. 4.

for delivery to Harold Carlstead, a certified public accountant who was married to her cousin."[239]

```
May 18, 1973

Today a Senate select committee will hold its
first public hearing on possible misconduct by
Nixon's re-election committee.
```

Three events precipitated February 7, 1973, passage by unanimous vote of Senate Resolution 60 creating a Senate Select Committee on Presidential Campaign Activities. District Judge John Sirica, who presided over the January 1973 trial of the seven Watergate burglars, openly shared his concern there must be more to the story. Detailed reporting in the *Washington Post* by Woodward and Bernstein uncovered several possible links to Nixon's re-election committee. As these alleged connections between those involved in the break-in and the Committee to Re-Elect the President emerged, the FBI opened its own investigation sending a message that Nixon's own Department of Justice believed there was potential wrongdoing.

Opening statements by the chair, North Carolina Senator Sam Ervin, and the other members signaled how seriously the panel viewed the Committee's mission. They scheduled televised hearings as a way to ensure transparency and generate public interest. Although, according to *Washington Post* reporter Jules Witcover, each member of the panel warned the public "…that the investigation doesn't intend to sacrifice thoroughness—or, when necessary, even boredom—for sensationalism, just to hold the TV audience."[240]

```
May 19, 1973

Elliot Richardson, Nixon's nominee to be attorney
general, says he plans to appoint Archibald Cox
as special prosecutor to investigate Watergate if
confirmed by the Senate. Cox, a member of
Harvard's law faculty, said he will accept.
```

---

[239] "Watergate Figure's Dead Wife Had $10,000 to Invest, He Says," *New York Times,* December 11, 1972, p. 33.
[240] Jules Witcover, "The First Day of Watergate: Not Exactly High Drama," *Washington Post*, May 18, 1973, p. 1.

Again, Mason provides the barest description of the day's news with no commentary. Although he does not mention it, Nixon supported the idea of a special prosecutor. The president hoped his endorsement would convince his detractors he too wanted to see anyone involved in campaign misconduct identified and held accountable.

Mason's cut and dry account of Watergate ended on July 13, 1973. If the Select Committee preferred thoroughness over sensationalism, as Witcover reported after the first hearing, America got a taste of both less than a month later.

July 13, 1973

Today is one of those days when I continue to worry our secret will never be totally safe. You never know what is out there or who knows it. Nixon must have assumed no one would disclose the existence of a taping system in the Oval Office. But that is what happened. Haldeman's former deputy Alexander Butterfield was being questioned during the Senate Watergate Hearings when asked about the accuracy of some of the comments by previous witnesses. The staff first asked if people took notes in any of the Oval Office meetings. He said he did not know. He was then asked about John Dean's previous testimony. Dean had suggested he may have been recorded. Butterfield just confirmed it.

I never saw a room empty so quickly. Until this morning, it was Nixon's word against those who accused him of possible crimes. Taped conversation should determine who is telling the truth.

Is there something or someone that could do the same to us?

Mason's concern about a minor player making the difference in a government scandal proved to be well-founded. Butterfield, a relatively unknown individual, changed the Watergate conversation in a matter of minutes. He was not even a White House employee at the time of the disclosure. In March 1973, after serving three years as Haldeman's deputy, he left his White House position to become head of the Federal Aviation Administration.

There was no advance notice of the bombshell Butterfield was about to deliver. Several members of the Senate select committee later admitted they had no inkling of what was to come. Committee staff and Republicans on the panel orchestrated disclosure of the Oval Office recording system on Monday, July 16, 1973. As Butterfield took his seat at the witness table, majority counsel Sam Dash deferred to minority counsel Fred Thompson.

> MR. DASH: Mr. Chairman, at a staff interview with Mr. Butterfield on Friday, some significant information was elicited and was attended by the majority members of the staff and the minority members. The information was elicited by a minority staff member. Therefore, I would like to change the usual routine of the questioning and ask minority counsel to begin the questioning of Mr. Butterfield.[241]

Immediately after learning of the recording system on July 13, staff scheduled Butterfield's appearance before the full committee for the next session the following Monday. The hurriedness with which the hearing schedule was changed to get this information before the committee members and the public is contained in Butterfield's one-sentence opening remarks.

> MR. BUTTERFIELD: Although I do not have a statement as such, I would simply like to remind the committee membership that whereas I appear voluntarily this afternoon, I appear with only three hours notice and without time to arrange for permanent counsel or for assistance by a temporary counsel.[242]

Nixon would not resign for another year. There is no doubt, however, Butterfield's testimony about the White House tapes foreshadowed the end of his tenure as president. Every national newspaper and network evening news program led with the latest update. At first, reports focused on Nixon's assertion the taped conversations were protected

---

[241] "Excerpts from Testimony Before the Senate Committee Investigation Watergate," *New York Times*, July 17, 1973, pp. 28-29
[242] Ibid., pp. 28-29

under a president's right to withhold confidential communications from the judiciary and legislature. In his next journal entry, Mason cites Nixon's claim of what is now referred to as "executive privilege," but does not use that specific term.

```
August 15, 1973

Pressure is growing for Nixon to release the
tapes. He went on TV tonight to respond to the
findings of the Senate Watergate committee. While
he acknowledged abuses by members of his campaign
staff, he claimed he had no prior knowledge of
their actions and promised to get to the bottom
of any criminal activity.

He also announced he would not give the tapes to
the Senate committee.
```

While not invoking the term "executive privilege," Nixon did describe the importance of confidentiality between a president and his advisors.

Each day a President of the United States is required to make difficult decisions on grave issues. It is absolutely necessary, if the President is to be able to do his job as the country expects, that he be able to talk openly and candidly with his advisors about issues and individuals. This kind of frank discussion is only possible when those who take part in it know that what they say is in strictest confidence.[243]

Presidential entitlement to confidential advice dates back to George Washington, but the first use of the term "executive privilege" is attributed to Dwight Eisenhower. He invoked the phrase when he instructed cabinet members not to share conversations related to the McCarthy-Army hearings. The expression lay dormant until once again applied to Nixon.

From this point on, until the final entry on November 22, 1973, Mason does little except note major milestones as the Nixon administration unravels. I can only speculate why. The most likely explanation being

---

[243] "Transcript of President's Speech to the Nation in Answer to Watergate Charges," *New York Times,* August 16, 1973, p. 24.

the extent of media coverage. The journal's original purpose was to tell a story no one else could produce. That was unnecessary when it came to Watergate with daily updates in every major newspaper, nightly news broadcasts and televised hearings.

```
October 10, 1973

Vice president Spiro Agnew pleads guilty to a
single count of tax evasion and resigns. Who will
Nixon nominate to replace him? Will he use this
opportunity to impair the Watergate
investigation? What if that had been LBJ?
```

The reference to President Johnson presents an important distinction between presidential succession in 1973 and 1963. Prior to ratification of the Twenty-Fifth Amendment in February 1967, there was no provision for filling a vacancy in the vice-presidency. If Lyndon Johnson had died before his inauguration to a full-term in January 1965, 71-year-old House Speaker John McCormack would have become the nation's commander-in-chief. In one more example of historical synchronicity, McCormack died on November 22, 1980, the 17th anniversary of the assassination.

In contrast, as Mason notes in the next entry, the search for Agnew's successor began immediately, setting the stage for one more anomaly in presidential history. Within a year, Gerald Ford would become the only occupant of the Oval Office without ever having been elected either president or vice-president.

```
October 12, 1973

Nixon nominated House minority leader Gerald Ford
to replace Agnew.
```

Ford emerged as the safe choice, likely to be approved by an overwhelming majority in both houses of Congress due to his personal relationships with both Republicans and Democrats. As expected, the Senate confirmed his nomination on November 27, 1973, by a vote of 92-3, followed on December 6 by a House vote of 387-35. Nixon may not have realized it at the time but replacing Agnew with the more popular Ford may have made his impeachment more likely. According to senior advisor John Ehrlichman, Nixon once described his first vice-president as akin to an insurance policy. "No assassin in his right mind would kill me. They know that if they did, they would end up with Agnew."[244] Images of Agnew behind the Resolute Desk would be equally abhorrent in the case of impeachment and conviction.

In contrast, Nixon saw Ford as an asset who could marshal his legislative agenda through Congress and shift the public's attention away from Watergate. According to *New York Times* reporter John Herbers, "The nomination of Gerald R. Ford, the House minority leader, as Vice President was expected to help President Nixon restore some of the power and prestige that his Administration lost as the result of scandals and crimes involving high Nixon officials."[245]

Based on his own actions, Nixon assured that would not happen. Following news of the tapes' existence, Judge Sirica ordered Nixon to turn them over so he could determine which conversations were relevant to the special prosecutor's investigation. The White House appealed Sirica's decision to the District Court of Appeals which affirmed the lower court ruling.

> October 19, 1973
>
> Nixon again tried to prevent release of his taped conversations. He offered to submit a summary of the tapes, verified by Mississippi Senator John Stennis, to the special prosecutor. Cox rejected the compromise and suggested he would bring the matter to the Supreme Court.

In a public statement on the afternoon of October 19, Cox explained his decision and his intent to continue pursuing White House compliance with rulings by the district court and court of appeals.

> *In my judgment, the President is refusing to comply with the court decrees. A summary of the content of the tapes lacks the evidentiary value of the tapes themselves. No steps are being*

---

[244] Ron Brodman, "Ehrlichman on the Nixon Years," *Washington Post*, December 14, 1981.

[245] John Herbers, "Choice of Ford Expected to Help Nixon Gain Power and Heighten '76 Competition," *New York Times*, October 14, 1973, p. 46.

taken to turn over the important notes, memoranda and other documents that the court orders require. I shall bring these points to the attention of the [Supreme] Court and abide by its decision.[246]

In response to Cox's defiance, Nixon then made a move that undercut what, up to that point, had been his almost unanimous backing by Republican members of Congress.

```
October 21, 1973

Last night Nixon ordered his attorney general to
fire Cox. Richardson resigned saying he would not
violate the promise he made during his
confirmation hearings that the Watergate special
prosecutor could operate independent of
presidential influence. Deputy attorney general
Ruckelshaus also resigned when asked to fire Cox.
Solicitor general Robert Bork finally carried out
Nixon's order.
```

After dismissing Cox, Nixon instructed the FBI to seal the offices of Richardson, Ruckelshaus and the special prosecutor. He also announced that further investigation and prosecution of criminal behavior under the Watergate umbrella would be the sole purview of the Department of Justice.

The events of October 20 became known as the "Saturday Night Massacre." The label first appeared in print on October 22 in "The Last Roll of the Dice? Nixon Political Clout Shrinks," an article by *Washington Post* political reporter David Broder. However, Broder introduces the term with the phrase "…what is being called," acknowledgement he did not coin the expression. The exact origin of "Saturday Night Massacre" remains a mystery, though several Washington insiders recall hearing it that same Saturday night at humorist Art Buchwald's birthday party at the Arlington, Virginia YMCA, though Buchwald never personally took credit.[247]

---

[246] John M. Crewdson, "Prosecutor Firm," *New York Times*, October 20, 1973, p. 16.
[247] Amy B. Wang, "Who coined 'Saturday Night Massacre?' A birthday party at a YMCA may hold the key," *Washington Post*, May 12, 2017.

For Richard Nixon, reactions to the Cox dismissal and the resignations at Justice were anything but humorous. They did not sit well with Democrats and Republicans alike.

> *Senior members of both parties in the House of Representatives were reported to be seriously discussing impeachment of the President because of his refusal to obey an order by the United States Court of Appeals that he turn over to the courts tape recordings of conversations about the Watergate case, and because of Mr. Nixon's dismissal of Mr. Cox.*[248]

November 1, 1973

Today, Nixon tried to counter all the talk of impeachment. He announced the appointment of Leon Jaworski as the new special prosecutor.

This proved to be one occasion when I found a minor error in Mason's journal. It was acting attorney general Bork who made the announcement with Nixon's approval. Bork went on to claim "Jaworski would have 'complete freedom' and the same mandate and guidelines to investigate wrongdoing in the Administration that Mr. Cox had before he was dismissed by the President on October 20."[249]

November 21, 1973

Jaworski informed Judge Sirica of a gap in a taped conversation between Nixon and Haldeman. Sirica used this new disclosure to again demand Nixon immediately turn over the original tapes.

This represented a change of heart by the district judge. According to the *New York Times*, Sirica had previously determined the tapes could remain in White House custody until the Supreme Court ruled on the special prosecutor's request. Sirica now felt the tapes needed to be examined by an expert panel for possible evidence of tampering.

---

[248] Douglas E. Kneeland, "Bork Takes Over," *New York Times*, October 21, 1973, p. 1.

[249] John Herbers, "Nixon Names Saxbe Attorney General; Jaworski Appointed Special Prosecutor," *New York Times*, November 2, 1973, p. 1.

> *Judge Sirica said he was taking the step "not because the*
> *court doesn't trust the White House or the President," but "in*
> *the interest of seeing that nothing else happens" to the still-*
> *secret tapes.*[250]

If took several more months to resolve the dispute over release of the tapes. In *United States v. Nixon,* by unanimous vote, the Supreme Court ruled general applicability of executive privilege does not extend to evidence in a criminal proceeding. Speaking for the Court on July 24, 1974, Chief Justice Warren Burger wrote:

> *In this case, we must weigh the importance of the general*
> *privilege of confidentiality of Presidential communications in*
> *performance of the President's responsibilities against the*
> *inroads of such a privilege on the fair administration of*
> *criminal justice. The interest in preserving confidentiality is*
> *weighty indeed, and entitled to great respect. However, we*
> *cannot conclude that advisers will be moved to temper the*
> *candor of their remarks by the infrequent occasions of*
> *disclosure because of the possibility that such conversations*
> *will be called for in the context of a criminal prosecution.*[251]

Some may wonder why Mason did not follow the Watergate story through to Nixon's resignation on August 8, 1974. I do not. The appointment of Leon Jaworski as the new special prosecutor provided a momentary bump in the president's support. Disclosure of the 18-minute gap in the June 20 recording of a critical conversation between Nixon and Haldeman nullified any goodwill associated with Jaworski's hiring. Once Judge Sirica ordered Nixon to turn the tapes over to the district court "for safekeeping," Mason must have assumed Nixon's fate was sealed.

---

[250] George Lardner, Jr., "Another Tape Found Faulty, Sirica Is Told; Haldeman, Nixon Talk Is Involved," *Washington Post,* November 22, 1973, p. 1.
[251] Opinion of Chief Justice Warren Burger, *United States v. Nixon,* 418 U.S. 683, July 24, 1974, p. 418.

He would not be wrong. The nine months between disclosure of the gap in the June 20 tape and Nixon's resignation on August 8, 1974, seemed like an eternity. In hindsight, the dominos started falling in rapid succession.

Mason's chronicle, with the addition of the final entry on November 22, 1973, had come to an end. He accomplished what he set out to achieve, documenting what he claimed to be the actual account of the Kennedy assassination. My work remained unfinished. Would evidence emerge in the succeeding years that could shed additional light on the journal's authenticity?

CHAPTER TWENTY-ONE

THE TORCH IS PASSED

Let the word go forth from this time and place, to friend and foe alike, that the torch has been passed to a new generation of Americans.

~John F. Kennedy, January 20, 1961

Carl Jung's theory of synchronicity is grounded in his belief there are no such things as coincidences. Our amazement when two seemingly unrelated events become elements of the same story lies less in their rarity than in our willingness to seek them out. Was I destined to complete what Mason had started? After reading the penultimate entry in his journal, the timing of his final post made sense.

The November 21, 1973, entry provided the rationale. Once Mason was convinced the American public had adopted Watergate as its focus of political intrigue, it was time to move on to the next stage of his life. And once he shut the door, he had no desire or need to track the process or findings of each additional probe into Kennedy's death.

Carl Jung would have argued, my role in this narrative was something more than a chance intersection between two individuals. At the same time Mason was winding down his 10-year memoir, I was in the process of selecting a topic for my doctoral dissertation. As an undergraduate political science major, my primary interest had been the electoral process. In graduate school, my interests turned to the three constitutional branches of the federal government.

The first challenge doctoral candidates face when it comes to a dissertation, their final academic hurdle, requires selecting a topic that adds to their chosen discipline's knowledge base. In other words, it must be unique and previously unexamined. One means to accomplish this goal is to pick up on a common theme and update it based on current events. The year was 1974. A literature search revealed little attention paid to the impact on congressional behavior following two major political events in the immediate past, Kennedy's assassination and Richard Nixon's resignation.

I retrieved a copy of my dissertation, placed it next to Mason's journal and flipped to the title page. The document had been produced on an IBM Selectric© typewriter with a courier font ball, similar to the ones the TEAM found on their desks when they first entered the command center at the Naval Annex.[252]

```
                  CRISIS AND CHANGE:
        COALITIONS IN THE UNITED STATES SENATE
      FROM THE KENNEDY ASSASSINATION TO WATERGATE
```

I took another look at the journal's title page. No question this was the kind of non-coincidence Jung urged each of us to step toward.

```
                  Personal Journal
            Special Agent  ███████████
            United States Secret Service
       December 4, 1962   November 22, 1973
```

The time frames were indistinguishable. Had some cosmic force intervened? One that could not be discounted or ignored?

Jung would argue my fate was cast. Even without prior knowledge of the effort Mason expended on his journal, there were other unfathomable agents at work. At their direction, I found myself more obsessed with the Kennedy assassination than someone who had been there. I had no choice but to pick up the mantle.

As Mason so aptly described it, Watergate was America's shiny new object. This redirection of the nation's attention gave Mason good

---

[252] "Courier" typeface was created for IBM typewriters by Howard Kettler (1919-1999) and first appeared in 1955.

reason to believe the truth about the TEAM and the ASSIGNMENT was now safe. Interest in debunking the Warren Commission findings or promoting alternative theories was overshadowed by televised Senate hearings, the drafting of articles of impeachment by the House Judiciary Committee and the trials of John Mitchell, H. R. Haldeman and John Ehrlichman.

Declining interest in publications and analysis about the Kennedy assassination supported Mason's new-found confidence. America now viewed Dallas in its rearview mirror. In the eight years following release of the Warren Commission report, bookstores were flooded with new volumes criticizing the commission's findings or promoting alternative theories why and how Kennedy was killed. The number reached a peak of 19 in 1967. During the height of Watergate, 1972-74, that number dropped to three.

What appeared to be the end of the Kennedy saga proved only a hiatus. Four months after Nixon's resignation, the nation's attention returned to the Kennedy assassination, prompted by the March 6, 1975, episode of ABC's *Good Night America,* with host Geraldo Rivera. Rivera's guests were assassination conspiracy theorist Robert Groden and comedian Dick Gregory. The defining moment came when Groden screened a copy of Abraham Zapruder's 8mm home movie, including the graphic sequence when Kennedy's skull exploded from the impact of the assassin's bullet. Previously, the public had only seen still frames published in the November 25, 1966, issue of *Life Magazine.*

The two-fold response was immediate and predictable. Many viewers and critics expressed outrage, questioning the appropriateness of airing the horror of a bullet striking the president's head. More importantly, images of the extreme backward motion of Kennedy's head upon the bullet's contact revived speculation about a second shooter and generated a new round of demands for release of classified evidence.

Under increased pressure to reopen the inquiry, both houses of Congress called for new investigations into Kennedy's murder. Two months prior to the ABC broadcast, *New York Times* reporter Seymour Hersh produced a detailed account of covert actions by the U.S. intelligence community raising questions about CIA surveillance of

American citizens and attempts to assassinate foreign leaders.[253] On January 27, 1975, the U.S. Senate, by a vote of 82-4, authorized creation of a Select Committee to Study Governmental Operations with Respect to Intelligence Activities, chaired by Idaho Senator Frank Church.

The inquiry revealed, at the time of Kennedy's assassination, the CIA engaged in efforts to take down Cuban president Fidel Castro. Public disclosure of the operation, code named AMLASH, raised the obvious question. Was Dallas revenge for the failed attempts on the life of the Cuban dictator? Lee Harvey Oswald's connections to both Russia and Cuba added fuel to speculation he may have been acting on behalf of a foreign government to even the score.

On May 26, 1976, the Church Committee released an "on the one-hand, but on the other hand" set of findings concerning the relationship between CIA covert operations and the assassination. Despite information previously unavailable to the Warren Commission, the Committee's report proved equally unsatisfying.

> *The Committee emphasizes that it has not uncovered any evidence sufficient to justify a conclusion that there was a conspiracy to assassinate President Kennedy.*

This general finding was tempered by several caveats.

> *The Committee has, however, developed evidence which impeaches the process by which the intelligence agencies arrived at their own conclusions about the assassination, and by which they provided information to the Warren Commission.*

> *Rather than addressing its investigation to all significant circumstances, including all possibilities of conspiracy, the FBI investigation focused narrowly on Lee Harvey Oswald.*

---

[253] Seymour Hersh, "Huge C.I.A. Operation Reported in U.S. Against Anti-War Forces, Other Dissidents in Nixon Years," *New York Times*, December 22, 1974, pages 1, 26.

*The Committee has found that even with this narrow focus,
the FBI investigation, as well as the CIA inquiry, was
deficient on the specific question of the significance of
Oswald's contacts with pro-Castro and anti-Castro groups
for the many months before the assassination.*[254]

I wondered how Mason reacted to this latest attempt to address the unsettled issues and persistent doubts about November 22, 1963? Was he amused? Relieved? The conclusions outlined in the Church Committee report were akin to an oft-told anecdote about economists. Like those masters of the dismal science, evidence presented before the members and staff of the Church Committee could also be laid end-to-end and they still could not reach a conclusion. Relief would derive from omission of any reference to Secret Service complicity. One more illustration how difficult it is to consider an alternative explanation when it seems so far outside the realm of possibility.

When I dropped by Mason's house that summer, I carefully avoided any appearance the sole reason for my visit was to cross-examine him about the Church Committee findings. Instead, during our conversation on a range of topics, I shared my own opinion of the Committee report.

*JS: I assume you followed the Senate hearings on CIA covert
operations? Except for the revelation about the CIA's efforts
to take out Castro, I'm not sure it clarified anything in the
Warren Commission report.*

MR: Agreed.

*JS: You must have been irritated, as someone charged with
protecting the president when you learned the CIA withheld
information about a potential threat.*

*MR: That's just the way it was. Back then, agencies did not
share a lot of information. Not much has changed. Look at*

---

[254] Final Report: Senate Select Committee to Study Governmental Operations with Respect to Intelligence Activities, Book V: The Investigation of the Assassination of President John F. Kennedy: Performance of the Intelligence Agencies, April 29, 1976, pages 6-7.

Watergate. Prior to release of the White House tape where he orders his staff to let Patrick Gray twist slowly in the wind, Nixon was able to convince the FBI director, at least until Haldeman and Ehrlichman went on trial, that Watergate was justified on grounds of national security. If the CIA and FBI had been free to share information, Nixon's justification for the break-in would have been quickly dismissed.

JS: But if you'd known about the CIA covert operations, would that have made a difference in how the Secret Service prepared for the trip to Dallas?

MR: Probably not. We had our hands full keeping track of locals who made it clear Kennedy was not welcome in their city. Concern about an international conspiracy would have been way down our priority list.

At the time, I had no reason to challenge Mason's implicit endorsement of the Church Committee's findings and recommendations. After all, the Secret Service was unscathed as the preponderance of criticism was directed at the FBI and CIA. The report posed no personal or professional threat to Mason or his colleagues. However, the Church Committee final report, rather than bringing closure to the issue, had the opposite effect.

Once the possibility of a conspiracy was re-introduced, the public appetite for more scrutiny of the Warren Commission Report was insatiable. Despite the 941 pages of documented findings and 25 volumes of transcribed testimony and exhibits, there were just enough questionable assumptions and inconsistencies to trigger an avalanche of new theories about who killed JFK and why. In response, the House of Representatives passed HR 1540 by a 280-65 vote on September 17, 1975, creating "a select committee to conduct an investigation and study of the circumstances surrounding the murders of John F. Kennedy and Martin Luther King, Jr."

Compared to the Senate Committee on Intelligence Operations, this second and last congressional investigation into the Kennedy assassination could have been orchestrated by director Mack Sennett of

Keystone Kops fame. At the outset, the House Select Committee on Assassinations (HSCA) decided not to recall witnesses whose testimony was available in the 16 volumes of transcripts appended to the Warren Commission report. Instead, it focused on evidence resulting from technological advances since the Commission concluded its work. These included ballistics data with emphasis on the credibility of the single-bullet theory, acoustical analysis of a police channel recording which captured gunfire in Dealey Plaza, and photographic evidence, including pictures and x-rays from Kennedy's autopsy as well as images of Lee Harvey Oswald.

Much like the Church Committee's conclusions regarding conspiracy theories, the HSCA final report, released on January 2, 1979, was either a glass half full or half empty depending on the reader's perspective. In support of both the Warren Commission and the Church Committee, the HSCA concluded:

- The shots that killed President Kennedy and wounded Texas Governor John Connolly were fired by Lee Harvey Oswald.
- Despite evidence that should have raised questions about Cuban government motives, there was no evidence of Cuban involvement. Nor Russian involvement.
- Neither the FBI, CIA nor Secret Service were involved in a plot to assassinate the president.

However, committee members refused to rule out the possibility of a conspiracy involving rogue anti-Castro Cubans or individual members of organized crime syndicates. Based on an independent acoustical analysis of a Dallas Police Department's Dictabelt recording as the motorcade worked its way through Dealey Plaza, the Committee established the high probability of a fourth shot which likely came from a second assassin stationed on the "grassy knoll."[255]

When I had the opportunity to discuss this latest investigation with Mason, I decided to take it head on. "It doesn't look like we learned anything new from the House select committee. If anything, they seem

---

[255] "Summary of Findings and Recommendations," Report of the Select Committee on Assassinations of the U.S. House of Representatives, March 29, 1979, pages 1-3.

to have muddied the waters." He simply nodded, bringing an abrupt end to what I hoped would be a longer conversation.

Similarly, I patiently waited to reach out to Mason about attempts to assassinate Presidents Gerald Ford (twice) and Ronald Reagan. In each case, my first instinct was to immediately call Mason to get his opinion. However, I feared such haste would put him on the defensive. I, therefore, made a mental note. The next time we were together I would casually introduce the topic. "By the way, I couldn't help but think about you when I heard about the attempt on President X by assailant Y."

This soft-sell approach worked. Mason's reaction after the failed attempts targeting Gerald Ford on September 5, 1975, by Charles Manson family member Lynnette "Squeaky" Fromme and 17 days later by Sara Jane Moore was surprisingly candid. He made the point that threat assessments in these latest cases replicated the same mistakes he and his colleagues made a decade earlier.

> *MR: It was no different back then. In 1963, the Secret Service almost exclusively focused on lone wolves who had a personal vendetta against a sitting president. After all, the three previous successful presidential murders had been carried out by an actor [Booth and Lincoln], a writer/lawyer who thought he was on a mission from God [Guiteau and Garfield] and an anarchist/steel worker [Czolgosz and McKinley].* [256]

That explained why, even when a person of interest appeared on their radar screen, scrutiny was inadequate, especially in the case of Sara Jane Moore. Moore had come to the attention of the Secret Service in early 1975 but was dismissed as a potential threat. Although she was detained by San Francisco police the day before Ford's arrival and charged with possession of an illegal firearm (.44 caliber revolver and over 100 rounds of ammunition), the incident failed to generate additional scrutiny in anticipation of Ford's visit. [257]

---

[256] James Carney, "How to Make the Secret Service's 'Unwanted List'," *Time Magazine*, August 3, 1998.
[257] Ibid.

Ironically, the occasion on which Mason let slip what might have been the closest indication of his involvement in JFK's murder had nothing to do with protecting a president. It followed the murder of former Beatle John Lennon in December 1980. I returned home to celebrate the holidays with my parents which, as always, included my spending time with Mason. I forget exactly why, but the conversation turned to Lennon and Mark David Chapman. Having taken place more than forty years ago, this is, to the best of my recollection, the conversation which followed his acknowledgement of the musician's death.

> *MR: You must have been devastated when John Lennon was shot. I remember how disappointed you were when the Beatles broke up.*

> *JS: I guess celebrities should have Secret Service-like protection too.*

> *MR: I think they do…now. They're called bodyguards. Not that it would make any difference. That Chapman kid was no different than presidential assassins who slipped through the cracks. He was not a professional killer. He owned a handgun, looked for an opportunity when he could get close to his target and pulled the trigger. Maybe his motive was premeditated but not the murder itself.*

Was this my opportunity to entice Mason to share something he had kept under lock and key for so many years? Would it be my only chance? You could call my desire to have this discussion with Mason premeditated. But here I was, in front of my target. Curiosity was my weapon. My ammunition, a dozen questions. I pulled the metaphorical trigger.

> *JS: I never thought of it that way. Is that why someone like Chapman always gets caught or is killed after the attack? They act on the spur of the moment. And have no plan to escape or what to do next.*

The bolt turned and the vault opened.

MR: Exactly. There are two kinds of assassins. You might call them "Oswalds" and "Rubys." Oswalds think they are going to get away with it. They approach an assassination as if it was a complex task with a checklist. Get to know the target by studying his movements. Carefully survey each potential crime location. Select a vantage point as far as possible from the victim. That often requires a long gun and the skill to hit the target from a distance. Then have a plan to dispose of the weapon and leave the scene of the crime. Oswald tried it twice, once with General Walker and then President Kennedy. Even when they think they got away scot-free, like James Earl Ray, after he murdered Dr. King, they usually still get caught.

For the Rubys of the world, getting caught and sharing their motive are essential. Chapman needed to get caught so he could explain how he was punishing John Lennon for claiming the Beatles were more popular than Jesus Christ. And Jack Ruby wanted everyone to think he did it to save Jacqueline Kennedy from reliving the tragedy during Oswald's trial. It didn't matter if that was the truth or a cover story to hide some other motive.

JS: Makes sense. Did you ever share this with anyone?

MR: Probably, but don't ask me who or when. It's been too long ago.

Just as quickly as the vault opened, it shut, only to be momentarily breached again when John Hinkley, Jr. shot Ronald Reagan on March 30, 1981. I stopped by Mason's house when I visited my parents the following April.

JS: Uncle Mason, doesn't John Hinkley fit your theory of Oswalds and Rubys. He had to know he would get caught.

MR: Or die. Pretty clear he wanted people to know he did it to get Jody Foster's attention. They found a letter addressed to Foster in the hotel room where he spent the night before the shooting.

As reported in the *Washington Post*, the first sentence of Hinkley's handwritten correspondence dated "3-30-81" read, "There is definitely a possibility that I will be killed in my attempt to get Reagan. It is for this very reason that I am writing you this letter now."[258]

Without the benefit of Mason's journal, the distinction between Oswalds and Rubys was an insightful paradigm of two contrasting modes of criminal behavior. When I reconsider it in the context of Mason's version of the assassination, our conversation takes on additional significance. I now understood one of the reasons the TEAM selected Oswald to be the assassin and why Ruby was the best option to eliminate him. I also could appreciate the TEAM's immediate concern when the post-assassination plan to extricate Oswald from Dealey Plaza evaporated.

They told Oswald a car would be waiting for him after he left the School Book Depository, the first leg of the promised escape route to Cuba via Mexico. Little did he suspect it was, in truth, a ride to nowhere. The original plan included immediate eradication, something that could not be guaranteed if he had shot Kennedy at close range. At best the assassin would never be identified. Even if the rifle on the sixth floor was connected to Oswald, his disappearance would generate a futile international manhunt for a suspect whose body lay buried somewhere off Interstate 35 between Dallas and Laredo.

My gallows sense of humor kicked in again. There was only one way to describe this step in the ASSIGNMENT, the "corpse protection program."

When the chaos in Dealey Plaza prevented Tinman from meeting Oswald at the predetermined location, Oswald panicked and went off script. The next best scenario would have been if Oswald had pulled his handgun when confronted by police in the Texas Theatre, resulting in a fatal shootout. Once he was taken into custody, silencing Oswald meant the ASSIGNMENT would go into overtime.

I often wonder whether Mason reassessed his legacy between the time he closed out the journal and his death. Or how he might grade the

---

[258] "Text of Letter to Foster," *Washington Post*, April 2, 1981.

ASSIGNMENT's impact when it came to Kennedy's place in history. After all, major civil rights legislation passed with bi-partisan support. When it came to national security, the Cold War had ended, and the Soviet Union was no more. Concerns about geopolitical conflicts were overshadowed by rogue terrorists. Except on rare occasions such as John Gotti's April 1992 conviction on 13 criminal counts, organized crime seldom made the front page or nightly news. Instead, stories of underworld activity were more likely the central theme of blockbuster movies such as *The Godfather* trilogy or *Good Fellas* and television series like *The Sopranos*.

One thing, however, did not change. At the time of Mason's death, there had been more than 500 books and major magazine articles about the assassination. The content of each fell into one of two major categories: conspiracy theories or efforts to debunk them. On the 35th anniversary of the assassination, *Texas Monthly* published perhaps the most comprehensive assessment of alternatives to the Warren Commission report. The November 1998 edition contained a series of articles addressing each major variant of what occurred in Dallas.

- *The Lone Gunman: Why the Warren Commission was right.*
- *The Two Oswalds: It's the most intriguing theory of all--two men with the same identity, one a patsy and the other a murderer who got off scot-free.*
- *The Cuban Connection: The Castro theory*
- *Hoover's Endgame: The FBI Theory*
- *The Red Scare: The KGB Theory*
- *Conspiracy A-Go-Go: The Shadow Government Theory*
- *Et Tu, Lyndon?: The LBJ Theory*
- *Saigon Surprise: The Vietnam Theory*
- *Married to the Mob: The Mafia Theory*

I have no doubt Mason would have been most intrigued by the following introductory passage by executive editor Pamela Colloff and crime reporter Michael Hall which set the stage for the rest of the issue.

What follows is an overview of the conspiracy oeuvre, though it is hardly exhaustive. We haven't included some of the shadowy figures—Umbrella Man, the Babushka Lady, Badge

> *Man—that populate the fringes of conspiracy-think. Nor do we examine the more far-out theories: that Joe DiMaggio, angered at Kennedy's treatment of his ex-wife, Marilyn Monroe, got his Italian friends to knock him off; or that the president, who was already suffering from Addison's disease, staged his own death, ensuring a glorified place in history; or that Frank Sinatra's drummer, Franklin Folley, was somehow involved.*[259]

There it was in black and white. Finally, someone other than Mason had raised the possibility Kennedy, to solidify his legacy, ordered his own death. However, Colloff and Hall dismissed this likelihood as swiftly as they raised it. How might Mason have reacted? Would he have been amused and sighed with relief knowing the version in his journal was still viewed as one of the "more far-out theories," in the same league as a hit job orchestrated by the Yankee Clipper?

Despite all the efforts by sanctioned governmental investigators, journalists and obsessed individuals to produce the definitive account of the assassination, none have satisfactorily ratified the Warren Commission's conclusions or any of the alternate narratives. With each, there remain persistent questions. And, although I have not found one significant inconsistency in the public record that would unequivocally debunk the journal's veracity, neither have I uncovered independent affirmation of its contents. Despite frustration over this ambiguity, I remain convinced there is some unturned stone that will help make the decision Mason entrusted to me.

---

[259] Pamela Colloff and Michael Hall, "The Conspiracy Theories," *Texas Monthly,* November 1998.

CHAPTER TWENTY-TWO

BEST EVIDENCE

Extraordinary claims require extraordinary evidence.

~Carl Sagan

My determination to solve "the crime of the 20th century" only intensified. I now felt compelled to re-read many of the volumes on my assassination bookcase, this time from the same perspective I applied to Mason's journal. Were there factual errors or chronological anomalies which raised doubts about each author's major assertions? Did his or her theory rely on now debunked details or was it in sync with the public record? I found myself returning more than once to the book that contributed to this obsession a quarter century before I ever became aware of Mason's manuscript, David Lifton's *Best Evidence, Disguise and Deception in the Assassination of John F.* Kennedy, published in January 1980.

'Best evidence" is a legal term of art, referring to situations when an original document or other evidence is not available. In the absence of the original, the best evidence rule allows counsel to submit secondary evidence based on circumstances which justify substitution of materials in lieu of the primary artifact. Lifton believed the Warren Commission erred when it relied solely on the official autopsy conducted at Bethesda Naval Hospital after the president's body arrived back in Washington, D.C.

The chaos, following the official announcement Kennedy had died, is well documented. Dr. Earl Rose, the Dallas medical examiner, was summoned to Parkland by state officials who insisted, regardless of the victim, the assassination was a state crime. It required an official autopsy by the local medical examiner.

Rose never got that chance. After Lyndon Johnson was informed of Kennedy's death, Rufus Youngblood, the Secret Service agent in charge of the vice-president's detail, advised Johnson he needed to get back on Air Force One and return to D.C. as quickly as possible. Worried about the optics of the situation, Kennedy advisor Kenneth O'Donnell told the chief-executive-to-be that Mrs. Kennedy intended to stay with the president's body until it was released for burial. Johnson agreed and told Youngblood, "I do not want to be remembered as the abandoner of beautiful widows."[260] A coffin with Kennedy's remains was forcibly removed from the hospital over objections by Dr. Rose, whom Secret Service agents pushed aside when he blocked the exit.

Ignoring observations by physicians who attended to the wounded president at Parkland Memorial Hospital, the Warren Commission never addressed discrepancies between the Bethesda autopsy and contemporaneous notes by Parkland doctors. Without photographs of the president's body, taken before it was removed from the Parkland operating room where he was initially treated and died, the attending doctors' descriptions of the president's wounds would have been admissible as the next best evidence.

The discrepancy between observations at Parkland and the official autopsy documented in Lifton's book is not what caught my attention. Lifton makes several claims which required extraordinary advance preparation, including alterations to the corpse between the time Air Force One landed at Andrews AFB and the beginning of the official autopsy. For Lifton's theory to hold water, three things needed to be true. One, there had to be advance knowledge that the Parkland doctors' notes might include information that contradicted any official account of Kennedy's murder. Two, without prior anticipation of a needed cover story, the time frame from announcement of the president's death (1:00

---

[260] Chris Jones, "The Flight from Dallas," *Esquire*, September 16, 2013.

p.m. CST/2:00 p.m. EST) to the arrival of Air Force One at Andrews (approximately 6:00 p.m. EST) provided the conspirators just four hours to set everything in motion. Three, for this covert operation to be conducted without suspicion it had to involve individuals whose presence at Andrews and Bethesda would not raise questions. These three prerequisites suggested the possibility of an inside job.

Several times during my pursuit of the true nature of Mason's journal, I wondered if, eventually, I might declare, "Enough is enough." I initially believed I would reach a point of diminishing returns when any new artifact duplicated information already gleaned from some previous record. I soon realized that time would never come. Every book, article or document raised new questions and opened another door to an endless maze of additional questions and possible answers.

I thought of inventor Charles Kettering who once said, "A problem well-stated is a problem half-solved." Perhaps I was asking the wrong question. Instead of concentrating on the breadth of research needed to satisfy my curiosity, what if I narrowed the scope? Instead of asking, "How much is enough?" my new emphasis was on quality, not quantity. A better approach was to take my cue from David Lifton. Lacking original documentation, I needed to identify the next "best evidence."

I had no smoking gun similar to the June 23, 1972, taped conversation between Nixon and chief of staff H. R. Haldeman. It would be different if Mason kept a copy of the instructions each member of the TEAM received when they first entered the operations center at the Naval Annex. Or photographs of the blackboards with the options, updates and procedural checklists. However, the TEAM dutifully assured no tangible trace of their work would survive their final day at the Naval Annex. Before sharing Mason's journal or my assessment of its validity, I needed a single historical artifact that would be the key to understanding the true nature of the document.

I metaphorically referred to this long-sought relic as my personal "Rosetta Stone." Much like the original, discovered in July 1799 during the Napoleonic invasion of Egypt, I hoped the archival equivalent of that granodiorite stele would help me decode Mason's journal, much as its namesake did with previously undecipherable hieroglyphic texts dating back to the third century BCE.

The term "Rosetta Stone" is now used more idiomatically in reference to a single piece of information or clue that sheds light on a series of events or issues. After so many years, I began to doubt one existed. But as is so often the case with a missing item, just when you stop looking, it shows up where you least expect it.

My "Eureka" moment began while rereading the October 25, 1963, journal entry. On previous occasions I focused on verifying whether the assault on Adlai Stevenson in Dallas might derail months of planning for the president's visit in November. This time, it was the second half that caught my attention.

> While I had Wizard on the phone, I took the
> opportunity to raise an issue the team discussed
> on several occasions. As unlikely as it may seem,
> what if Wizard made up the story about JFK
> ordering his own assassination? What if we were
> being played?
>
> I told Wizard we wanted confirmation from the
> President. Wizard offered to see what he could
> do.

I knew I would not find a listing in the presidential appointment calendar "Meeting with four Secret Service agents to discuss President's assassination." What other evidence might corroborate Mason's account? A passenger manifest for Air Force One? A list of individuals who met with the president at the Waldorf-Astoria? These documents potentially contained more than evidence of the meeting; they might also provide clues to the true identity of Wizard, Scarecrow, Tinman and Lion. If one of them was still alive, I potentially had a second or third source to corroborate the narrative.

Another dead end. Air Force One manifests in the National Archives cover flights beginning with the Carter Administration. And if visitor logs from the Waldorf-Astoria ever existed, they had not been preserved. One more reminder the administration had no legal obligation to maintain any of this information until Congress passed the

Presidential Records Act in 1978. There still remained my one "go-to" source of Kennedy's movements.

During JFK's 1,036 days in office, Evelyn Lincoln maintained two daily reports for the president. The first, identified as "The President's Engagements" was a bare-bones schedule of events, where he needed to be, when and the purpose of each event.

A second set of documents contained a detailed record of activities and movements from the time the president started his workday until he retired for the evening. There were to exceptions: family vacations and the death of infant son Patrick in August 1963.

I pulled entries surrounding the November 9 meeting assuming they followed the normal protocol. The November 8 "Engagements" page (below) ended with Kennedy's departure for New York to attend a dinner hosted by the New York City Protestant Council.

THE PRESIDENT'S ENGAGEMENTS

Friday, November 8

9:30 a.m.	Receive delegates to 1963 Session of Management Council of Consultative Committee on Postal Studies
10:00 a.m.	H.E. Habib Bourguiba, Jr. Ambassador of Tunisia
11:00 a.m.	H.E. Mohammed Yazid Special Representative of President Ben Bella
11:30 a.m.	Samuel Barber Gian Carlo Menotti (Off record)
12:00 noon	Dr. Glenn Seaborg (Off record)
12:15 p.m.	Meeting on wheat.
1:00 p.m.	Lunch
4:00 p.m.	Congressman Barratt O'Hara Archie J. House National Commander, United Spanish War Veters
5:00 p.m.	Depart for New York.
	Attend dinner sponsored by Protestant Council of the City of New York.

I then compared the proposed schedule with Mrs. Lincoln's detailed activity record for the same day (page 2 below).

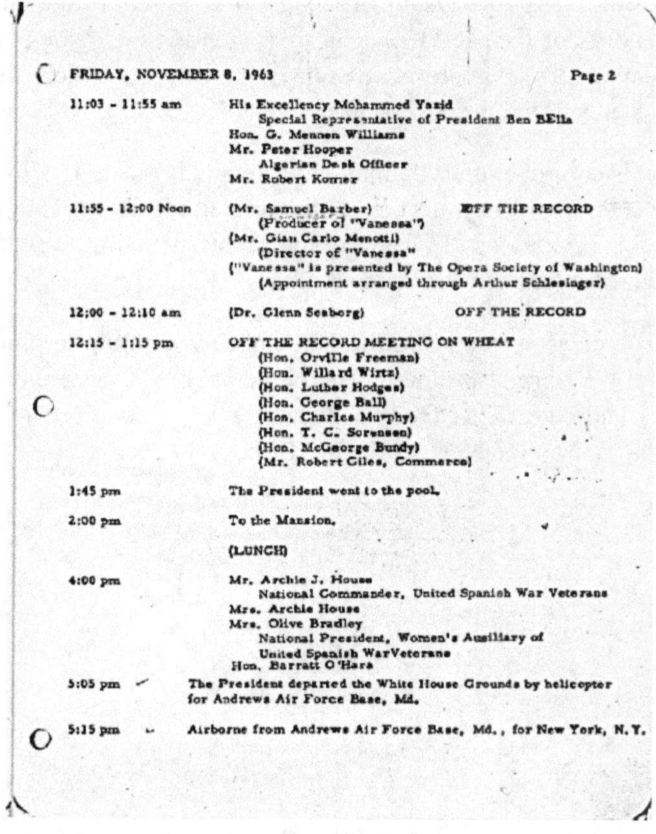

FRIDAY, NOVEMBER 8, 1963   Page 2

11:03 - 11:55 am   His Excellency Mohammed Yazid
                            Special Representative of President Ben BElla
                        Hon. G. Mennen Williams
                        Mr. Peter Hooper
                            Algerian Desk Officer
                        Mr. Robert Komer

11:55 - 12:00 Noon   (Mr. Samuel Barber)   OFF THE RECORD
                            (Producer of "Vanessa")
                        (Mr. Gian Carlo Menotti)
                            (Director of "Vanessa"
                        ("Vanessa" is presented by The Opera Society of Washington)
                            (Appointment arranged through Arthur Schlesinger)

12:00 - 12:10 am   (Dr. Glenn Seaborg)   OFF THE RECORD

12:15 - 1:15 pm   OFF THE RECORD MEETING ON WHEAT
                            (Hon. Orville Freeman)
                            (Hon. Willard Wirtz)
                            (Hon. Luther Hodges)
                            (Hon. George Ball)
                            (Hon. Charles Murphy)
                            (Hon. T. C. Sorensen)
                            (Hon. McGeorge Bundy)
                            (Mr. Robert Giles, Commerce)

1:45 pm   The President went to the pool.

2:00 pm   To the Mansion.

                        (LUNCH)

4:00 pm   Mr. Archie J. House
                            National Commander, United Spanish War Veterans
                        Mrs. Archie House
                        Mrs. Olive Bradley
                            National President, Women's Auxiliary of
                            United Spanish WarVeterans
                        Hon. Barratt O'Hara

5:05 pm   The President departed the White House Grounds by helicopter
                        for Andrews Air Force Base, Md.

5:15 pm   Airborne from Andrews Air Force Base, Md., for New York, N.Y.

With one exception, the president's 15-minute delayed departure from Andrews Air Force Base, the versions matched. More importantly, the official record now put Kennedy in New York City for his November 9 meeting with the TEAM.

When I returned to the "Engagements" file, as expected, there was no schedule for November 9 or 10. Kennedy was headed to Atoka for a weekend with family and friends. These "personal days" are further documented by the now famous home movie from November 10, 1963, of the president being nuzzled (some say eaten) by Caroline's pony Leprechaun.[261]

I expected a parallel gap in Mrs. Lincoln's daily recap of Kennedy's activities. Instead, there was a hand-written note (below). [262]

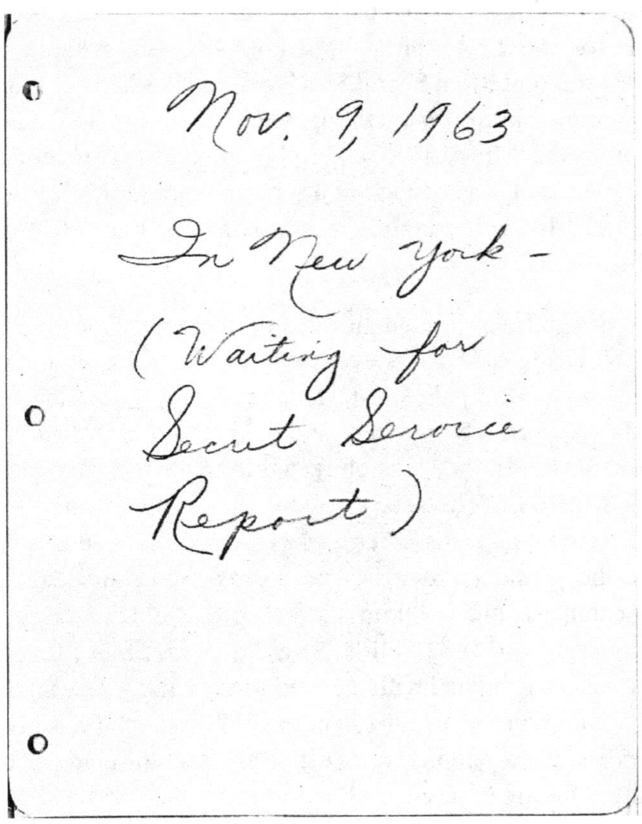

At first, I felt that rush of euphoria Pierre Bouchard, a soldier in Napoleon's army, experienced when he first uncovered a rock inscribed with both Egyptian and Greek characters near the city of Rosetta. Or as so often happens in fictional courtroom dramas, the satisfaction a

---

[261] "The Newspaperman: The Life and Times of Ben Bradlee," Kunhardt Films and HBO, December 4, 2017.

[262] Evelyn Lincoln, Presidential Appointments, John F. Kennedy Library and Museum, Content ID #26059865, November 9, 1963, p. 14.

prosecutor feels when the prime suspect breaks down on the witness stand and admits, "Yes, I did it." Mystery solved. The search for truth is over.

Nonetheless, my elation was short-lived. A second glimpse at the handwritten document suggested I may have prematurely jumped to a conclusion. One thing was beyond dispute. The president traveled to New York for the Protestant Council dinner. But what about the parenthetical reference to a Secret Service report? Who was waiting for it? Did "report" imply something other than an in-person oral presentation? Had Mrs. Lincoln simply jotted down a reminder to herself the president was expecting a written communication from the Secret Service? If so, it certainly would not have been related to the ASSIGNMENT.

Two other possibilities immediately came to mind. One was a more thorough debriefing of Adlai Stevenson's trip to Texas in anticipation of the upcoming campaign trip to the Lone Star State. Threat assessments are routinely updated, and despite the president's lack of concern, the Secret Service was obligated to make the president aware of any risk situations. The second involved an ongoing disagreement between Kennedy and his Secret Service details. Despite agents' objections, the president regularly requested they stand back during public appearances, making him more approachable. During a *New York Post* interview in 1983, retired Secret Service agent Floyd Boring recalled a discussion he had with Kennedy following a campaign trip to Florida. Boring quotes JFK, "It's excessive, Floyd. And it's giving the wrong impression to people. We've got an election coming up. The whole point is for me to be accessible to the people."[263]

The true test, however, was to flip my first assumption upside down. Instead of validating Mason's journal, there was a chance it proved just the opposite. What if, rather than authenticating Mason's account of the assassination, the November 9 note was the catalyst for a counterintuitive, fictional version of the events leading up to the death of a president. I constructed the following scenario.

---

[263] Larry Getlen, "JFK Told the Secret Service to Keep Its Distance on Assassination Day," *New York Post*, May 16, 2021.

As a member of the presidential detail on November 22, Mason likely anticipated a request to testify before the Warren Commission or, at a minimum, be deposed by Commission staff. In that event, he reviewed Lincoln's appointment book to refresh his memory of every interaction with Kennedy prior to the assassination. He sees the November handwritten note and wonders why it differs from every other daily record.

Even though he is aware of nothing that might suggest it was directly related to the events two weeks later, his imagination gets the better of him. Others would write books promoting outlandish conspiracies theories based on less circumstantial evidence. Aspiring authors are always told to write about what they know best. John Grisham turned his knowledge of the law into bestselling novels. Likewise, Patricia Cornwell penned 24 books featuring fictional public coroner Kay Scarpetta, drawing on her experience as technical writer and computer analyst for the Virginia state chief medical examiner. What better plot for a novel or screenplay than a version of the Kennedy assassination in which Secret Service agents are the central characters.

If nothing else, I now had a better understanding why Mason typed the last entry in his journal in November 1973. He knew it was time to step aside from a project to which he had devoted a decade of his life. He had accomplished his goal, whether that was to document the truth about the Kennedy assassination or create a fictional account in which numerous famous and infamous characters became part of the story. Medgar Evers and Byron De La Beckwith. Frank Sinatra, Sam Giancana and Johnny Rosselli. General Edwin Walker. Marilyn Monroe and Judith Campbell Exner. Mason had taken me on an 11-year journey which, after crisscrossing more than a decade of history, ended abruptly on November 22, 1973. Then, emulating Tom Hanks' portrayal of Forrest Gump on his final cross-country run, Mason declares "I'm pretty tired. I think I'll go home now."

After 19 years, I too am tired. However, I remain unconvinced I achieved what I set out to do. There is substantial evidence that suggests Mason's chronicle is true. Yet, the November 9 handwritten memo, which appears to be the last piece of the puzzle, is still circumstantial. Without confirmation by a second source with direct knowledge,

Mason's account remains one person's word against multiple official and independent inquiries, none of which hints at anything akin to this outlying variation of a monumental chapter in U.S. history.

CHAPTER TWENTY-THREE

A TIME TO REFLECT

Paper is to write things down that we need to remember. Our brains are used to think.

~Albert Einstein

I stared at the two paper-filled boxes in front of me. One contains the document bequeathed to me by Mason Rhodes. The second, more voluminous than the first, holds all the notes and exhibits I have assembled over the better part of two decades. If Einstein was correct, both are compilations of events Mason and I felt a "need to remember." I have always referred to Mason's chronicle as his "journal," largely due to its chronological nature. In contrast, I considered my additions to be research, although, it too is documentation of a different kind of journey.

I still did not know what it all meant. In which case, Einstein might urge, "It is time to brush the paper aside and start using your brain." Or as I used to tell students in my creativity classes, "We have a hard time making sense of our lives when we are too busy doing. Learning comes during the quiet moments when we can reflect on our actions."

True reflection is not as simple as asking, "What is this trying to tell me and why is it important?" It requires recognition that facts have more than one interpretation based on the context in which they are gathered and the diverse experiences of individuals who try to make sense of them. The search for meaning does not end with our first impression of what we see, hear or sense. It forces us to keep looking for the next right answer.

Although I have yet to find definitive proof of the true nature of Mason's journal, I never doubted the journey was worth the effort. As a result of this deep dive into a period of consequential American history, I found myself engaged in the equivalent of a Jackson Pollack masterpiece spattered with new insights about both the events of November 1963 and a valued mentor who was there.

So Many Dots; So Many Connections

Once I began comparing Mason's journal to the trove of available information resulting from the official and independent investigations of Kennedy's death, I understood how so many versions of one event could materialize. The Warren Commission asked Americans to believe there was a straight line between Point A and Point B. A repatriated defector, unhappy with his country's policy toward Cuba, took out his anger on the president of the United States. The body of evidence more closely resembles a painting created using the pointillistic technique of George Seurat than the brush strokes of a Rembrandt or Michelangelo. It is a canvas littered with constantly fluctuating flecks of information that can be rearranged to produce unlimited configurations.

Nor does it matter where one commences his or her respective inquiry. The cluster which contains the initial entry point will quickly merge with another. Mason's narrative is a perfect example. Initially, the TEAM viewed organized crime and national security as unrelated options. Sam Giancana felt betrayed when the Justice Department prosecuted him despite allegedly helping Kennedy win the presidency in 1960. From a totally different perspective, Mason and his colleagues regarded opponents of Kennedy's foreign policy toward the Soviet Union and its satellites as a completely separate alternative. We now know the two were inherently linked. When you add Kennedy's insatiable sexual appetite two new players join the cast. Judith Exner who served as a liaison between Kennedy and Sam Giancana. And FBI director J. Edgar Hoover who twice recruited Robert Kennedy to warn his brother of the national security threats posed by the commander-in-chief's extra-marital affairs.

Depending on the skill of the investigator, each dot or connection can contribute either enlightenment or misdirection. For those who begin with no preconceived conclusion, the first dots represent a portal into a vast web of material to which they assign an unbiased value. However, if their goal is to confirm a preconceived theory of the case, they are more likely to cherry pick those factoids most likely to substantiate a preordained conclusion.

Believing Does Not Make It So

In 1962, Daniel Boorstin, American historian and the 12th Librarian of the U.S. Congress, published his most prescient book *The Image: A Guide to Pseudo-Events in America*. Decades before the internet, Facebook, Twitter or 24-hour cable news, Boorstin wrote:

> *In this book I describe the world of our making, how we used our wealth, our literacy, our technology, and our progress, to create the thicket of unreality which stands between us and the facts of life. I recount historical forces which gave us the unprecedented opportunity to deceive and to befog our experience.* [264]

Boorstin defines "pseudo-event" as a non-spontaneous, planned creation "for the immediate purpose of being reported or reproduced."[265] In the world in which I have been immersed for the greater part of two decades, the "event" consisted of three indisputable observations: the president's assassination, Jack Ruby's murder of Oswald, and Ruby's trial. Everything else were "pseudo-events," including the Warren Commission, publication of Mark Lane's *Rush to Judgment*, Oliver Stone's *JFK*, etc.

The danger Boorstin foresaw was that pseudo-events make facts irrelevant. Rather than objectively capturing irrefutable evidence, they represent speculation and opinion. One need go back no farther in history than the January 6, 2021, attack on the U.S. Capitol to appreciate Boorstin's visionary wisdom. The findings of the House Select

---

[264] Daniel J. Boorstin, *The Image: A Guide to Pseudo-Events in America*, Antheneum Publishers, New York, 1962.
[265] Ibid., p. 11.

Committee to Investigate the Attack on the Capitol changed few minds about what happened that day. Depending on where individuals get their information and with whom they converse, they remain convinced those who breached the Capitol were either insurrectionists or patriots.

I share this perspective because I now possess a journal, which if and when released, would surely fit Boorstin's definition of a pseudo-event. Which, in turn, forces me to ask two obvious questions, "Have I given Mason's account more attention than it deserved? And if so, why?" Maybe it was our personal relationship. Would I have done the same if I had found the manuscript in the drawer of an antique desk purchased at an estate sale? Was it because I trusted him and could never imagine his playing such a hoax on me or the public? I was both honored and humbled when he chose me as the recipient of what he referred to as his most valued possession. Thus, it became equally valuable to me. I wanted it to be true.

I keep telling myself I have done my best to objectively seek the truth. After all, I was trained in and have devoted much of my professional life to objectivity and the art of critical thinking. However, one's biases only hibernate, quickly awakened when the conditions or situations are favorable.

Did It Matter?

From a historical perspective, whether Mason's journal proves to be fact or fiction, the events of November 1963 remain grounded in the very first entry when he recalls John Kennedy's question, "If you had a choice, would you rather have been President Woodrow Wilson or Abraham Lincoln?" If he did order his own assassination, did the president make the right choice? And to what extent was his decision a product of the times?

The methodology and information available to empirically assess public reaction to events or a president's approval rating were more limited than those in use today. There was nothing comparable to the Gallup poll of presidential approval during Wilson's term of office, much less Lincoln's. Therefore, there is no statistical record of these earlier presidents' favorability before and after major events.

Even if polling data were available, the standards by which print and broadcast news media cover a president's professional and personal life have also changed. There are no longer unstated "rules of the road" between the president and the media which make certain aspects of the chief executive's life off-limit. Every utterance is captured on always present video and audio recording devices. Every gaffe or stumble becomes "must see TV" on cable news, YouTube or Twitter. Media, which once simply reported polling results, now influence them.

Imagine earlier presidents making the same decision today under these totally different conditions. Could Wilson have survived press scrutiny of his absence from public view? In November 1966, to stave off rumors of a more serious illness, the White House felt compelled to release a one-minute video of President Johnson at Bethesda Naval Hospital following a 53-minute procedure to repair an abdominal hernia and remove scar tissue from his vocal cords.

To calculate the impact of such events on a president's political standing, one need only examine the Gallup approval rating before and after public notification. For example, Reagan's approval rating, once doctors announced he would fully recover from a gunshot wound, rose dramatically from 53 to 67 percent.

Downturns in a president's approval seem more connected to his performance in office than his health. In contrast to Reagan's 14-point jump in favorability following John Hinkley's attempt on his life, he experienced an even greater decrease (a decline of 16 percentage points) within days of his November 25, 1986, acknowledgement of the illegal Iran-Contra arms deal.

Kennedy's circumstances appear more analogous to those of Franklin Roosevelt. Both entered their presidencies with known physical issues, even if not fully exposed. And similarly, every effort was made to hide the extent of their infirmities from the press and voters. FDR often used a wheelchair in private but refused to do so when it came to public appearances. Likewise, Kennedy exchanged crutches for a back brace when in the company of others except family and immediate staff.

One might conclude Kennedy need not be concerned his various maladies would become a threat to his political future. But aspects of his situation differed from Roosevelt. Everyone assumed Roosevelt would not seek a fifth term, assuming World War II ended before the 1948 election. In contrast, Kennedy would face increasing discomfort and periodic absences from public view during a rigorous re-election campaign, raising questions about his fitness for another four years in office. Such inquiries could open the door for a Republican victory in 1964 and a new chief executive who did not share his priorities.

Or was the momentum of Kennedy's agenda before his death irreversible regardless of who occupied the Oval Office? Like so many other questions raised by Mason's account of the assassination, a definitive resolution whether the 35th president of the United States accomplished what he intended to achieve by ordering his own death remains elusive.

In the introductory class on research methods at every university, lesson #1 is the difference between correlation and causation. Was Kennedy's death a prerequisite for passage of the civil rights and voting rights acts? Or the next round of bilateral nuclear arms control negotiations with the Soviet Union? Or were the forces leading to these policy breakthroughs already in motion and irreversible? The demand for civil rights legislation was bolstered by video of violence directed at racial minorities and the bombing of the 16th Street Baptist Church. The first nuclear test ban treaty was signed 10 days before the assassination.

Despite advances in the application of scientific method to the social sciences, proving a causal relationship between one historic event and another cannot be done absent two critical requirements. First, there must be a control group. Second, the investigator must be able to replicate key elements on which the statistical relationship depends. To satisfy these methodological standards, the researcher would have to recreate the same conditions and series of events that existed in the fall of 1963 minus the assassination. Then observe whether the policy outcomes remain the same had Kennedy lived. Passage of civil rights legislation. De-escalation of the cold war. Increased Department of Justice prosecution of organized crime. The 1969 moon landing.

Perhaps these achievements might have occurred anyway. To this day, historians debate whether realization of Kennedy's "New Frontier" would have been derailed by the Vietnam War as happened with Johnson's "Great Society" domestic agenda. Despite speculation JFK would not have ordered the military buildup in support of the Saigon government, there is evidence to the contrary. The number of military advisors in Vietnam had already increased from an initial May 1961 deployment of 500 to 16,000 at the time of the assassination. Still Kennedy maintained the South Vietnamese people and their government would determine the eventual outcome of the civil war with the North. Consider Kennedy's remarks during a September 2, 1963, interview with Walter Cronkite at the president's home in Hyannis Port, Massachusetts.

In the final analysis, it is their war. They are the ones who have to win it or lose it. We can help them, we can give them equipment, we can send our men out there as advisors, but they have to win it, the people of Vietnam, against the Communists.[266]

A copy of the full transcript was immediately sent to U.S. ambassador Henry Cabot Lodge in Saigon with a note confirming the administration's policy to limit U.S. engagement. On October 2, 1963, after a 10-day tour of Vietnam, Defense Secretary Robert McNamara and General Maxwell Taylor issued a public report which predicted a withdrawal of the first 1,000 advisors by the end of the year.

Without a control group, the probability of different outcomes, if Kennedy had not been an assassin's target or survived the assault, is mere speculation. All we know for sure is the war in Southeast Asia continued for the next nine years and cost the lives of 58,300 members of the U.S. armed forces. To categorically argue Kennedy would have taken a different tack is intellectually suspect.

Which raises the possibility the singular beneficiary of the president's death was his personal legacy. Before there would ever be images of an infirmed John Kennedy, the idea of "Camelot," with a young, energetic leader at the helm, was frozen in time. A legacy embellished by his family and inner circle, documented by sympathetic historians like

---

[266] President Kennedy interview with Walter Cronkite, CBS News, Hyannis Port, Massachusetts, September 2, 1963.

William Manchester in *The Death of a President* and Arthur Schlesinger in *A Thousand Days*. Or tributes by the president's lifelong friends such as David Powers and Kenneth O'Donnell in *Johnny, We Hardly Knew Ye*.

The Missing Link

I have one lingering frustration. The above reflections are mine. Having read the journal following his death, I never had the opportunity to ask Mason about his takeaways. Although speculative, I do believe he left clues throughout the journal.

I gained an appreciation for each of the moral quandaries Mason would face during and in the aftermath of the ASSIGNMENT. Of course, he was afraid if what he alleged was true. He had participated in the planning and execution of a felony. Then, for the next decade, he feared one of the inquiries into the assassination, official or unofficial, would unearth the truth. And, for the remainder of his life, Mason also pondered the personal and public repercussions of sharing an account he promised he would never disclose or put to paper. Mason never explicitly mentioned his apprehension how disclosure might be received. Yet, I know it must have been a consideration. Why? Because I find myself in the same predicament.

Which brings me to the last significant issue of conscience Mason and his cohorts faced, the mental tug-of-war between duty and principle. Through an intermediary, the nation's commander-in-chief, for whose safety they were oath-bound to protect, had recruited the TEAM to engage in a legally and morally questionable operation. A tall order which must have weighed heavily on their consciences throughout the planning phase of the ASSIGNMENT. The kind of enigmatic decision you might want to discuss with a close friend or confidante, an option unopen to them.

As the fateful day approached, of course, they wanted confirmation the president had authorized his own homicide. In the October 24, 1963, journal entry, Mason told Wizard the TEAM needed to hear such a haunting directive "straight from the horse's mouth." This, too, I now understood more directly. Had not Mason charged me with an equally daunting task? Was I not at a crossroads between conscience and duty?

Except there was a difference. What *was* my "assignment?" Mason left no explicit instructions or desired outcomes. There was no manila envelope with conditions that must be met. Just the opposite. He might just as well have said, "Here it is. You figure out the rest."

The circumstances of my assignment were quite different from Mason's experience on January 9, 1963. Imagine if, on that day when the TEAM was summoned to the Old Executive Office Building, Wizard had laid out the situation as follows. "The president is terminally ill and may not make it to the end of his first term. He is frustrated with the lack of congressional progress on his agenda. And the FBI director is blackmailing him. Do what you think is best." In what has become the standard response when someone wants to avoid a decision of this magnitude, the TEAM's unanimous response would have been, "Sir, *that* is above our pay grade!"

I believe I exhausted every available resource in hopes of authenticating the journal. The only outstanding issue is what to do next. Disclose the journal's existence and content? If so, in what form, as originally given to me or annotated based on my research? And how would I disseminate it?

I could emulate Daniel Ellsberg, who in February 1971 handed "The Pentagon Papers" to *New York Times* reporter Neil Sheehan, leaving the decision to publish up to the paper's editors and legal counsel. I could transmit the journal to one of several internet sites such as Wikileaks to be anonymously published on-line. Or mimic former government officials and celebrities and produce a tell-all book.

Although I thought about consulting someone, I continued to fear any intentional or inadvertent leak of the journal and its content would preempt most, if not all, of my options. And the only person who would fully understand the importance of absolute confidentiality was not available. Though maybe he was.

In their book *Creativity in Business*, Michael Ray and Rochelle Myers introduce an exercise to get in touch with a trusted ally. Some people choose a historical figure. Others, a deceased relative. I knew there was only one person in whom I could confide, someone Ray and Myers would call a "wisdom keeper or spirit guide—an inner person who can be with you in life, someone to whom you can turn for guidance."[267]

In life, Mason often filled a similar role for me. It was time to contact him. I closed my eyes and imagined I approached his front door and rang the bell. And there he was, just as he appeared each time I visited his house. He motioned for me to come in and take a seat in his study. Everything was the same, including the chess set on the side table by his chair. And as Ray and Myers suggested, I followed their script to open the conversation.

> *Be my guide. Introduce me to new ideas. Help me make a wise decision. Lead me to the source of my creativity.*[268]

Let me reassure you, I was neither under the influence of alcohol nor hallucinogens. Nor had I recently been diagnosed with a brain injury. I did not expect Mason to physically materialize, nor did I think I would hear the actual sound of his voice. The power of this exercise is rooted in the proposition our inability to make decisions is not about the choice. We already know what we want or need to do. The struggle is finding the confidence in that decision and acting on it. The spirit guide is only a catalyst who helps us acquire the necessary level of assurance in our own judgment.

> *MR: Jonathan, it's good to see you. It's been too long.*

> *JS: Uncle Mason, I've missed you. And regret I never had the chance to say goodbye.*

> *MR: But we're here now. Is there something you want to talk about?*

> *JS: I think you know. It's not that I'm ungrateful for the gift you gave me. It was obviously very important to you. And*

---

[267] Michael Ray and Rochelle Myers, *Creativity in Business*, "Getting in Touch with Your Inner Guide," Main Street Books (1986), page 37.
[268] Ibid., page 37.

became important to me, taking up much of my life since I first read it. But I still have so many questions.

MR: Go ahead. Ask.

JS: Why did you wait until you died to share it with me? Did you think I might betray your confidence?

MR: I was not protecting myself. I was more concerned about you. If I had been there, you would have constantly been asking me if this or that was okay or worried about what I wanted. I took the story as far as I felt I could. I knew you would pick it up. You didn't need me looking over your shoulder.

JS: Story? Is it just a story?

MR: Of course, it's a story. Everything is a story. [He laughs.] The question is whether it is a true story.

JS: And you're not going to tell me that. Are you?

MR: I'm afraid not. Because it's a magical story, capable of being anything you want it to be. If presented as fact, it would re-write history. As theory, it could encourage generations of curious individuals who weren't alive in 1963 to keep looking for the truth. As a novel or movie, it could entertain. Or it could remain our secret.

JS: I never thought of it that way.

MR: I'm not so sure of that. A person doesn't spend 19 years of his life working on something without some idea why he's doing it. Now, go do it.

JS: I still have so many things I want to ask you.

MR: If you didn't already find the answers in the journal, I have none.

And just as Ray and Myers said he would, Mason ended the conversation with the following.

> *Call on me whenever you need me. I will always be there for you.* [269]

That evening I picked up a legal pad and wrote across the top of the first page, "Decide what to do; then do it!"

As fate would have it, each time I thought I had completed my research for this manuscript, the National Archives would release newly declassified, assassination-related documents. However, each release of withheld artifacts associated with the government investigations into Kennedy's death fell into the category of "something old, nothing new."

With each document dump, news outlets reported most of the new material was duplicative of already available content. The only difference was fewer redactions. Each time frustrated researchers, myself included, were left to wonder why the FBI, CIA or other national security agencies refused to fully comply with the 1992 congressional mandate to make the entire collection available to the public by October 2017.

During his 2016 campaign, Donald Trump assured voters that he would not stonewall release of all remaining documents. He did not keep that promise. President Joe Biden then set a new deadline—December 15, 2022—for full compliance with the statutory mandate. On schedule, there was another release of over 13,000 previously unseen documents and exhibits. After reviewing the new material, University of Virginia faculty fellow Steve Gillon assessed the latest tranche of documents.

> *There are little things that we discovered from the documents, but nothing that changes the fundamental narrative that Lee Harvey Oswald was the sole assassin in Dealey Plaza that day.* [270]

---

[269] Ibid, page 38,
[270] Matt Kelly, "Details, But No Big Revelations in Latest Kennedy Assassination Documents," *UVAToday*, January 10, 2023.

Still, the Archives, with presidential approval, withheld information the intelligence community deemed too sensitive to release. There may be valid reasons for this. Each of the official investigations delved into covert intelligence activities which might have directly or indirectly been the catalyst leading up to November 1963. Gillon speculates the remaining material may prove extremely embarrassing for the CIA. Or maybe it was not the information but disclosure of intelligence gathering methods and sources still in use. One other possibility. Former CIA officer David Priess suggests, though unlikely, one of the CIA operatives or sources involved in such activity "could still be alive and at risk from disclosure."[271]

Although there was nothing in this latest release that confirms Mason's account, neither was there anything that categorically invalidates it. And I become more convinced any future releases will be more of the same. In November 1973 Mason understood he had taken the narrative as far as he could. I may have reached that same milestone.

---

[271] Katie Bo Lillis, "JFK Researchers Underwhelmed by Latest release of Assassination Documents," CNN, December 15, 2021.

CHAPTER TWENTY-FOUR

BEYOND A REASONABLE DOUBT

Even if you are a minority of one, the truth is the truth.

~Mahatma Gandhi

More than 19 years after receipt of Mason's journal I still have unanswered questions. Although I never found any major anomalies to definitively disprove his account, neither did I uncover one primary source who would corroborate it. Even if those sources were once out there, like Mason, they have most likely gone to their respective eternal rewards. Furthermore, if Scarecrow, Tinman, Lion or Wizard retained any evidence of the operation, to my knowledge, it remains beyond my reach. At best, the journal is a classic case of "he said; everyone else said."

Why has it taken 19 years to reach this point? I keep convincing myself there are good reasons. Career. Family obligations. Community projects. But those are just excuses. I somehow made time to dissect, fact check and re-check every detail in each journal entry. And yet, I still procrastinated when it came to forming an opinion about the veracity of Mason's account of the events surrounding November 22, 1963.

In the context of my own journey, the sense of indecision Mason expressed in the handwritten note that accompanied the journal now makes complete sense.

> *This box contains my most valued possession. It contains something I have shared with no one. Maybe I should have, but I was afraid.*

The emergence of long-lost or suppressed artifacts of historical importance has, on occasion, brought clarity and insight. Among the most recent examples is Mark Felt's 2006 memoir *A G-Man's Life: The FBI, Being 'Deep Throat' and the Struggle for Honor in Washington.* In 1972, Felt was deputy director of the FBI when he befriended Bob Woodward, providing critical information about the extent of the Nixon re-election dirty tricks campaign and how to expose it. For 33 years, Deep Throat's identity remained a mystery until Felt authorized Woodward to tell the whole story in 2005 with publication of *The Secret Man: The Story of Watergate's Deep Throat.*

No one questioned the authenticity of Woodward's or Felt's account. The two central characters were still alive and submitted to numerous interviews during which they brushed aside any challenges. To make sure, I Googled, "Mark Felt was not Deep Throat." Not one direct hit. The identity of Woodward's "mystery ally" remains unchallenged to this day.

On the lighter side, there was a 2017 interview with movie director Peter Landesman in which he discusses *The Silent Man*, his film about Felt and how he aided the *Washington Post's* coverage of Watergate. Landesman said the only thing his subject regretted was the code name Woodward and Bernstein gave him.

> *[Deep Throat] was a porn reference and was actually one of the reasons Mark felt so ashamed. He was a real Christian, and that actually was a big deal for him.*[272]

---

[272] Tashara Jones, "Mark Felt was 'ashamed' of Deep Throat nickname," PAGESIX.COM, September 22, 2017.

In contrast, the perpetrators of manufactured historical artifacts suffered a less noble place in the annals of journalism and literature. In 1970, Clifford Irving and Richard Suskind claimed Howard Hughes asked Irving to ghostwrite his autobiography. To bolster their claim, Suskind enlisted the help of skilled forgers to create correspondence in Hughes' handwriting. Irving and Suskind used the documents to secure a $765,000 advance from McGraw-Hill for rights to the forthcoming volume. All of this was achieved despite the fact Hughes was not dead. He maintained a reclusive lifestyle, constantly relocating between residences in the Caribbean and Central America.

When McGraw-Hill partnered with *Life Magazine* to publish excerpts of Irving's draft of his book and copies of the forged documents, Hughes scheduled a January 1972 conference call with representatives of several national newspapers. He denied ever having met Irving or even talking with him. Later that month Irving confessed to the fraud, was sentenced to 17 months in prison and returned the $765,000 to the duped publisher.[273]

In 1981, Konrad Kujau, an East German dealer in black market Nazi memorabilia, offered what he claimed to be Adolph Hitler's personal diaries to *Stern*, a weekly German news magazine. During the preceding decade, Kujau produced and sold forgeries of alleged Hitler paintings, personal notes, war poems and a handwritten draft of *Mein Kampf.* Based on the commercial success of these items, he began a more ambitious project, a 60-volume diary he attributed to the German *Führer*. Kujau claimed the diary had been discovered in the storage hold of a crashed plane in which Herrmann Wilhelm Goering, an early member of the Nazi Party and trusted Hitler confidante, was a passenger.

The document's magnitude became a factor for historian Hugh Trevor-Roper who was among the first individuals asked to examine the diary. He gave the following reason he considered the work's physical immensity important. "Who, I ask myself, would forge sixty volumes

---

[273] "CRIME: The Fabulous Hoax of Clifford Irving," Time Magazine, February 21, 1972.

when six would have served his purpose?"[274] Within days of Trevor-Roper's assessment, Rupert Murdoch offered *Stern* $3.3 million for the U.S. and British Commonwealth serialization rights. Despite lingering concerns about the document's authenticity, *Stern* announced the diary's existence and forthcoming publication in a press release dated April 2, 1983.

Ironically, Trevor-Roper was also among the first to raise serious doubts about the diaries. His concern was triggered by inconsistencies in different versions of the story behind their discovery in Goering's plane. Skepticism grew based on Hitler's medical records. Hitler's personal physician Dr. Theodor Morell diagnosed the *Führer* as suffering from Parkinson's Disease. Yet the handwriting in the diaries showed no evidence of such an affliction. Similarly, other doctors who examined the diaries found it inconceivable Hitler penned the final entries following an arm injury sustained during "Operation Valkyrie," a July 20, 1944, assassination attempt initiated by the head of the German General Army Office Friedrich Olbricht.[275]

In August 1984, Kujau and his accomplice Gerd Heidemann were convicted of stealing more than $3.2 million as a result of their fraudulent scheme. During sentencing, Judge Hans-Ulrich Schroeder suggested Kujau and Heidemann were not the only ones at fault. He accused the publisher of a lack of due diligence, more interested in the diaries' commercial value than their accuracy. "The negligence of *Stern* has persuaded me to soften the sentences against the two main co-conspirators."[276]

The dichotomy between the truthful unmasking of "Deep Throat" and the forgeries associated with Hughes and Hitler added to my indecision over what to do with Mason's journal and the notes and commentary I added to the mix. Before taking that last step, I needed to determine whether Mason's work and mine would be received more akin to Woodward's and Felt's or Irving's and Kujau's.

---

[274] Robert C. Williams, *The Forensic Historian*, Routledge Taylor & Francis Group, London and New York, 2013, p. 24.
[275] Joachim Fest, *Plotting Hitler's Death: The German Resistance to Hitler, 1933-1945*, Weidenfeld & Nicolson, 1996.
[276] Dan van der Vat, "Bunker Bunk," *The Guardian*, July 9, 1985, p. 21.

From the outset, I knew the decision to release the journal and my subsequent analysis was mine and mine alone. There was no Mark Felt or Bob Woodward who would defend the work based on their first-hand participation and knowledge. And any possibility the content might leak if I sought the counsel of others was a risk I was unwilling to take. Therefore, to reach a definitive verdict regarding disposition of the work required an objective process and criteria. My choice of the word "verdict" in the previous sentence is no accident. It became the foundation on which I decided to reach my ultimate conclusion.

What better venue for seeking the truth than a courtroom. Let me, therefore, share what I dubbed the civil case of *Sheppard #1 v. Sheppard #2*. I created this imagined debate as a more serious and intellectual equivalent of the representations in cartoons and situation comedies when superimposed contenders materialize on each shoulder of the indecisive protagonist. In reality, they are nothing more than an animated version of a list of pros and cons on a legal pad, giving voice to the items in each column.

In pre-trial motions, both parties requested the judge establish the rules of evidentiary standards and burden of proof. In most circumstances this is governed by whether the defendant is charged with a criminal offense (violation of a statute or regulation) or is engaged in a civil dispute between two or more individuals. Some cases involve both. O. J. Simpson was acquitted of murder in his criminal trial but found guilty of wrongful death in a civil suit filed by Nicole Brown's family. The former required a unanimous verdict of proof beyond a reasonable doubt, the latter by a preponderance of the evidence by only a super majority of nine of the 12 jurors.

As previously noted, this case most resembled a civil suit. However, on such a sensitive matter, relying on a preponderance of the evidence seemed inappropriate. I needed to be sure. Therefore, in my third role as Judge Sheppard, presiding officer of this moot court, I chose to make proof beyond a reasonable doubt the standard by which I would ultimately rule.

In his opening statement, the plaintiff claimed the defendant Jonathan Sheppard #2 was in possession of historical artifacts of which he came into possession some 19 years ago. The plaintiff stipulated the defendant's ownership is not in question. However, he suggested the federal government could make a case Mason's journal was a record of events to which he only had access due to his position of employment. Plaintiff further believed the contents were of such national importance any decision about their disposition superseded the defendant's personal ownership rights and must be released to the public.

Defendant Sheppard argued the journal had historical significance, if, and only if, the purported facts contained within were authentic and could be validated. Otherwise, Mason's journal could be a work of fiction for which the intellectual property rights lawfully transferred to the defendant upon the author's death. Defendant also argued his additions to the original work now qualified the document as a "joint work" which extended the period of copyright protection to "70 years after such surviving author's death."[277] Based on ownership, defendant Sheppard contended he and he alone should make the decision if, when and to whom the material became available for external consumption.

Following opening arguments, both sides found themselves in a common situation many trial lawyers face. Without witnesses or original receipts, e.g., the contents of the manilla envelopes on each TEAM member's desk when they first entered the operation center in the Naval Annex, they had to rely solely on circumstantial evidence.

Plaintiff Sheppard contended the journal itself was sufficient to convince future readers of the possibility it was true. He even invoked the same rationale used by Trevor-Roper during his initial assessment of the fabricated Hitler diaries.

> *Did agent Rhodes really need 10 years to tell this story? The gist of his narrative begins in December 1962 and ends 11 months later. And could have been laid out as a 25-page manuscript. The effort expended, and detail contained in the account, were needed to prove his case. If his purpose in creating the journal was to simply suggest there is one more*

---

[277] Title 17 U.S.C. Section 302 (b) (1978).

possible motive driving Kennedy's assassination other conspiracy theorist overlooked, there were much less demanding ways to do exactly that.

He then used Defendant's additional 19-year effort against him.

I want to acknowledge the work of Defendant Sheppard. His effort and the quality of his work does more to bolster the journal's validity than anything Rhodes wrote. Having compared virtually every word of the account to the public record, he found nothing that definitively disproved the journal's veracity. Quite the opposite. He produced the one document, Evelyn Lincoln's November 9, 1963, handwritten note in the president's daily activity log, which he, himself, admits is the best evidence the journal is authentic.

His third point focused on the Defendant's responsibility to clear the content with the federal government if he chose to publish the journal.

As stated in our opening argument, plaintiff does not contest the ownership of the journal or defendant's analysis. There remains, however, the question of prepublication clearance. Defendant will likely argue everything he used in his assessment is in the public domain and unclassified in accordance with the President John F. Kennedy Assassination Records Act of 1992. However, when Rhodes created the journal, he had access to unredacted versions of all this material. At a minimum, a galley of any pending publication should be submitted to the Defense Department Office of Prepublication and Security Review prior to its release.

Plaintiff then presented evidence related to the historical significance of any material which might shed additional light on the unresolved questions associated with "the crime of the 20th century."

The American public demands and deserves transparency when it comes to the assassination of any major figure, much less the president of the United States. Congress acknowledged this when it passed the Assassination Records Act. It requires every piece of evidence associated with the

Warren Commission and other official investigations be made public. It did not apply to independent investigations. This legal loophole should not, however, relieve anyone from their patriotic and moral obligation to share significant information associated with the events of November 1963. If Defendant wants to hedge his bets as to the authenticity of the journal or protect himself from potential civil liability, there are mechanisms to do that. Include a disclaimer that any statement not backed by fact is an opinion or the information may be "imperfect" but represents a best effort to verify the underlying data. Obtain permission of individuals identified by name. Or remove inflammatory, sensitive or embarrassing information.

Defendant Sheppard was more than prepared to respond to his adversary's case point by point.

Your honor, I am not prepared to make a categorical declaration the journal is true. But first, let's assume, for argument's sake, it is. Does Plaintiff not appreciate Mason's involvement in the story does not end with Kennedy's death? He has a secret he fears could be disclosed at any time. It is only when the public's attention turns to Watergate does he let his guard down. Wrongfully so, I might add. Would plaintiff have done the same if he was in Mason's shoes?

Now let's assume the story is not true. That is the better reason to compare it to the Hitler diaries. It is more difficult to make a falsehood seem real. And how did Konrad Kujau hope to do that. By devoting so much time and effort to his fabricated work he could fool a distinguished historian such as Hugh Trevor-Roper. In either case, the length of the journal or time Mason spent drafting it is of no significance one way or the other.

And I am flattered Plaintiff is so enamored by my own contribution to the historical record. And he is correct when he suggests the November 9 entry in Evelyn Lincoln's appointment book is a titillating piece of evidence.

Unfortunately, he does not consider the counter argument. What if Mrs. Lincoln's handwritten note proved to be the kernel of an idea that resulted in Mason's creating a work of fiction. An anomaly in the president's daily itinerary any Secret Service agent assigned to the presidential detail might have seen.

Let me provide another example where the answer to the question "which came first?" completely changes one's assumptions about the journal's validity. Mason's January 20, 1963, entry goes into great detail about how he sifted through the FBI records when it came to Americans who defected to the Soviet Union. It was the process by which he claims the team eventually settled on Oswald as the best candidate to groom to be the assassin.

As part of my research into whether Mason's process was viable, I came upon a March 1979 report prepared for the House Select Committee on Assassinations by staff researcher Johanna Smith. It was titled, "The Defector Study." As part of its investigation into Oswald's pre-assassination behavior, Committee members asked staff to compare his experience with other defectors who sought asylum in the USSR. Like Mason, Smith began with a CIA list of individuals who had defected to the Soviet Union between 1958 and 1964. Also, similar to Mason's process, she eliminated persons who expressed no interest in returning to the U.S., narrowing the list of individuals worthy of further scrutiny to 23. For those who survived this triage process, Smith then created in-depth profiles, not unlike those Mason provided to the team.

One of two things could be true. Two individuals, Rhodes and Smith, tasked with similar assignments could have independently established the same procedures. Or, having discovered "The Defector Study" as I did, Mason determined that was exactly how he would have conducted his own research if asked to identify a presidential assassin. Since there are two plausible explanations, I feel less than qualified to definitively pronounce who was the chicken and who was the egg.

When it comes to the priority of official information contained in both the journal and in my subsequent commentary, Plaintiff conveniently overlooks two important factors. The prepublication review process to which plaintiff refers was part of the Cabinet reorganization following World War II that established an Office of the Secretary of Defense. The review function evolved over time and is now housed in the Defense Office of Prepublication and Security Review. Its mission to review written materials for public and controlled release, however, has not changed. More importantly, the two regulations which govern its authority, DoD Instruction 5230.09 and 5230.29, only cover DoD information.

During the time period covered in the journal, the Secret Service was under the jurisdiction of the Treasury Department. The Treasury Secretary had no mandated prepublication review authority nor did the Department house any entity with that responsibility.

It was on Plaintiff's last point, Defendant's moral and patriotic duty to release the journal, that the proceedings, which up until this point had remained relatively civil, turned contentious.

Plaintiff suggests Defendant would be immoral and unpatriotic if he chooses not to make the journal available for public consumption. To bolster this claim, he argued Mr. Sheppard #2 need only include a disclaimer or admission of possible imperfections to avoid legal liability. Perhaps Defendant skipped his Torts 101 class on the day devoted to disclaimers or slept through the lecture. Disclaimers are less than iron clad. I could waste the court's time with an encyclopedia of legal precedence based on cases, particularly those involving contract disputes, where a disclaimer held little if any water. I trust the judge is familiar with more than I could provide.

Equally important, disclaimers can have unintended consequences. Ask the late Supreme Court Justice Antonin Scalia. In his 1998 dissent when the Court ruled 6-3 that Texas' anti-sodomy law was an unconstitutional invasion of privacy, he pointed out the majority opinion included a disclaimer. "The case under consideration does not involve whether the government must give formal recognition to any relationship that homosexual persons seek to enter." Scalia should have stopped while he was ahead. He continued, "When sexuality finds overt expression in intimate conduct with another person, the conduct can be but one element in a personal bond that is more enduring, what justification could there possibly be for denying the benefits of marriage to homosexual couples?"[278] Much to Scalia's chagrin, the Supreme Court referenced this exact argument when it legalized gay marriage 12 years to the day on June 26, 2015, in Obergefell v. Hodges.

Can Plaintiff guarantee a disclaimer would protect the defendant from any legal liability in today's litigious environment? Or that there will not be unintended consequences of forcing the release of a private citizen's property. I think not.

Both parties' more combative approach carried over to the closing arguments. Plaintiff went first.

We have presented evidence Defendant possesses a significant historical document which should be in the public domain. Instead, he has selfishly chosen to keep it to himself. Nor has he allowed anyone else to examine the document in order to affirm or debunk its content. How does this differ from Henry Wade's closing argument in Jack Ruby's trial when he compares Ruby to a self-appointed vigilante? When it comes

---

[278] John Geddes Lawrence and Tyron Garner v. Texas, Case No. 02-102, June 26, 2003.

to disposition of Mason Rhodes' journal, Defendant wants to be the Judge, the Jury and the Executioner.

I will close by asking the one question I hope Judge Sheppard will take into consideration. That question in Latin is "Cui bono?" In English, who benefits? It could be historians, journalists, the American public, all of whom will have a chance to read and evaluate this latest addition to the catalogue of assassination exhibits. Or it could be one individual who will have the right to decide the journal's fate. And its commercial value.

We have no argument Defendant has a right to compensation for the time and effort he spent these many years dissecting the journal's content. We do, however, question whether he has the same monetary rights to the journal itself, especially since he acquired it through an accident of time and place. What do we mean by that? Assume the journal is valid. But for the fact a Secret Service agent moved into Defendant's neighborhood and befriended a young boy obsessed with the slain president, we would not be here today.

Convinced he sufficiently covered the main points during his presentation of the evidence, Defendant Sheppard chose to use his closing statement to counter Plaintiff's argument related to intended beneficiaries.

It is easy for someone who has nothing at risk to suggest legitimate stakeholders should ignore the consequences of their action. Clifford Irving and Konrad Kujau went to prison. Hugh Trevor-Roper, for a while, became a laughingstock, a sucker for having fallen for Kujau's hoax. Pulitzer Prize winning Washington Post writer Janet Cooke, who penned a bogus tale of a an 8-year-old heroin addict, ended up working at a department store in Kalamazoo, Michigan for $6.00 an hour. Oprah Winfrey's reputation as a literary expert was damaged when she initially vowed for James Frey, the author of "A Million Little Pieces," an Oprah book club selection which proved to be a fabrication of Frey's life story.

Nor does it have to be a complete forgery. Consider the number of writers and speakers accused of plagiarism, whether intentional or not. Famous writers including Stephen Ambrose, Alex Haley, Helen Keller included verbatim material from other sources without crediting the original author. The Boston Globe suspended columnist Mike Barnacle for a month after he lifted uncredited one-liners from books by George Carlin. Joe Biden's first run for the presidency was derailed when he appropriated lines from a speech by British member of Parliament Neil Kinnock. And, in 2016, former First Lady Melania Trump never lived down her almost verbatim rendition of Michelle Obama's speech at the 2008 Democratic Convention.

A journalist, author, scholar and even a judge, for better or worse, is responsible for any work product they share in the public arena. However, they should not be forced to release it until they are satisfied it is ready for public consumption and believe they can defend it against challenges. Your Honor, we would not expect you to hand down a decision in this case until it met these same criteria. Defendant only asks he be held to the same standard. Thank you.

Plaintiff waived his right to rebuttal. The judge announced a recess, pending his decision. The two parties did not have to wait for long.

Both the plaintiff and defendant have presented compelling cases. The plaintiff was correct to focus on the significance of the journal, even if it is only a theory. Mason Rhodes had first-hand knowledge of what it means to be a Secret Service agent. Even if he was not part of a conspiracy to assassinate the president, there is information in the journal which adds to our understanding of how the Secret Service strives to protect the nation's leaders and the conflict of conscience that can arise when a president directs agents to do something which is contrary to their primary responsibility.

However, the controlling factor in this case is not the significance of the content but its ownership. There is no dispute that the defendant owns his analysis of the journal. So, the only issue in question is the property rights associated with the journal. Although Mason Rhodes was a federal employee during part of the time in which he purports to have created the narrative, precedence suggests the government has no claim to the content in this case. If it did, the U.S. Treasury would be the recipient of royalties from every former president's memoir. Therefore, the journal belonged to Rhodes who had the right to transfer the copyright to the individual or entity of his choice.

And, as informal as a handwritten note might seem, the letter to the defendant which accompanied the physical transfer of the document is beyond challenge and makes him solely responsible for its future disposition. It would be different if Rhodes left specific instructions what to do with the material after his death. But he did not. To quote the letter, "I leave that up to you. I am sure you will make the right choice."

I, therefore, rule in favor of the defendant and order all records of this trial be sealed until such time the defendant requests they be unsealed. As for the defendant's need to determine the veracity of the document, this court offers no opinion. Mr. Sheppard, I hope you find the answer you are looking for.

I now found myself in the same position after first reading the journal. It is still hard to imagine Mason Rhodes, someone to whom I had been so close, would have agreed to plan, much less carry out, Kennedy's murder, regardless of the circumstances. Yet, 19 years later I have been unable to produce any indisputable grounds to conclusively reject Mason's version of history. On the other hand, everything I uncovered which would corroborate the journal is circumstantial in nature. I have not been able to identify, much less locate, another first-hand witness.

In journalistic terms, I hold the equivalent of a sole-sourced news story. The lack of corroborators is an important factor, as there are myriad examples how substandard reporting has ruined the careers of up-and-coming journalists, and on occasion, the publications for which they worked. Most recent is the 2014 *Rolling Stone* story, "A Rape on Campus," alleging several students at the University of Virginia sexually assaulted a female student during a fraternity initiation. Failure to verify questionable aspects of the "victim's" account resulted in *Rolling Stone* retracting the article, issuing an apology by the writer Sabrina Erdely and facing three defamation lawsuits, two of which were settled out of court and one in which Erdely was ordered to personally pay $2.0 million in damages to Nicole Eramo, UVA's associate dean of students.

In the end, it still comes down to the public's right to know versus protecting my professional standing as a social scientist whose research and findings should never blur the lines between fact and fiction. Yet, I must admit, Plaintiff Sheppard asked an important question in his closing argument. *Cui bono?* Who benefits? If I choose to publish the journal and my subsequent research, each individual gets to make his or her own assessment. If I keep it to myself, I avoid any risk of sullying my academic reputation.

My research into and teaching of the creative process taught me never to be satisfied with the obvious choices. Nor should I ever be content with "yes" or "no" as the only options. As I would tell my students, "You need more than a Plan B. Success depends on finding the next right answer and the next. Even if it turns out to be Plan Z." There must be a way to both share the journal and protect my professional integrity. I just need to find it.

EPILOGUE

On November 22, 2023, the 60th anniversary of the event which triggered (pun intended) this extensive chapter (again) in my life, *In the National Interest* opened at the Avalon Theater in Washington, DC. At the premiere, my wife and daughter both nudged me when the opening credits rolled across the screen.

Screenplay by Jonathan Sheppard
Based on a story by Mason Rhodes

Reviews were mixed. The *Washington Post* described the film as "a fascinating, well thought out delivery of an implausible story." The *New York Times* was less charitable. "One would think all the JFK conspiracy theorists would have either given up or passed away by now." The film had limited distribution and in the few "art theaters," which screened it, attendance was, to say the least, underwhelming.

As you might expect, the harshest criticism came from the Kennedy family and the Secret Service. The John F. Kennedy Library and Museum issued the following statement on the family's behalf.

> *Some may find Jonathan Sheppard's account of the president's murder intriguing, even compelling. We do not. To suggest John Kennedy authorized (if that is the correct word) his own assassination is abhorrent to everything he stood for. He was only 46 years old. Does anyone really believe someone, with so many promising years ahead, would consciously choose to end his own life? Not see his children and grandchildren grow up? Not fulfill the promise of "The New Frontier?" Mr. Sheppard, shame on you!*

In a press release, the Secret Service dismissed the film as fiction without judging its entertainment value. They did, however, express some surprise that any agent might have played a role in its creation.

> *Even in the case where an agent is fabricating an alternative version of history under a pen name, I am concerned whether this act violates the oath to which he or she swore upon entering the service. Unless required to testify in a criminal or civil proceeding, an agent is expected to operate within a "barrier of confidentiality." There is the possibility Mason Rhodes never existed. Perhaps Jonathan Sheppard created him, just as he fabricated this absurd tale. Merely claiming "agent" Rhodes drew upon events at which he was present, even if the information was used solely to buttress the veracity of an overall fanciful narrative, appears to cross the line. I would encourage present and aspiring writers with wild imaginations not to follow this example.*

Despite the lukewarm reception, I have no regrets. I have never second-guessed why I chose this course to share Mason's story. I owed it to my benefactor. Upon his death, he gave me a gift. And I felt obligated to pass it forward.

There are still as many questions as there are answers. And even if I take Mason's account at face value, I only do so based on my own assessment. Mason wanted me to seek the truth for myself. Others deserve the same respect. It is not up to me to pronounce definitively whether the story is an accurate account or a fabrication.

I still believe there may be some shred of clear-cut evidence out there that will ultimately resolve the issue. After all, it was 50 years before Evelyn Lincoln shared Kennedy's unsent love letter to Mary Pinchot Meyer. Despite promises by every succeeding occupant of the Oval Office to declassify *all* the records, documents and exhibits produced by the Warren Commission and the House Select Committee on Assassinations, we do not know what remains in the National Archives warehouse.

As it stands, maybe this was just a story about time. How any search for the truth never loses traction when there are so many versions of a singular event. The public's interest does not diminish as each successive narrative promises new facts or a different perspective. That is why promises by each newly elected president to finally release the

Kennedy assassination files in their entirety still command front page headlines.

I have taken my research as far as I can. I still comb the internet for news of another book or article about the assassination. Or news of a deathbed confession by another member of the TEAM. I wonder if another similarly obsessed individual will find other previously overlooked artifacts such as the November 9, 1963, entry in Evelyn Lincoln's appointment book. Hopefully, a similar discovery will inspire other Don Quixote-like quests for definitive answers to still unresolved questions. After all, is it not in the national interest we continue to pursue the truth about John Kennedy's assassination and other major events which help us understand history and ourselves?

Acknowledgements

First, I want to thank the sponsors and curators of the following digital repositories without whom I could not have told this story.

WIKIPEDIA
John F. Kennedy Library and Museum
Mary Ferrell Foundation
TimesMachine/*The New York Times*
Washington Post Archives
Newspapers.com by Ancestry
National Archives and Records Administration
FBI Records: The Vault
Archive.org

I also thank the many friends and family who encouraged me to pursue this project. In particular, I want to acknowledge my former Miami University colleague Todd Bailey, whose legal knowledge and experience was indispensable, especially when drafting the penultimate chapter "Beyond a Reasonable Doubt."

Finally, none of this would have been possible without the support of my wife Brenda and our daughter Shana, both of whom provided valuable feedback throughout the process. In addition to their substantive contributions, they were always there to share the excitement of each creative breakthrough and the frustration of the occasional writer's block. For that and so much more, I will always be grateful.